THE GODS OF DARK SWELL

THE GODS OF DARK SWELL

CHAMPIONS OF THE REALM

BOOK I

DAVID DOWELL

Library of Congress Control Number:		2016917665
ISBN:	Hardcover	978-1-5245-1866-0
	Softcover	978-1-5245-1865-3
	eBook	978-1-5245-1864-6

Print information available on the last page.

Rev. date: 08/02/2017

To order additional copies of this book, contact:
Xlibris
1-800-455-039
www.Xlibris.com.au
Orders@Xlibris.com.au
747285

CONTENTS

PROLOGUE

The Creator

H E HAD NO idea what would happen when he stepped through, yet he didn't turn to look back and there were no sideways glances.

He wasn't afraid.

Striding up the last few steps, he reached the large, oval of silver that floated shimmering in front of him. Without hesitation he stepped through.

The journey was instantaneous. One moment he stood on the steps of his palace at home, the blistering sun beating down on his back. The next moment he was in a new world, a light breeze cooling his brow and the feel of soft grass beneath his feet.

He looked around and saw five others step from portals the same as his.

He looked at each one of them in turn, as they stood looking around at one another and at the land around them. He guessed they were all of a similar age to him.

Eventually his focus was drawn to his surroundings, his attention immediately drawn to a path. It was a well-worn track; like that an animal would make travelling the same path day in and day out.

There was no one else around and no signs of other life.

'I guess we follow the path,' one of the other boys said. He was much shorter than the rest, but older than his stature suggested.

No one answered him, but they all followed as he made his way towards the path.

They walked in silence, the track leading them away from the portals and through a land of long grass, small hills, and a scattering of trees. It was a beautiful landscape, but at the same time, it didn't feel right. There were no birds and no indication that any animals lived here. There weren't even insects crawling on the ground or buzzing through the air around them.

Eventually, they came to the top of a small rise and the boy saw below them a clearing. Still silent, they all made their way down to it.

Here the grass was shorter and colourful pillows were strewn around the clearing in a large circle. It was the first sign that someone else was on this world.

The boy counted six pillows, each one placed on the ground in front of its own large, oval-shaped window. They were similar to the portals through which they had all stepped; only these ones were completely translucent.

Still none spoke. They just stood around, waiting and hoping that someone or something would appear.

The boy recalled the looks on each face when they first exited their portals. It suggested to him that none of them knew what it was they had been chosen for, or where it was they had come to.

He was the first to sit down on one of the pillows. The rest followed his lead.

None of them saw where he came from, yet they all turned as one to look at him as he entered the clearing.

He moved to the centre as the gentle breeze blew, stirring his long, black mane of hair. The sun was bright overhead, its aura burning in the centre of the pale blue sky.

The man's features were not old, nor were they young. He was striking in his appearance and to all those that looked upon him he seemed to be in the prime of his life.

Dressed only in white breeches, he stood proudly, his skin shimmering between colours as he slowly turned to look upon the six that were seated on the grass around him. They in turn gazed at him, their focus drawn to his eyes whenever he looked in their direction; dark, circular chasms that appeared to hold within them aeons of wisdom and knowledge.

Anticipation and awe were clear to see on each face, as they waited for him to begin.

He turned as he spoke, slow deliberate words that held his audience.

'You have all been chosen to partake in a game.' He paused to look at each in turn before continuing. 'Yet what you are about to embark upon is so much more than any game you could imagine, with a reward for the victor, greater than anything offered anywhere within the universe you all live in.'

None of the six stirred as he spoke. Their eyes widened and their hearts beat faster, but none thought to interrupt him. They were captivated with each word that left his mouth.

'You have been chosen based on your potential to do well in this game, nothing more. You are going to work hard, very hard, before it even begins, but I trust you are all eager to impress.'

The 'windows' before them began to hum, as each one lifted off the ground. An image appeared on each, blocking him from their view, as he continued to speak.

'These are your *eyes*, through which you will play the game.' He paused to give them a moment to take it in. 'The picture you see before you now is an image of the world I have created. The world in which this game will be played out.'

There were a couple of excited murmurs as the world appeared in front of them. As they looked at it, the image zoomed in and they saw before them a large swathe of land, surrounded by ocean.

'Each of you will be given a realm in which your chosen race will be placed. Your first task shall be to prepare this realm and strengthen your race, before the game itself will begin.'

The images disappeared as suddenly as they had appeared and each of their *eyes* sunk back down to touch the ground, translucent once more.

'This is not the first of these worlds that I have created, sculpted, and nurtured. There have been games on worlds before this one, worlds where races have fought battles, destroyed cultures, and annihilated their own civilisations.' He paused again before continuing.

'The world you have just seen I will be giving to the six of you to nurture as your own. Perhaps one of you will be the architect in finding that long sought-after balance. Maybe one of you will be the one to shape your own civilisation for aeons to come. Perhaps this world will become the one to endure, a world that will avoid the reaping others have suffered.' He stopped so that he could look again at each of those seated before him.

'Each of you has just celebrated your twelfth cycle. You will have six more to learn how best to develop the realm that will be given to you. At the end of that time, on the day of your eighteenth cycle, your race will be chosen and the game will begin.' Still none of the six stirred as he spoke.

'You should trust me when I say that the stronger your realm, the greater your champion's chances will be in the end.' He spoke the last part quietly, emphasising its importance.

He paused in his turning and slowly sat down on the grass.

He raised his hands to the sky, looked up, and spoke in a booming voice.

'I am the Creator and I bid you welcome to my Home World.'

He lowered his arms and looked straight ahead.

'The world that I have created for you I have named Dark Swell. It will be here that you chosen few will be my Gamers of Destiny. You are going to be the G.O.D.'s of Dark Swell.'

A small, barely perceptible grin formed on his face.

'Now let us begin,' he said and vanished.

The six of them looked around, shocked both at what the creator had said and his disappearing into thin air.

It was the short boy who again spoke first.

'It looks like we are going to be here for a long time,' he said. 'My name is Kabir.'

No one answered him straight away. They continued to look around the clearing, some touching the window in front of them.

One of the girls stood up and walked around hers, trying to see how it worked.

'I don't think we are supposed to stay here,' Kabir said, as he too stood up.

'So where are we meant to go then?' the girl asked, as she stood behind her window.

'There,' he said, pointing to a trail at the edge of the clearing. It was at the opposite side to the one they had come in on.

The boy hadn't seen it before Kabir pointed it out.

The rest of them stood up and walked over to where the track began.

It led into a thick forest of trees, with a huge mountain range rising in the distance behind them.

As with the path, the boy hadn't seen the mountains before now. There was something strange about the world they were in, he could feel it.

'My name is Linf,' the girl said, as she walked up next to Kabir. 'I hope it isn't just me, but I'm sure those mountains weren't there a moment ago.'

Kabir just nodded at her, as did a couple of the others.

They all walked in to the trees and before they had travelled more than five minutes, they came to another clearing. This time they saw much more than a few cushions.

There were wooden buildings spread out amongst the clearing and a narrow stream running through the middle of it. They could see gardens and crops and pens with animals inside of them, as well as many wandering free.

As the last of them stepped out from under the shade of the trees, the Creator appeared again, walking towards them from the middle of the clearing. None of them saw where he came from. He was just there, walking casually, as if it were nothing out of the ordinary for him to appear out of nowhere.

'Welcome to your new home,' he said, spreading his arms wide. 'It is here that you will live while you study in preparation for the game. You will not return to the clearing again until the game begins; however, the rest of the land here is yours to explore as you see fit.'

Again, none of them spoke. The boy had so many questions, yet he too didn't ask the Creator anything each time he paused.

'Everything you will need for the next six years is provided for you. Food to tend, game to hunt, shelter from the weather, and most importantly, the books and parchments you will need to study for the realms you will be given.'

The boy looked around again as the Creator stopped and looked at them. The mountain range was gone, replaced by rolling hills that now surrounded the clearing they stood in. He could see animals walking along the ridge of the nearest one. Some of them stopped to look down at them.

He was stunned at what he saw, but his attention was drawn back to the Creator as he continued speaking.

'There are lists of races for you to study. You are required to choose one, but you have six years to make up your mind. I trust you will make the most of the time you have been given.'

Once again he vanished from sight.

The boy looked around and saw a couple of the others looking at where the Creator had been standing only moments earlier, their mouths open in shock.

Others were looking around at the hills, their expressions probably mirroring his own.

He looked around to see where the Creator had gone, but he gave up after a little while. The man was no longer with them.

He assumed he would appear again soon enough.

None of them saw him again for almost six years.

CHAPTER 1

The Day of Choosing Approaches

TIME PASSED QUICKLY for the six gamers.

Through discussions, they discovered each of them had been relative loners within their own worlds, preferring their own company to that of others.

The place they had called home for the last six years had suited each of them. They all spoke with one another about day-to-day activities and helped hunt and gather food together, but when it came to their studies and the game itself, they kept most of their thoughts to themselves.

It was a game they were going to play, with a promised reward like no other. The reward was one topic they were all happy to discuss and speculate about, but they were each acutely aware those they now lived with were going to be their opponents when the game began. Until they knew all of the rules, they hadn't wanted to risk giving anyone else an advantage. Information could be power.

There were only a handful of days remaining when the Creator finally appeared before them again.

All six happened to be within the centre of their little village when he walked casually from the forest, striding along the same path from which they had first arrived.

He waited until they had all moved over to where he stood before he began to speak.

'In two days' time, you will make your way to the clearing where I first spoke to you.' He spoke softly and with no emotion.

'Once there you will inform me of the race you have chosen and I will reveal to each of you which realm shall be yours.'

They were almost eighteen cycles now, but the excitement they all felt was as intense as it had been when they first arrived.

'The moment your *eyes* come to life is the moment the game begins.'

They were so close now. All of them felt ready, but there was still much they didn't know.

'You will only be able to see into your own realm. That which happens within the rest of Dark Swell will remain a mystery to you until the Naming Day arrives.'

That was one question answered, the boy thought.

'You each have finite resources to choose from the lists you have studied. Each 100 years you can contribute again, right up until the Naming Day in 2,000 years.' The Creator spoke now of that which they already knew, but their attention remained focused.

'Time moves differently within the clearing where your *eyes* are. Two thousand years on Dark Swell will move quicker than the time within my Home World. Whenever you step outside of the clearing to eat and sleep, the years will pass quickly there. You must be mindful of this. If you miss your chance to contribute then you lose that opportunity. You cannot carry over any resources unless you are sitting in front of your *eye* when that time arrives.' He paused then and looked around at them.

'Do any of you have any questions?' he eventually asked. It was a simple question, but it was enough to stun each of them.

Of course we have questions, the boy thought, yet he couldn't focus his mind enough to ask any of them.

He looked around at the others, waiting for one of them to ask something so that he could clear his mind.

They all looked as stunned as he.

'Then I will see you in two days,' he said and began to turn away.

'What does our champion need to do in order to win the prize?' Brindel asked. 'There was no reference to it within that which I have read.'

The Creator turned back to face them.

'It is a game,' he said in answer. 'I certainly don't want to give away the ending.' He smiled and turned once more, walking slowly back into the forest.

THE TIME HAS COME

Coming and going from the place in which their *eyes* had been set up, they had almost gone through the days given to them to make their contributions.

Decisions had been made and changed. Some as they re-evaluated their fortunes, some thrust upon them by events that were out of their control.

Some of those races within the realms had prospered more than others, yet as the end of their involvement was nigh, all races had survived.

All six were still in the game.

As they sat looking through their *eyes,* there was perhaps one thing they all had in common, one thing that consumed most of their thoughts.

Even after almost 2,000 years had passed since the game began in the world of Dark Swell, plus the many years before that were spent on study and research within the home world of the Creator, each of them, except for one perhaps, still wished for one thing: more time.

There was less than one week until the Naming Day and none of them would move now from their seat on the grass.

Not until they were ready to name their champion.

They each had one more opportunity to intervene before they must seek out the Creator and tell him which of those that lived within each realm would be the one they hoped would make it to the end.

Within their own minds, each of the six had decided on which of those within their realms they would choose as their champion. The one they deemed most worthy from their entire race.

The moment the gamer selected their champion, they would take on the name of the gamer, as if they had never had another.

Now it was simply a matter of waiting until they would officially name them to the Creator.

A lot can happen in a few days.

CHAPTER 2

Death of a Champion

REACHING DOWN NEXT to where he sat, one of the six took hold of a small rod. Made of no material found on Dark Swell, it held within it the power for one within his realm to harness the weather; to bend it to their will for a time.

There was no other item more expensive in the game. In all the worlds created before this one, none had been able to procure it, until now. It was worth ninety generations of resources combined.

The gamer who now held the rod had sat back for years with no influence, his plan decided upon 2,000 years ago. He had known it was a considerable risk he took, but he believed it would work for him in the end.

Yet for most of those two millennia, things had not gone as he had foreseen or hoped.

Looking at the rod, he basked in the realisation that events had somehow come together. He was suddenly in a position where he could still be the one to prevail.

Now he decided to gamble once more, but it was no greater risk than any other he had made before this day.

Right up until today he had intended to give the rod to another within his realm. That had been his intent for a long time.

Yet his mind was sharp and he believed his skills at evaluating the cause and effect of decisions was unequalled within this game.

Another path had opened to him that might still see him victorious and he was excited by it.

His thoughts moved fast and continued to calculate the likely outcomes against those less likely. His confidence grew in the choice he now made.

With a flick of his wrist, a small movement that belittled the game-changing occasion it represented, the rod was cast through his *eye* and into the world of Dark Swell.

Unerringly it fell, the end of the rod lodging itself into the hard rock at the feet of an elf.

Standing alone on the out crag of a mountain, the elf looked down at it with a bemused look on his face. He hadn't sensed it coming. Strange, he thought, as he looked up into the sky above him. He saw nothing flying above and there was nowhere from which it could have fallen or been cast. This part of the mountain had no overhang and no peak nearby. There was nothing but the empty sky above him.

Turning back to the rod, the elf bent down and grasped hold of it. To his surprise, it came easily out of the rock.

He could not take his eyes from it—eyes that burned with the colour of rich flames. Within the rod he saw swirling clouds. A faint breeze blew from one end of it.

There were no archaic words spoken within his mind and no runes upon the surface of the rod. It was smooth and dark, yet somehow he knew what it was the moment he grasped hold of it. As he peered at it, an item more breathtaking than anything he had ever seen before, he inextricably knew exactly how to use it.

With his heart beating fast and a crooked smile on his face, he raised the rod, pointed it to the sky, and called forth the powers of the storm.

The gamer placed his arm back onto his lap and continued to gaze into his *eye*. He didn't intend going anywhere in the near future, even had he been given a choice.

A small grin formed on his face, which quickly turned into a larger one.

If his eyes weren't all white they would have sparkled.

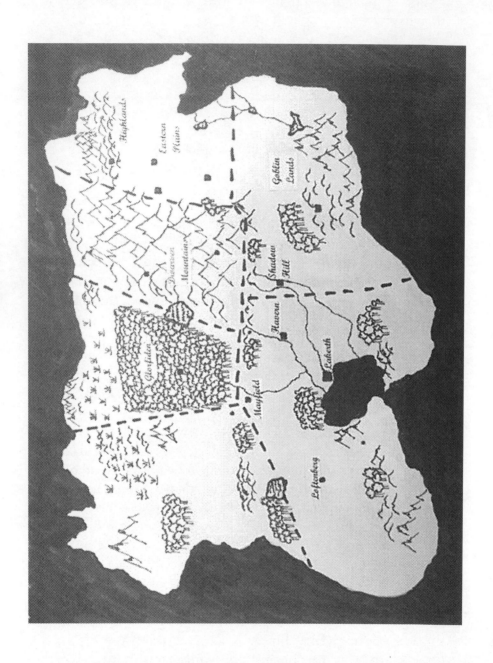

CHAPTER 3

MENDINA—The Gamer of Destiny

MENDINA WAS ONE of only two females in the game and she had been the first of them to choose her race almost 2,000 years ago.

Her home planet had been a dry, arid land where her people spent most of their lives indoors, the landscape outside making it barely habitable. Mendina was among the majority in her world who had never been fortunate enough to travel elsewhere. Only the elite in their society were allowed to travel, either by transport or portal.

Her only way to learn of the beauty within other worlds had been through books, illustrations, and stories told to her by her elders. There was little technology within the squalor where she grew up, and by the time she was almost old enough to be allowed to use and view it, she had sat the test and been spirited away to the home world of the Creator.

For her, the elves had been an easy choice.

She had been captivated with the thought of magic even before she had heard of the game.

In the years since she had arrived here and began learning about the game, and then through the years spent studying it, she had discovered that elves were the strongest in magic of all those races she had to choose from.

Her first real decision had been which race of elves she would choose. The choices available to her were as varied and numerous as the habitats available.

Woodland Elves, Dark Mountain Elves, Swamp Elves, Desert Elves . . . the list went on and on.

Each of these would have their magic based in whatever environment they lived in.

Yet her choice in the end had been an easy one, decided purely on what she believed an elf should be. What she had grown up believing them to be. Mystical creatures living within the forest, secluded from all others and masters of their home and habitat.

Her plan had been simple enough to begin with. She would have a select few that would have greater access to the powers she would give to them. The rest would be their protectors, less powerful but skilful with sword, bow, and magic. She assumed the trees and their solitary nature would be her best defence early on against any that may try to destroy her.

The first of her race she chose to give as much magical prowess as she was able, so they could secure themselves within their woodland realm. She had been confident none of the others would pose a threat early on. She had hoped their magic would keep them safe from the others and that come the time to choose her champion, she strongly believed that none would be able to match her.

Every 100 years, she had added to the magical source within her forest realm from which her elves drew their power. She had also given to them more skills and a greater knowledge with which to use those powers. They were strong in many of the elements, not just those relating to the forest.

Her eldest became even more powerful as each generation passed.

The elves were also longer lived than other races and one lifetime for them was far greater than 100 years. Mendina saw this as yet another advantage in choosing her woodland elves.

Looking down now at her beloved forest, she knew that she got that part right.

The champion she intended to choose had already lived for hundreds of years. She doubted his powers would be matched by any other within Dark Swell.

She had been both surprised and delighted when she had discovered that no other gamer had chosen elves or any other race strong in magic. Humans could be strong using it, but they didn't come close to the elves.

Her champion had been selected a long time ago and he was perfect.

She was only days away from naming her champion and she couldn't wipe the smile from her face.

CHAPTER 4

Mendina—The Champion

THE RUMBLE OF thunder in the distant sky was getting louder. The elven girl looked up and saw a blanket of darkness rushing towards Glorfiden. Great billows of dark clouds looked to be racing one another across the sky, clashing strikingly with the glorious blue above her.

Strangely she felt as though she should be heading back home, back to the Great Trees in the centre of the forest, even though she was still within the protection of Glorfiden. The storm did not have a natural look to it. Intermingled within the clouds sparks of lightning seemed to crackle, giving the impression that the storm had a life force within it.

It sent a chill through her body and she began to feel afraid. It was a fear totally foreign to her within the boundaries of her home.

Just a few more berries, she thought, and she would be back before the torrential rains arrived. The clearing where she was standing was flush with the red berries she favoured and she had walked a long way to get them. They grew only in this part of the forest and she hadn't been here for many moons.

'It looks as if there is going to be a major lightning strike in that one.'

The elf spun around and drew the jewelled poniard from her belt.

Already it was darkening, though it was only mid-afternoon and she could only make out a shadowy humanoid form that had spoken.

It stood under the bough of a large oak at the edge of the clearing twenty paces away and wore a cloak with the hood pulled down enough to shadow its face.

'Do not be afraid, little one. I am a friend.'

It pulled back its hood and the man the elf saw standing there was only a boy.

He was short for a human, standing little higher than an adult elf. His hair was a bronze unlike that of human or elf. His ears were human, his voice and speech were certainly that of a human, but his eyes showed him to be one more akin to those of the forest rather than one of the desecrators of the land. Even in the gloom, she could see his eyes. An intent but mischievous look was held in those eyes.

He would have been no more than twenty in human years, which in the equivalent to elven years in maturity would have left him only a year or so older than herself.

She took all of this in through a glance and was intrigued, but wary. She was also concerned how he had crept up on her amongst the trees of Glorfiden.

She quickly reached out her senses to them, but they did not respond. She felt an emptiness in her mind that worried her even more as she held the dagger out further. She thought suddenly of her pet that she had left at home today and regretted the choice. He was a fine guard and she felt safe when he was around, but she hadn't wanted to aggravate his injury.

'Please put away your needle. I would not harm you.'

He spoke with a strange accent, but in her elven tongue.

'What are you doing in Glorfiden? And how did you sneak up on me?' The elf girl was surprised at how her voice came out quavering, but this all felt wrong. The storm and this strange being that spoke with too much confidence. She wanted to leave.

She could sense the trees again and they were scared. She was certainly unnerved.

'The trees sense no threat in me, therefore there was nothing for your elven senses to pick up from them.' He spoke with a smugness she did not like.

'You could not know of our bond with the trees of this forest,' she said as a matter of fact. 'You are not of Glorfiden.'

The man stood there and smiled and stared at her with those eyes of his, eyes which looked as though they saw right through her. She could feel herself beginning to panic.

'Please,' he asked again, 'put away your dagger. I truly mean you no harm.' He smiled first but then his face grew serious.

'However, Mendina, you can sense their fear as well as I. That storm is coming closer. I would prefer that neither of us is standing here when it strikes.'

Mendina heard what he said and agreed she would rather not be here, but her curious elven nature would not yet let her go.

'How do you know my name and how do you feel what the trees sense? Who and what are you human?' she asked more confidently now, although she still held her dagger in her hand.

'Please do not be so naive, Mendina.' He spoke as if to a child and she liked it not. 'I am but half-human. My father, as yours is, was an elf. But he is gone now.'

She sensed him drop his guard as he spoke suddenly of his father and Mendina grew more confident. 'But how do you know my name, halfling?' she saw the insult sting. 'Have you been spying on me?'

He hesitated now. 'I admit I have been . . . watching over you. You intrigue me, elfling.'

Now it was she who was insulted. Elfling was a name they called spoilt children.

'Who was your father?' she asked as rudely as she could.

'He was a warrior from Glorfiden. His name was Jarkene.' He spoke to her again in the same calm, confident voice he had begun with.

Mendina was visibly shaken and she felt her eyes widen and her jaw drop. Jarkene!

She knew that he had a son named Mortinan and had taken a human as his wife. She also knew, as did all the elves, that both mother and son had died.

There was a sudden, brief shaking of the earth itself, as the thunder boomed above the forest and her thoughts scattered.

'Please come with me.' She heard the catch, and was it fear in his voice? He held his hand out to her. 'Already the evil strikes,' he said.

As in the fashion of a mighty seer and before Mendina could begin to ask what he meant by the evil, the first blinding flash appeared and ended with a crack and eruption of flame.

The strike was less than two leagues from where they stood.

'There is enormous power in that storm. I would strongly suggest that you come with me. To head back to your home would put you head-on into the storm and I fear you would not outrun it.' He stepped closer to her.

She held the dagger out menacingly. 'Stay where you are, halfling. Why should I trust you?' Yet her voice betrayed the panic she felt. The trees were indeed restless and they were afraid.

'The trees trusted me little elf, so can you.'

Mendina heard the truth in those words, but she was from a stubborn and suspicious race.

'The elven lords would not let anything happen to Glorfiden,' she was sure of that.

The elven king Glendrond and his two sons Perillian and Quaneillan were the most powerful sorcerer—warriors in the land as far as she was concerned.

Yet she was afraid. The rains that accompanied any storm in Glorfiden to quench the flames were not there. There was only a howling wind, becoming more ferocious as they spoke and seemingly capable of blowing any blaze into a fiery inferno.

'That may be,' he yelled over the wind, 'but the Lords are not here.'

He reached out his hand to Mendina and she hesitated only a moment before running to him and clasping hold of it. Together, they turned and fled the storm.

'Where are we going?' she soon asked, realising she was going in the opposite direction to her home. She had to yell to be heard over the deafening thunderclaps and whip like cracks of lightning bolts, as they continued to crash through the underbrush of the forest.

'We go to my home,' he yelled back as they both struggled to run parallel to the wind's howling barrier, 'on the edge of Glorfiden.'

Mendina let go of his hand and came to a halt, her eyes wide.

'I will not leave the forest, halfling!' she screeched. 'Your human folk have desecrated the land outside of the boundaries of Glorfiden. I will not go with you.'

He gave an anguished sigh. 'I told you it is on the edge of the forest. Your delicate senses will not be harmed by what lies outside.'

Mendina stood firm, her arms by her side. 'I will not!'

'Please,' he asked again and she could see he was worried now. 'Look at the storm, Mendina. To be out in this is at one's most deadly peril.'

She looked back over her shoulder. The lightning looked to be out of control. She had never seen such a storm. She could not have even imagined one like it.

They had stopped again in a clearing and the storm behind them was clearly visible as the lightning bolts continued to light up the sky.

They seemed to be striking in a random fashion, yet no bolt struck near another. The storm seemed to be maximising the destruction where each one struck.

Then all of a sudden, as the two looked on, the storm ceased.

The thunder disappeared and the lightning was no more. All that remained were the clouds, black as night and covering most of the forest, but now with an orange tint to them from the fires that burnt unabated across the north and west of Glorfiden.

In their part of the forest all was quiet, but it was an eerie silence.

Mendina looked at the halfling. She thought for a moment that he had forgotten she was there. His forehead was crinkled and he looked to be concentrating on something. After maybe a minute or two, his expression suddenly changed into one of either fear or awe—or both.

Mendina looked back over the forest and saw a horror that rooted her to where she stood and one that did not let her scream.

Forked bolts lit up the sky as if it were sheet lightning, but no longer in a random fashion. With double the ferocity of before, they all hit in the one place.

Mendina came out of her trance and spoke two words. 'My home.'

Mortinan reached out and grabbed hold of the elf before she could flee. As adept as he was in the forest, he didn't fancy his chances of catching up to a panicked elf in her own domain.

'My home!' she screeched this time as Mortinan grabbed hold of her and she came back to her senses. 'It is attacking my home!'

'Whatever it is,' Mortinan spoke in a hushed voice to himself, 'it has a purpose, Mendina. And I feel it has power your home will not withstand.'

Patient no longer, he lifted the girl with an ease that did not befit his lean build. He pinned her arms as best he could, knowing how willing she was to use her dagger and fled the storm towards the safety of his own home and his mother.

After what seemed like hours but was in truth barely one, Mortinan and his captive came to the edge of the forest.

The storm was still raging at their backs but the lightning strikes were less frequent now and their power had diminished. To Mortinan, it seemed that it was just casually completing the task which it had been sent to do.

The trees had withdrawn completely a short time ago, after Mortinan had been privy to their pain and anguish on his run back here to the edge.

The animals were nowhere to be seen or heard.

This part of the forest and no doubt the other parts that had survived was still in shock and struck mute by the suffering they could all sense coming from the centre.

The thick smoke still billowed, putting a grey tinge into the black sky above. It made it look more evil than before.

Mortinan wondered if the many hues this storm cloud had taken were something akin to a demon's rainbow.

Mendina had stopped kicking and biting at Mortinan only a short time ago, having drawn a great deal of blood and given him more bruises and lumps than he had accumulated his whole life.

Evening was drawing on and Mortinan could see the smoke coming from his house about 400 paces to the right of the path they were on.

'May I put you down lady and pray you do me no more harm. I am not far from collapse,' he thought as he said it she would not, that she would flee instead. As he placed her gently on her feet, she took a step back and glared at him.

'I should kill you, halfling, for the insult you have given me.' He could see the pain and fatigue in her eyes, for her home and for the trees that cried out on their flight through Glorfiden.

'I meant no insult, Mendina, and my name is not halfling.' He said it as neutrally as possible, not wishing to give her an excuse to kill him or to run.

She looked at him for a short while. Mortinan was relieved that looks themselves could not kill. Not from an elf anyway.

'What then is your name, "halfling"?' she eventually asked, even though she already knew the answer.

Mortinan ignored the tone in her voice and introduced himself as pleasantly as he could in the circumstances. 'I was named Mortinan, but my mother just calls me Mort.'

He took a deep breath and continued on. 'I did what I thought to be the right thing to do and I stand by that decision. There was an evil in that storm. I could sense it and it would have been your death had you entered it. Although I felt your desire to return home and I would have acted the same way had it been my home, you would not have been able to help.' He felt they were harsh words, but they had to be said.

Mendina lowered her eyes, put her hands to her face, and started to cry.

Mort had readied himself for an outburst, even an attack, but this he was not ready for. His heart went out to her but he could not move. He just stood there stunned.

Finally, he did move towards her, his arms held out for an embrace.

As soon as his arms were around her, he felt a sharp prick of pain in his stomach. Backing away, he saw the dagger that was in Mendina's hand, a trickle of blood on the point. Her eyes held the look of a large predatory cat.

'Already you have touched me one time too many boy,' she shot back at him, tears streaking her cheeks. 'To do so again will be the last thing you ever do, halfling!'

Mort was taken aback by this sudden ferocity from the tiny elven girl. So far, she had proven herself fragile and afraid. Now she was an elf as in all of the stories Mort's mother had told to him. He made no further move towards her.

'Very well,' he said, 'but will you please come with me to my mother's house. She will want to meet you and we will be safe there for a while.'

Mendina did not respond but the fire seemed to have left her and her eyes fell to the earth again.

'Please, Mendina. The house is on the edge of the forest and our land is respected and well looked after.'

She did not respond.

'My father Jarkene, he lived there for a while. My mother and I learnt much from him.' Mort would beg now but not force her to go. The immediate danger had passed.

Mendina looked up at him. She could see the pity in his eyes. Once it would have angered her, but he looked so pathetic she almost laughed.

'Where is your father now, boy?' she asked him, although again she already knew the answer.

He did not answer her.

'Where is he, Mort?' she asked again.

'He is gone now,' he finally answered her, 'but he was a great man. I will tell you of him later. It is a subject that hurts but one of great pride to me.'

It was he who lowered his head this time.

'Please,' Mort asked her one more time, though he spoke in only a whisper, 'come with me. No harm will come to you, Mendina. I swear this on my life.'

He looked up and into her eyes and she noticed for the first time the myriad of colours that were held in his gaze. This truly was the son of Jarkene.

'I would very much like to hear your story, Mortinan,' she said with genuine interest. Her thoughts picked up again now from where they had been interrupted by the storm. He was supposed to be dead! 'And I would also like to meet the human female capable of winning the heart of an elven lord.'

'Elven lord?' Mort asked her and she saw that he was genuinely surprised.

'It seems your mother did not tell you all, for whatever reason you must ask her.' Mendina also spoke softly now, although she was surprised at Mort's last words. There were too many questions running through her head at the moment and too many answers that she didn't want to know. She needed time to gather her senses.

'Now I am weary and a place to lie sounds a good idea. I must think on what has happened, Mort, before I go home tomorrow.'

Looking at this tiny creature, who for months now had been foremost in his thoughts, Mort continued to feel things he was totally unsure of.

Love, it could be, a love story like one his mother had told him.

Respect for the bravery she was showing at a time when her family and friends may have all perished in the storm.

She was a creature of beauty and charm and Mort swore to himself that he would do all he could to protect her. He wanted nothing more than to be able to care for her now that all her family and friends may have perished.

Whatever spell she had cast upon him was swift, ruthless, and complete.

Without turning to see the final death throes of Glorfiden, Mort and Mendina strode off towards his house and his mother, leaving the burning forest behind them.

'There you are dear,' Mort's mother said to Mendina as she handed her a steaming cup.

Mendina tried to smile as she took the cup, peering at it and then taking a small sniff of the aroma. She blinked in surprise as she recognised the smell to be that of Featherleaf Tea. She sipped and then stared at Mort's mother.

'It is wonderful,' she said. 'I did not expect to be sipping it in a place outside of Glorfiden. I thought that the Featherleaf was found only in the heart of the forest and no human, or half-human,' she added looking over at Mort who stood by the fireplace staring at her, 'has ever been close to that part of Glorfiden.'

'Jarkene brought some with him when he would stay here with me. He put in a small plant for me on our anniversary some years ago. It prospers still,' she added in a sweet but sad voice.

Hours ago, Mendina would have been outraged, but this woman in front of her was nothing of what she had been told humans were like. The Elven Council made no secret of what they thought of humans and all elves were brought up to believe it.

However, on her way in, Mendina had seen with her eyes and felt with her senses that this house and its surrounds were as well kept as any in Glorfiden.

Or as they had been in Glorfiden.

The Council had also said that both of the people in this room with her had died.

She looked again at Mort's mother and thought for the twentieth time since they had arrived that not only was she shocked at how pure the land was where Corein lived, but she was also taken aback by her appearance. She would have to be in her early fifties, yet her beauty had not paled at all through the years.

Elven women were known to have a beauty unsurpassed by any in the land. Some females among the race of men were said to be beautiful in their own way but none came close to the ethereal elegance of the elves. Yet here was a lady whose elegance and refined features would have held her in high regard amongst her own people. Mendina also saw a strength and determination in her. In the short time she had spent with her, she could already begin to see why Jarkene had sacrificed everything to be with her.

'Do not fear the worst yet child,' Mort's mother said, interrupting her thoughts. 'The elves have always been a bastion against evil.'

'Do you read minds my lady Corein?' Mendina asked.

'No, but I have become quite good at reading faces,' she replied with a tinkle of a laugh. 'Jarkene was not one for always speaking his mind, so at times his face and his eyes were the only communication I got from him. Elven men are as proud a race as there has ever been I think, yet the most secluded, both in their homes and in their hearts.'

Mort felt the pain in her words as he felt his own pain, but the time to ask his question was now. He could contain himself no longer.

He had stood patiently while his mother soothed Mendina's nerves and tried to allay her fears and he felt that she had worked a miracle.

'Mother. Was Father truly an elven lord?' he asked with no lack of scepticism, thinking Mendina had not possibly meant what he thought she had. It was not possible. As soon as the words were out of his mouth he felt foolish for asking it and wished he could take the words back.

Corein sat down slowly and looked up at her son.

'I have prepared myself for this ever since you glimpsed Mendina in the forest and could talk of nought else since that day.'

Mort blushed and stole a glance at Mendina to gauge any reaction. When she did not even twitch he looked back to his mother.

'I was sure once you introduced yourself to her,' Corein continued, 'that she would know who you were. I was right,' she added with a touch of regret in her voice.

Mort did not think it would be safe if his heart were to beat any quicker than it was now.

Corein looked now into the fire as she spoke.

'Jarkene was a Lord of the Forest, Mort. He was the third son to Glendrond, Protector and Nurturer of Glorfiden.' She spoke with as much gusto as she would talking about the weather.

Mort was dumbstruck. Of all the stories his mother had told him, of all the questions he had asked for as long as he could speak, at least half revolved around Glendrond and his two sons Lords Perillian and Quaneillan.

They were his heroes and his inspirations. They were the greatest warriors and mightiest wielders of the magic among all of the elves.

His mother had never spoken of a younger brother.

The fact that his father was also a Lord and brother and son to *them* hit him like a giant oak crashing down on top of him. His head started to spin, he had no way of controlling his thoughts and emotions and with a thump of skull on wood he crumpled onto the floor.

Corein just sat there and stared at her son, the blood beginning to trickle from his wound. Mendina glanced at her with a stunned look and then got up and went over to him.

'He has knocked himself out Lady Corein, why do you just sit there?' As gently as possible, she lifted his head into her lap. 'And his head bleeds. Can I have a cloth please?' she asked Mort's mother, who continued to just sit there and stare at her son.

'He is not ready yet,' she said to no one. And then with a sigh, 'As if he ever could be.'

Mendina stared at her, wondering what had happened to the lady she had met earlier.

Corein must have noticed the way Mendina was looking at her as she turned and spoke to her, as if to an infant.

'Wait a moment, Mendina, and watch.'

'What do you mean wait a . . . oooh.' Mendina felt a sharp tingle on her hand where it rested near Mort's wound. She looked down and the steady flow of blood slowed to a trickle and then stopped, all in a few moments. A blue nimbus of light, or it could have been a thousand tiny specks of light, hovered around it. Then as suddenly as they appeared they were gone. Mendina parted his hair and saw nothing. There was no wound. Only the sticky blood in his hair showed there had ever been a cut.

Mendina gasped and stared down at Mort's face.

'But . . . but. . .' she stammered. 'You are human. He is from a human womb. It cannot be. Only Glendrond and the elven lords have the Healing.' It was Mendina's turn for her thoughts to go into a spin, but she did not faint.

'He is the son of Jarkene, Mendina, and I'm sure he possesses all of the powers of an elven lord, although he has no idea.' Her voice was alive now, challenging Mendina to dispute her. 'With your high and mighty elven philosophy, surely you did not think that the human trait of the child would dominate the elven side. Especially when it is that of a Lord!' Corein had raised her voice at the end but she quickly brought herself under control.

'Mendina, he is aware that he can perform magic, it could not be contained within him. But he thinks even the least powerful elf can do what he does and much more.'

'I am sorry, Lady Corein, for insulting you.' Mendina knew a little of what had happened to Jarkene and understood in part why Corein would not hold the elves on the friendliest of terms.

'He is not ready, Mendina. And now I am afraid what will happen to him.' Her voice retreated back to one of sorrow and regret.

'What do you mean not ready? Not ready for what?' Mendina was still quite stunned by his ability to *heal* but she wanted to tread lightly with this woman.

'Not ready for anything to do with the elves and their ways.' Corein turned now and looked directly into the eyes of Mendina.

'Certainly not ready for what you have in mind for him my dear.' The last said with a trace of warning in it.

Mendina knew she must have looked stunned by the accusation and she was. Stunned by how easily this human could read her thoughts.

'I do not know what you mean,' she said in a neutral voice.

'What if you cannot find Glendrond when you return?' Corein asked her.

'Nothing could possibly happen to the Protector and Nurturer my Lady.' Mendina was surprised by Corein's words and also by her strained conviction. 'Nothing!' she added, this time sounding more sure of herself.

Both women stared at each other until a moan from Mort brought Mendina's attention back to him.

Mort awoke and thought he was in a dream.

He looked upon the most stunning creature he had ever glimpsed. Her hair was a light brown and long, with the most glorious light green eyes he had ever seen. They seemed to glow and draw him into their depths. He smiled up at her and whispered, 'I love you.'

With a thump, his head hit the floor and he heard the voice sing, 'I think he is still delirious and may be suffering from concussion, my lady.'

As tiny little men began to thump the inside of his head with mallets, he suddenly remembered where he was and the memories of only moments before flooded back into his consciousness. He was the son of an elven lord!

He sat up and his mind began to swim away again, but before he passed out a second time, his mother's voice broke through. 'Your father was a Lord Mort. Stop fainting!' He mistook her fear for anger.

He looked at her and stopped, but then started to ask the first of his one million questions. All on the tip of his tongue battling for priority, but he tried anyway.

'What happened to. . .' he began, but his mother stopped him again with the raising of her hand.

'Today has been an enormous day Mort, Mendina.' She looked across to the elf. Mort thought he sensed something new between them but he had no idea what and he couldn't focus any of his thoughts long enough to come to any conclusion.

His mother continued.

'I think it is time for us all to rest and not dwell any further on what has happened today. Tomorrow is a brand new day, with new beginnings.' She stood as she finished talking and said to Mendina, 'You may sleep in Mort's room tonight.'

Mort's eyes lit up and his heart began to beat as it had before.

Corein looked at her son and sighed, looking at the ceiling.

'You will sleep out here in the living room, Mort.'

'Of course, Mother,' he replied quickly, as if he had not been thinking anything to the contrary.

'You have a responsibility now, Mort,' Mendina spoke from where she sat behind him. Mort turned and stared at her.

'You are the son of an elven lord. I do not doubt that,' she spoke matter-of-factly. 'Glorfiden has just been attacked without warning and maybe without survivors.' Her voice caught a little then, but she continued.

Mort could only keep staring at her as she stared at him. He looked quickly at his mother and saw that she was glaring at Mendina.

'Therefore, you may be one of the last remaining elves or half-elves, with any real power. You must come with me to Glorfiden tomorrow and see if there is any who live. If not, then you will find who was responsible and we will both see they suffer for what they have done.'

Mort thought that he could see tiny flames dancing in her eyes.

'I have no real power,' Mort said to her.

'You have,' Mendina began.

'Enough!' Corein stood and looked down at Mort and then Mendina. 'I have heard enough.'

Mort's eyes nearly popped out of his head hearing his mother yell.

Mendina calmly stood and looked up at Mort's mother with anger in her eyes and something else he could not fathom.

'He must come with me,' she said quietly and calmly, 'and he will punish all that were responsible. If something has happened to the Nurturer and his sons it was done with surprise. We will have the surprise this time. We have an elven lord's son who they do not

know even lives! Their guard will be down and we will crush them!'
Mendina slowly made her hands into fists as she finished talking.

Mort thought for a moment that she wasn't acting much like an
elf. Then he again remembered the stories his mother had told him of
wars that the elves had fought. They had been ferocious and merciless
at times. Mort could certainly believe that of them. Even the female
elves, who were both warrior and magic user.

Yet he had no idea of this immense power that he supposedly
had, a power both Mendina and his mother seemed to believe was
within him.

'Mort, come over here.' His mother held out her hand to him.

Trying not to turn and look at Mendina's face, without luck, he
slowly lifted himself up and stood next to his mother. The flames
were her eyes now and Mort was startled and afraid. He dared not
ask her what it meant.

'Mort, take Mendina's hand.'

He tried to let go of his mother's. 'The other hand Mort,' she said
to him with as much patience as she could.

Mort blushed and slowly extended his other hand.

'Why?' Mendina asked and the flames flickered.

'Take his hand, Mendina. I wish to show you some of his power.'

'What are you talking about, Mother?' Mort asked. He had no
idea what she meant by that.

'Take his hand, Mendina,' was all that his mother said, not taking
her eyes from Mendina's.

Slowly, the elven girl reached out and clasped hold of Mort's
hand. It was tiny and soft and Mort looked down at her. Mort heard
his mother speak a few words. They sounded Elfish, but he had never
heard them before and he didn't understand what they meant.

He began to feel a tingling sensation in his head, or more
accurately, in his mind. He felt something course through his chest
and into his arm. It then flowed through his fingers into Mendina
and was gone.

Corein let his hand go and he looked around at her. He could
feel and see that she was exhausted. She sat down in her chair and
closed her eyes.

Mort looked back to Mendina, who still had hold of his hand.
The flames had gone from her eyes and been replaced by tears. She

looked at Mort, let go of his hand, and fled from the house. Mort started to follow her.

'Let her go, Mort. It is best that she is left alone for a while.'

'But it is not safe outside,' he said to her in a pained voice. The look Mendina had given him had been one of incredible sorrow and disappointment.

'She will not go far, only to the trees, Mort,' she said in a frail voice.

'What did I do to her mother? Did you see how she looked at me? She hates me now.' He didn't know why he thought that but he was sure of it.

'You did not really do anything to her Mort. I did.'

'You did?' Mort exclaimed. He would be glad when he could sit and put all of his thoughts together. 'You cannot perform magic mother, how could you do anything to Mendina? I felt whatever it was going through my mind.' He was sure that it had.

'I used you as a medium. Jarkene showed me how it is done and I will show you one day, but it is enough to know that Mendina was at a point where her senses had been overcome Mort.'

Corein looked at Mort's puzzled face.

'Did you see the flames in her eyes, Mort?' she asked.

'I didn't want to mention anything about that while she was here,' he replied, still not understanding anything that was happening.

'I have seen that look in the eyes of elves before. I saw it in the eyes of your father, the very last time I saw him alive.' Tears were in his mother's eyes now. 'It is a bloodlust of the elves. It rarely happens, only after something terribly dramatic happens to one of them.' She paused for a moment to compose herself. 'There is a method to prevent it,' she continued, 'through the touch of one powerful enough and a few spoken words.' The tears flowed freely now and for some reason Mort knew what his mother was going to say next.

'I understand, Mother,' Mort said in a strong voice, trying to give her strength through his words. 'You did all that you could I am sure.'

She stared at him and then put her head into her hands.

Mort could hear the muffled words she spoke. He understood a little more now. She had told him how his father had died. Now he had some idea of why.

'He would not let me help him, Mort,' she sobbed. 'I could have helped him, but he was so angry. I could have helped him.'

Mort knelt down and held his mother. Neither spoke any further before they both fell into a deep sleep. Mort kneeling by her chair, his hand in hers and her tears in his hair.

Mendina came back into the house a few hours after dark and sat quietly down on the floor. Corein and Mort both woke as she came in. Mort stood up but stayed next to his mother.

'My apologies, Lady Corein, we are all aware of Lord Jarkene.' Mort noticed that her voice was very formal. 'If I may stay here for the night until the fires have burnt out, then is there still a place that I may sleep?'

'Of course, Mendina,' Mort's mother replied kindly, 'Mort's room is through there.' She pointed to a door behind Mendina.

Mendina rose. 'Thank you,' she spoke to them both and then retired to Mort's room.

Corein said goodnight to Mort and went to her own room.

Mort walked over to the window facing out on to the forest. It was a dark night outside, made even eerier by the silence coming from the forest. Mort had never heard it so quiet and it sent a chill down his spine. Yet it also sparked anger within him. Mort had always loved the sounds of the forest, especially at night.

Now someone or something had taken it from him. That something had also upset Mendina and he could only assume had also devastated her people. His people also, he thought for the first time.

Mort had never had a bad temper. He had only ever seen the beauty in things. He had seen how harsh nature could sometimes be but he understood its purpose. He believed everything possessed some form of beauty and goodness.

Now he was not so sure. For the first time in his life, he began to feel the stirrings of hate. Even though he knew his mother was right in quenching the bloodlust, he also knew that if Mendina asked him to do something for her, he would have to say yes. It scared him that he may act against his mother's wishes, but the spell Mendina had cast upon him still held firm. He wanted to help her however he could and he knew not the power that was within him.

The next morning, Mort awoke from where he had slept on the floor and walked out into the kitchen. His mother and Mendina were both up. Neither was talking.

Mort's mother turned around and looked at him. He saw sadness in her eyes, and he knew his mirrored the same look.

He looked down and saw a pack at her feet.

'Thank you,' he said. 'You are not coming with us?'

'There are enough supplies there to sustain both of you for quite a few days Mort.' She spoke in a soft voice and tried to smile, but he could see tears begin to well in her eyes.

Mort didn't think she was going to come, but he hadn't fully thought through the pain it would cause his mother. He had been too caught up in wanting to help Mendina.

'I won't be gone all that long mother,' he replied.

'I know,' she said and walked up to him and gave him a hug. She kissed his cheeks and the top of his head and then hugged him again. She held him out at arm's length.

'I'm proud of you, Mort. You have always been a wonderful son. You are strong and caring to a fault. But listen to me now.' She looked across at Mendina and then back to her son. 'The two of you lack experience outside of your homes.'

Mort stared at his mother and tried to take in all she said, but he felt empty inside.

'Mort, you have powers I cannot begin to describe,' she continued, 'but Mendina can help you in a small way with those.' She paused then as tears streamed down her face.

'It's okay mother,' he said. 'I will be home soon.' He reached down and picked up the supplies pack and flung it over his shoulder.

'I love you, Mother,' he said. He looked to Mendina, who was watching them both with no expression on her face. She turned away when he looked her way and walked out the front door.

Mort smiled at his mother and then followed her outside.

They walked in silence for most of the morning. Mendina led and Mort followed. This part of the forest hadn't been burnt by the fires that had engulfed the centre, but the trees were still mourning and had withdrawn.

The animals hadn't returned either. Mort had no idea where the ones that survived may have fled. He looked ahead and could see thin wisps of smoke in the distance where trees still smouldered.

He had never been anywhere near the centre of the forest, although he had always wanted to see the elven city. Now he would get his chance and he was dreading it.

He could feel the anguish radiating from Mendina. She continued to look straight ahead as they walked and Mort just followed, trailing along behind like a lost puppy.

Around midday, Mendina stopped and sat at the base of a tree. She looked at Mort. 'We should rest a little and have something to eat.'

Mort sat down next to her and opened the pack his mother had given them.

There was plenty of food to eat but neither felt like much, so they picked at some bread and continued on.

Mendina was in a hurry to reach the elven city before night fell. But they had moved quickly throughout the day and both were mentally and physically tired when they reached the first of the burnt-out trees in the middle of the afternoon. Neither of them crossed over the wide but shallow stream that had acted as a saviour for the trees on this side of the water. The winds had obviously not blown across the water or else this barrier would not have been enough to save them from the burning sparks.

Both looked across at the once mighty trees that were now blackened husks. Mort could feel the despair that washed over Mendina, even sharper than the hollow anguish that she had been radiating throughout their journey that day. He also felt a profound sadness. This once mighty forest, alive with fey creatures and proud trees, was now a wasteland. The sun shone freely now to the forest floor as wisps of smoke still rose out of the ashes. Many of the giant roots and trunks still smouldered and burnt underground.

'We should rest here for a while,' Mort suggested after a time of standing and staring. 'I think we both need to regain some strength before we move on.'

Mendina said nothing. She gave no indication that she had even heard him speak.

They both sat for a short time, and then, without a word, Mendina rose to her feet and began to walk across the stream.

Mort picked up his pack and followed after. He didn't know what he could possibly say to her, so he said nothing. In truth, he was relieved to stay quiet.

The despair he felt from Mendina did not diminish as they walked through the burnt-out part of the forest. The further in Mort walked, the number he himself became.

After another couple of hours walking, Mort's perception of the forest began to change, as Mendina's pace increased.

He could feel the forest within him now, stronger than he ever had before. The wind that blew gently against him and the ground he walked on were amplified. His senses were heightened tenfold. But he also felt emptiness like he never had before.

'It is close now,' Mendina said suddenly. She hadn't spoken for hours and Mort was slightly startled at the sound of her voice.

He looked ahead and the blackened tree husks were a memory only.

There were no burning husks standing before them. Instead, trees lay at odd angles out of the ground, as if they had been blasted out. Some were splintered and smashed apart. Others were uprooted and twisted among the others.

Mendina was walking ahead of Mort. He stopped to stare at what was ahead of him. Mendina halted about twenty paces in front of Mort at the twisted and splintered remains of a once mighty tree.

He saw her fall to her hands and knees. She put her head to the ground between her hands and began to sob. Mort stayed where he was.

He no longer felt pity and sadness for Mendina. The anger that had been born in his belly the night before now rose to his chest and to his head. He could literally feel his head begin to throb.

Unbeknown to him, the powers that his mother said were within him had their origin here in the centre of Glorfiden. And although the elves had been all but wiped out, that power remained and it recognised Mort.

Mendina bowed before the mighty tree. Even in death, it was still a marvel to her and much loved. She kissed the dirt that its trunk had spat from the earth. It was worse than she could have imagined. The heart of Glorfiden should have been visible to her now but instead she saw a bleak landscape of destruction. The trees were no more. Her home was no more. The elves were no more. She wasn't even sure if the power of Glorfiden was still alive.

She thought she could feel it within her still, but it seemed less than before. This fact was frightening to her because it was a source that was shared by all of the elves.

As she knelt and began to draw a small amount of the magic into her, she felt a massive amount of it suddenly drawn to a space behind her.

She turned and looked at Mort. He stood a short distance away and was looking straight at her. She took a few steps towards him, frowning at the way he was staring at her. As she moved yet closer she realised he wasn't staring at her. She didn't think he would be able to see her at all.

The magic that Mendina could feel pulsing through him was extraordinary. She thought she could almost see it, such was the intensity. A barely perceptible aura surrounded him.

She panicked for a moment thinking that it may be the bloodlust within him, but his eyes were clear.

Without even meaning to, Mendina felt herself draw some of the magic from him. She soon realised that Mort was in fact feeding it to her, although not by choice. He was trying to draw so much into himself, that the excess which had nowhere else to go was finding its way to her. She felt more alive than she ever had. Her body tingled with it.

It lasted only a short time before the stream of power ceased, but she was still buzzing with it when she realised Mort had stopped drawing it in.

She was concerned at how much he still held within him. It must be enormous.

She looked intently at him and saw that his eyes remained distant. She knew his mind was still elsewhere.

Minutes passed and Mendina stood transfixed by him, waiting to see what would happen, when Mort suddenly let out a long breath and fell to his knees, much of the power slowly draining from his body and mind.

Mendina walked over to him and lifted his body up. His eyes, the colours still swirling in them, looked dim. His breathing was laboured, but he looked at her this time and not through her.

'I found him.' he managed to say in a strained voice before his eyes closed and he collapsed into a deep sleep.

Mendina did not want to stay here next to the mangled trees, but she was tired as well and knew she couldn't drag his prone body anywhere else, let alone carry him.

She sat next to where he lay; all his features and clothing covered in ash and numbly looked around her waiting for him to wake.

Mendina fell asleep sometime after dark and didn't awaken until the sun was rising. She opened her eyes and looked over at Mort. He was still asleep but his breathing was steady now and the colour had returned to his face. She stretched her arms and legs as she stood, her body sore from a night sleeping on the forest floor.

She reached down and gently prodded him in the shoulder.

He woke at her touch and sat up looking at her.

Before she could ask, he rubbed his eyes and spoke to her.

'I found him, Mendina,' he repeated again in a voice choked with emotion.

Mendina was excited by his words, as she had been the night before when he first spoke them to her. Her mind had raced at the time and she had wanted to shake him awake on several occasions, but had decided to let him sleep.

Mort could see her eyes dancing and her senses alive with hope.

'Where is he, Mort? Where is the Protector?'

Mort lowered his eyes. He had been foolish. He should have guessed what his words would mean to her.

He looked up at her, at the hope in her face and the expectation in those perfect features. He saw them dashed as he spoke and his heart became even harder.

'Not Glendrond. I'm sorry. I didn't find him.' He saw the hope turn to confusion and then anger.

'What are you talking about!' she said in a shocked voice. 'You said you'd found him!'

'No. I found the one who did this.' He spoke in a quiet voice. 'I followed the power, the magic that brought the storm to Glorfiden. . .

He paused now because he didn't know how to say the next few words.

Mendina grabbed him by the front of his shirt and lifted him to his feet.

'Who did this? Who did you find and where is he?' Her words were forced and she choked on them as she spoke.

Mort just looked at her with a sad and forlorn look.

'Who?' she screamed at him, pushing him in the chest.

'I followed it to the mountains, to a man sitting by himself on a cliff ledge.' He spoke quietly, looking at the ground.

Then he looked up at her with a pained expression on his face and tears in his eyes.

'I found my father, Mendina . . . my father is alive.' He stepped back from her, gently took her hands from his shirt and turned to face the other way. He didn't want to see the look on her face any longer.

He stood there for seconds more staring towards the distant mountains before he spoke again.

'Jarkene sent the storm,' he said to her in a strained voice.

'My father destroyed Glorfiden.'

CHAPTER 5

KABIR—The Gamer of Destiny

K ABIR HAD CHOSEN and then re-chosen a number of times in the months prior to the game beginning.

Back when it began, they were told that their realms weren't created until after each race was decided. No one would have been comfortable choosing a realm of dwarven warriors with the chance they would end up in a woodland realm. Therefore, their choice of race was all they had to concern themselves with before anything else.

Like Mendina, magic had been his first and most obvious choice. It would make for a powerful champion, but it was expensive.

Amassing numbers had been another choice he had tossed aside after settling on it for a time. He had almost committed to that one.

A small statured man with little physical strength, Kabir was intrigued with the magic the game offered. The others would assume that his would be a champion strong in magic. He did not intend to be so predictable.

Part of their training had been in learning about those they would be competing against.

As a result, none of the others spoke much about their own home worlds or about their own thoughts and strategy. Information and intelligence were an important aspect of the game. They asked each other questions to clarify rules within the game and they asked each other what they knew of other worlds, but rarely anything of consequence was shared. Most of their topics concentrated instead on the mundane.

Others weren't so forthcoming even with small talk. Kabir didn't think of himself as arrogant, but he knew he came across less friendly than some of the others. Yet he felt at times that they looked down upon him and he didn't appreciate that. It helped fuel his competitiveness, which he took as a good thing.

He was also smart enough to know that part of his feeling that way was his own insecurity.

He had been short amongst the other children from his world, but it wasn't until he had been brought to the Creator's world that he realised that his people as a whole were short in stature. He had felt his lack of height even more so then.

Perhaps this was part of the reason why he had in the end settled on barbarians.

Yet even after he had informed the Creator, he still wasn't totally comfortable with his choice.

He had studied their kind and believed that a single barbarian would be a strong champion. He had always imagined being taller and the hulking highland barbarians were certainly that. Although lacking in any magic and easy prey early on to those with magic, he knew that before the time came to choose his champion he would have defences against the magic that some of the others would invariably select. He suspected that Mendina would choose elves and although they would be powerful from the very beginning, he didn't believe they would venture out of their own realm to try and attack others. He assumed that most; if not all of those in the game; would stay where they were to begin with and try to build up their strength first.

Once he had committed to his choice he turned his mind to what resources he would need to strengthen his realm. Prey to eat; that would survive the harsh climate they lived in and provide good nutrition. Predators to assist with their learning and ability to fight, hunt and become feared predators themselves. Barbarians were not a prolific race and the population would never grow to the proportions others would, but their habitat would be good protection against invasion.

His predictions had panned out exactly as he had envisaged them in his mind when the game had begun all those years before.

His allowance to spend was limited and he had only been able to contribute each 100 years, but the resources he needed grew less on each occasion.

Over the past 1,000 years, he had devoted nearly all of it into an item that he was confident would protect his champion.

He was excited at the prospect of the game finally beginning. All of their hard work and study would soon be at an end and the real game would begin. There would be no more decisions and choices to make.

Looking at the one he had chosen as his champion, he was more than a little proud. Although they had never been told they would be judged or graded on their performances, Kabir knew that in many ways they would be and future prospects probably depended on a good showing.

The skills shown even getting to this point would be noted also, of that he was confident.

Their selections in relation to their choice of fauna, flora, and habitat were important in the development of their races and the ultimate skill of their chosen one.

He was unsure what happened to those of them that weren't successful in this game. He had spoken to the others in length about it, but if any of them knew they weren't sharing. They all seemed to be in the dark about it as much as he was. Those few that had left his world in years gone by to play their own game had never returned. Their fate remained unknown.

None of those he was competing against in Dark Swell had come from the same world. They all had different personalities and he wasn't aware of any friendships that had developed. He certainly had no one that he confided in. His infrequent discussions with Mendina were the closest thing he had to either friendship or companionship. They were all solitary and none trusting of the others.

Their time here since they were young had revolved around education. They all took it seriously, some more than others. The honour of being selected had been much sought after on his home world and he assumed it was the same for the others.

Yet before they arrived here, none knew exactly where they were going or what they had been chosen for. It was a time honoured tradition that just prior to the age of 12 each child was tested in the capital, on the chance that the Creator should appear to choose one of them. The elders said that it was an honour for those that were chosen and that their futures would be one of excitement, prestige, and privilege.

Of course, he was only 12 at the time and his thoughts were simply of the mystery and adventure such a journey would lead him to.

Since the day he had been chosen his efforts and desire had increased beyond measure, and he had put his heart and soul into his studies and then into the game.

Now all he had to do was sit back and see how his champion would fare.

CHAPTER 6

Kabir—The Champion

KABIR COULD NOT remember being this nervous before. His coming-of-age three cycles ago had given him less trepidation and he had been only 18. Yet back then, he hadn't felt the same excitement either.

A thrill coursed through his body and mind and he thought of all the stories told to him while he had grown into a man. They all started here and they all spoke of the thrill of the beginning.

He was the first for many cycles who had chosen the path of adventure.

Now he was leaving his clan. He was leaving his father and he was saying good-bye to his younger brother Wilhelm.

His father Rondig he would miss. Rondig was a respected man in their upland village of Deerstep. He was a strong warrior and he had taught Kabir all that he could, until Kabir had surpassed him and he could teach him no more.

Rondig had not encouraged his son to leave Deerstep. He had understood and helped Kabir where he could, but he had heard of the world outside and he feared that he would not see his son again.

In the end, when he saw there was no swaying him from his chosen path, Rondig had given Kabir his sword. The greatest treasure he owned, it was a mighty weapon crafted by the smiths of old and handed down. Not many of the older crafts remained in the village of Deerstep.

Kabir would miss his father, but he was not saddened.

Wilhelm was the one who nagged at his free spirit.

Wilhelm idolised his brother and Kabir knew it. It had torn at him more and more as the day of his leaving grew nearer.

Wilhelm was still 6 months from his coming-of-age and although not the brutish warrior Kabir was, his brother was strong and possessed a wit that he admired enormously. Wilhelm was an intelligent fighter and fast. Kabir himself was a giant, even among the men of the highlands and his strength was unmatched.

Their mother had died when Wilhelm was seven cycles, in a raid from a distant warrior clan. Kabir had been only 11 at the time and had killed the man responsible using a small axe used for chopping splinter. He had been charged by his father to protect her, though his father never blamed him for her death. Neither did his little brother. Instead Wilhelm had gone everywhere with him. Kabir was his role model and his idol.

Motherless, Wilhelm's wit and temper would often get him into trouble with elders and other boys his age and older. Kabir was always there to sort it out. Many an arm and leg he had broken in defence of his little brother.

They were as close as brothers could be.

Leaving Wilhelm stung Kabir and the pain would not abate.

Yet he would never show that pain to the outside world. Never had he shown weakness to his brother. He had not even wept at his mother's burial, although her death had tolled more deeply on him than any knew.

He was a warrior now, soon to be an adventurer and his heart needed to be like stone if he hoped to get very far.

The night before his departure, Kabir and Wilhelm went up into the mountains from their shallow valley to say their farewells.

They walked to a creek where they had duelled together on countless occasions and sat with their legs in the water as they had done when they were small boys.

'I will follow your tracks in six months' time at my coming Kabir and I will find you,' Wilhelm told his brother in a serious voice.

'If only Wil,' Kabir replied in a soft voice and then paused. 'But you know as well as I that the elders choose your path, not I nor even the gods. At 21,' he went on, 'you can come find me. In fact, if you do not then I will come back here myself and thrash you for it.'

They both laughed for a brief moment and then sat staring at the waters. It was a clear night, although the moon was only a quarter full.

'So be it.' Wilhelm pledged after a while. 'And I will already be renowned throughout the land as the brother of the mighty Kabir. Feared throughout the land by all men and the toast of virgins in every cottage and castle.'

'Ha, you have that right Wil.' Kabir chuckled. 'So in the mean time you will be strong and you will continue to push yourself. So that when you join me, one or two of the scrawnier maidens I will give to you and you will not disappoint them.'

Wilhelm gave Kabir one of his mischievous grins.

'You had better make the most of it big brother, because when I join you I fear that only the farm animals will be satisfied to have you over me.' He made the sound of a sheep lost in the night.

Kabir reached across and grabbed his little brother in a headlock and threw him headfirst into the water. Wilhelm surfaced spluttering, stepped back onto dry land and sat back down next to his brother, shaking the water from his dripping hair.

'My apologies mighty warrior,' Wilhelm said in all seriousness, shivering a little from the freezing cold water. 'I meant no affront to your enormous ego, which I thought large enough to withstand much more than that.'

Kabir laughed. 'You never were one to learn a lesson very quickly. I will continue this with you at a later date little brother.' He stood then and looked down at Wilhelm, who was now sitting and staring at the water.

'I will not be here to watch over you now Wil,' he continued in a serious tone. 'But the gods see you and you cannot fool them.'

He reached down his hand and Wil grasped it but did not rise.

With a final farewell that required no words, the brothers said good-bye and Kabir strode back down to the village to finish his preparations.

In the morning Kabir departed to a rousing send off.

Wilhelm still sat up by the creek. He had not gone to see his brother off. He could not. Instead he had sat there all night, looking into the flames of the small fire he had lit, thinking of what life without his brother would be like.

It was true that he thought the world of his brother and had learned much from him as a warrior. It was also true that his brother had been there to 'rescue him' on numerous occasions. Yet in truth, on many of those occasions he hadn't needed rescuing.

For Wilhelm was the only one, including his brother, who knew how much the death of their mother had really affected him.

Wilhelm knew that Kabir missed her and thought of her every single day, reliving the nightmare of watching her die over and over again. It was at times when he saw it getting to his brother that he would help move his mind on to other more immediate things . . . And it usually worked. Kabir would be at him for days mothering him, guilty at leaving Wilhelm without his real mother.

Wilhelm knew that Kabir felt terrible for leaving him, that it played hard on his mind.

They were brothers and they were best friends and Wilhelm knew that Kabir feared what would happen to his little brother without him there to protect him.

But Wilhelm held no concerns for himself. He practised hard against the other boys and men in the village and held his own against most. But he never tried too hard, much to his brother's disgust. Kabir kept at him, telling him of his potential if he tried harder, but Wilhelm didn't feel the need to prove himself. He enjoyed his brother's attention.

In his own time when he went into the mountains for solace, he practised hard. Very hard. And he knew not only his potential, but that his own skills and desire were well above the others in the village. Maybe even close to those of his brother.

So as he sat there by the stream and as his brother rode away wracked with guilt for leaving, Wilhelm felt similar emotions. He worried how his brother would cope without his little brother there to take care of him.

Wilhelm already knew that the adventurer's life was for him and he began making the preparations in his head for when he would leave.

He respected the elders and he respected his father enormously.

Nevertheless, in six months' time he would begin the search for his brother.

Kabir pulled up his horse and looked back at his home for the last time.

His brother had not been there to see him off, but he had not expected him to be.

Turning back to where he was headed Kabir felt only loneliness, not the exhilaration he thought that he would be feeling.

He had no set destination and he had no companion. He would have loved for his brother to have come along with him, but neither his father nor the rest of the clan elders would ever allow such a thing. A man was a man at twenty-one and not before. Wilhelm would have to wait.

He thought of what his brother had told him last night, of being feared by all men and the toast of all virgins. He thought if he could harness his loneliness and guilt into making his brother proud, then he would find it much easier to continue.

He began to feel his anxiety wash away as he imagined them riding together. He could but hope and wait for the day when his little brother could join him.

Driving his boots into the belly of his mount, Kabir rode down off the valley summit and into the world beyond.

He rode strongly for two days through the highlands of his people where he had hunted many days and nights. He intended to put behind him the land he was familiar with as quickly as he could. The familiar settings stung him with memories of his brother and he needed to be far away from it soon so that he could concentrate on the task ahead.

Although that task was unknown, there was so much potential for his sword that he wanted to be strong of mind; stronger even than the steel of his own enormous bulk and the sword at his back.

He wanted his father and especially his brother to be proud of him. Kabir remembered the stories of those who had left for adventure, found it, and come back to the highland to retire and tell of their experiences and mighty deeds. They had never stayed long. An adventurer's retirement was never long lived. Those of the highlanders who were born with the blood of adventuring were forever on the move.

Kabir was one such highlander and his expectations were enormous, expectations that didn't have to wait long before being given their first exposure of the roads ahead.

It was dusk of Kabir's fourth day from his village.

The hills and valleys of his home he had left behind him the day before. He'd ridden down from the last valley onto a stretch of land that lay flat, but for the sparse growth of small tangled trees and bushes that protruded from the high grass.

These were the grasslands that Kabir had heard told of and they stretched for many leagues to the south of where he was. Very few adventurers from Deerstep came this way and those that had did not head south, but rather skirted the boundaries in order to avoid the villages both east and north of Deerstep. Kabir also had no desire to venture through or near any other village. Although there hadn't been a major skirmish or battle for over ten seasons, not many of the highland clans were friendly to one another and they protected their lands fiercely.

To the west of where he stood was a mountain range, seemingly small from this distance, but a range of colossus' that dwarfed those where he came from. To the far-east would be the roar of the ocean and the end of the world beyond that. He decided that he would ride as far south as he could before turning his sights to those very mountains and the glory contained in the lands beyond.

He had been searching for somewhere suitable to rest for the night, but had seen nothing that resembled shelter from the chilly night air.

He spurred his horse forward south in a challenge to the new land he had entered. He would ride the night out if he had to.

Yet as soon as the sun had vanished below the horizon, Kabir's mount stumbled in the grass and both rider and horse went crashing to the ground. The impact with the earth knocked the breath from his lungs as his back hit first, yet he managed somehow to push himself clear of his horse as it skidded through the grass.

'Fool,' he muttered angrily to himself as he stood gingerly up off the ground. 'A lot of good I'll do killing myself galloping at night.'

Walking over to his horse he swore in anger and in sorrow. His horse had not stumbled back to its feet. In the remaining dim light from the glow of the quarter moon, Kabir could see from the angle of its neck that it would not rise again.

He stood for a moment transfixed by it all and then went to see what it was his horse had tripped over.

He soon located what he was looking for but was surprised by what he found. Stretched between two of the small trees scattered throughout the plains was a fine, but strong piece of rope. Someone had deliberately set a trap. Even in the daylight, Kabir doubted that he would have seen it, but he still cursed himself again for his foolishness.

He walked back to where his horse lay, removed all of his supplies from it and spread them out on the ground. He then put out his blankets and lay down on the hard ground.

Deciding to wait until first light to move on, Kabir tried to get some sleep. It didn't take him long to find his way to the path of dreams.

In the morning, Kabir rose and looked at his things. Some of them he would have to leave behind, so he grabbed those he thought most important. Water was essential. He hadn't seen any since he left the highlands and didn't know which direction the next stream or river lay. It would take him days to walk back the way he had come, but he didn't want to risk venturing any further into the vast plains without a horse.

He grabbed his blankets also. He didn't fancy freezing to death during the cold nights.

Some food, his flint and his sword were the only other items he took.

His bow, arrows, and his traps were left behind, too cumbersome to carry on foot, as was the greater proportion of his food. He would have enough food and water to last him several days. Once he was back in the highlands, he knew that he would have no trouble finding either.

Saying a farewell to his mount, Kabir began his trek back towards his homelands, where he would have to start afresh after he managed to secure himself another horse. His pride was hurt, but his body was still whole. The fire in his belly now burned even stronger.

After several hours, Kabir stopped to rest. The plains had seemed far less daunting when he had been riding on his horse. On foot, the grass reached his hips, and although pushing through it was not hard, it was tiresome.

He sat near one of the trees and took out his water bottle and some food.

After a short while, he packed up his things and was about to set off again, when he heard a rumbling in the distance coming from the east.

He moved behind the cover of the tree and looked to see what it was that approached.

After a while he began to make out small shapes, which soon became larger, much larger. He had never seen such horses before. The one he had ridden here on could have one been one of their foals.

There were between fifteen and twenty of them, each with a human rider on their backs. Although they were heading in his general direction, if he stayed where he was they looked likely to pass him by about one hundred paces to the north.

Feeling brave and a little bored, Kabir stepped out from behind the tree.

He heard a few short shouts and watched as about six of the horsemen came towards him. The others fanned out in groups of three or four, circling the area where he stood.

Kabir raised his arms above his head in a gesture of peace and to show that he had no weapon in his hand.

The six horsemen stopped about ten metres in front of him. Three of them held arrows poised and aimed in his direction. Two scoured the surroundings and looked to the others that had circled around. The other one stepped his horse closer to Kabir, stopping about 5 metres in front of him. The bowmen all still had a clear shot at him.

Up close, Kabir couldn't help but stare at the horse standing in front of him.

Half again as tall as he was, it had a short but thick coat of hair, with a light-brown colouring.

'What are you doing in the plains highlander?' the one closest to him asked. 'Are there any more of you?'

Shorter than the men of the highlands, the plainsmen sitting astride their horses in front of him still looked to be competent fighters.

As a man who spent most of his life fighting and hunting, Kabir was well able to judge a man's ability by the way he held himself and his weapons.

The bows were larger than his own, but he suspected that with little cover in the plains they would need to shoot larger distances. The men who held them taut and ready to fire did not seem to be straining at all. They were all well practised and adept.

The man who spoke to him held his sword in his right hand. It was pointed behind him by his side, but it looked well used and well cared for. The plainsmen had an air about them that spoke volumes to Kabir. They were shorter than his people and darker skinned, but they were strongly built and lean.

He knew that if he antagonised them, or if they just wanted it done, he would die now on this spot.

'I am alone. My name is Kabir.' Kabir replied.

'What are you doing in our plains?' he asked again.

'I have just left my home in search of adventure. I wish to make new friends and offer my sword to those that will have it.' Kabir decided that the truth was his best option. He had nothing to hide.

The man closest grinned at him.

'An adventurer!' he exclaimed in a loud voice, turning to his men.

Several chuckles came from the archers and those that now stood their mounts behind him. Kabir had known they were there but didn't turn. He did not want to offend the man he spoke to, who was obviously their leader.

'So I ask you again, highlander, what are you doing in *our* plains?' The leader asked it louder this time with an emphasis on the 'our'.

Kabir was confused and beginning to get a little impatient, but he held his temper in check again.

'Again, my name is Kabir and *I* seek adventure.' He emphasised the 'I', for no other reason than he was beginning to dislike the attitude of this man who looked down on him from his horse.

Their leader appeared to think for a moment and then asked another question.

'It would seem that you seek death, not adventure, travelling the plains on foot highlander.'

'My horse fell back there,' he indicated the direction with his head. 'It tripped on rope and broke its neck.' He thought about not speaking his next words, but he wanted to know. 'Did your people put them there?'

'No,' was all he said as he put his sword back into the sheath attached to his horse's saddle. It showed Kabir that the plainsman did not consider him a threat any longer and he did not intend to try and gut him with it either.

'If you could point me in the direction of the nearest water, I'll be on my way,' Kabir said. They obviously weren't going to ask him to join them any time soon.

The plainsman pointed in the direction that Kabir had been going, towards the highlands. He had hoped for more but wasn't surprised.

The plainsman leaned down on his mount, in a more relaxed posture.

'How well can you use that hulking sword on your back, highlander?' he asked, a small smile showing at the corner of his mouth.

Kabir's eyes lit up at the tone of the plainsman's voice. This was the opportunity he had been hoping for. A chance to prove his worth without ending up stuck with arrow tips.

He also read into the tone that they weren't too upset by his trespassing on their plains, as he wasn't any threat to them.

'I can use it quite well,' he said. 'If you are having any troubles in your land, I may be able to assist you and you in turn may be able to help me.'

'Help you?' The plainsman was obviously amused by Kabir's words. 'You are getting ahead of yourself, I think highlander.'

'Not at all,' Kabir replied, his arrogance returned in full. 'I will show any of you that are prepared to step off those giant horses just how well I can use my hulking sword.'

The leader of the plainsmen laughed and turned to the five horsemen behind him.

'Tremill!'

One of the plainsmen that had stood with the archers rode his mount forward and stopped next to his leader.

'Some swordplay with the highlander.'

Tremill dismounted gracefully from his mount and took his sword from its sheath.

Slender and straight, the sword looked like a dagger compared to Kabir's two-handed long sword. Kabir nodded to the leader and then again to Tremill, as he pulled his sword out from its sheath behind his back.

If you were a stranger and walked upon the scene now, it would look like a man fighting a boy. Tremill stood a foot shorter than Kabir, his sword almost the same. The barbarian looked like he could swallow him in an embrace.

But Kabir saw an adept warrior, if only by looking at the way he moved and held his sword. For all his arrogance, he never assumed anything about an opponent and always paid them every respect. Even after he had defeated them soundly.

Tremill was one of the finest swordsmen among his tribe. He looked at Kabir and saw only a slow, heavy fighter. He saw that even though Kabir was a giant, his sword was too big to swing effectively and his build was too bulky. He knew that Kabir was probably a fine warrior in battle, but against a fast and skilful opponent one on one, he would be out of his depth.

Kabir stepped forward and raised his sword above his head. He swung it in a full circle around his head and made for a sideways blow at Tremill's head.

Tremill ducked and moved in to stick the highlander in the stomach. The barbarian's swing had been even slower than he'd expected.

The next thing his brain registered, instead of his sword-piercing Kabir's torso, was a heavy blow to the back of his head and sprawling face first into the ground.

The highlander had moved too quickly for him. The sword stroke at his head had been a deliberate ruse to put him at ease and act too quickly. He felt the pointed end of the highlander's sword at the back of his neck, pressed far enough in to draw blood.

'I take it that you yield plainsman.' The highlander's deep voice seemed to boom in his ringing ears.

Tremill just lay there, furious at himself for falling to the highlander in front of all these men. He knew that he wouldn't hear the end of it until he had beaten all of their heads together.

'Impressive,' the leader said to Kabir. 'Now step back.'

Kabir stepped back from Tremill and returned his sword to its sheath.

'Not so fast highlander,' the leader continued. 'You did say that you would show any who would step off their horse, am I correct?' The last part spoken as he jumped from his horse and on to the ground. He took his sword from its sheath.

Kabir nodded his head to their leader and again took his sword out.

'My name is Denizen highlander, and if you can best me with that field plough you call a sword, then I will offer you that adventure you seek.'

'Denizen, my name is Kabir,' he repeated as a show of respect for the plainsman giving his name, 'and I accept.'

The two began to walk in a circle, tracking the movements of the other as they did.

Denizen was the only one amongst this group that could better Tremill with a sword and he held Kabir's victory in high regard.

The highlander had been deceptively fast, moving his body out of the way of Tremill's sword and then striking him in the back of his head with the pommel of his own. Denizen realised that Tremill had underestimated the highlander and would have a headache to remind him of it for a while. The highlander could use his giant sword with ease and was much quicker than he looked.

A dangerous adversary, but Denizen was older and more experienced. He would wait until an opening showed itself.

Kabir moved in at the plainsman, swinging his sword in wide arcs, keeping his opponent back. He had the advantage of height and his sword was longer. He didn't want to give his opponent the chance to get close to him.

Kabir noted that Denizen's feet moved well and his defensive movements were fluid. He moved with the grace of a fine swordsman. Kabir kept at him, raining blows at his head and body. Denizen continued to move backwards, jumping out of the way or moving his body to avoid the barbarian's sword, until he was finally forced to use his sword to block one of Kabir's attacks. Kabir anticipated that he would now finally try and counterattack, but what happened took them both by surprise.

Denizen's sword shattered as he held it by his side to block a sweeping blow aimed at his torso. Kabir kept his wits enough to stop his own sword biting deep into the side of the plainsman, but he could see that the impact severely jarred both of Denizen's arms, as his grip loosened on what was left of his sword.

It was the first time Kabir had used his father's sword in combat. Thinking back, it was the first time he had seen it used in any sort of contest. His father had never used it in practice, but he was bullish when he insisted Kabir take it in place of his previous sword.

When he had first held it, he had admired how light it felt and how keen the blade was. But it wasn't until this moment that he realised just how fine a gift it was his father had given him.

Kabir looked from his sword to the plainsman. Denizen still stood with a bewildered look on his face.

'That didn't seem to be an even contest,' Denizen finally said to the barbarian. His expression made his displeasure plain. 'Is that a dwarven blade?!' he asked, his question laced with suspicion.

Kabir shook his head and was about to answer when suddenly some of Denizen's men began shouting and shooting arrows into the high grass surrounding them.

Kabir stood there confused, until the creatures they were shooting at leapt from the grasses and attacked.

He had never seen the like before. They seemed to be half wildcat and half insect. Their heads were human shaped but with two giant bulbous eyes and mandibles. Their bodies were the same shape and size as a large wildcat, but with claws instead of paws.

It was this body and their four legs that had enabled them to get so close through the grass without being spotted.

The plainsmen had been too engrossed in the fight and hadn't been watching for the tell-tale movements in the grass.

The first man to yell had been taken from his horse as one of the insect creatures leapt from the ground. It had crashed on top of him and pierced his chest with its front claw.

Unknown to Kabir, the plainsmen had fought with the insect creatures for many years and knew how to fight them.

Denizen called his men to him as he leapt back astride his horse.

In a single contest, the insect creatures moved too quickly and were too powerful, however, in a group Denizen and his men could watch for each other and fight them as a unit.

Denizen could see once he was back on his horse that there were more of them than he had seen together in a long time and he knew they would not make it out of this alive.

The surprise attack had seen four of his men fall before they could begin to regroup and the insect creatures were among them now.

Kabir took it all in quickly. The creatures were quick and lethal and struck at the chest. It was a quick kill point.

The first one that came at Kabir went straight for his heart with its front claws as it jumped at him.

Kabir waited until the last moment and twisted his body out of the way as his sword tip crashed into the back of its insect head.

Unlike its smaller cousin, it didn't twitch and throw itself around. This insect had a spine and it died instantly.

Kabir almost didn't see the next one until it was upon him. Instead of leaping through the air like the one before, this one had crouched and ran at him through the grass. Its claw came at his leg, hoping to bring him down to the ground first instead of a quick kill.

Kabir's sword came down in a sweeping motion and severed the claw from its leg. He turned then and brought his sword down again through the back of its head as its body swept past him.

Three of the creatures saw their fellows fall to Kabir and moved at him at the same time. Kabir grinned and had decided on his first two moves just as they got to him. He moved in a backward arc, stepping away and to his right, away from the one that came at him from his left. His sword swung around as it went past him and cut through the hardened husk of its rump as he completed the arc. The creature skidded along the ground, smashing into one of its pack that was rushing at Kabir from his right. The third leapt through the air, avoiding the others as they crashed in a heap a short distance away. Kabir let himself fall backwards to the ground, swinging his sword in front as he did, slicing the insect creature from front to back.

The other regained its feet but was quickly skewered by arrows as two of Denizen's men found their mark.

Kabir had time to look around and saw Denizen fighting furiously with two more of the creatures. No longer on his horse, the creatures were swinging their claws at him from close range and Denizen was struggling to keep them at bay. His left arm hung limply by his side and blood streamed from an open wound in his scalp. The blood was limiting his vision and Kabir guessed he was moments away from a fatal strike. Without his sword, he had been forced to fight them with only a long dagger.

The Highlander let out a blood curdling roar, momentarily stunning both man and insect creatures, as he bounded over to where Denizen stood.

He moved in next to the plainsman as one of the creatures moved forward, just out of reach of Denizen's dagger but within reach of one of its own swinging claws. Kabir's sword was much longer than the plainsman's blade and it sunk into the creature's head. He moved to the side of the other, which quickly fell to Denizen's dagger as it moved its attention to the barbarian.

As quickly as that, the skirmish had turned against the insect creatures. Denizen's men had been given time to form up again and their arrows were now raining death. Three more of the plainsmen had been taken from their horses before they had managed to regroup, but Kabir's kills had been the difference in giving them time, distracting many of the others in their attack.

Those that remained alive turned to run, but none made it outside the range of the longbows and the arrows rarely missed.

Kabir got to Denizen as Tremill did, the plainsman putting a hand out to him.

'Thanks for your help, Highlander, but I will take care of him.' His tone was not harsh, but clearly he still wasn't completely trusting of Kabir.

Kabir took a step back, accepting that his help was not needed here.

Denizen indicated for Tremill to stand back. 'I don't need care, Tremill. I can walk. See to the men and the horses. We need to move as soon as we have everyone on a horse. Alive or dead, we're all heading back to camp.'

Tremill signalled to another plainsman on horseback and they began to move from man to man, checking on each and barking orders.

Denizen turned to Kabir.

'My thanks, Kabir. All those that live here owe their lives to you, of this I have no doubt.' He gave a short nod of his head to emphasise his words.

'I'm sure the same fate would have befallen me if not for your men.' Kabir was solemn in his reply and returned the short nod. Now was not the time for his usual brashness.

'You are welcome to return to our camp, to meet our leader, and to honour our dead,' Denizen offered. Kabir nodded his head in acceptance.

'Good,' Denizen replied. 'I will find you a horse shortly when we are ready to leave. We will speak of you replacing my sword later.'

The barbarian was smart enough not to reply to his last comment.

Kabir moved over to his belongings and took out an old rag, wiping down his sword with it. He looked admiringly at it as he did. The blood and other substances that had come out of those creatures wiped easily from its surface. He inspected the blade and saw that there wasn't a mark on it. Not a dent or scratch could be seen, as if it had only just been cooled in the forge from where it was created. A mighty gift indeed he thought again, as he slung it back into the scabbard on his back.

The trek back to the plainsmen's camp took the rest of the day. Kabir's horse—Denizen had said its name was Firth, which meant 'loyal' in their old tongue—was a fine beast and receptive to his commands for the most part. He heard a few chuckles from some of the men when the beast decided it wanted to stop for a rest or to eat some of the shorter grass they rode through, but overall he was impressed with it.

He had ridden the smaller horses from his home all his life, but he knew his skills paled to those men he now rode with. They seemed one with their horses, an extension of them rather than just a man controlling their movements with prods, kicks, and reins. Kabir watched them for much of the ride, hoping to glean an insight into whatever secrets they must use to do it, but he was no closer to working it out when they finally arrived just before dusk.

The camp sprawled out before him was exactly as he had been told it would be. Tents and enclosures for the horses. Somehow they had managed to find shaded areas to rest their horses, which surprised Kabir due to the sparse number of trees he had seen all day. Obviously, their steeds were their lifeblood and they treated them accordingly.

A young man approached him as he stopped behind the others.

'You ride Grinsom's stallion barbarian. One of the finest we have.' He didn't say anything else as Kabir dismounted and collected his saddle bags. He just took the reins from him and began to walk off with Firth.

'Hold there,' Kabir said to him.

The man paused but didn't turn his head.

'I am sorry for the loss of Grinsom and am honoured that his horse was able to bear me here.' He said it with a strong but sincere voice.

The man still didn't turn but inclined his head a little in acceptance of his words.

'What will happen to Firth now?' he asked.

This time the man, who not long ago would have been a boy, did turn his head and looked directly at Kabir.

'Usually, whoever kills one of our warriors claims his horse.' He paused before continuing. 'As it was one of the insect filth, Denizen will decide whether to give it to his son or to another more worthy of the honour.'

Kabir was surprised to hear this. Who could be deemed more worthy than the son of the man whose horse it was?

'What is your name?' Kabir asked.

Again he paused before answering, 'Gristenn, son of Grinsom.' He quickly turned again and walked away with the horse.

Kabir frowned and turned to follow Denizen into the camp.

They walked in silence until they reached a large tent, which was obviously that of their leader. It was as plain as all of those throughout the camp, but this one was larger and had two men standing guard outside it. The guards were taller and larger than those in the hunting party he had run into, but looked no less agile and dangerous. Probably more so, being in charge of the safety of their leader.

Denizen pulled aside the flap and beckoned for Kabir to follow him. No one asked him to relinquish his weapons, which he was thankful for. He doubted he would have handed his sword to them.

They walked in and he saw a man standing over a small table, nothing fancy, but it looked well made. Being nomadic, they had no large, bulky items anywhere that he could see within the tent, which made sense.

The man standing at the table was old, but still had a warrior's build and a steely gaze as he looked up and directed it at Kabir.

'You are welcome in my tent, Highlander,' he spoke in a deep, kind voice, but with an unforgiving undertone. 'I have heard already of the skirmish with the insects and your role in it.'

'I am pleased to meet you. . .,' he left the last bit hanging, waiting for him to introduce himself. 'All horsemen must be like this,' he thought to himself.

They stood for a time staring at one another until their leader spoke again. 'I am Crenshen and you have my thanks.'

'I am Kabir of the Highland village Deerstep and I am sorry for the men you have lost today.' Crenshen beckoned him to a cushioned seat to his left and then took a seat before him, with Denizen to his right.

'You are an adventurer Kabir?' he asked.

'I am. Seeking glory and wealth,' he replied with some of his bravado. 'But if there is no wealth to be found, I will happily accept the glory.' The corner of his mouth curled a little. Not an arrogant smirk, it was more just the thought of that glory that made him almost smile.

'We have a dilemma, Highlander, and it would have been an opportune occasion to ally ourselves with some of your people.' He looked disappointed and troubled.

'I am but one, but I am happy to assist with whatever dilemma ails your people,' he replied. He was unsure of what his people could assist with that these warrior horsemen couldn't cope with in their own homeland.

'I see your confusion, Kabir, and it is well founded. We don't need help when it comes to fighting in the plains. However, these insects have been attacking our hunting parties for many months now and seem to be getting bolder every week.' He spoke with some anger in his voice now. 'We are losing men. Only a handful before today, but this was by far the largest and most organised group we have encountered. I fear this will only increase.'

Kabir waited for him to continue, but when he did not, he chimed in. 'So you plan to take the fight to them, I assume?'

'That is the dilemma,' Denizen spoke for the first time since he had mounted his horse earlier today. He had his arm in a sling now, the result of his bicep being slashed open, but he showed no sign of the pain it must be causing him.

Kabir gave him a confused look and he continued.

'We know where they live. All of them. In the same place.'

'I take it they don't live in the plains then,' Kabir surmised.

'No, they do live in the open plains and in an open battle on the plains we would crush their shells and send every last one of them to the underworld,' Denizen answered with little emotion in his voice.

Kabir was confused again and he knew his face was an open book.

'They are part insects Kabir and their lair, although in the plains, is inside a vast dirt structure that none of our people have been inside. We assume it goes underground and is their colony, much as that of an ant. We can't fight them inside their home with our horses,' Denizen finished and looked back to Crenshen.

'I believe, based on what I have been told of your fighting today, that a horde of your people would do untold carnage inside their fortress of mud, which is why I was disappointed only one of you is here in my plains,' Crenshen finished.

An idea came to Kabir almost immediately. It wasn't what he had in mind when he had set out on his adventuring, but it still offered an opportunity for glorious battle and to be remembered by this group of plainsmen, who he already respected. They were fierce adversaries on their plains, atop their horses. They had adapted their skills to suit horseback, but they all appeared ready-made warriors and they had swords which they used well. Denizen, more than well.

'I see that you are time short, Crenshen,' Kabir began with all of his bluster, 'but I would be pleased to offer you my services in training your men in combat on the ground. A month or so under my direction and I am confident you would be able to send your men inside their dung pile and lay waste to the inhuman creatures inside.' He finished with a steely gaze to show the seriousness and confidence in his words.

Crenshen seemed genuinely surprised by the offer, if not all that taken by it.

'I appreciate the offer, Kabir, but I don't believe you can retrain men that have spent a lifetime learning the skills they have now, especially from someone so young. It wouldn't be enough. We would not prevail.'

'I would be honoured to go with your men, Crenshen,' Kabir continued, becoming more excited by the prospect as he spoke, completely ignoring the comment about his age. Older men had underestimated him before. 'I would be there with those in the front, and if their lair is like that of an ant, then the tunnels or corridors or whatever they have, will not be wide.' He paused for a moment. 'In fact,' he said in his most serious voice, 'I think that I will go there anyway. It sounds like a mighty challenge.' He finished with a grin.

Crenshen stared at the barbarian as if he were mad. Denizen had a small grin on his face, knowing full well from the short time he had known him that this crazy Highlander would probably do it.

He would die in the insect lair, but he would probably kill a lot of them before he did.

No one spoke for a time. Kabir waited for Crenshen to speak, Crenshen just continued to stare at him.

Finally, the leader of the plainsmen spoke.

'Our options are scarce, so although you speak like a man wanting to die in battle, I will let you train some of my men. A select number that already fight well on the ground. We have little to lose as we cannot fight them in their mud castle and they don't come out in enough numbers at once for us to cripple their attacks.' He sighed, as one resigned to the fact that he had no other options. 'You can begin tomorrow and I will rethink the idea after a week.'

Kabir smiled but then grew serious as Crenshen continued.

'Then in two days, after their bodies are readied and their loved ones say their farewells, the men we lost today will be honoured.' Crenshen looked to Kabir. 'There will be a man outside to take you to your tent. Go and rest, barbarian.'

Kabir rose and walked from the tent.

CHAPTER 7

LINF—Gamer of Destiny

L INF HAD BEEN a lot like Kabir in her thought processes. She chopped and changed her mind, weighing up the strengths of magic versus that of warriors versus that of numbers. The races that each gamer had to choose from had strengths and weaknesses already predetermined, along with their basic personality. This had all been set out by the Creator in their studies. Yet it didn't prevent them from adding their own touches and trialling different things during the 2,000 years prior to the Naming Day. The choices were many and varied and each had specific advantages and disadvantages.

In the end though, she had gone with numbers to stock up her realm.

Goblins were the most prolific of breeders amongst the races and excellent warriors as well. They had an inbuilt resistance to many forms of magic, and although limited in their use of traditional magic, she already had a strategy in mind which would give her champion an advantage to bolster the list of advantages the goblin already had.

Initially, she had concentrated her efforts on building up their numbers. She knew that her champion would come from an elite few of the stronger goblins, but survival was her main concern to begin with. Goblins were able to live in almost any environment and she wasn't averse to having them spread out into the realms of others, even if she couldn't see what they were doing there. She had studied the race deeply and had a fair idea what they would be getting up to. They weren't a creative race. A goblin's way was a 'survival of the fittest, take what you can' kind of mentality. They suited her intentions quite well.

She had hoped to try and wipe out a couple of the others early on if she could, before they were able to build up their realm's strength. Unfortunately, the others had been able to secure their realms sufficiently prior to her goblins' efforts to spread out.

There had even been times when other races had invaded her own realm in an effort to wipe them out.

A couple of times, they had come close, but hers was a hardy race and they repopulated quickly.

Within the world where she had been born, there were a lot of mystics and charms. Her mother had been one and had taught her the intricacies of her craft. There had been no real magic there, nor was there on any other world that she was aware of.

Unlike the worlds of the Creator, not like there was on Dark Swell.

Yet her upbringing on her home world had given her the spark for many ideas that she was able to use within the game. She had been able to imbue her own race with whatever powers and magic her mind allowed her, what her spending allowed her and of course what the Creator himself allowed. Fortunately, his restrictions had been few throughout the 2,000 years.

She was still amazed at what they were able to do within the world they had been given to play in.

Now they were close to the end, and she was confident in the one she would choose. She would be surprised if any of the others were able to predict how strong her champion was going to be.

CHAPTER 8

Linf—The Champion

'GET OUT OF my way, grunter!'
A foot struck out at the miserable pile of filth squatting in Greeble's path.

Linf had been waiting for most of the afternoon for Greeble to return, tediously scavenging for food, but without any luck.

Yet her mind was on another task, as the poison-tipped short sword, barely concealed by the rags that she wore, told of another, darker purpose. Greeble had what was coming to him and then some.

Linf had waited too long for this moment. Years of humiliation, sickening beatings, and constant hunger were to be nothing more than a memory after today.

She was disappointed that it would be over for him so soon, but she would not risk doing it any other way.

'Get out of my way grunter,' the younger goblin mimicked back, a wicked hint of malice in her voice that Greeble had never heard from the runt before. If Linf ever made a sound in his presence, he would beat her for it. Alarms rang through his head and with reflexes that many had underestimated before from a goblin of his size, Greeble leaped backwards and drew his sabre in one swift motion. Even as he had begun to move, Linf was knocked back. She staggered backwards and was almost knocked from her feet. It was as if she had been struck by something physical, yet she had seen nothing come near her. In the time it took her to steady herself, Greeble was already in his fighting stance and moving towards her.

It took him a little longer to crash into the ground as the potent poison took hold of his nervous system, Linf's short sword protruding guiltily from his abdomen.

Her first reaction at seeing her tribal chieftain's body convulse and then drop to the muddy pool at her feet was that of unbridled joy and pride. She had killed the mighty Greeble! They would respect her now, and best of all, they would fear her.

Linf leaned over Greeble's motionless corpse, impressed with the potency of the poison the pixies had given to her.

A few days' past, she had accidentally saved one from a falling branch.

She had in truth been waiting patiently in hiding for one to come by. One had, so she lunged quickly at it, only to have a branch fall on her where it had been standing moments before she startled it.

The pixies knew very well her intentions but decided to reward her nonetheless, offering for her to name her gift, thinking it would be food or gold. Linf chose the poison she had heard other goblin runts talking about.

Angered, but true to their word, the pixie's gave it to her. Her ribs and skull they had also helped mend. Linf thought of them only as stupid little creatures, easily fooled.

Linf had never had reason to think well of anyone or anything.

Still leaning over Greeble, she tore the sabre from his still warm grasp, carefully placing her own sword back into its sheath.

'Nice sword, Greeble,' Linf said to her ex-chieftain. 'Mind if I use it?'

She brought the sword down on Greeble's neck with a clean strike and then sent his head bouncing down the path with a swift kick.

'I would say that is the quickest you've moved for a long time, Greeble,' Linf commented to herself and then burst into a fit of laughter. It was all too good to be true.

Suddenly drawn away from her own world, Linf began to notice the women standing around watching her and then down the track a few of the men running her way. The looks on their faces showed they were none too happy with her heroic deed.

In her own secluded existence, Linf was unaware that the killing and looting had been good of late with Greeble in command.

Confusion reigned in her mind as they drew their swords and she saw the killing lust in their eyes. She quickly realised whose death they had in mind.

Without hesitation and with the practised throw of one who is skilled in the art of fleeing, Linf swung Greeble's sword in a wide arc and let it go.

It crashed into the leg of the nearest pursuer, Greeble's second in command Merthic and put him to the ground. It momentarily stopped the others also as they paused to watch him fall.

'Kill it!' Merthic howled as he sat up clutching his leg. 'Kill it,' he said again less forcefully, suddenly realising the impact the blow would have on his chances of fighting for the place of Chieftain. He would have none and his foes would not chance him recovering his health. The sword may as well have gone through his neck.

Linf knew it, too, as she paused for a quick grin at Merthic. 'Two swine in the one afternoon,' she thought. She turned and sprinted towards the east end of the village as a crossbow bolt sang through the air, crashing into a hut where her head had been moments before.

Linf's village was a large one as far as goblin settlements rated in present-day Dark Swell. King Dayhen continued to keep a reign on their numbers, as his ancestors had after the Raiding Wars, when the goblins would stream from the hills and mountains destroying all in their way.

But that was a long time ago and their culling of goblins decreased every season as the memories faded.

There were at least 10,000 occupying whatever space they could claim and hold on to. Greeble, being chieftain, had his hovel in the centre and that was where Linf had ended his reign.

Fortunately, for Linf, the rest of the huts and holes were scattered in a random fashion, which made the pursuit a difficult one.

As Linf darted around huts and along dirt tracks used as roadways through the village, the sounds of her pursuers—though no less determined—began to drop back. Linf was very quick for a goblin and the fear of capture lent wings to her feet.

After a few minutes, as she neared the edge of the village, the sounds of her pursuit had become goblins yelling out to others to look out for the young runt who had killed Greeble, rather than the mad pack following her trail. She was still not safe but her lease on life appeared to have been extended.

As she was looking over her shoulder with a grin, Linf crashed into something and was knocked flat on her back, the breath knocked right out of her. She shook her head and tried to take in as much air as she could. Looking up, she saw the face of a large adult goblin, a snarl on his face and his hand balled into a fist.

'You stupid piece of filth,' the goblin spat down at her. Her first thought was that she had been caught, before quickly realising that this brute had probably only stepped outside to see what the yelling was all about in the distance. He doesn't know what happened, Linf re-assured herself, but she still didn't want to stay here and explain herself. She would probably get a hiding anyway.

Linf stood up with a sorry and terrified look on her face, her hands behind her back. The goblin reached out a hand to grab her by the collar, clearly not threatened by the cowering little goblin in front of him. He staggered back as Linf swung her poisoned blade, cutting a large gash in his forearm. The goblin roared with anger and then shock, before collapsing backwards, his mouth frothing as he hit the ground.

Putting the sword back in its sheath, Linf started to take off again when she felt hands around her ankles. She tried to run but instead fell forward onto her face, screaming as she went down from the agony that suddenly lanced through her left calf. She looked back and saw a female goblin tearing into her leg with her teeth. She let go for a moment and looked at Linf.

'You killed Harfick, you runt. I will rip out your heart with my teeth!' she screamed, spitting out bits of flesh as she spoke.

In a horrified panic, Linf ripped her right leg free from her grip and kicked the other goblin as hard as she could in the face. She heard bone crunch and saw a spray of blood from the goblin's shattered nose, but the grip on her other leg did not loosen. Instead, her assailer lurched forward and tore another chunk from Linf's lower leg. The young goblin screamed with the agony and again kicked down, this time connecting to the temple. The grip on her ankle loosened momentarily and Linf managed to drag herself out of reach. The crazed goblin wench made another lunge towards her and for a third time Linf's right foot cracked into her face. She was knocked back, blood covering her face. Snarling still, she readied herself for another lunge.

'You stupid cow-dog!' Linf screamed through the pain. 'You die, too.'

Linf's last kick had given her the time she needed to draw the short sword from her sheath before she took hold of her leg for the third time. This time instead of kicking her, Linf leaned her body forward and rammed the sword into the top of her skull, just as her teeth were about to once more tear into her leg.

The older female goblin did not get up this time.

In a daze from the horrendous wounds she had sustained, Linf somehow managed to haul herself to her feet. In a mad adrenalin inspired charge, she half hopped, half stumbled forward towards the edge of the Goblin settlement, not knowing when or if the pursuit would catch her and in no condition to care. All her thoughts, when she could think at all, were of moving forward and not stopping.

Linf didn't know how long she had been running, but she had crashed through the undergrowth surrounding the settlement what seemed like an eternity ago. As the last of her strength left her and the numbness killed what was left of her adrenalin, she collapsed in the outputting roots of a huge oak tree. Pulling herself into a concealment of sorts, she lay her head down. The young goblin then closed her eyes and decided to let death take her.

Her last thought was that at least death would not be as bad as her life had been.

Linf awoke and saw that it was morning in the forest now. Her first thought was of hunger, as it always was when she awoke. That was shortly followed by how painful her leg was and how weak she felt. She was disappointed that she wasn't dead yet. Damp, with no food and her life force slowly ebbing away, Linf began to think about what it would be like to be dead. Such thoughts had never really entered her mind before. She had always been too busy surviving to give it much thought, but she was tired now and the pain was increasing as she came further out of sleep.

She had survived yet again, but knew that this time she was dying.

Her thoughts turned to the fat swine that had ripped her leg apart like a ripe fruit. Linf hoped she was feeling like she was right now. 'I should have gutted her like her slug of a man,' she said quietly to herself. Then she remembered that she had killed her, too. A small smile flitted across her face before being replaced by an anguished look of intense pain.

'You are an angry one, aren't you?' a voice said from the air in front of her. It was goblin speech, but not spoken by a goblin.

Linf squirmed back deeper against the trunk of the tree, letting her breath out as her leg moved and the pain caused her body to shudder. She could see no one and the air gave no scent out of the ordinary.

'Am I halfway to the next hell hole already?' Linf grated to the air through the pain.

'Perhaps, goblin-child,' the voice said, 'but I am from this side of the gate, not the other.'

Out of the air, a body formed in front of her. First the head and then the rest of it. A cloak of some sort had concealed it from her, including its scent. Even in her weakened state, Linf could appreciate what a fantastic cloak it was and how nice it would be for her to have it. She could sneak up on anything she wanted and kill it before it even knew she was there. She would never go hungry again.

Then she remembered the human in front of her, a very ugly human with long white hair. Linf wanted to tear its throat out but knew she couldn't even move.

'Just kill me then,' Linf managed to hiss through gritted teeth.

The human smiled at her then. 'A disgusting look,' Linf thought, but she recognised the look of pleasure on its face. It just made her want to kill him even more.

'Wow. I most certainly will not be killing you, my beauty,' the old man chuckled, 'but I will need you to pass out now so that I can

take you home and get you all mended.' The last sentence he spoke
to himself in the human tongue, before pulling out a small blowgun
and shooting Linf in the neck with a dart. It would slow her heart so
that she didn't die as quickly and shut down her brain, so she didn't
wake and kill herself trying to claw his face off.

As gently as he could, the old man picked up the limp body of
the young goblin and walked with her back to his own place deep
in the forest.

Linf opened her eyes and saw a rearing white horse in front of
her. As awareness crept back, she also felt something banging into
her head, from the inside out. She thought that someone must also
be holding a burning torch to her left leg. The pain was unbearable
and she again passed from the waking world.

The next time she awoke, she again saw the white horse. This
time, the banging had lessened to a small thudding and the pain in
her leg was now only excruciating. She was able to keep herself from
passing out again and on second inspection saw that the horse was
just a large rug attached to a wall in front of her. She had seen a rug
with a picture on it once when she had crept into Greeble's tent one
day to steal some food. She remembered getting caught and beaten
to within a fraction of her life.

Pain was no stranger to this small goblin.

She lay there for a time looking at the rug. Not through any real
interest, but through years of experience in lying down in pain. She was
aware that if she moved, the pain would be greater. Instead her thoughts
began to gather themselves and she tried to work out what had happened.

She remembered killing Greeble and wounding the swine
Merthic. She remembered her flight through the village and killing
another large goblin. After that, she didn't remember anything
specific. The only other thing that she remembered was that she was
dead. And her situation was no better than it had been. She risked
lifting her head a fraction to see if she was still in the same filthy
body she remembered. The pain brought a tortured scream from her
throat and she lay back down again, sucking in great gasps of air. She
teetered again on the fringe of consciousness and then fell over it.
She was still Linf, the goblin runt.

She awoke again, but this time there was no horse in front of her. This time she looked upon a creature uglier than the pig-ugliest goblin wench she had ever seen.

It was old, she could tell that much by the crinkles covering what she supposed was its face. The nose was small and its eyes a clear blue. Its hair, which ran straight down the sides of its head and she assumed down its back also; was white. It smiled at her with white teeth, all straight across and with no gaps in them anywhere. They all looked blunt, as if it had filed them down! She sneered at it.

It moved its mouth as if to talk, but she heard only a soft, mumbled noise come out of it. Maybe it was trying to talk to her she thought.

'Where am I?' Linf managed to grate through clenched teeth, those that she had left.

The thing grabbed something that was hanging around its neck.

'How you survived, even with my help, I don't know,' it said to her in a soft voice.

'So it does speak,' Linf thought, and 'it saved me.' She no longer sneered. Now she just fixed it with a stare of pure loathing. This dung heap had saved her life!

'Either you hate all humans, young goblin, or else you're none too happy to be alive. I guess you've had it pretty hard looking at you. Oh well, things can only improve from here.' It smiled at her again with its putrid teeth showing. It then walked up to her and poured something into her mouth. Before she could react by spitting it back into its face, the thing grabbed her throat and rubbed it, forcing her to swallow the filthy draught. She tried to spit phlegm into its face but was wracked by a fit of coughing, which sent a whole new wave of pain from her leg to her head and she again passed out.

When next she woke, Linf found herself again staring at the white horse on the wall.

This time she didn't feel as much pain. Instead, looking at the horse, she felt hungry. She had tasted horse flesh before, one day when she had been lucky enough to stumble upon a carcass in the forest. She had managed to feast herself upon it before other goblins smelt the stench and came running through the bush, chasing her from it with clubs and fists. Horse flesh was the finest meat she had ever tasted.

The only thing she could think of that was good about the human wench saving her was that when she got better, there may be some horse around that she could kill before they caught her and killed her.

The human male was called Brax and he was far from an ordinary old man.

Brax had been excited when he found Linf. Although weak and close to death, he could still see the anger that burned within her small, frail body. This little goblin had an intensity he had never felt before in any goblin and they always had plenty of hate within them.

Brax had nursed her while she regained enough strength so that she wouldn't die, but it wasn't until she finally came out of her unconscious state that the old man truly felt the potential Linf had inside her.

There was no fear inside this one, he thought to himself. Remarkable that in all the time he had been feeding off the fear and hatred of creatures, he had never found one without fear, but still with such burning hate. The small goblin in front of him appeared to have fed all of her fear into her hatred for the world and most probably those that contributed to her miserable existence. The old man was excited about this one. He had found creatures that had no hate, but that was because they had given up all hope and just wanted to be done with this world. Those were of no value to him.

His power and life essence came from the pain, the anger, and the pure hatred creatures had. He had learnt how to draw it out of creatures, absorb it into his own body, and boost his own skills and strengths.

The old man was born an ordinary human over 200 years ago. His family and friends had long since died, but his power continued to burn. He was not as strong now as he had been a century before, but he was still stronger than anything in these parts. The goblins that settled nearby knew of a presence in the forest and scared their young with it, but those that came across Brax never returned to tell any of his true existence.

The essence of fear and hate they provided him were sustaining, but not the same as when he lived among men, whose fears were so much greater than those of goblins. But there were wizards among men and organised and skilful hunters. His strength was dealing with the few, not fighting many or those with true magic.

He eventually found his current home in these forests away from man but close to goblins. Goblins were fierce fighters but their loyalties were questionable and they weren't apt to put themselves in danger to help others.

Thus Brax had been able to wander the forest taking prey as he desired. He had also been able to accumulate a number of treasures from his victims, of which they had been ignorant to their true values.

As his powers and treasures grew, so too did his desire to return to the settlements of men. He had unfinished business to attend to.

He thought to himself now that he may finally have found one that could give him the strength and power to do it.

He didn't exactly foresee how that would pan out, though. Not for a second could he trust a goblin.

For days, Linf came in and out of sleep and each time she did she felt less pain in her leg and in the rest of her beaten body. However, her temper got worse and the pain in her head refused to lessen. She remembered the old man coming in when she awoke and just standing next to her. She didn't know why he just stood there with a blank expression on his face, but her hatred for him continued to grow. He kept ignoring Linf's taunts and insults, which only served to make the little goblin angrier still.

Brax was feeling better than he had at any time since he came to live in the forest. The raw anger and hatred coming from the young goblin were intoxicating and intense. It was easy to anger her as well, which only fed his ecstasy. He found that by ignoring her, the goblin burned with an intensity that Brax found somewhat difficult to absorb at times. This didn't concern him, however, as he was in no hurry. He would be smart with this one and continue to absorb her hate until he knew he was ready to leave. It could take weeks, but it would take the goblin that long to heal properly anyway and he would of course be taking her with him. He felt that he had, remarkably, only began to tap the hatred within her.

After another few days of Linf being angry and the old man coming in and standing next to her, she suddenly decided not to get angry anymore. Just like that, the anger left her. Mostly. She still burned with the need to kill the old man in the slowest and most excruciating way possible, but she managed to convince herself to put that to the back of her mind. For now. Instead, she just looked at the old man as he came into the room.

Brax walked to the side of the bed Linf was on and looked down at her. He smiled and Linf felt the stirrings of hate begin to rise, but she pushed them back down again and just returned the old man's stare.

The old man began to chuckle. This was the first time Linf had gotten a reaction from him in some time and it was then she knew that she was on to something.

Linf grinned back and then chuckled herself.

The old man stopped smiling and walked out of the room.

A short time later, he walked back in with something in his hands. When he got closer, Linf saw, after she had first smelt it, that he had the leg of some small beast. So far, Linf had been fed nothing but hot, flavoured water and bread. Goblins were not meant to live on water and bread. It was cruel beyond words.

The smell and sight of the hind leg was mesmerising for Linf. She no longer saw the old man, just the leg, as it came closer to where she lay.

She watched as it came within biting range and as she leaned forward to take it in her mouth, the old man pulled it back and put it to his own lips. Linf watched in horror as he took a large bite from it and started to chew, the juices running down his chin.

The anger Linf felt before came rushing back to the surface, bringing with it more hatred than she thought even she could feel.

Brax lowered the lamb shank from his lips and looked at Linf. He opened himself up to the torrent of hate that he knew was coming.

It hit him like a giant wave from the Dark Swell and physically knocked him backwards into the wall. He hit it hard and crumpled to the floor, still conscious but dizzy and weak. He had tried to take in too much anger. It was something he hadn't done for many, many years and on that occasion it had been from almost two dozen people at once.

He had been forced to expel as much of his power as he could in a short space of time, so that he could get his senses back and not risk any permanent damage to his body or his mind. It was that expelled power that the goblin had struck him with, without even knowing she did it.

He felt suddenly weak but had strength enough to stand and look down at this most remarkable creature.

Linf watched as the old man crashed into the wall and slumped to the floor. She was looking around to see who or what else was in the room with them, when she felt a surge of something in the air. It seemed to caress her body, which latched on to it as a fly catcher snaps at its prey. Whatever it was seemed to seep into her body and fill her with a new found strength and energy, such as she had never felt before. It was intoxicating. She flexed her injured leg and felt nothing. No pain, not even an itch. She flexed the bonds that held her captive to the bed and she knew that if she put enough effort into it, she could snap them.

Linf looked around the room again but neither saw nor smelt anyone else in the vicinity.

The old man was slowly getting back to his feet now, holding his head in one hand as he pushed himself up off his knee with his other hand.

He stood and looked over at her.

Linf smiled back at him, knowing for sure now that for whatever reason, this old man wanted her angry all the time. She decided once more that she wouldn't be angry at the old man from now on.

She also knew this time the old man had gone too far and somehow Linf had hurt him. She had thrown him back against the wall.

The old man continued to stare at her, but there was no expression on his face. No smile and no chuckling. Just a blank stare. He bent over, picked up the shank, and put it into Linf's mouth. Linf clasped down on it. There was no way she was letting go of it if this was another trick, but the old man just turned from her and left the room.

Linf began to take small bites, lest she let it fall from her mouth. Then she remembered the bonds. With considerable effort, the bond on her right wrist snapped, freeing her hand. It had taken more of her strength to break it than she thought it would, so Linf simply grabbed the shank from her mouth and began eating it in a more goblin-like fashion, not bothering to free her other arm.

When she had finished it, bone marrow and all, she lay back down.

She was still hungry and could have eaten five more of them, but she was satisfied for the first time in a long time. She was also pain free for the first time in a long time and she wanted to know how that happened.

She knew magic when she saw it, but she never thought in her wildest dreams that she could use magic. She liked it, wanted more of it, and she knew where she had to get it from. When she was rested, she would go and pay the old human a visit.

Eventually, they all ran out of anger and hate and even fear, but Brax had been doing this a long time and he had pretty much seen it all. When he walked in there and saw Linf smile, he knew that it wouldn't be long before she would start to work it out and try harder not to get angry and to suppress the hatred.

But Brax knew there was always a way and generally when he found that trigger, the hate and anger would be greater than it had been before. Humans and goblins were similar in many ways, not least of which was their basic needs and wants. Brax would find out what their desires were and work on exploiting them. Family and friends were another step in the process.

Linf was different than most others, so Brax didn't have many options with her. She had no family and no friends. She had suffered all her life and she had no fear of death.

So when he walked into the room and saw her smile and then chuckle, he knew that the angry little goblin had worked it out and had decided to resist. But Brax knew that Linf was hungry.

Food was the greatest weakness for goblins and Brax had used it many, many times before. Although the broth and bread had been important for Linf and her injuries to begin with, he could have started feeding her properly days before now.

When he took the shank from her mouth and then crashed into that wall, he wasn't surprised at the reaction, just at the extent of the flood of anger that came from her.

When he stood up and saw his excess power being absorbed by Linf, he was more than a little surprised. He was astounded.

He had thought himself unique, the only one in this realm with the power to absorb anger and fear. Yet without doubt, the goblin strapped down to the bed in front of him had it too. He knew she was more than just a source of power to him now, she was a threat. He didn't believe the goblin knew about the powers she had, or if she did then she had no idea how to use them. She wouldn't have let him torment her for as long as he had otherwise.

So she was no threat to him for the present.

As this realisation occurred to him, he suddenly saw in this young goblin a potential ally, something he could bend and train to his advantage. Another weapon to use against those from whom he intended to take back what was rightfully his.

He suddenly no longer wanted to anger Linf. Instead, he stooped, picked up the shank, and popped it into the goblin's mouth. He then walked out of the room and into an adjoining room. He moved to a picture and looked through the eye of a beautiful woman sitting beside a river and into the room where Linf lay. He wanted to see how much the little goblin had absorbed and what it did for her.

He still had to be very careful.

The goblin was certainly dangerous now and he was fairly certain that she knew it too.

As he watched, he saw the goblin break her bond and grab hold of the shank. The strength it would have taken to break that bond sent a chill through Brax. For a moment, he thought very seriously about ending the goblin then and there. He was still a lot stronger than her and could kill her quite easily, but the potential he saw was what really scared him.

He calmed himself and began to think. He had time to make more assessments as things progressed. If the goblin started to become too strong, then he would end her then. In the meantime, he would continue to use her to strengthen his own powers and he would watch her very closely.

But before any of that happened, he would need to get stronger bonds.

CHAPTER 9

VALDOR—Gamer of Destiny

NONE ARE AWARE of what the others have chosen until all have submitted their race of choice to the Creator. Valdor thought he knew the other players reasonably well and had made his choice based on the assumptions he had surmised in his own mind. He liked the idea of magic, but he quickly discarded the elves. He believed that Mendina would choose them and he wanted to have his own race to build and nurture, free from any alliance.

The dwarves had the ability to make magic items, but their strengths were too one-dimensional to his liking. Goblins, orcs, ogres, trolls, and the like were too unpredictable, as were the other humanoid races that favoured the crueller and darker side of life.

He eventually settled on men as his race of choice. They possessed the qualities of many others in varying degree, yet had more flexibility. They could use and make magic, they were fine warriors, they could adapt and live in most environments, and they were traditionally quite prolific.

His plan at the beginning had been to build them up as quickly as possible and then nudge them to branch out, using magic and martial ability. His initial plan had been to give them abilities in both and wait to see how they developed before contemplating what sort of champion he would eventually decide upon. It would also give his realm a spread of strengths to draw on against his enemies. He remembered well the Creator saying how important it would be to have a strong realm to assist their champion.

It hadn't been until he had studied several generations that he knew where his champion would be selected from.

At the beginning, he hadn't pictured himself choosing a monk as his champion, but the fit was right and he had needed all the time he had left to get them where he wanted them to be.

The world Valdor had come from had been a strict and disciplined world. He knew that his choice had a lot to do with that, but he believed it was a good idea to stick with something he was familiar with. He knew the strengths that came with a strong and focused mind and a disciplined martial existence.

He still had those within his realm that could use magic and he knew their proficiency would increase over time without an excessive amount of assistance from him. They continued to help strengthen his realm, but most of his resources he gave to his monks.

The champion that he would be choosing was stronger than he had envisaged at the beginning, yet one that the others would not see as a threat.

He believed otherwise.

CHAPTER 10

Valdor—The Champion

VALDOR WALKED THE corridor of the Chapel in Loftenberg as he had done every morning and night he had been here over the past twenty-eight years.

At the age of 4, those chosen for the path of monkhood were taken to the training grounds at Loftenberg and remained there until they were deemed ready to serve their king. This was the way of the monks for as far back as memory went. They were raised as pious and loyal men, faithful to their chosen God and their king and trained as warriors.

In a land where danger stalked every road and roamed darkly through each forest and mountain track, it was necessary to have those dedicated men to defend the people of the land. The monks of Loftenberg had seen the need and had taken it upon themselves many years before to protect the people of the land.

The king's attention had been drawn to their feats as the monks became renowned for their fighting prowess and stoicism.

Possessing no family ties nor ever taking a wife, they had only one purpose. They were defenders of the people, and when they became the king's men, their involvement soon spread throughout the kingdom. They soon became not only the defenders of the people but defenders of the entire realm, protecting those that couldn't defend themselves, as well as their king. They became known as the

King's Shield, their loyalty given willingly to the king; ready when necessary to give their lives.

Valdor, the youngest ever within their order to be granted the status of King's Shield, was today about to embark on the most important assignment given him so far in his short life. The king's daughter, Princess Areana, who was housed at Loftenberg for the southern winter, was to be escorted to the palace in Lakerth to be wed to the Duke of Letheris.

Lord Thaiden, Commander of the King's Shield, had chosen twenty of the Shield's finest to accompany her on the journey south.

The reason for such a large personal guard, where usually three or four were sufficient, was the sudden increase in slayings and disappearances throughout the King's Realm over the past few months. There is an evil abroad, the king's sorcerers were proclaiming, and the monks themselves could feel it in the wind and on the ground they trod.

Lord Thaiden was not going to chance the safety of the princess.

Valdor stopped outside of the chapel door and reached to open it.

'Valdor, hold thee a moment.' Valdor recognised the voice, though the footsteps had told him already that his friend approached.

Valdor turned to wait for Catlin as his friend and fellow monk strode towards him.

He and Catlin had been through much together in their acolyte days. Catlin was Valdor's senior by nine years, but they had both reached knighthood at the same time. Catlin when most others did, Valdor when none had before.

They were as close as two monks in a reclusive order could be, having spent quite a deal of time testing one another in all of the various skills a monk required.

However, it was held that too close a friendship could interfere with a monk's loyalty to God and king. Neither believed this to be true. Both would see the other fall beneath the spiked club of a mountain troll if their king were in danger and needed their help. They both stood fast to this belief. Both still hoped it would never come to pass.

'It is a fine day, Valdor,' Catlin said cheerily to her friend. 'It is a fine day indeed.'

'You are in fine spirits this morning Catlin,' Valdor replied with a thin but sincere smile.

'I most surely are my friend, for today I journey to the palace of our king, to see his pride be wed and a new prince regent proclaimed.'

Valdor couldn't remember seeing his friend as excited about anything.

'You speak truly,' Valdor replied with an optimism in his voice that Catlin had rarely heard in all of her time spent with him. 'It will be the finest hour since our gracious Queen did depart this cruel world, leaving our sovereign king without a son, and without the will to ever take another wife again.' A cold sadness returned to Valdor's words as he remembered the queen.

Only twice in his life did Valdor see Queen Kainet, yet he knew that none would ever leave such a mark upon him as she had, even the king.

The first time he was struck with such a remarkable sensation, that when he had visited Lord Thaiden to query it's meaning, he was firmly instructed to ignore it, to never be influenced by it. It was not a component of his duty.

He had accepted the word of his Lord but was still bothered by the ordeal. To a pious man, such feelings were difficult to understand. It would be some years before he saw her again.

Six years before today and two years before Queen Kainet would be struck down with a sudden illness and no medicine or magic in all of man's realm would be able to save her, Valdor saw her again.

It was the day of his knighting and the Queen was there to congratulate her king's newly fledged protectors of the realm and to give them her blessing.

To Valdor, her presence was overwhelming. He had to use all of his disciplined willpower to refrain from staring at her beauty and obvious charisma.

Yet when the Queen came to congratulate him, he could not bring himself to look upon her. Kneeling in front of her, his head bowed, Valdor knew it was an insult to royalty but he was unable to raise his eyes. He feared what it would do to his already thumping heart and frail nerves. He could sense Thaiden's eyes boring a hole through him, but he would not look. He could not look at her. He just stayed head bowed and waited for the Queen to move on.

Instead of moving on, the lady had put her hand under Valdor's chin and gently lifted his head.

'Why does thou have tears in thy eyes Knight?' her touch chilled him, while her voice sang to him.

Valdor knew he would sooner grow wings than be able to mouth any sort of a reply so he stayed silent. He looked at her with eyes that had never felt the drop of tears in a life unimaginably difficult, but which held them now. Valdor stared as if confronted by a god and the tears turned into a stream down his cheeks.

'Such a young and handsome knight,' she sang to him again. She seemed to look into his soul. 'My husband the king truly has the finest and most loyal of men in all of the land.' She stepped back and said in a loud voice, 'My blessing to you all. Be faithful, be strong, and live long.' She then stepped into the throng and the ceremony continued. Valdor never saw her again.

The day Valdor heard the Queen had died, he felt a great part of himself die also—a part that he knew could never be made whole again.

'Hopefully, you will not mourn so heavily now the king has himself an heir,' Catlin said without much conviction.

'Perhaps my friend,' Valdor replied as if talking to the air itself.

He turned and looked at Catlin for a moment and then pushed open the chapel door.

Together, they walked into the Loftenberg chapel, each for the last time.

The sun was peeking from the tips of the Westerling Mountains as the Princess Areana and her troop of King's Shield rode from Loftenberg. Only when riding for battle had such a large number ridden together at the one time. Such were the times they lived in.

Although in the cities and large settlements life went on as usual, in the remote villages and solitary farms, death and destruction were becoming commonplace and more horrifying every day. Even the soldiers the king sent out did not always return. Those that did either saw nothing or came back less of a person than when they had gone forth.

Valdor and Catlin rode beside the princess' coach. As yet neither had seen the Princess Areana. Valdor had heard it spoken that she was more beautiful than her mother the queen had been. He paid no heed to gossip.

Princess Areana was a small and solitary girl who seldom ventured into public, preferring instead her own spaces and a garden to walk in, be it at Loftenberg in the small confines reserved for the royalty, or in the vast-walled gardens of Lakerth, where she would lose herself for an entire day at times. It was her own private sanctuary and she was looking forward to returning there. She was not particularly looking forward to her marriage, being just turned 16 and only meeting her betrothed on one occasion years ago.

She remembered the Duke of Letheris as a kind man, in so far as a warrior can be kind. She also remembered him being so big as to scare her a little even now, thinking back on her encounter when she was 12.

The large and gruff-looking Knights scared her a little also, as she peered from the curtains of her coach. She had heard many tales of the Monks of Loftenberg as she had grown up. They were the 'King's Shield' and they were the fiercest warriors in the land. She also heard they hardly ever spoke. Still, she was very happy to be travelling with them, knowing their sole purpose was to keep her safe.

Her eyes locked onto one of the Knights, as his met hers. For a moment, she thought she saw an expression of sadness on his face, if that were possible for one of the King's Shield, and then one of surprise, even less likely. She looked again, and he was looking straight ahead, his face made of stone. Her mind playing tricks on her, she surmised. They had already travelled a few hours and it had become quite stuffy inside her coach.

She turned to the man seated opposite her.

He was an elderly man. She wasn't sure of his age and couldn't even begin to guess, but she knew he was old. He was a scholar and he had been her teacher and mentor all her life.

Always kind and considerate to her, he was the father she never had, as her father was too busy being king.

He had guided her mind in many other ways and she loved him dearly, although he did get on her nerves at times. She did so love her privacy and he always seemed to be able to find her no matter where she was. Even in the garden at Lakerth where she knew all of the hiding spots.

She guessed he had been there longer than she and probably knew some places even she didn't.

'Bored already, princess?' he asked her in a pleasant voice.

'Yes, Heridah,' she replied and then in a sweet voice, 'do you think we could stop soon. I do so need to stretch my legs.'

'Certainly, my dear, shall I inform Lord Thaiden of your request?' he mocked her, she knew. Thaiden was the only man in the realm that her eyes and smile had no influence over. He was the Commander of the King's Shield and she liked and respected him, except for when she wanted him to do something that he did not want to do. Sooner turn back the Dark Swell itself than bully Thaiden.

Suddenly, the curtain at the entrance to the carriage was swung open and none other than Thaiden himself stuck his head in. His horse was trotting under him, though you would have thought that the carriage was stationery such was his poise.

Areana looked at Heridah with a smile. He returned a frown, knowing that an argument was about to break out.

'Thaiden,' she began, 'I think that it is about time. . .'

'My princess. Heridah,' he interrupted, much to the princess' ire, her eyes shooting sparks at him. 'There is a disturbance up ahead. We will be halting for a short while. Do not be alarmed, but I ask that you stay in the carriage.'

Before either could respond, he had closed the curtain and she could hear his horse galloping ahead as more hooves crashed to a halt outside the carriage, setting up a guard ring around the princess.

'I will find out what is happening,' Heridah said to her, and before the princess had a chance to close her mouth and say something, he had stepped from the carriage.

After coming to grips with being ignored twice, the princess sighed and realised she should be used to it by now. Then the royal side of her denounced those thoughts and wondered why she let them get away with it.

The regal princess stepped from the carriage to see what was going on.

She took not three steps when she was suddenly picked up from behind, giving a startled squeal. She was put back into her carriage, not roughly, but with little dignity.

She turned around and looked into the face of the same King's Shield she earlier had the emotion-filled illusion of. The stinging rebuke hesitated on her tongue as she once again saw the same confused and startled look on his face. It was gone again in a second, but she knew it had been there.

'How dare you!' she hissed at him, her senses flooding back to her. 'You have worked your last days as a King's Shield. How dare you lay hands on me!' She was only just warming up on him. 'I will have your title stripped and you will be flogged for this. You are an insult to my father's good name.' Areana saw her words sting him more and more as if each were a physical blow. 'Do not come near me again. Leave now!'

Without hesitation, Valdor bowed, turned, and rode away, his head held low in a most extraordinary pose for one of the Shield.

Lord Thaiden saw Valdor riding from the princess' carriage, his head bowed.

'Hold there, Valdor,' he yelled at his knight.

Valdor reined his horse in immediately and waited for his Lord.

'Why are you leaving your post?' he demanded.

Valdor looked at him with a blank stare. 'Her Royal Princess bid me remove myself from her service my Lord.' No emotion was betrayed in his words.

'Go to the front and help sweep the forest,' Thaiden spoke to him and then turned towards the princess' carriage. He didn't even look to see if Valdor obeyed him.

Areana felt a whole lot better. That had done the trick at getting rid of her frustrations. She sat back down and smiled to herself as Heridah opened the curtain with his mouth wide open.

'I want not a word from you, Heridah, other than to tell me why we have stopped.' She knew he must have heard some of what she said. He had always been critical of the way her temper sometimes made her a little too harsh on people. She disagreed. People needed to be told or they wouldn't learn.

'Princess, it is only a precaution.' Heridah replied. 'We have stopped so that the scouts can more thoroughly search through the forest ahead. They saw some movement ahead. Nothing to worry about.'

'I wasn't worried,' the princess replied. 'And do not talk to me like a child, Heridah.'

'Then do not act like a child, Areana. The King's Shield are here to protect your life.' Heridah spoke to her in an angry and disappointed voice the princess did not hear too often. 'They are not,' he continued, 'your servants to bully around.'

Areana responded, expectantly, in her most haughty manner. 'He handled me, old man. No one lays their hand on my person. He's fortunate I don't have him flogged for his insolence.'

'I would not advise such an order, my lady.' Heridah spoke now, unbelievingly to her ears, with real anger. 'And I don't know of any who would even contemplate flogging one of the King's Shield, certainly not Valdor. If you knew his story my lady, you would not speak with such petulance.'

For a short time, Areana was speechless. She literally could not talk. How could Heridah speak to her in such a manner? How dare he!

Before she could think how to respond at being spoken to in such a way—not even her father spoke to her like that—the curtain to the carriage was pushed open and Lord Thaiden put his head inside.

'Who in blazes do you think you are?' Thaiden roared at the stunned princess. 'How dare you speak to one of my men like that!' Areana froze, stunned not only by his words, but the way he spoke to his princess. This on top of Heridah's outburst.

'I am your princess,' she replied. Nothing else came to mind, but her stubborn royal spine was obviously still there somewhere.

'Princess.' He almost spat the word. 'Respect is earned, girl, not given to you at birth. Valdor has earned it and then some.' In his anger, Lord Thaiden had returned to the common tongue of his birth land. 'You will apologise to Valdor, Princess, and you will be sincere.'

The way he looked at her then almost made the princess jump from the carriage and run to find this knight they had both obviously suckled from birth. Almost.

'I doubt my father would be pleased with the way you have both spoken to me just now. I think I am the one who will receive the apology.' She returned Lord Thaiden's stare, though she felt like wailing. Her cheeks were aflame.

This retort resulted in Thaiden pushing himself into the carriage, only his legs now outside. The princess involuntarily moved back from him.

'Thaiden,' Heridah interrupted. The princess looked at her old friend and saw that he also looked a bit shocked at Thaiden's outburst. 'Give me a moment alone with Areana.'

Areana looked back at the Lord of the King's Shield. He gave a curt nod and was gone from the carriage.

Areana turned to Heridah and opened her mouth but was again interrupted.

'Please, Your Highness.' He now spoke to her in a quiet voice, but for some reason, her mouth closed and the tongue lashing flew from her mind, replaced by nothing. A tranquillity, completely at odds to the way she knew she should feel.

'Let me tell you a short part of the story of Valdor,' he continued. 'For in truth, Princess, although he is but young, he is already spoken of in legend in the ranks of the Shield and the full story would take some time.'

Areana bit her tongue as her thoughts returned to her, but she silenced them and chose instead to listen to her teacher.

'Valdor, as most knights, was brought to the monks at Loftenberg at a very young age. He has not seen his parents since. They are dead to him. Such is the way of the King's Shield.'

'I know that already, Heridah. For the king and their God,' she could not help interrupting. She was still furious, after all.

'Yes, Areana,' Heridah replied with a thin smile. 'Valdor was an exceptional youth, both in his studies and his physical prowess. He was bettering students twice his age. Students of exceptional skills themselves. So it was that he was sworn in as a King's Shield at the age of twenty-five cycles.'

Areana's eyebrows rose at this.

Heridah continued. 'On that day, he was, as were all those accepted into the ranks, blessed by your mother, may her soul forever run free.'

Areana's eyes glazed over, as they always did when she thought of her mother.

'When your mother came to Valdor to give him her blessing, he would not look up at her.' Heridah tried to continue but was stopped short by the princess.

'He what? How was he ever allowed to be a King's Shield at all?' Her anger suddenly threatened to boil over again.

'I should have said he could not look up, Areana. He was spellbound in a way. Have you ever been in love, Areana?' Heridah asked and sighed. 'It is a most extraordinary sensation.' Areana wasn't sure whether to be stunned at Heridah saying this man loved her mother, her father's wife, or the unspoken thought that Heridah had once been in love. She couldn't picture that so she went with the first.

'He was in love with my mother? Is this supposed to endear the man to me, Heridah?' She had no idea where he was going with this story.

'Not that kind of love, Princess. Not like out of a tale told to you at night. It was like the love a man has for his god, or in this case, his goddess.' Heridah paused for a moment. 'He physically could not look at her. His body must have become like stone, such were the emotions he felt. To a pious man, this must have been a torment.'

'But instead of continuing on, your mother lifted Valdor's chin and looked him in the eyes. Eyes that I could see were bursting with tears, for I was there. Thaiden told me later that even through all of the enormous hardships and obstacles Valdor had been through to achieve his place among the Shield, those were the first real emotions he had ever seen in the man. He knelt there for hours after everyone else had gone. Her death hit him hard, Areana. Thaiden told me he turned from stone into a glacier.'

'My mother was the most beautiful woman alive.' Areana said softly and then in a louder voice. 'These feelings do not make the man special.' Her anger had not subsided.

'Valdor has saved the lives of many, many people, Areana. He has single-handedly fought off half a dozen armed men with nought but his bare hands. He. . .'

'Yes, yes, he is a legend, Heridah, you have already told me,' Areana interrupted this time. She was still unforgiving and certainly not about to apologise.

'Six men,' Heridah continued, 'who tried to abduct you when you wandered off alone one afternoon in Loftenberg. You were only 5 years old.'

A memory came to Areana of when she was very young, indeed she could have been about five. She remembered the secret little door she had found while hiding in the garden. It came to her now as if she were reliving the event all over again.

She had not wandered very far from the door she had found. It was late in the afternoon and the shadows of the wall crossed over much of the street that she was on. There were only a few people about, all with their hoods down shielding their faces from the cool air. It was nearing the snow season and the cold days had already arrived. The princess looked behind her, expecting to see somebody coming for her from the small door, but no one had. She walked back to the door, but it closed before she got to it and there was no handle on this side. In fact, she couldn't even see a door there anymore. She turned again and saw several men walking towards her. One of them pointed at her and they all looked. The one who pointed walked up to her with a large grin on his face. 'Managed to escape from the palace, have we?' the leering smile she remembered well. He reached for her, talking as he stooped to grab her, 'I'd say you'll fetch a few gold coins here or there. I'm sure you will.' They had all seemed so large and she recalled the sudden terror she had felt, not having been out by herself before and not knowing what this man was doing to her.

She was not exactly sure what happened next, but she remembered bodies began flying everywhere. The one with the nasty smile was flung backwards from her.

She remembers the sound of swords leaving their sheaths and thought they were going to cut her into pieces. But of course it didn't happen. Not one of them ever laid a hand on her.

The next thing she remembered was being handed to one of the palace guards and taken before her very upset mother and furious father.

She looked at Heridah. 'That was him.'

Heridah started to reply when suddenly his eyes went white, as if they had clouded over and he lunged at the princess. His hands found her throat and he squeezed. Areana tried to scream, but she could not even draw breath. She began battering at his arms, but the old man was strong and she was but a young lady. She reached for his face with her fingers, but his arms were held straight. Areana could not see him anymore. Stars were appearing before her eyes and she hit his arms harder as the last of her strength left her.

As suddenly as he had attacked her, Heridah let go. Areana sucked in deeply, filling her lungs with the most glorious air she had ever tasted. Her vision returned and she looked across at Heridah. His eyes were back to his normal light brown and he was looking at her with a shocked expression.

As Areana got enough breath into her lungs to start breathing less frantically, she let forth with a loud scream.

'No need, my princess. I was not myself. I am back again. You are safe.' Heridah hurried with the words, as if he feared not to be heard.

Unconvinced, Areana screamed again. As she finished, the carriage doors were flung open from both sides and two of the Shield were inside, their short swords drawn. Unsure of what was happening, one of them grabbed hold of the princess and stepped back outside with her as more of the Shield took up positions around her and at intervals away from her.

The one who remained in the carriage was shortly joined by Thaiden, who, with one look at Heridah, ordered his man out and sat down opposite the old man.

Thaiden waited for the old man to speak.

'Somehow, someone took control of my mind, Thaiden.' Heridah was back to his calm self again and spoke clearly. 'I don't know who, or where from, but he very nearly succeeded in killing the princess. I found myself again with only moments to spare.'

Thaiden raised his eyebrows. 'Who could do that to you, Wizard? I thought you had spells to stop that sort of thing happening.'

'We do. I do.' he replied distractedly. Heridah's mind was racing in thought.

'Is the princess safe with you now, old man?' Thaiden asked. His thoughts were only on how he could best protect the princess.

'What?' Heridah replied, still obviously a bit rattled by what had happened. 'Yes, of course she is.'

Thaiden again raised an eyebrow.

'I was taken by surprise, Thaiden. It will not happen again. She is as safe with me as she is with anyone.' He still sounded a bit shaken. 'I think that whatever was up ahead has now gone. It was obviously a ruse to have my thoughts elsewhere and your men.'

'Agreed old man. We will make as much haste as we can.' He turned to leave.

'Can you talk to her for me, Thaiden?' Heridah asked. 'It may take a bit of convincing to get her to trust me again.'

'She trusts you more than any, Heridah,' Thaiden looked at the Wizard, the one chosen from among their ranks at the birth of the heir. Always the most powerful wizard at the time was chosen to care for royalty's first born. Thaiden thought to himself that if the most powerful wizard had been possessed by something, then the world of men was in serious danger. He could see the same thoughts mirrored in the eyes of Heridah.

'If she will not ride with me in the carriage Thaiden, then I shall ride my Dragon horse.' He paused. 'Choose from your men one to watch the princess in here. Valdor would do fine.'

'Valdor? Are you sure, Heridah?' Thaiden was not one to take orders from anyone, especially to do with his men. However, Heridah was a trusted friend, one of the Black Wizards and first in charge of the princess' safety. He respected the order of rank.

'Valdor. Now, we must make haste, Thaiden. I need not tell you these are dangerous times. I believe that we are in extreme peril.'

'Then we must be even more wary,' Thaiden replied, backing out of the carriage to start giving his orders.

Heridah halted him with his next words.

'You misunderstand me, Lord Thaiden,' Heridah spoke in a hushed but serious voice. 'I did not mean simply this trip and the princess. I mean all of the lands.' Heridah seemed to have his composure back once again. 'There is an evil abroad Thaiden and its power seems to be far greater that we would like to dare contemplate.'

'What would you have us do then?' Thaiden asked.

'Always the practical one, aren't you? Do you ever get flustered or surprised?' Heridah said with a small smile. He was glad to have men like Thaiden on their side.

'What is the point of that wizard, it only interferes with rational thoughts that can actually help.' Heridah wasn't sure if he was serious or not. His next words were. 'Do we speed up and sacrifice caution in order to get you back to your fellow wizards, or do we increase our caution for the princess and sacrifice time. They are my two choices.' Thaiden paused for all of two seconds. 'I choose haste.' Backing all of the way out of the carriage, he began barking orders.

They continued with their journey. The princess stayed in her carriage the entire time, not wanting to leave it and not wanting to see anybody. She refused any company, so Heridah had Valdor ride just outside of the carriage while he himself rode a short distance to the rear. Several other of the guard rode at points around the carriage, further back still. There were no delays for the next three days and nothing slowed their progress, yet Heridah and the King's Shield became no less vigilant.

On the fourth day out from the incident with Heridah and the princess, Thaiden suddenly called a halt. He rode to where Heridah had stopped his horse at the rear of the princess' carriage. They had halted in a small clearing with trees all around them. The King's Shield spaced themselves in a semi-circle, a small distance in front of the carriage, but well back from the trees.

'There is movement in the forest ahead,' Thaiden reported. 'We will stop until the threat is cleared. I know not the numbers of creatures or what they are. They are not of this realm,' he finished.

Heridah cast his mind forward into the trees. He could sense many small minds waiting in the trees. Of minor intelligence, they were nevertheless capable of thoughts above those of a wild animal. He also sensed an evil intent.

'They have been sent to wait for us, Thaiden. I don't like it.' Heridah was cautious, but not afraid. 'I also sense something else with them, but I cannot make out what it is, or how many.'

'Is this something you can help with wizard or shall my men clear a path?' Either way suited him. He had blind faith in the ability of his men and he had also seen Heridah at work.

'I shall try,' Heridah replied.

Reaching his mind forth into the forest ahead Heridah called on the power of wind. Beings flew from the trees directly ahead and went crashing onto the ground below. From there, they were pushed along the dirt to either side. Like cutting through a cake, Heridah pushed more wind into the forest and then flung all in its way to either side. For a distance of fifty paces across and in front of them, all of those waiting were moved aside and a barrier formed. The barrier stretched all around them and behind.

Thaiden barked a few orders and his men formed up quickly in front of and around the carriage. All moved off into the forest with Heridah at the rear.

The spell was a simple one for Heridah but it was draining. It didn't stretch as far as he would have liked, but the larger it was, the more it would drain him. It was also not the strongest of barriers, but the creatures surrounding them were not powerful enough to breach it.

As they reached the forest, Heridah looked across at the barrier he had created. Swarms of the small creatures were pushing against it and striking it with small swords. Others were using claws from their elongated arms or arrows from the small bows that many of them carried. The sounds they made were shielded from the party, but the King's Shield could see the anger and malice in their faces.

Similar to men but standing only 3 feet off the ground, they were skinny and covered in fur. The faces were long and the mouths huge and filled with small pointed teeth. It looked like they had taken a portion from their small legs and added them to their long arms, which they used efficiently to swing through the trees.

For hours they walked this way as Heridah steadily weakened. The creatures were relentless in their efforts to try and batter their way through the shield of air and as such Heridah was unable to search ahead for a clearing. All of his concentration was on maintaining the barrier, but Thaiden assured him that a large clearing was only a couple of leagues further on.

Heridah knew that once they got to the clearing and the creatures were brave enough to attack, the King's Shield would soak the ground with their blood. If they chose not to attack, then it would take them a long time to circle around. This would give him time to rest and hopefully give them a start at the other side of the clearing.

As Heridah's thoughts turned to the rest he would soon be getting, he felt something new gently pushing against his barrier. At first, he could not tell what it was, only that it was something more powerful than the creatures in the trees. It was directly in front of them, yet still hidden around the next bend on the trail. He wasn't yet able to see what it was.

Seconds later, he knew exactly what they were, as they shot forth balls of fire which burst through his weakened defence.

'Thaiden!' he yelled.

Thaiden swung around on his horse to face the wizard.

'Are you too weakened already, wizard? You have. . .' but he stopped on seeing the look on the wizard's face.

'Ogre-mages ahead,' he said in a loud voice, tinged with fear. 'They're coming through the barrier.'

Thaiden wheeled his horse around and barked out to his men what was coming through but they were already upon them.

Six of them had pushed through the barrier of air and already two of the King's Shield lay severely wounded from the first fireballs that were shot through the air barrier. The monks were sturdy and skilful, but both of those that fell were hit with two balls of magic fire. Their defences weren't adequate to stop destructive spells hurled at them from such a short distance.

Heridah had no choice. 'The shield is down,' his voice boomed as he flung the mages back with thickened balls of air, fired out so fast that the mages didn't have opportunity to release any more shots of their own.

Almost immediately, the swarms of hairy creatures were among them, squealing and howling in their own high-pitched voices.

Heridah had moved to the front of the carriage to confront the ogre-mages. Two had regained their feet and were coming again.

Ogre-mages were from the wasted lands and hadn't been in these parts of the land for living memory. They were strong in body and mind. Evil magic users who used fire as their magical base and used it with devastating effect. The two bodies of the King's Shield that lay writhing on the ground reflected this. They didn't look like they would survive their hurts. Six together was unheard of even to Heridah, except in times of war and only then on the battlefield.

Yet Heridah was the greatest wizard the humans had and he had recovered from his initial shock. Although wearied from his barrier he still had reserves untapped and unlike the ogre-mages, Heridah was a master of all the elements. He had fought ogre-mages before and he knew how to kill them.

The ogre-mages had hoped to use the element of surprise to conquer their foes, for they knew there was obviously a wizard among them. They had waited until they knew the wizard would be tired from his use of the shield. They had held off their attack for that very reason, but the clearing ahead had forced their hand earlier than they would have liked.

They hadn't expected to find a wizard this powerful. The lead ogre-mage, Shazriz-Pith, was the first to recover from the balls of air that had knocked them back. The force of it had surprised him, but he had sensed it in time to put forth a small shield which limited the impact.

He felt satisfaction at the two burning monks in front of him, but the rest of the King's Shield had moved back near the carriage to fight the Squargrin. He would burn more when the wizard lay dead. For it was only the wizard who had moved forward to meet them. Shazriz-Pith could see that he was tired and his breathing was laboured, but he wouldn't underestimate this one.

Moving behind a tree, he could see two of his fellow ogre-mage back on their feet and moving forward. He was hidden from view, but he wouldn't need to see the wizard to know what he did next.

He saw both of the mage's hands raise and point towards the wizard. Both began to cast fireballs and he could sense that they were drawing on everything they had. As the fireballs began to leave their fingers both mages were engulfed in flames. Then they simply exploded.

Shazriz-Pith had heard of this happening to mage before in the past when confronting some of the human wizards. This one definitely had incredible power. He had thickened the air around both of the mage just as they released their fireballs. He had left enough air around each to allow the flames to ignite. Then when the balls had released, they had smashed back into those that had cast them. Not only did it take power, but the timing of such a spell had to be perfect. If cast too soon, the mage would have sensed it and stopped the spell. If cast too late he would open himself to the fireballs. Seconds later another of the mage exploded in a ball of fire.

The other two remaining in front of the wizard saw this one explode and stopped their own fireballs.

Shazriz-Pith's mind was racing, but he remained calm. Rather than step out to help his fellow mage, he made the decision to wait and watch what happened to the remaining two.

One of them cast a wall of flame at the wizard. Shazriz-Pith knew that the wizard would now be surrounded by flame, his visibility taken from him. The second mage then shot forth his fireball. He didn't explode this time, which was promising, but Shazriz-Pith was not yet ready to step out into the open.

Moments later he was glad he hadn't.

The mage who had cast the firewall reeled back as his head and body were ripped apart by shards of ice the size of arrow tips. The second had time enough to put up an intense wall of flame, which stopped the shards tearing him apart also. They stopped in a hiss of steam as the flames extinguished the ice. Yet putting up the firewall blinded the mage momentarily this time. As he took the wall down to strike again at the wizard, an ice shard the size and length of a human arm, but with a pointed tip, crashed into the mage's chest, hitting with such force that the embedded shard poked out from his back.

Shazriz-Pith knew that he would have to move now. This wizard would be able to sense him and he was an easy target there for someone with control of so many elements. His fire was more effective when he could see his opponent.

Shazriz-Pith stepped out and looked straight at Heridah. The wizard's breathing was even more laboured now, but Shazriz-Pith knew that he only had one chance to win this battle. The time behind the tree, although only seconds, had given him opportunity to choose his spell.

He raised his hands and prepared to cast a fireball straight at the wizard. Flames danced on his fingers and he began to cast. He felt the air surround him as the flame left his fingers and he was engulfed in fire. But instead of a fireball, he changed the spell—a subtle change only—and a burst of liquid fire streamed from one of his fingers instead. White hot, it pierced the shield of air easily and arrowed straight at the wizard's chest.

Heridah was exhausted. It had taken enormous concentration to kill off five of the mage. They had been powerful, but also somewhat predictable.

The last one stepped from behind the tree. Heridah knew he had been there and was about to wrap him to the tree so that he could question him. A live ogre-mage was risky, but he wanted information on what was going on in the wasted lands.

Heridah also knew this one was the most powerful of those that had been sent to meet them. He was prepared for something different from him, so he was a little surprised when he sensed that it was casting another fireball at him.

Heridah waited until the last moment and then put the shield of air around it. He saw the flames engulf the mage and thought it over, but then he felt a subtle change in the mage's spell. His fatigue nearly cost him his life, as he saw the stream of white-hot liquid flame coming straight at him.

He was sure that any other wizard would have died in that instant. The air shield disappeared in an instant and the flames around the mage were extinguished.

Heridah sucked all of the heat from a small area in front of his chest and forced into it as much moisture as he could summon. A thick block of ice formed in the air in front of him as the bolt of liquid fire struck. The ice exploded and knocked Heridah back through the air. He smacked into the base of a tree behind him and the breath was knocked from his lungs. He knew that he was open now to the fireball that would come next. He also had just enough time to know that he couldn't do anything about it.

Shazriz-Pith saw the ice form and then the wizard crash into the tree behind him. He wasted no time. The flame again flickered from his fingers as the fireball was aimed straight at the prone wizard.

The ogre-mage was smiling as Thaiden's sword was driven through his throat. Shazriz-Pith slumped to the ground, the fire dying on his fingertips as his life left him.

Thaiden rushed over to Heridah as the wizard sat up holding his head.

'Are you able to fight still, old man? The battle is not finished.' He spoke to him as if they were still on horseback conversing about the journey.

'I am good, Thaiden. Go.' Heridah waved his hand at Thaiden, indicating for him to move on. Thaiden didn't break stride as he raced back towards the carriage and into the middle of the Squargrin.

Valdor was at the front of the carriage as the ogre-mage raced through. If he had hesitated a split second longer, he would have been engulfed in flame. His dive sideways had saved him. Millon and Werkith hadn't been as quick. He saw them struck as he came back to his feet. At the same time, he heard Heridah yell that the shield was down and knew that the wizard would deal with the mages. He turned to face the mass of creatures that streamed through the trees towards them.

The rest of Thaiden's men had remained in place right throughout the march, ready in case the shield faltered. They were the finest trained soldiers in the lands and their silence was far more terrifying than the squeals from the creatures attacking them.

The Squargrin had massed and numbered in their hundreds, but the Shield were more than ready and they moved to maximise both attack and defence. Several of the King's Shield moved around the carriage, none getting in the way of another and yet leaving no gaps. Arrows flew at them, but they came without the strength or accuracy of an elven bow and the king's men moved with exceptional speed.

Amazingly to the creatures themselves, none of the arrows hit their marks. They quickly decided to close in with their short swords and long claws and in no time were amongst the Shield.

As adept as they were in the trees, on the ground, and having to move within striking distance of their own short weapons, they were no match for Valdor's sword.

It sung through the air, each swing a killing strike. Valdor didn't waste any of his energy and he didn't have to swing twice at the same creature. But he could also see that the creatures were coming through the forest in greater numbers than any of them had thought. A few had already made it to the carriage before they were dealt with and the mass continued to thicken. All of the King's Shield had relinquished their mounts. The creatures were too small and would easily get under their horses.

Valdor heard explosions to the front where Heridah was fighting the mage and then in no time Thaiden was by his side.

'We cannot hold them off. We cannot remain here, Valdor.' Thaiden spoke quickly but in the calm voice of one who had been in many battles before.

Valdor had summed it up the same way.

'Get three others and take the princess into the woods. Hack through them, Valdor, and keep moving. Go forward and get to the clearing.' Both men continued to fight as Thaiden spoke. They both moved with the fluency of master swordsmen and the bodies of the Squargrin began to mount at their feet.

Valdor moved to the carriage and indicated to the three closest to him. Victor, Grenthem, and Catlin moved to the entrance of the carriage and Valdor put his head inside. Arrows crashed into the carriage next to his head but he didn't flinch. He knew if any of the creatures found their aim, then the arrows would be cut short by those at his back.

Princess Areana was backed up against the rear of her carriage. She looked up with a startled expression and was relieved to see Valdor's face.

'Princess,' he said in a calm voice, 'you must come with me.' He reached out his hand.

Her eyes bulged. 'I'm not going out there!' she squealed.

She had peeked out a few times during their latest trek through the woods and had seen the creatures teeming on the other side of Heridah's shield. She hadn't been aware that there was a wizard with them, but she was extremely glad they had one.

When she heard the explosions at the front and then Heridah yell that the shield was down, she immediately thought the worst and had jumped to the back of the carriage. Her heart had raced when the door opened and then jumped with joy at seeing Valdor.

'You must come with me, Princess,' Valdor said again and then saw her hesitate once more. 'Or you will die in this carriage.' He looked her straight in the eye for the first time as he said this.

Those last words obviously got through to her as she jumped up from her seat and into his arms.

'You must run behind me,' he said gently as he put her on the ground, 'but you will be safe.' He took the time to give her what he thought was a reassuring look and then turned to face the swarm of Squargrin.

Valdor knew the reason Thaiden had chosen only four of them to take the princess through to the clearing was speed. If their run through the forest was slowed, then the creatures would swarm them and they would be lost.

Valdor started out in front. He began by cutting a swathe through the Squargrin directly in front of him and then picked up speed. He realised quickly that the Squargrin had guessed they would make a run for the clearing and the numbers in front of them were too many. In the trees, and on the ground, there was no way they could fight them all and run with the princess as well.

Then the path in front of them was cleared of Squargrin as they were swept aside and back into the trees either side.

Heridah's parting gift, but the barrier didn't stay this time. Heridah had only time to cast a quick spell their way before the creatures again swarmed around him and Thaiden and his attentions were drawn back to them.

Valdor sprinted forward, not wasting any time. Catlin was at the rear and she urged the princess forward.

It wouldn't be long before the creatures began swarming through the trees again and got in front of them, so the five of them moved as quickly as they were able.

The princess was only small, but she was surprisingly quick. Valdor knew that it was her fear that pushed her to speed and that fatigue would soon overtake that emotion.

After a short distance, he began to see the creatures appearing again in the trees to both sides of him. He wasn't sure how far away the clearing was.

Catlin and the other two shields struck away the odd arrow that would have found its mark, while Valdor set the pace for them and waited for those that would soon come at them from in front.

They continued to run, but eventually the numbers in front grew again and their pace slowed as Valdor was forced to start fighting against those that came at him.

They fell quickly, but as quickly as Valdor's sword dispatched them, they were replaced by more and then more again.

Valdor saw Grenthem take a blow to his shoulder, and in the time it took him to change his sword arm, another had pierced his thigh with its sword. Neither strike were deep or serious, but it slowed him slightly. Too many more and he would be hard pressed to help defend both himself and the princess.

Valdor knew they were in trouble. Without a fit sword to the right of them, they would be overwhelmed.

Grenthem continued to hack at the creatures as they came at them, but his stride was slower now as another sword strike breached his defence and he began to lose blood from his wounds.

Then Catlin was struck in the chest with an arrow, as the small missiles now teemed from the trees all around them. The arrow that struck her pierced her skin but did little serious damage. Her strikes and defence remained steadfast.

Valdor looked past the swarm in front of them and could now make out the clearing ahead. He knew that they would make it in only a couple of minutes more.

'We are almost upon the clearing,' he said in a loud voice. 'Hold firm!'

They got only a few metres more when Valdor was stopped by the thud of an arrow penetrating flesh, but it was not his.

The princess fell as an arrow—missed by the flailing sword of Grenthem—struck her in the side. Even had he not been injured, it couldn't be known whether he could have stopped it. There were just too many of them.

Valdor whirled as he heard the arrow strike and bent over the princess. The other three closed in around them and tried valiantly to stop the swarm of arrows that were now coming at them.

The Squargrin sword attacks had steadily slowed as the bodies mounted and they had instead fallen back and fired their arrows at the small party. Their aim had improved as the party they tracked had tired from their wounds and been forced to slow.

Now that Valdor had stopped to check on the princess, the Squargrin didn't even bother attacking them at close range. Most of the arrows now flew straight at their targets and no matter how good these warriors were with their swords, they could not stop all of them.

Valdor lifted the princess in his arms, covering her vital areas as best he could and they set off again.

Grenthem, however, was no longer with them. An arrow had pierced his defence and embedded itself in his eye socket. For all their strength and hardiness, that was one spot all monks were vulnerable. Grenthem's body lay lifeless on the ground, having fallen moments before Valdor and the other two started their final dash towards the clearing.

Catlin and Victor looked to Valdor like pin cushions, several arrows protruding from their limbs and shoulders. They had been forced to concentrate on stopping the arrows that would have struck vital organs. They could not stop them all.

As they ran to the clearing, Valdor was also struck by a number of the arrows that teemed through the air like insects. Only a few of them embedded themselves in his flesh. The others seemed to bounce off, leaving small gashes or cuts where they struck.

He had only one arm to fend them away with. He was more concerned with keeping them from the princess.

They all ran tightly together now, Catlin and Victor shadows at Valdor's side.

Finally, they burst through into the clearing and ran a further fifty paces before the arrows stopped raining down on them. The Squargrin bows didn't have the power to hit them at that range.

Catlin and Victor braced themselves for the oncoming Squargrin charge as Valdor lay the princess down and checked her wounds.

He gasped as he saw a second arrow protruding from her chest. It had narrowly missed her heart, but her breathing was shallow and she was unconscious. The first arrow had struck her in the side just above the waist and was not life threatening on its own.

Valdor quickly pulled some bandages from his belt pouch and bound it around the arrow in her chest and then around her other wound.

This took him very little time. The King's Shield were well practised in treating wounds. He was also well practised in seeing what kind of wounds people recovered from. These were not those. He believed that she would die soon.

Valdor stood and turned around as the creatures began breaking from the trees.

Out of their element, the Squargrin would not have ordinarily run to attack on foot, especially against those that had shown themselves to be masters with the sword.

But these Squargrin had enormous numbers and they had seen that those they chased had taken many wounds. They would have assumed those they faced would be greatly weakened.

This was true for both Catlin and Victor. Both were unsteady on their feet, blood streaming freely from their wounds now. But they would not lie down until they were dead and both had plenty of life left and plenty of lives left to take away.

If it had been just the two of them, they would have fallen quickly. Their wounds were many and both knew they could not survive against such numbers. Neither were concerned with their own imminent deaths however. Their only thoughts were to protect the princess for as long as they were physically able.

'Both of you stand by the princess.' Valdor's voice was still strong and his breathing was not yet laboured, even after their run and the wounds he had suffered.

Both of his companions looked back at him. Catlin saw the look in his eyes and looked down at the princess. She also knew from a glance that Princess Areana would die soon.

Both she and Victor stood either side of the princess' still form, swords steady in their hands and their breathing coming back under control. The sight of the princess and the look on Valdor's face had bolstered their own determination to yet another level.

Valdor stepped a few paces in front of them and faced the horde of Squargrin coming at them.

'No more shall die at the hands of these foul creatures.' His voice held no emotion.

'We shall send them all, every last one of them, back to their homes in the pits of whatever swamp they sprang from. Let none live,' he said quietly as the first of them struck.

Valdor moved with the grace of a dancer and his sword moved from one Squargrin to the next. This time, his sword killed several in the same fluid movement as his injuries were ignored. The bodies began to pile up all around him. He stepped back a pace as those that he had slain mounted and the rest continued to swarm around him.

Initially, very few got past Valdor, but those that did were quickly put to the sword by either Catlin or Victor.

Yet their numbers continued to grow and they soon began to circle around and push forward. With no trees to swing from and shoot their arrows out of, the Squargrin were clumsy and they soon began to realise that these monks weren't as tired and hurt as they had believed.

Even with the swelling numbers, the ferocity of their attack diminished as those in front saw the death being dished out to them by the possessed swordsman.

Valdor did not miss a step and his sword sang death, a song the Squargrin were beginning to grow tired of hearing.

After a few minutes, both Catlin and Victor were labouring again as those Squargrin close enough to both her and Victor chose to attack the two of them rather than try their luck with Valdor.

Victor's sword was beginning to grow heavy as the loss of blood began to tell. Valdor heard the death cry of his fellow knight as one of the creatures' swords got through his tired defence and pierced his stomach, the blade driving its way up into his heart.

Valdor stepped back quickly to take his place by the princess.

Fortunately the Squargrin must have thought the princess dead already, so none wasted their energy trying to strike at her after Victor fell.

Seeing Victor fall, the Squargrin attacked with renewed ferocity, but Valdor's sword still did not waver and the stoic Catlin remained on her feet, her own sword doing enough to keep the creatures at bay, even if her killing blows were fewer.

Then suddenly, the Squargrin began squawking among themselves in a different pitch and they stopped moving forward. With the same gangly lope as they used to run across the clearing, the remaining numbers stopped their attack and ran back towards the trees where they had come from.

Valdor and Catlin remained where they were, still shielding the prone princess. Neither of them understood what had just happened.

When he saw the last of them reach the trees, Valdor turned and knelt down beside the princess.

'She does still breathe,' Catlin spoke softly to Valdor in a voice weary from pain and loss of blood.

Valdor didn't speak. He removed the blood-soaked bandages and tore some more for her, cleaning the wounds and then rebandaging them.

The princess was still breathing, but her pulse was weak. Valdor felt helpless, kneeling by the princess with nothing to do but watch her die. There were no more foes for him to slay and nowhere for them to go. They couldn't move her. She was too near to death already.

Valdor looked up when he heard the sounds of footsteps coming again from the forest, but he knew these weren't the same beasts returning.

He saw now why the Squargrin had fled.

He saw first the solid form of Thaiden striding towards them. He hardly looked out of breath, which didn't surprise Valdor. Heridah was by his side being helped by two of the Shield. Only eight others were with them. Valdor knew the rest must have fallen to the beasts that had attacked them. A huge cost, he thought briefly, but looking down, he realised that the cost was not nearly enough. They all should have fallen before the princess did.

He didn't rise nor look up at his Lord as Thaiden knelt looking at the princess. He was roughly pushed aside by the wizard as Heridah fell to his knees next to her.

Heridah said nothing as he looked her over but Valdor saw the look of fear in his eyes. Heridah slowly and carefully pulled Valdor's makeshift bandages from her.

The wizard pulled something from inside his robe and spoke a few quiet words as he rubbed it gently into her chest wound.

The princess' breathing was spasmodic and Valdor knew that her life left her. Not even the wizard could cheat death.

'Thaiden,' the wizard roared without taking his eyes from her prone body.

'I am here,' Thaiden said to him in a soft voice.

The wizard reached over and grabbed hold of Thaiden's forearm.

'Forgive me my friend,' the wizard said, 'but you are the strongest still among us.'

Heridah reached his other hand out and touched the wound in Areana's chest.

'None interfere,' the wizard said in a loud voice and Thaiden echoed the order just before he doubled over in excruciating pain.

Valdor had never heard Thaiden make any sound other than a sharp order or war cry. His scream took him aback and his first instinct was to stop the wizard from performing whatever wizardry it was he was doing.

Then he noticed the body of the princess convulse and grow rigid. Her eyes opened and her mouth formed a circle, but no sound came out.

Valdor stood there transfixed for what seemed like minutes as Thaiden writhed in agony, the wizard's grip somehow holding him where he stood.

Heridah eventually let go of Thaiden's wrist and the screaming stopped.

Thaiden collapsed to the ground unconscious, but Valdor saw that his breathing was still steady.

Areana's eyes closed again, yet Valdor could tell by the colour of her skin and her breathing that she was no longer at death's door, although she was far from healed fully.

Heridah sat back exhausted. Unlike the princess, his skin was ashen and he looked on the verge of collapse. He looked quickly at Thaiden and then turned to Valdor.

'She is not yet saved, Valdor,' he said to him, 'but she is well enough now to be moved.'

'I understand,' he said. Valdor could feel his own wounds now as the adrenalin let go of its control over his body. They hurt him, but he showed none of it and pushed it to the back of his mind.

The monk bent down and carefully lifted the princess into his arms. He looked at Heridah, who spoke to him in a serious voice.

'We will follow you as quickly as we may, but I intend to make it difficult for them to follow you.' His eyes had an intense look in them and Valdor knew that many more of the creatures that had been stalking them would die today at the hands of the wizard.

That part of it made no difference to Valdor though. His only concern was to get the princess to the capital as quickly as he was able, to allow those with the powers to heal bring her back to full health.

Valdor looked down at the girl in his arms and swallowed nervously at the sight of her.

Then he looked up in the direction of the Capital and began his journey, striding away from the small group as they turned their attentions to their own wounds.

He moved quickly, as the milling creatures began to make their way around the clearing.

CHAPTER 11

BRINDEL—Gamer of Destiny

B RINDEL WASN'T A short and sturdy man like Kabir. He was tall and lean, with chiselled features and a short cropped beard. The people from his world were all athletic and intelligent. There was no caste system and no classes of wealth, due to the fact they all excelled at most endeavours they turned their minds to. They were forever challenging themselves to greater exploits, rejoicing in the success of others and sharing the glory and accolades. His was a happy childhood, spent in a loving family that thrived on any challenge life threw at them.

Yet when he began studying the races within the game he took an instant liking to the dwarven culture. The more he read about them, the more taken he was by them.

Perhaps it was their resilience, their sense of home and family. He wasn't sure of the exact reason why he was drawn to them, but his decision was made early. It wasn't all fanciful though. He knew that they would give him a worthy champion when the time came.

They were extremely strong, adept in crafting weapons of magic and their home was a mighty defence in itself. Dwelling deep in the mountains, he was sure he would not have any trouble defending his realm. This would give him plenty of time to develop a champion he was confident would be the match of any.

A ready supply of sustenance was the only area of any concern for him. The mountains did not provide a lot in that way. He would need to find a place away from the mountains that was able to be protected and sustainable for growing crops and hunting game. This he wouldn't be able to secure until the game actually began and he could search his realm through his *eye*. A lot of his spare time at the beginning went into different scenarios for whatever may be available. Still, he had been happy with his choice and had gone into the game with plenty of confidence in his dwarves.

Once his realm had been shown to him, he saw that it suited his race perfectly.

A mighty mountain range traversed it from the northern tip, almost to the water's edge and then all the way down to its southern frontier.

And a frontier it was.

The mountains went both east and west at his southern border, as good as sealing it off from his neighbouring combatant. From the north, it also branched out and down along the western border for a distance. Where it ended there were low hills which fed their way into a large lake.

This layout had exceeded his wildest expectations.

His only concern had been that the lake itself bordered his western neighbour, so he had needed to be mindful of who they were in the early stages.

If they had been Linf's goblins, then he was at risk of having his race wiped out very early in the game.

This area was to be his food and game source and he had needed to devise of ways to protect it.

As it turned out, Mendina's elves were the ones who bordered his western frontier and they hadn't journeyed near to his lake until much later on.

By the time they came into conflict with one another, both were firmly entrenched within their respective strongholds and neither a genuine threat to the other.

There had been regular skirmishes and battles, but Brindel looked at these as important steps to improving his defences against their magic and ultimately strengthening his champion.

Yet as the Naming Day approached, he still hadn't decided which dwarf was to be his champion.

He had narrowed it to a select few, but his thoughts were that maybe this time he wouldn't be as predictable as he had been so far.

Before the game began and then throughout the last 2,000 years of Dark Swell, the gamers had been in each other's ears. Some things were said to try and psych the others into mistakes or letting slip with pieces of information. Other things were said simply out of spite or competitiveness. The one thing he knew was important to them all was keeping the others guessing. Up until they had all played their final piece and selected their champions, moves could still be made based on facts and assumptions they had gleaned through their discussions.

This was why he, and no doubt the others as well, had strived to be as unpredictable as he could think to be.

Maybe his champion needed to be one that his foes hadn't also used their skirmishes in order to devise ways of dealing with his strongest defences.

He looked again into his *eye* at the one who might change everything for him in this game—a dwarf that would definitely surprise the others.

Especially those miserable elves.

He had taken a particular dislike to the elves.

CHAPTER 12

Brindel—The Champion

'THAT WAS THE last straw,' Brindel thought to himself as he left the king's chamber.

'Very pretty, Brindel,' his king had said to him. 'I have a daughter who might like it.'

'Very pretty indeed,' he fumed, as he snatched the gauntlets back from the king's guard and stormed out, trailed by the raucous laughter of those he left behind.

He would never say it out loud to anyone else, but his king was a fool. And he wasn't anywhere close to as funny as he thought he was. None of them were.

He realised before he went in that the king suffered his presentments as he would the jests of a fool. Yet each time he still went in convinced that this would be that time they would appreciate his work. He supposed he was just as big a fool.

In fact, no one in the whole Northern Mountains took him or his works seriously and he had decided as soon as the words left his king's mouth this time that it was time for him to move on.

The dwarves of the Northern Mountains were a warrior clan and they were idiots.

The fiercest of their cousins and the easiest to anger, they also liked to laugh and jest at each other's expense. But Brindel had never been one to take kindly to their constant torment.

The worth of a dwarf in his small kingdom was determined by their deeds on the battlefield and the myriad of tests and tournaments they held regularly inside their mountain kingdom.

Brindel was a part of the clan, but he was no warrior by trade. He was a blacksmith, which in any other clan would have had him highest in esteem and hierarchy. He was sure of that.

He had seen the weapons, armour, amulets, and trinkets that made their way into his mountains from their southern cousins.

They were certainly wonderful to look upon, he would give them that. Some were even well wrought with the charms and runes needed to protect the wearer or user from the spells of their enemies.

But here in the North, there were very few blacksmiths. The ones they did have made items fit only for practice or for children. That was their intent of course, but not Brindel's. His works were not intended for practice, let alone children!

His clan, however, were mercenaries, trading their fighting skills for payment.

The payments they favoured were usually the weapons and armour from those in the south and whatever other charms they had for sale.

Southern dwarves made the best armour, axes, and hammers in the entire kingdom according to his king and brethren and so Brindel was considered an oddball in his own clan.

Not only was he considered strange within his own kingdom, but those in the South frowned upon his work as well.

He had gone down there a long time ago at his king's behest.

'To learn from those who do it best' had been his words.

Yet they had derided him as well for the items he made. They were different to theirs, ugly to look upon and so inferior and of little use.

Brindel conceded even to himself that the works he produced weren't much to look at a lot of the time, but he knew that those materials that made an object shine and sparkle often didn't provide the best protection.

He knew that his were powerful, especially against elves, but because none were willing to try them during combat against those with magic, his works had never been proven.

'Ignorant fools!' he cursed to himself as he walked into his chamber.

He walked straight to his cupboard and began pulling out all of his belongings.

Soon he had a large pile strewn across the floor.

He knew that he wouldn't be able to take everything so he began throwing aside those items that he wouldn't need. The pile soon began to grow smaller.

He picked up the pair of gauntlets he had just taken into the king's chamber and looked admiringly at them again.

They had no diamonds, no gold, silver, or gems on them and were made of leather, yet this piece had taken some making. He smiled at the satisfaction he had felt when they had finally been completed.

The materials he had needed for this piece alone had taken him months to locate.

The hide was that of a beast only found in the highest steppes of the mountain in which he lived and even once he'd found it he'd still had a hell of a time catching and then killing it. A deer of sorts, it had been very agile and could bound around on the slopes like it were on flat ground. Its hide was so strong he had to put a spear through one of its eyes to bring it down. The other two he had thrown had bounced straight off it.

Not only was it tough, but it had a fierce resistance to cold, even before he had added all of his own augmentations. Black pebbles were attached to it from the fingers to the wrist, covering much of the surface. They were a dull black and not much to look at but they were strong. Oh boy were they strong. He had found them deep within a cavern underneath their stronghold, in the dark recesses of an old mine long since abandoned. Those that had mined there had left these stones behind, seeing no worth in them. Brindel instead had woven spells into them which not only increased their already strong nature but would absorb the impact of any blow struck against them. He had seen straight away that they were perfect for his works in armour. No other material he knew of could absorb anything near to what these could without shattering first.

He slipped the gauntlets over his hands and onto his wrists. These he would not be leaving behind.

Once he had decided on what he would be taking with him, he got out his backpack. This was just a large sack with straps woven into the front of it for him to carry his spare clothes and food.

Dwarves didn't have beasts of burden and they didn't ride horses. Their constitution was well known and they could walk for days without rest, even burdened with all of their worldly possessions.

Once packed, he flung the sack over his shoulders, strapped his axe on to one side of his belt, and his hammer on to the other and left his room.

A dwarven child came running up to him as he left his chamber. 'Going somewhere, Brindel?' he asked curiously.

Kagen was one of the only dwarven youngsters that had really appreciated his works. His father had bought him several items over the years at his son's behest. He had been happy to do it, too. Brindel's pieces cost much less than those from the South.

'I am lad. Definitely going somewhere,' he said gruffly. 'It is exceptional timing on your part though,' he said a little more brightly.

'I was just off to tell old Branwen,' he continued, 'that I won't be coming back here in a hurry and have no more use for my chamber or everything left in it.'

Kagen looked disappointed, but Brindel could also see the look of lust in his eyes that all dwarves get when they know they are a chance to receive something valuable.

'Go on now.' Brindel indicated his chamber with a flick of his head. 'Take whatever you like before all of the ungrateful sods arrive to pick it clean.'

Kagen stayed where he was, looking up the gnarly older dwarf.

'Why are you leaving?' he asked with genuine care in his voice, while still managing a quick glance at his surroundings to see if anybody else was nearby that may have heard what Brindel had just said.

'Why do you think I'm leaving young Kagen?' he asked and then sighed.

'Is it because no one likes the ugly things you make?' the boy asked.

Kagen was a good young dwarf, Brindel thought and brighter than most in these halls, but not very tactful. He had always seemed genuinely interested in listening to Brindel relate how his pieces were made and the efforts he went to create them.

Brindel noticed that he wore on him now all of the pieces his father had bought for him from his workings.

A pendant around the boy's neck he had made of hardened ice that he found in a glacier at the northern end of their mountain range. He had fused it together with spells at the time he found it and then encased it in the membrane from a fire drake's wing. There was no other place he knew of with ice that solid. That had been another epic adventure that he had been lucky to escape from with his own hide.

It kept the wearer safe from intense heat, which he thought initially to impress the Southern dwarves with. Such an item would be invaluable to them working in their furnaces deep in the mountain where they lived. But surprise, surprise, they had spurned him yet again.

Still, he was glad the boy had it now. He liked him and it might save his life one day. He had a matching one he wore within his own tunic.

'Yes, boy. It's because they're all morons!' he shook his head and tried to keep his temper in check in front of the young dwarf. 'But it's also so I can see more of the world and try to find some true marvels to shape into items that will be a sight to behold . . . and also wipe the smirks off all of their stupid faces.' He couldn't help himself. He was a Northern dwarf after all.

'Well I like the ones you make,' he said.

Brindel looked at him. 'This child likes them,' he thought to himself. Great! If he had doubted himself at all before, now he was sure that he was making the right decision.

As he patted the young one on the shoulder and walked past him, he said over his shoulder, 'Make sure you grab the helmet with the black stones.' He had tossed up between that one and the one he now wore. It was a magnificent piece and he was glad that at least the boy was the one who was going to get it.

Actually, *glad* was probably too strong a word for the boy getting his piece for free. He was satisfied instead that none of the other ignorant tossers were going to give it to their doubly ignorant offspring. At least the kid appreciated its worth.

He didn't bother turning to see the boy race into his old living quarters. This place held nothing for him now.

After letting old Branwen know that all the property he had left behind was for anyone who wanted it and got to it first, he made his way to the Western hall and then out through the main gates.

The doorway here was not huge. Designed so that it could be shut quickly and easily, it was still incredibly thick and dense and the hinges and pulleys that were used quite complex. If enemies were somehow able to gain entry before the gates could be closed, the hallway leading to it was not wide and barely high enough for the tallest dwarf to walk through standing up.

Any enemy foolish enough to try and make it through would have a tough time of it trying to fight a horde of angry dwarves in such a small space.

None had yet succeeded in making their way into the caverns behind since their kingdom was first carved out of the mountain many, many moons ago.

Brindel looked out and about now as he crossed beyond the threshold of his home. They weren't all that high up into the mountain here.

Getting down to their food supply would have been too onerous and time consuming even for a dwarf, if they had made their home high up into the mountain.

It also suited their mining exploits, as many of the fantastic jewels and minerals they found in the lower depths of the mountain and they didn't have to mine so far down from here.

He looked across and could just make out the distant trees at the northern end of Glorfiden.

The home to the dwarves' mortal enemy, the elves and dwarves shared a mighty lake between the mountains and the forest. Game was plentiful in and around the lake and many fierce battles had taken place throughout the years between the two races. Neither wanted to share the bounties with the other and compromise had never been an option.

Brindel knew it would be foolish to go too close to the lake and surrounding valleys and fields when by himself.

However, he also didn't much feel like journeying through the harsh climate and difficult slopes of the mountain. Not in his present mood anyhow.

He could have gone through the myriad of tunnels and waterways within the mountain and found himself much farther south and on the other side of the mountain range, but again he didn't much feel like tramping through the underground for weeks on end either.

Although it was very un-dwarfish of him, he wanted to be outside. He wanted to hunt for a little while in the valleys closer to the mountains without going down in to the lower ones, where the elves also hunted and gathered.

He just wanted some time to himself under the sun and the stars, away from his forge and the snickering of his clansmen.

Making his way down into the closest valley was easy going. There was a well-worn track which had been used by dwarves since the first day they came to this mountain range. It was wide enough for several dwarves to walk abreast, as they sometimes did when heading down to fight any major battle with the elves. It was true that there were other less-than-friendly creatures about that needed exterminating from time to time, but these always came from the eastern side of their mountain range. Nothing could access this side unless it came over the mountains or went around it to the north.

Brindel had never heard of that happening, so he walked along with an easy lope and not a care in the world.

After three or four hours of steady travel downwards, he came to the first of the valleys above the great lake. From here, he turned south, deciding to skirt both the mountains and the lake. This path would eventually take him past both the lake and the Southern Mountains and into the lands of men, his chosen destination.

The dwarves were not held in high regard by men.

Brindel himself had never been into their lands, but many of the Southern dwarves had. When Brindel had been in their kingdom, they had told him of their journeys into those lands to the south.

Apparently, a long time ago, the trade between them and men was a healthy and profitable one for both sides.

But his cousins in the south had said men started to become greedy for the wealth they saw coming out of the mountains and their bargaining became increasingly unreasonable. The language his southern cousins used had been much more colourful.

They told him that men also started settling closer to the dwarven kingdom and even tried gaining access to their caverns, some by stealth and others by force.

Both methods were easily disparaged after only a few attempts, but suspicions and hatreds grew and after a time only a select few men were allowed to trade with them.

This only made the rest of the men in the area and some further away, jealous of the wealth that those select few were amassing.

Today, there are many men who not only distrust dwarves but openly dislike them.

Brindel wasn't worried though. He was confident in his abilities to look after himself. He also suspected that in such a place he would be able to make himself quite a lot of gold and, just as importantly, find those that would appreciate the works he made.

The going was a little more difficult now that he had to climb in and out of the valleys. There were loose rocks strewn across the path from falls much higher up in the mountains, but his footing was sure, and although it slowed him a little, it didn't hinder him.

He kept his eye out to the west towards the lake for any signs of an elven hunting party, but for two days, he had seen nothing.

In the mid afternoon of the third day from his home, when his supplies had begun to dwindle, he decided it was time to venture into the low lands for some game to hunt, or if that were sparse, he would go to the lake for some fish to catch.

It was nearing winter, and not surprisingly, he saw very little in the way of game. He decided not to bother with his traps but instead kept walking until he came to the shores of the lake. He was near to the southern reach of the large inland waters and the danger was real now that elves could be nearby.

He picked out a spot where he was confident there would be fish biting. He had arrived in time to set up his lures well before the sun would be setting.

As he was setting up his third line and hook to drop into the water, he looked across, sure he had seen movement along the edge of the lake about a league from where he sat.

He looked again but saw nothing. He strained his eyes and concentrated on where he thought he had seen the movement.

There were trees near to that point of the lake and he knew that it would be easy for some sneaky elves to hide themselves without being seen. Even moving through the trees, he knew he wouldn't see them.

'Sneaky bastards,' he said quietly to himself. He couldn't be sure it was elves that he'd seen, but he wouldn't assume it wasn't. He had deliberately chosen this spot, as there were no trees closer to him than those he now turned his attention away from.

He slowly and subtlety turned his body and his face in such a way that any arrow shot at him would not find its mark in his flesh. They could pepper his armour day and night with their pesky arrows and they wouldn't leave a mark. But to reach their target, they would have to leave the safety of their trees and expose themselves.

He was confident that most spells wouldn't get past his defences. It would take a strong one to do that and he was yet to meet one of those. They tended to keep to themselves and away from these parts, for whatever reason he was thankful.

He awkwardly flung the last of his lines into the water and stuck the wooden stick into the wet ground where he stood.

He sat down, again awkwardly as he tried to leave no area exposed for their arrows. He then moved his head and tried to look using his peripheral vision at the area where he had last seen them.

Again, he saw nothing in the trees, so he moved his head slowly further left and saw three of the cocky tree lovers walking casually towards him. One of his lines snapped taught as a fish tugged at his line.

'Oh that just tops it,' he said out loud. 'You're not only dealing with an irritable and hungry dwarf, but now you've cost him his meal!'

He stood now and faced them, drawing his axe at the same time as two of the elves let fly with their arrows.

All pretence of trying not to notice them was gone. Knowing now what he faced, Brindel felt much more at ease. He knew their aim with their bows was remarkable. From this distance, he knew they wouldn't miss. From this distance, they could probably shoot him in the eye if they wanted to.

Raising his weapon in front of his face, both arrows clattered off the axe head, falling broken on the ground at his feet.

They stopped at the point where they had fired off their arrows. Even outnumbering the dwarf three to one, they weren't stupid enough to get too close to him. At least a couple of them would have battled dwarves before. They wouldn't have let these elves so near to the dwarven kingdom without at least a couple of seasoned campaigners in their midst.

'Get away with your pretty bows and your ceremonial swords you cowards!' Brindel yelled to them. He knew they would be able to hear him, but whether they understood him, he didn't know, nor did he care.

'Just so you know, if you try any spells on me, you'll be disappointed. You may even upset me enough that I'll come and chase you, pointy ears!' He spoke in the common tongue. He wanted them to hear his insults, especially when he thought of something really clever to say.

One of them walked forward in front of the others.

'Oh good,' Brindel thought. A bandy of wits. He was just getting warmed up.

But the elf said nothing to him. Instead, it walked closer to the banks of the lake and started pulling water from it into the air.

Brindel rolled his eyes.

'Didn't you hear me, tree lovers?' he yelled, as he began an easy lope towards them. As he ran, he spun his axe in a circle in front, holding it with both hands as he did. Flames began to appear in its wake as he spoke a few quiet words in his dwarfish tongue.

The elf closest to the lake turned to him after he had covered only ten strides and with a movement of both his arms in Brindel's direction, sent the deluge of water heading straight at him. It was intended to smash into him and knock him backwards on to the ground, where he would be much easier to spike with their arrows.

Instead, the water hissed into steam as it touched his axe, the fire rune blasting it into a fine spray.

Brindel continued to run at them, no longer interested in curses and insults. The arrows were flying thick now, but as the first stage of panic set in, their resolve began to wane. Clattering off his armour or falling to ash if they struck his axe, nothing was getting through his defences.

The two that had been shooting arrows started moving backwards as they fired their arrows. Their sure footing kept the arrows on target, but the speed they were firing at slowed as they kept looking to see how close Brindel was getting. The third elf, a little shocked at the power of this dwarves' magic resistance, resorted to pulling out his sword.

Brindel grinned at him as he finally closed the distance.

The elf sprang back from the dwarf's first swing of his axe. He had the advantage of reach and swung his own sword in an arc at Brindel's neck, thinking to slice right through the padding he had there.

Unlike other dwarves, who preferred chain mail and steel plates for their armour, Brindel liked the greater movement his leather armour provided. It was also incredibly strong. He had no chain mail protection at his neck like other dwarves, so it was one of the few vulnerable places he had.

Fortunately, he was fast. His axe had many charms and spells crafted into it, one of which gave it very little weight.

He was able to swing it with a speed that seemed impossible for a weapon of its size.

The elf's swing had been met by the blade of his axe on its inward arc and the jolt almost shook it from its hands. That initial shock was all the time Brindel needed to step in and with a downward motion, his axe head sliced straight through the elf's leg, entering just above the knee and severing it cleanly.

As the elf fell screaming, his sword falling from his grasp and his body no longer shielding the dwarf from his brethren, Brindel again raised his axe to his face. Two more arrows clattered to the ground in front of him.

Seeing their strongest fall and their arrows useless against this one, both of them turned and ran.

Brindel didn't bother chasing them. He stood there and watched as they fled back to the trees from where they had come, disappearing again from his sight.

He moved to the other side of the one who had fallen, so that his back was to the elves in the trees. He didn't put it past them to try and put more arrows into him, but his helmet came down to the armour at his back, so his neck was shielded from them.

He looked down at the one who had fallen. He was still alive, although his already pale features had turned whiter still as the blood pumped from his wound.

'I gave you fair warning,' he spoke nonchalantly to him. He felt no guilt or sympathy towards the elf, but he didn't feel the need to see his suffering. He swung his axe down into the chest of the dying elf, burying the edge in the ground underneath him. Blood spat from his mouth as he died, and Brindel pulled his axe away. Stooping down, he picked up part of the elf's cloak to wipe the blood off his blade. A blast of fire impacted him from behind, but the flames quickly dissipated. He felt the blow, but it did him no hurt and he gave it no notice. He remained looking at the elf lying at his feet. He pushed aside the cloak and saw that apart from his clothing and weapons, he carried nothing else.

No food, Brindel thought to himself disappointingly. He would have to go back to his fishing spot at the lake and hope at least one of his lines was left standing and not swimming in the depths of the lake with the first one.

Without a care in the world, he strode back to where he had left them.

He was almost there when the last of them was uprooted from its spot in the mud and dragged quickly into the waters. He lunged at it but wasn't quick enough to grab it.

Cursing to himself, he sat on the bank and looked back over towards the trees. The elves hadn't returned, as he knew they wouldn't. Not yet anyway. He knew they were still watching and would wait until he had gone before claiming the body of the one he had slain.

His attention was then drawn to the skies above the trees where he looked.

Dark thunderclouds were rolling in from the northwest and they looked ominous. He realised quickly how fast they were moving. It didn't look right.

'Oh well,' he spoke out loud to himself. 'No point sitting here hoping for a fish to jump out of the water and into my lap.' He stood up and walked back towards the valley he had walked down from to get to the lake.

He was confident of at least finding some sort of shelter from the storm, if not as confident at finding something to eat.

His stomach continued to grumble as he got up and started his trek back into the hills.

He reached the top of the first rise as the first wave of lightning strikes lit up the sky above the elven forest.

Brindel turned around when he heard the first crack of lightning.

He stared at the sky for some time. The clouds had stopped moving east and had settled above the centre of the forest.

'What are those deviants up to now?' he said aloud to himself, then crinkled his forehead in thought as lightning strikes began to pepper the forest all around the centre.

It was at that moment it dawned on him that it wasn't the elves that had created this hellish storm. Someone or something had sent it there.

He sat down to watch, silently cursing again that he had nothing to snack on.

'Not the same watching without food,' he quipped and chuckled to himself.

Brindel's jaw had dropped when the storm unleashed all of its fury into the centre of the forest.

He knew that the elves' city must have been there, where the sky had lit itself up with forked bolts.

He didn't close his mouth again until after the light show had run its course and the storm began to lose its momentum.

He realised then that it wouldn't be heading his way.

'Thank the kings of old,' he said out loud. 'I don't think I could have found shelter outside of the mountain itself to protect myself from that!'

Even his armour would have melted down to nothing and his body inside of it fried from the power of those bolts.

He knew there was no way any of the elves could have survived. Not from that. Not a chance.

He was stunned into silence. Even his mind took some time to truly acknowledge the impact of what had just happened.

Then he thought of those elves that had fled from him earlier.

Turns out they might have been the lucky ones. Possibly some of the last remaining elves left in the land. He was almost glad he hadn't killed them. Poor bastards going home to nothing and no one. At least he hadn't been responsible for nearly wiping out their entire population.

They were good sport at times and he would miss fighting them.

CHAPTER 13

MORTINAN—Gamer of Destiny

ORTINAN WAS UNLIKE any of the others competing in the game.

He had always been solitary, even amongst the royalty of his home world, and he was a deep thinker. His strategy was going to be unlike any before him, that he was aware of.

When he had made his decision not to choose any of the races made available, he had sought advice from the Creator and laid out his desire.

The Creator had shown little emotion and confirmed to Mortinan that it had not been done before. He conceded that it was permitted.

Mortinan knew the Creator would be doubting his seriousness in the game, but to him this game was everything. He would be inconsolable even if his champion did very well. He was here to win. There was no consolation prize.

He had always resented everything he had been given in life. Stepping through that portal from the palace steps had been the most gratifying thing he had ever done. He wanted very badly to have something that he could say was his through no gift or assistance from any other. He intended to earn his victory in this world.

Mortinan had chosen a half-elf. A bonding between a man and an elf.

Of course, there was no such race. His entire game was based on the proviso that both elf and man would be chosen, that their realms would be close enough for each to interact, and that there would be a pairing between a human and elf at some period prior to when he must choose a champion.

His first gamble was that his realm would border that of the elves. This would enable him to keep his input to a minimum. It was permitted to put within your realm any race of people that hadn't been chosen by any of the others. This was one of the reasons he chose a half-elf. He had a fallback plan if he needed it.

As there were numerous types of elves and a myriad of different human races, if he was unfortunate in his placement then he would have to create his own to enable his half-elf champion to be born.

Before he took such a step, which would require him to spend more than he hoped to contribute early, he needed to determine who was on the borders of his realm.

To draw them out early, he created an oasis at the corner of his realm that bordered two of his opponents' realms.

Not only did he make that small area of land picturesque, but he devised to fill it with game to attract the inhabitants of his fellow participants to determine what races lived there.

The first to show themselves to his *eye* were Mendina's elves. They lived to the east of his land and he still remembered the flood of relief he felt on that day. It was then his plan truly began to take form and was the day he decided he would no longer have himself a plan B. His half-elf was to be his all or nothing.

There were still a lot of 'maybes' to his strategy, but he thought that if what he saw in his head came to fruition, he would be very hard to beat.

His would be a champion none could match.

When the others learnt he had chosen a half-elf, none could see how he would achieve it without considerable luck. Still, his was not in any danger in the early stages and he would have to spend next to no resources for a very long time. Each of the gamers had finite resources, but he intended to pool nearly all of his.

The others may come to see his plans eventually, but for now, they wouldn't see why he did it, nor what he could hope to see happening in the very near future.

The wealth of his little area had, as he had predicted, eventually attracted men to his realm. It took many years after that of the first elf to enter his land, but they soon set up a village and his plan was complete.

Luck had played some part in his eventual champion being born, but he had never doubted it. Not even as the Naming Day drew near.

He would have preferred for his champion to have been born earlier, but he still saw within him the potential to be victorious.

Looking into his realm and with a small grin on his face, Mortinan flung the rod into his *eye*, landing it at the feet of the banished elven lord. . .

CHAPTER 14

The Naming Day

THE SIX GATHERED in front of their eyes and for the first time in a hundred years, not since the last spending day, the Creator was there with them.

This was the most important day since the game began.

Today, each champion would be named and the six would finally be able to see into the whole world of Dark Swell, not just into their own realm.

Today was Naming Day and there was a great deal of excitement amongst them all.

It was called Naming Day not only because each gamer selected his or her champion but because that champion then took on the name of their gamer. No other creature within the world of Dark Swell could have that name except the respective champion. Whatever name each champion had prior to the Naming Day no longer mattered, nor was it kept within any record.

Once the name was given on Naming Day, it was the name they had been born with and it was as if they had never had another.

Mortinan looked across at Mendina. He had expected her to be visibly upset at her elven kingdom being wiped out only yesterday, but she looked surprisingly pleased with herself. He didn't think any of her Lords would have survived the lightning, but he was doubting himself for the first time in a long time. There would be no reason for her to be feigning confidence. Not today anyway. He didn't think she would have chosen the exiled Lord. She wouldn't have been foolish enough to risk choosing one that she didn't even know still lived. She couldn't have guessed that he would use one of her own to destroy Glorfiden. Unless she felt she had nothing else to lose.

His own champion had made it safely back to his home after the storm, so he knew he was safe. He had since returned back into the forest with the elven girl and Mortinan was unaware of his current location and status, but he was confident that there was nothing in Glorfiden that could endanger him.

Yet as he continued looking at Mendina, he was concerned now for the first time. What did she know that he didn't?

He would find out soon enough, so he tried to put it to the back of his mind.

The others all looked calm and excited at the same time, as expected.

Mortinan had calculated what each of the other's strength would be right at the beginning of the game.

He had based his own strategy on what each of the others' champion would bring to the table. Each of them would try to be unpredictable in their own fashion, but his plan gave them nothing to plan against. He thought he had succeeded quite spectacularly there. His plan from the beginning was to have a champion skilled in magic and to take out any other powerful in magic before the Naming Day.

He thought he had until he saw Mendina's face.

Mendina would have powerful magicians leading the elves, which up until a short time ago would have been far too powerful for the other champions to conquer in a one on one battle. He still couldn't work out why Mendina still looked so content. He couldn't stop looking at her.

He eventually dragged his eyes away from her and turned his gaze to Brindel. His dwarves would be strong in battle and have magical weapons and armour to protect themselves. They may have honed their skills against the elves, if their realms bordered each other. If they did, then they would have fought many times over areas where both races most likely hunted and harvested, but he was confident in the power of his champion regardless.

Kabir had chosen a barbarian and would have a mighty warrior with some magical charm to help him out.

Kabir's barbarian shouldn't pose much of a threat and he didn't rate him.

Valdor had chosen humans and their variety was enormous, so his was a selection that was difficult to gauge. He hadn't specified any particular class of human and he would have been vulnerable early on, but he had survived and may even have flourished. His could be sorcerer or warrior, thief or assassin, cleric, monk, or druid. His was a difficult one to make plans against. He would have the added advantage of a strong realm and many allies to assist him. Mortinan saw him as his greatest adversary.

As for Linf, he still couldn't understand why she had chosen goblins. Weak, selfish, and unpredictable, they seemed like a poor choice. Their numbers were prolific, so the only advantage he could see had been at the beginning, where she could use their numbers to try and wipe out other races.

Mortinan thought that would have been her strategy, but here they were at the Naming Day and everyone was still in the game. Linf was not a threat.

Mortinan's thoughts were interrupted then as the Creator stepped into their circle.

'Welcome,' the Creator spoke to those gathered. His voice was low, but his words clearly heard by all present.

'Today is, to me, the most important day in the history of Dark Swell.' He spoke with a pride in his own creation but also for the efforts of his gamers.

'You all sit before me today still a part of the world and the game. This pleases me.' He smiled and there appeared a shine to the chasms of his eyes.

'It is rare indeed that all combatants survive to the Naming Day. Many of those that have, their worlds have not prospered, and their champions were predictable and boring. Many hid within their realms, just waiting for the Naming Day and hoping they had a champion strong enough.' His words held an excitement within them that none of those seated around him had heard before.

He looked around at them and suddenly smiled. The creator smiled. A genuinely happy smile.

The gamers were stunned but infected by the Creator's reaction they all smiled back.

'This world I have watched and the characters within it have intrigued me throughout. I have seen the motives behind moves and delighted in some of the ingenuity. Moves have been outstanding and most unpredictable.' He continued to smile as he spoke. 'And then, just yesterday, Mendina had almost all of her elves vanquished by Mortinan's storm. A brilliant strategy came to fruition, yet a twist even I didn't see was born. As you will soon find out,' he looked directly at Mortinan, 'Mendina is still very much in this contest.'

He turned his attention to Linf.

'And who could have seen your champion, weak and pathetic that she is, killing the strongest goblin I have ever known. He would have been a worthy champion, yet I still hold out hope that your replacement may grow to be even greater.'

His smile didn't waiver.

'I also feel that you too are still very much in this contest.'

The gamers looked around at each other, each still smiling and relaxed in the knowledge that there was nothing else they could do now to help their champion. Even Mortinan was smiling, but inside his stomach was churning as he tried to think of what twist the Creator was referring to.

Then the Creator spoke again.

'Before I open up your eyes to the whole world of Dark Swell,' the creator continued, 'I will speak to you each in turn and give you my thoughts on your efforts so far and my insights into the merits of your champion.'

The gamers were all surprised at this and delighted. They hadn't expected the Creator to be so involved on Naming Day. From what they had read about other games, Naming Day was just about naming each champion and opening up the eyes for them to check things out themselves. There had been no ceremony and no commentary mentioned in the texts on previous worlds.

Mortinan's mind stopped thinking then. His questions would soon be answered and he relaxed somewhat.

The Creator moved his focus to Brindel first.

'Your dwarven champion is not the kind I usually see Brindel. Yet in this company, I should have expected nothing less. An outcast armourer in a tribe of warriors seems on the surface to be a strange and foolish decision. Born of a warrior class, he can fight. His skills are less than his fellow tribesmen, but compared to those of other dwarven tribes, he is well above average. His skills as an armourer are believed by his kinsmen to be far less than those of the tribes that specialise in these craft. Obviously, you have seen what I did. His skill in weapons and armour are unorthodox and his pieces are far less attractive than those the others create. The magical properties are designed to ward against destruction magic, such as fire and missiles, yet also have properties which defend against earthen magic and other elements, such as those used by many of the elves. Dwarven armour is usually gifted with these; however he has developed his already exceptional skills and has armoured himself against other kinds of magic and elements for which his brethren are not known for. To put it simply, his armour is quite amazing.'

'As for his weapons, just as effective against magic. A truly worthy champion Brindel,' he concluded. 'I will enjoy watching his progress.' Brindel nodded his head low in respect to the words spoken by the Creator.

The Creator turned his focus to Kabir. Mortinan would be second last and Mendina last. How fitting he thought.

'Your barbarian champion is exactly the kind I usually see Kabir, but I am no less disappointed. His fighting prowess is elite among the barbarian tribes and he has *that sword*.' The Creator emphasised 'that', again with a small grin. 'This is where your barbarian differs from those used in other worlds and why he is still a chance among this extraordinary field. You chose just the one sword to imbue with all of the powers you could purchase throughout the past 2,000 years. It is a weapon of incredible power, of which even your champion is unaware. This, I believe, has tempered his enormous ego enough that he respects his foe and is still cautious and thoughtful in his decisions. A fine champion was needed for your weapon and I believe you have found one.'

Kabir was chuffed and looked around at his companions with a pleased look on his face.

Next, he spoke to Linf.

'Unlike all of the others here, Linf, yours still intrigues me most as she has not yet begun coming into her true powers. As I said earlier, slaying your would-be champion seemed a terrible blow to your chances. Yet she is strong now, with the potential to be stronger than any other goblin has been before her, even her father Greeble. I'm sure you'd confess there was some luck that led her to her magical mentor. Still, her inborn magic resistance and stoic, stubborn nature as a goblin that enabled her to use this magic to her benefit, were traits of the goblin that drew you to them in the first place. In a final battle of champions, I don't believe she would be a match for the others. But there are so many opportunities before then, where her powers could be used to destroy those that are unsuspecting of this unique creature.'

Moving in order around the circle, the Creator moved his gaze to Valdor. Mortinan was curious to see what class of man he had used for his champion.

'Valdor. In regards to power gained through both crafted and inborn magic, your monk is by far the weakest of all selected here. However, with martial skills above all of those in his elite order, he is still not a champion to be dismissed easily. A small order, their skills have been honed for hundreds of years and powers purchased and imbued into their fabric, into the very cells of their body. This has crafted a class of man stronger, more enduring, and far more skilful than those I have seen on other worlds. Combined with a strong realm and users of magic within it, again I say, a worthy champion and one that could also wreak havoc before any day of reckoning may arrive.'

He finally moved his attention to Mortinan.

'You made the most outrageously risky course of play I have ever seen, bar none. I thought for a long time that you had wasted your opportunity to be a part of this game, but the patience and foresight seem to have worked out for you in a most satisfactory way. Your champion has exceptional magical prowess and pitted against any other champion, once he has fully realised those powers, he would be unmatched. But he is still raw in his abilities and has none of sufficient skill to teach him to his potential. No one that is, except for his father.' He paused before continuing. 'I don't see that coming to pass, do you?'

The Creator looked at Mendina before swinging his gaze straight back to Mortinan.

'As for Mendina's champion, I shall address you again, Mortinan.'

Mortinan looked back at him with a puzzled look on his face.

The Creator grinned as he spoke, 'I shall address you because her champion is a very unremarkable female elf, with below-average magical and martial prowess. You skilfully killed off her chosen champion. A champion I had feared would have made the conclusion almost forgone such was the power he possessed. Included among his death were any that would have made a worthy secondary champion, except one. I assume Mendina chose not to risk selecting a champion that may not still live. A decision she may come to regret.'

'Yet other elves still live within Glorfiden who are considerably stronger than the one she has chosen,' he continued. 'Hers has nothing in the way of any special talents and in a battle with any of the other champions she would be vanquished quite easily.'

Mortinan was baffled. His relief when he heard she hadn't chosen Jarkene was immense, yet the Creator had sounded sincere when he said she was still very much in the contest.

Finally, the Creator concluded his thoughts on Mendina's champion.

'The reason I address you in regard to Mendina's champion is because this very unremarkable "female" elf,' he emphasised the word female, 'has already stolen the heart of your most worthy champion Mortinan.'

Mortinan hadn't bothered paying much attention to their interaction when they had returned from the forest. He had seen that the elven girl was as the Creator described her. Unremarkable.

Now his heart sank. The implications for him became apparent immediately within his brilliantly analytical mind.

His champion would not let anything happen to Mendina's champion. He would protect her from those wishing her harm. He and Mendina may as well have had the same champion.

He looked over at her now and it suddenly dawned on him exactly where her look of confidence came from. Not just from the fact that his champion would protect hers. If it were just that, then Mortinan wouldn't be feeling how he was right now.

Mortinan's heart sank because if there came a time when Mendina was in mortal danger, then his champion would do absolutely anything he could to save her. He would risk his life for hers and he would die before letting anything happen to her.

Mortinan was doomed and he felt sick.

CHAPTER 15

Good-bye to the Forest

NO WORDS WERE spoken for a long time after Mort told Mendina who he had seen. Shock was her initial reaction. Jarkene was dead. All of the elves knew that. He had died years before. Then again, so had Mort and his mother.

A number of questions formed in her mind, but looking at Mort, the questions died on her lips. She wanted to ask him if he was sure, but he was talking about his father. Mort wouldn't mistake his father for anyone else, and even if his memories were askew, an elven lord is not mistaken for any other.

She tried to turn her thoughts to what they could do now. She knew Mort had power in him. He was born of an elven lord and yesterday evening she had experienced a taste of the power within him.

But she knew even the power he held, the potential he had with that power, would not be nearly enough against Jarkene.

For them to go against his father would be sending them both to their deaths. Even after what he had done, Mendina still wasn't sure exactly how Mort was feeling. About what his father had done and the fact he was still alive.

She looked over at Mort again and saw the shock still present on his face at what he had seen.

She decided that question and answer time could wait. For now, she just wanted to be out of Glorfiden and away from the pain of its destruction.

'We should move now, Mort,' she spoke in a quiet voice, walking over to him. She gently grabbed hold of his arm to get his attention and spoke the same words again.

Mort looked at her.

'Where do we go?' he asked.

The simplicity of the question and the deadpan voice took her aback. She hadn't thought about *where* they could go, only that she didn't want to remain here any longer.

'I have no destination in mind, Mort,' she answered. 'We just need to go somewhere else.' She hesitated and then added, 'Do you wish to go home?'

Mort looked at her. He did want to go home. He wanted to tell his mother what he had seen. To ask her again what had happened to his father and again why she hadn't been honest with him. He wanted to ask her to come with him and find his father. Wanted her to be with him when he asked his father why he had destroyed the elves. Most of all, he needed her there to try and stop him from killing him. That was the strongest of his emotions. To kill his father. To avenge the many deaths of a people he never had the chance to meet. His people and his family.

He wanted to avenge the abandonment he felt for both himself and his mother. For the pain his father had bestowed on his mother.

And yet if all that were pushed aside and somehow justified in his mind, he still wanted to kill him for the pain he saw in Mendina's eyes. He knew her pain wouldn't go away, that it would continue to grow as she began a life without her family and the rest of the elves.

He owed it to Mendina to try and he knew his mother would never understand. She would try to convince him otherwise and he didn't want that to happen.

He knew he wasn't ready to face his mother yet.

'No, Mendina. I don't want to go home'. He still spoke to her in a voice without emotion.

However, the next sentence held plenty of emotion.

'My mother wouldn't approve of the help I will now seek from you.' He knew his eyes held the look of murder in them, as he saw the same mirrored in hers.

After a short time, where they continued to stare at each other, Mort spoke again.

'I need you to help me with the magic inside me, Mendina. We both know I'm not ready yet. Let us just walk in a direction and I will learn all I can along the way. If you are willing to assist me?' Mort asked it in question form, but he knew that their paths were the same now.

He was shocked and saddened by the things he had seen in the past few days, but the fire within him still burned for this elf. If anything, it had magnified. He was content to be with her and he knew that whatever her feelings for him, she needed him now and would stay at his side.

'Let us leave then, Mort,' she said and turned away from the heart of Glorfiden. 'We won't come back here again.'

Mendina began to stride away and Mort watched her walk off before picking up his things and moving off after her.

'Never say never,' he said quietly in answer to Mendina's last words, as he quickly tasted from the pool of power again that dwelled within the centre of Glorfiden. It was intoxicating.

Thoughts that the elves hadn't been completely wiped out in his father's attack convinced him they would both be back.

They were both still alive after all.

He would see the forest grow again.

They walked without talking much for the rest of that day. Intent on reaching the edge of the burnt trees, it wasn't until an hour before dusk that they finally reached the Trilling River. Much wider than the small stream they had crossed on their journey into the forest the trees on the other side still stood proud and strong.

Mort could feel their sadness radiating across to him on this side, but he could also feel the life pulsing through them. It was a welcome feeling for them both after the horror they had been through, especially for Mendina.

Mendina walked them to the edge of the river and stood in front of a number of burnt husks that were once elven river craft.

She sighed, a resigned sigh. She had prayed they would still be intact but she hadn't been very hopeful.

She leaned down and scooped water into her hands, washing away much of the ash from her hands and cleaning as much of her exposed skin as she could. Mort knelt next to her and did the same.

Mort looked up when he had finished and saw that the river currents were strong and the water was flowing fast. Swimming across would prove to be very difficult.

'Mort, do you see the boats on the other side?' Mendina asked as she pointed to a spot across the water.

'Yes I do,' Mort replied, 'but I don't see how that helps us.'

'Then it is time for your first lesson in the use of magic from an elf,' she said.

Mort looked at her and raised his eyebrows.

'They are a long way away, Mendina,' he said sceptically.

'Mort,' she said patiently, as if to a child. 'Your powers are greater than you think. I know you are beginning to believe that now. And belief in yourself is very important.'

'Elves are strongest,' she continued, 'in the use of earth, air, and water magic and in communicating with the wild animals and trees of this land.'

'My mother told me pretty much the same thing,' he replied. 'Elves prefer it above fire and electrical magic. They concentrate on that which is natural to the earth itself and which is not solely destructive by nature. Am I right?'

'That's true; however, these elements are still very powerful when used against our enemies,' she continued, with a zest in her voice. Her voice reminded him then of when she had flames in her eyes in his house only days ago and he quickly checked to see that she was okay.

He saw that her eyes were still the same alluring light green as she continued.

'These elements can be used to achieve amazing things, especially when used by the more gifted of magic users.' She looked straight at him, her eyes piercing.

'So what do I do here then?' he asked, still sceptical. Being able to draw in the power from Glorfiden was one thing and following a trail of magic that he could see, but he had no idea how to actually use the elements to untie a boat and bring it across such a wide river.

'You must feel them, Mort. You feel the wind on your neck, in your hair. Lift your hands and feel the breeze run between your fingers. You need to concentrate to begin with while you are learning to use it. After practice, it becomes second nature to you, but we will start with concentrating.' She stepped in front of him and grabbed his hands in hers. He knew he wouldn't be able to concentrate on magic if she kept holding his hands.

'First though,' Mendina asked, 'your mother said that you have used magic before. What sort of things are you able to do?'

Mort tried to listen to the words coming out of her mouth, but all he could think at that moment was putting his arms around her and holding her tight. Her lips were perfect.

'Mort!' she said loudly. 'Are you listening to me?'

'Sorry,' he said coming out of his trance. 'Uh . . . I can sense the creatures of the forest and the trees, but you knew that already.'

'What can you do with the magic?' she asked him.

'Just small things. I can take fruit from the highest branches by tickling them with the wind, a small gust is all because I can tell if they are almost ready to fall.'

'So you can use the wind. Go on,' she said again. She knew this was important but she also needed to be over the other side among the trees again.

'Sometimes when I was tired, you know only because I'd been working hard and it was getting late, not because I was lazy. . .'

'Mort, I'm not judging you, I just want you to answer my question.' He could tell that she was losing patience with him. He didn't like disappointing her.

'I would move the earth to help plant vegetables and trees. I'd make a hole using magic. It was a little harder than moving the air,' he finished.

'Good,' Mendina said, 'you can perform earth magic. What about water? Have you ever done anything with that before?'

Mort thought for a bit. He hadn't really *used* water in that way before.

'What would I have needed to do with water before?' he asked. 'I used buckets to carry it from the stream. So no I don't think I have. Sorry.' He hoped she wasn't disappointed in him.

'Many things, Mort. You can use it to help push boats along when you have no paddles or sails to use the wind. You can slow or even move its path, to redirect the water where you want it to go. It can be used as a shield against fire. There is almost always moisture in the air if you are ever thirsty. All of the elements are useful in so many ways.'

'I never thought of it in that way before,' he said, his mind racing. 'So I need to change the direction of the river so that the boats come to us,' he said excitedly.

'No, Mort,' she said with an exasperated voice. 'Even if you were able to do such a thing, which I highly doubt, that would send the entire river in this direction drowning us most horribly.'

'Oh. I see.' Mort replied, feeling foolish. 'So what then?'

'You only need to guide the boat here using the currents that are around it,' she explained. 'You need to see the water around it and send the magic there, directing it to your will.'

Mort thought he understood what she meant, but he couldn't possibly make out the water around the boat from here.

'But I don't think I'll be able to see the magic from all the way over there, Mendina. I'm not sure how I will be able to control it if I can't see what it is doing?' He finished with a bemused look on his face.

Mendina stared at him for a moment trying to comprehend what he had just said to her.

'What do you mean when you say that you can see the magic, Mort?' she asked in a voice already tired from trying to teach him. She was considered young amongst her own people and here she was trying to explain to the son of an elven lord how to use magic.

Mort looked at her with a confused look on his face. Surely, she knew what he meant?

'When things are close, I can send the magic to them. I can see it leave my body or my hands; however I choose to send it. I can then wrap it around what I want to move or I can use it to push the breeze.'

Mendina was stunned. She had never been able to see the magic. The first time she had caught even a glimpse of it was when Mort had drawn so much of it into himself. And even then it had seemed just an aura, a barely perceptible haze.

'What does it look like, Mort?' she asked, a look of wonder on her face.

Mort looked confused.

'Are you testing me, Mendina? I assure you that I can see it as you do.'

None of the Lords in Glorfiden were ever involved in the teachings of magic. They were friendly and kind to all of the other elves, but they kept to themselves most of the time and she could not recall ever hearing any of them talk about their magic in any detail.

All of the elves knew that their powers were well above their own and in battle the stories lent credence to that belief.

But it had never been mentioned that they could actually see the magic. She herself could feel it pulse within her and she could feel it when she used it, her senses keen to anything she did.

'The elves I know can't see the magic, Mort.' She spoke to him in a voice that she hoped hid the excitement she felt.

Mort seemed taken aback by her statement.

'Then how do you use it?' he asked genuinely surprised. 'If you can't see it then how do you control it and direct it?'

'I can feel it. It's hard to describe but it's like an extension of yourself.' She wasn't sure how to explain something that just was. Like explaining how the sun's warmth feels on your skin or the wind feels in your hair.

'I can feel it, too.' Mort chimed in as soon as she finished her sentence. 'Maybe that is how I can move the boat over here. I'll just feel it.' He looked at her and smiled, an unconvincing effort to try and show her that he understood her completely.

'I'll give it a try,' he said simply and directed his will towards the other side as he had when using air or water. Both techniques had been similar.

'Wait. . .' Mendina began, but she felt that he had already begun.

She looked across at where the boats were and a great whoosh of water impacted one of them, sending it flying into the trees and breaking it apart. The remnants crashed into the ground.

Mort could sense the irritation in the tree that the boat had struck.

He looked across at Mendina. 'You said to wait, didn't you?' he asked meekly.

She looked at him and as patiently as she was able said, 'You need to practice control first, then you can attempt to move the boat.'

'I understand,' Mort said, turning away from her and looking intently back at the water across the river.

Then a thought occurred to Mort and he turned back to Mendina.

'Mendina. . .' he began and then paused, realising how many times he spoke without truly thinking first. But on this occasion, he decided to ask the question.

'The boats on this side that are destroyed, they were here to get across to the other side of the river correct?' he asked.

'Of course,' she replied, not without some impatience. Her mind was still trying to come to terms with Mort's ability to see the magic. This could make her assistance much less helpful than she had hoped or it could make it easier.

'And no one but the elves use these boats correct?' he asked, the excitement building and his heart beating faster.

'No one else comes into our forest Mort,' she said matter-of-factly and with a tinge of annoyance and anger.

'Then what are the boats doing on the other side? If all of the Elves were in the centre of Glorfiden, why are there boats on the other side of the river?'

'They would be brought back across when. . .,' she spoke slowly and Mort saw the sudden realisation dawn on Mendina's face as she spoke.

'You are not alone,' Mort said.

He felt mixed emotions as he thought about what that meant. He was happy that Mendina's pain would be less, that she wasn't the last of her race. Yet he couldn't help but feel some sadness. He knew it was selfish but he felt their bond weakened at that moment. She no longer needed him and him alone. She would have others to lean on and to share her grief.

'They may have just been left there,' Mendina began, but she couldn't keep the excitement from her voice, betraying her doubts.

Mort tried to push the selfish feelings he felt to the back of his mind, thinking instead what this meant to Mendina.

'What purpose do you cross the river here for?' Mort asked.

'Gathering and hunting,' she replied. 'As you can see, the forest skirts the mountains up ahead there and we sometimes travel large distances in areas where there are no settlements of men. We do sometimes run into those horrible little dwarves but we try to avoid them. They may not even know what has happened here.' She finished.

'They would have seen the storm and felt what happened, as we did,' Mort said. 'They wouldn't know the extent of it, but they would know.'

'Yes.' Mendina continued his thoughts. 'And they would head straight back here. They won't be far off Mort.' She stared at him now and the first true smile he had seen lit up her face. Mort's selfish thoughts disappeared at seeing her smile. It was without question the most extraordinarily beautiful image he had ever seen and he basked in her delight.

'We will wait for them on the other side of the river, Mort. They will come back here to cross,' she continued. 'So now you practice and we will soon cross the river.'

She sat down on the edge of the water. Her smile had gone but Mort sensed an immense load was lifted from her. She seemed almost content for the time being.

Mort turned his attention back to the water and began to caress its flow, feeling much more relaxed himself now.

With the gift of concentration without distraction, Mort found the task to be far less difficult and daunting than he had thought only minutes before.

He picked up a small stick and tossed it in the water and with an ease that Mendina thought a beginner should not possess, moved the stick through the gentle waves and out into the middle of the river. He then lifted the stick clear out of the water, brought it back, and laid it gently in Mendina's lap.

He smiled at her and turned his attention back to the boats.

'Water is pleasant,' he said with some of the confidence he showed when he first spoke to Mendina prior to the storm, 'but I'm still more comfortable with air.'

Mendina followed his gaze back to the boats. She looked on in astonishment as one of the boats began to rise from the bank. It hovered for a moment as the rope tying it was unwound and then began to fly across the river mere feet above the water.

The boat was halfway across in little time and Mendina looked at Mort. His breathing had grown heavier, but he showed only a small amount of strain as the boat moved closer to their side.

As it neared the edge, she began to see the strain showing on his face and his body start to tremble, yet the grin never left his face.

He is powerful, Mendina thought to herself, as the boat thudded into the bank only a short distance from where she sat.

Mort's breathing was heavy, but he looked over at Mendina now and his eyes were glowing. Mendina had seen many novices when they first started using magic and none were ever able to move something as large as a boat, let alone fly it across the Trilling River. She wondered then how a half-elf could be so strong, even half an elven lord. Then she remembered Corein's words.

'*Surely you did not think that the human trait of the child would dominate the elven side.*' Dominate no, she thought, but she did think that the elven side may be lessened somewhat. She may have come to respect Corein in the short time she'd known her, but years of elven teachings still maintained that the elves were superior in all things magic. Yet here stood a half-elf with the potential to be one of the most powerful magic users in the land.

And although she knew she could have helped him somewhat in honing those skills, to have elves still alive that could show him even more excited her so much that it seemed to lessen the pain of what had happened. Or at least take her mind from it.

'Let us go across now,' Mort said to her with his head tilted to one side and a small, funny smile on his face. She suddenly realised she'd been staring at him and looked away.

Mendina stood and walked over to the boat. She stepped in and took a seat. Mort followed her and picked up one of the oars that was inside it.

He pushed off with it and their boat drifted unerringly across to where the others were tied on the opposite side of the river.

Mendina jumped out and walked over to the trees. She sucked in a sweet lung full of air and sat then with her back to one of the trees. Mort heard her begin to communicate with one of them but quickly tuned out. He realised it was not a conversation for his ears. Instead he tied up the boat and got out some food for them to share.

Now that they were out of the ruined forest he realised he was ravenous. He began to eat and wait for Mendina to finish with the trees.

Mendina returned to Mort as the sun finally began to sink below the tree line. Mort had built a small fire from the few dry branches of those that had washed up on the shore.

'The trees tell me there is a band of elves heading this way. They have camped about half a day's walk and are heading in this direction.' Mort could see from the flickering flames that she had a small smile on her face; however, her eyes were again withdrawn and sad. 'We should rest', she continued and then lay down on her side and tried to find sleep.

There was no way Mort was going to be able to sleep tonight. Mendina's proximity and the thought of meeting more elves excited him, but more than that was the power still pulsing through his being. He felt more alive than he ever had.

CHAPTER 16

Jarkene Returns

A S THE STORM dissipated above the forest of Glorfiden, Jarkene sat back down against the hard rock of the mountain crag on which he had been standing.

The power required to send the storm and keep it going for as long as he did had been much, much more than he could have envisaged.

The rod he still held in his hand was something otherworldly, he had no doubts in his mind about that.

Now that he had finished his efforts at destroying those that had banished him and done much worse, he turned his mind to the rod.

There was no longer a breeze coming from it, nor were there clouds swirling within its surface. It looked to be nothing more than a simple rod, a beautifully made one at that.

He suspected it was recharging. He hoped that a rod of such power had not spent itself in one use. He too was tired and also needed recharging.

Although the rod was the true instrument of power in calling forth the storm, Jarkene still had to expend a lot of his own energies, knowledge, and skills to control the elements within it.

His will it was that had stopped the storm above the place where he had once lived.

His will it was that had halted the first round of lightning.

His will it had been that had directed and kept concentrated all of the bolts in those terrifying clouds.

He dropped the rod into his lap, closed his eyes, and fell into a long and deep sleep.

He didn't know how long he rested on that lonely part of the mountain. It could have been hours or days.

He looked down at the rod and immediately felt a breeze coming from it. Ever so soft, but it was alive again and he smiled.

Turning his attention to the forest, he could see the blackened centre from his vantage point and thin tendrils of smoke reaching towards the sky from the mighty trunks that continued to smoulder.

He was saddened at the destruction of the trees. They were a terrible consequence of the vengeance he had rained down on those he once called his family.

He was also a little numb at the demise of his people and felt lost now that it was all over. For years, his thoughts had been consumed with how he was going to get back at those who had taken everything from him.

In the recesses of his mind, he knew that he had gone a little mad from the isolation and his own despair, yet he retained enough of himself to recognise some guilt at the death he brought to so many innocent trees. He was thankful for that. He could also feel a growing sadness for the death of all those elves who had played no part in what his family had done to him decades ago.

Then something drew his attention to the sky above the forest and the hairs on the back of his neck stood up.

They were faint and strangely unfamiliar, but he wasn't mistaken in what they were.

Someone was reaching forth, following the trail of the storm he had sent. The magic from the rod had been so immense that part of it still lingered in the air and it was drawing whoever it was straight to where he now sat.

He was unable to determine who it was that was looking at him now, but he knew there were only three elves alive that would have the power to do it.

The rage that had left him after the storm finished began to grow within his chest again. A small grin made its way to his face. He had a renewed purpose.

If it was his father, he wasn't sure if the rod alone would be enough to vanquish him. He was far more powerful than his offspring and Jarkene was sure there were things Glendrond was capable of that even he wasn't aware of.

He knew that another storm directed at him, and him alone, may be able to blast him from the earth, but that would take time and whoever it was knew where he was. He was also aware if he had somehow survived then he might have a defence against it. That concerned him, but in the back of his mind, he didn't think even Glendrond could have withstood that storm.

More likely, it was one of his brothers. One of them must have been away from the centre of the forest when the storm struck. Perillian he surmised. He knew his brother still liked to patrol the outskirts in search of those daring the borders of their lands. He had seen him a couple of times in recent years.

Regardless of who it was, he knew he now had no choice but to chance a return to the forest. The wards his father had put up against him would tell him straight away if it were Glendrond who lived or one of his brothers.

If there was no shielding up when he tried to enter then he would know the mighty Nurturer and Protector was no more.

With the power of the forest and the rod he now held, he knew that he was more than a match for his older brother.

Picking up his staff, which had long since been drained of any magic, Jarkene began the long trek into the valley below him.

The journey down was long, but it wasn't a difficult one for him. He had travelled it so many times in the last thirty years that he could have done it blind folded.

There were fell creatures that roamed the slopes that he had to walk, but they had learned to stay clear of him over the years and he made his way to the bottom of the mountain without incident.

Walking the gentler slopes of the valley, he picked up his pace, eager to test the boundary of the forest that had been forbidden to him for so long now. He ached to taste of the pool of magic within the centre of Glorfiden.

After what seemed an eternity, he made his way to the top of the final rise and looked down upon his home. Only a short clear patch of ground separated him now from the edge of the first trees that were the boundary to the realm of Glorfiden. He had never been able to see or even sense the barrier his father had formed. It kept none out but him and had been a large part in fuelling the anger which had ultimately led to the destruction of so much.

He remembered the first time he had tested the strength of the barrier. He had been told by his father that it was there and that he would not be able to breach it. But he had to see for himself. Being away from the magic for so long initially had been too sore for him to take.

He had simply tried to walk through that first time. As soon as he tried to step past that first tree, a tremendous pulse had gone through his body and he had been flung back about twenty paces. He wasn't sure how long it had knocked him unconscious for.

After that he had thrown whatever magic he could at it, but no matter what the spell was that he cast, they all went straight through and only impacted the trees beyond.

The barrier hadn't been designed to keep magic out, just him.

He had retreated back to the valleys then for a while, before making his way into the mountain.

He had been beyond the mountain as well, journeying over it and around it to the lands beyond, but he always came back. Something within him needed to be able to see the forest he had been cast out of.

The lands beyond the mountain were dangerous ones and without the magic source to draw upon, there had been many times when he had been forced to hide from creatures of one kind or another in order to let the magic within him regenerate. Initially, he had his staff, which was made of a wood from the centre of Glorfiden and with which he had been able to store magic drawn from the pool of power in the forest. It held a lot, but it had run out a long time ago.

He had stopped going beyond the mountain three years ago and now he had no intention of ever returning there again.

His pace slowed as he drew closer to the edge of the forest. His heart started to beat faster and a cold sweat had broken out on his forehead.

He got to the very edge and involuntarily stopped. He tried to sense if there was a barrier there, but as before, he felt nothing. He confessed to himself he was putting off what he knew he had to do.

Taking a deep breath, he stepped forward into the forest.

Bracing himself for an impact he almost stumbled as his foot touched down on the soft earth underneath the trees.

The first thing he could sense was the trees. They were restless, but he guessed because they were so far away from the centre, they weren't as distraught as he had expected.

The second thing he could sense in the far distance was the magic source.

Even here on the outermost point of the forest he could feel it and he began almost immediately to draw it to him.

He had forgotten how good it felt. His chest heaved as he breathed deeply of the fresh forest air for the first time in thirty years and an old, familiar feeling came to his face. He smiled. A smile of pure ecstasy.

He was home and now he needed to find his brother.

CHAPTER 17

Fight Well or Die Trying

KABIR AWOKE IN his tent early the next morning. He had slept well and was keen to get up and about and attend to the men he would be training.

He didn't think they would begin their first lessons until after the burial of those men that had died on the plains. When Denizen came to his tent shortly after he had arisen and washed, he was more than pleased with his greeting.

'Are you ready to begin, barbarian?' Denizen hadn't entered his tent but spoke in a loud voice from outside the flap.

Kabir couldn't hide the smile on his face as he stepped outside. Denizen took a step back as he exited, obviously not expecting the barbarian to be ready so early.

'Greetings, Denizen,' he boomed. 'Please take me to them. I look forward to seeing what I have to work with.'

Denizen frowned at that comment.

'These men are not children, Highlander. They are skilful with sword both on horseback and on the ground. I would appreciate that you realise that.' He spoke politely but with an edge to his voice.

Kabir laughed then. A hearty laugh.

'I meant no offence.' Kabir chuckled at the seriousness of his new friend.

'Quite the opposite, Denizen. I am merely curious to see how long it will take until we are ready to storm this Insect fortress and put the whole stinking dung heap to the torch.'

He held an arm out indicating for Denizen to lead on.

Denizen shook his head and started walking towards the practice arena. This crazy barbarian was going to take some getting used to but he had to admit to himself that he did like him.

They didn't have far to walk. The camp wasn't a massive one and the arena, or rather the space of dirt where there were no tents set up or horses tethered, was in the middle.

Kabir was surprised to see a large number of people both young and old encircled around the area set up to train. It would appear that everyone who had no pressing task to attend to had come to watch.

Inside the area were about forty men. Kabir hadn't known what number he would be training, but he had hoped for more.

He grabbed Denizen gently by the arm to stop him.

'Is this all the men we will have?' He asked in a serious voice.

Denizen's expression was again one of annoyance and so Kabir spoke again quickly before the plainsman could respond.

Holding up his hands, Kabir added, 'I mean no disrespect, but if their lair is like an ant's nest, then we will need to spread your men throughout the tunnels.'

Denizen looked to visibly relax when he realised no insult was meant.

'These are our best barbarian.' Denizen spoke with pride. 'Crenshen wants to see the results after one week before he commits any more men to this. He is still far from convinced and I was surprised he has given you this many.'

Kabir nodded then, sure in his skills and ability to teach these men. In truth, he had never had opportunity to instruct so many seasoned warriors and he was excited by it.

'Then let us stop standing around gossiping like old women and start fighting.' Kabir grinned as he finished and patted the plainsmen solidly on the arm.

They walked over to the men that stood around waiting for the barbarian to arrive. Each of them had the same curved blades sheathed at their sides. The sheaths were a thin, plain leather that seemed to be more of a wrapping than something designed to carry and protect their swords, which themselves hung loosely from a cord around their waist.

Kabir raised his eyebrows as Denizen took his place among the men.

'Very well,' he spoke in his best booming voice. 'My name is Kabir and as you know, I am a barbarian from the North of here, from the village of Deerstep.' He looked around at them all. 'I'm sure you've all heard of it.' He added.

None of the men fanned out in front of him moved or made a sound. They just stared at him with the same blank expression.

'I am considered to be the funniest person in my village,' he continued, 'and quite adept with the sword.' He knew they would warm up to him soon.

He looked at Denizen. 'You have practice blades?' he asked.

He patted the sword at his waist. 'We have only these Kabir.'

'You practice with sharp blades?' Kabir was surprised they weren't all hobbling around with limps and missing limbs.

'We do most of our fighting on horseback, barbarian,' Denizen explained. 'Our ground fighting is done only after each progresses through stages and is at a level where they are evenly matched. It is more like a dance than a brawl.' He looked seriously at Kabir. 'There are some who are hurt if they get tired or are clumsy, but that is rare. We don't practice our killing strikes on each other. They are performed only during our *Piqest*.'

He turned and signalled for one of his men to step forward. Kabir recognised Tremill. He stared at Kabir with a look that showed he hadn't yet had time to sort out those men that had seen him bested by the barbarian.

'Show the barbarian the Seventh *Piqest*,' Denizen ordered.

Tremill gracefully pulled his sword out from its sheath and began a series of movements, which to Kabir did look like he was dancing. Sword thrusts were combined with slashes, combined with fluid movement of his feet and body. His arm was an extension of his sword and all of his strikes were designed to flow on to the next, whether it was a defensive posture or an attacking thrust.

After a minute or two, he stopped, sheathed his weapon, and went back to stand with the other men.

Kabir was impressed with the grace and some of the moves were ones he hadn't seen before. He nodded his head in admiration, hiding the disappointment he felt inside. He knew that he needed to see more before he could judge them fully but already he could pick huge holes in their training. He understood that fighting another, be it a man or some other ungodly creature, was a series of movements where one strike or counter needed to move seamlessly into the other and that the wrong selection could mean a catastrophic injury or even death.

Yet he couldn't get past the fact that these men didn't train against one another with practice weapons. Sword fighting was an art, but there were so many variables. Only through gruelling practice and fierce sparring could you truly reach your potential. He saw in these men the potential to be just as effective in killing their foes on the ground as they were on horseback, but he knew he needed time.

He didn't know how much time, but it wouldn't happen in a week.

Still he had been given the week to show Crenshen what he could do and he didn't intend wasting a minute.

'I am glad I knocked your man down as early as I did Denizen,' Kabir said to him while looking still at Tremill. It was meant as a compliment, but when Tremill heard the snigger of a couple of others standing amongst him his eyes narrowed even more and Kabir could almost see the thunderclouds circling his head.

'Shall we begin then, barbarian? These men are very interested in seeing how you may be able to assist us. As am I.' He finished with a small bow. He showed no discomfort from his injured arm.

'I would like to, Denizen, but first one more question. Do you have many spare swords?' He spoke seriously. He thought it best not to try and be too humorous all the time. At least until he had earned the respect of those here.

'We have a number of spare swords barbarian, but not forty. If we could gather those of the old and fallen I could get enough, but why practice with those when each here has his own?' Denizen wasn't sure where Kabir was going with this question.

'If you could gather enough for each man here Denizen before we start. I will then need all of their edges blunted.' He knew the plainsman wouldn't like it, but there was no other way. They were time short and he needed for them to fight with weapons of a similar weight and shape and something that wouldn't kill half of them before the week was out.

Denizen frowned and didn't answer for a time. He eventually barked orders for some of the men to collect enough swords for each man and to then take them to the sword makers and have them blunt the blades on each.

Kabir nodded his head in thanks. It shouldn't take too long. He was sure they would have stone wheels and instead of using them to sharpen the blades they could blunt the edges by pushing them directly on to the stone.

The swords began arriving in small bundles as Kabir and the rest of the men assembled waited patiently.

In a much shorter time than he thought it would take, forty-two blunted swords arrived and were stacked up in a bundle near where Kabir stood.

He walked over to them and inspected each as he handed them out to those that would be using them. He was satisfied that none would be able to deliver any serious damage. They had even blunted the pointed ends which he had forgotten ask of them.

He guessed those who made the swords probably knew a bit more about it than he did.

Selecting his own practice sword, he stood back in front of them all.

'We can now begin,' he said to them. 'I want you to remove the swords at your hips first and then partner up with someone else. Give yourselves room away from each of the others.'

When that was done and they were spread throughout the practice arena, he walked to the centre. Denizen walked with him.

'Now I want you all to start fighting each other, as you would normally.' None of them moved. He assumed they were confused due to their assumption that he would be teaching them new ways to fight.

'Begin!' Denizen roared at them and as one they began to fight.

'Thank you,' Kabir said as he turned his attention to the man as his side.

'I too am confused as to why you want this Kabir,' Denizen answered in response to his thanks, 'but they need to learn to listen to you.'

'My thanks for that, too,' Kabir smiled at his new friend. 'I need to watch them for a while first to gain an understanding of how your men fight. I need to learn before I can teach.'

Listening to himself, Kabir thought he sounded like one of the elders back at Deerstep. There were some mighty fighters among those in his village, but the one he thought of now had been both a great fighter and an amazing teacher. He thought of his father Rondig and smiled.

'Shall we begin,' he said to Denizen as he began to walk among the paired combatants.

The first thing he noticed was the movements of the men around him. Like Tremill, they all had an animal-like grace with their footwork and sword strokes and the whole scene looked like one of the celebrations in his village when everyone would meet at the Great Hall and dance.

This was far too choreographed for his liking.

He walked between two men and indicated for them to stop.

'You both move well. Your defences are clean and your strokes efficient but this time I want you,' he pointed to the larger of the two who he noticed had excellent defensive moves, 'to kill him.' He pointed then to the plainsman's opponent who had been the more aggressive of the two.

He stepped back from between them and watched.

'Go,' he said, and they began.

The larger of the two moved forward immediately, swinging his sword in an arc at the other one's head. He ducked under it easily and had his sword ready for the next swing, which he anticipated would come as an upward stroke at his side.

This too was parried aside as he moved away from his opponent. The larger one came at him again swinging his sword at his torso this time. His opponent again deflected away before moving again into position for the next similar stroke.

'Stop,' Kabir said, moving forward and standing next to the larger man.

'Go and stand next to Denizen over there.' The man nodded and moved over next to his usual instructor.

'Okay,' Kabir said, holding his new sword out in front of him. His other sword was still strapped to his back. The only time he removed that from his person was when he slept.

'This time, I'm going to attack you as one of those creatures would come at you. Are you ready?' The man opposite him nodded his head and took up a defensive stance.

As quick as a striking snake, he lunged forward at him, his sword arrowing in at his chest. His opponent was quick and managed to step aside and knock Kabir's sword away with his own, still balanced and ready for the next strike. As his feet touched the ground, Kabir began his next swing towards his torso, from his stooped over position. However, Kabir's reverse sword strike stopped before it got to him and instead his leg swept out and took his opponents own out from under him. The man fell on to his back as Kabir's sword cracked into his shin. The plainsman let out an involuntary yelp from the pain, but Kabir hadn't finished with him yet.

He lunged at him again with his sword aimed at his torso, but the plainsman still had his sword ready and deflected it once more. As his sword clattered away, Kabir let the momentum take it down and into the other shin before stepping back and allowing the man the chance to stand. He got up gingerly with a scowl on his face.

Kabir noticed that those others closest to him had stopped their own contests to watch him fight.

'I am not here to embarrass you.' He said it loud enough for all of them to hear. 'I am here to show you how to fight these creatures from the ground.'

'The first lesson I have shown is that they do not fight as you do. They will try to rip your heart out with their claws and if that doesn't work they will take out your legs so that you can't stand.' He paused to look around and make sure all were listening.

'If you can't stand then you can't fight. Each of their moves is not always to kill straight away, but rest assured, each stroke is designed to kill you eventually.' He still didn't think it was time for jokes so he kept his words and his tone serious.

'This time when you are fighting I want one of you to try and take out the other man's legs while the other tries to stop him.' He paused again.

'And I want you to use every dirty trick you can think of. There are no rules when I instruct. It is a life and death struggle and I intend it to be the death of those evil insect spawn hiding in their mud hole and not yours!' He raised his voice for the last part hoping to inspire them, but they just turned back to their opponents and began sparring once more.

'Inspiring,' Denizen said to him. Kabir turned around and saw a small grin on the face of the plainsman.

The barbarian gave him a blank stare in return and then burst into laughter.

CHAPTER 18

Teaching a Goblin New Tricks

THE NEXT MORNING, Linf awoke and her leg hurt again. Whatever had numbed the pain the evening before was no longer helping. She was disappointed but still excited about absorbing more of what it was the old man had given her. She had felt alive for the first time and was hungry for it, which in turn reminded her how hungry she was for food as well.

It wasn't long before the old man walked into the room carrying a bowl with something that smelt very good.

He laid it next to the goblin and left.

Linf looked down at the food, scarcely believing her eyes. Inside the bowl were chunks of meat. Nothing but chunks of meat. She quickly scanned the room. A lifetime spent protecting what little food she could scrounge had made her wary.

She looked again at the door, expecting the old man to be standing there with something attached to the bowl so at the last minute he could drag it away. But he wasn't and there was nothing tied to the bowl.

Linf leaned down, grabbed the bowl, and hugged it to her chest. The meat smelt fresh.

She grabbed a piece and put it to her nose. She couldn't smell any poison so she shoved it into her mouth and started to chew. It was good, very good. It didn't take long to finish everything in the bowl. She then threw it into the wall and lay down, satisfied for the first time she could remember.

She thought of how good it felt having a stomach full of food. No hunger pains and no never-ending quest to find scraps to live off.

Her thoughts drifted to why the old man had given her such a fine meal. Why feed her when all he had been trying to do since she had been there was make her angry. Now he didn't want to anger her anymore and the goblin thought she knew why.

He was afraid of her. Afraid of what had happened when she took the magic from him. Afraid that she would do it again.

She smiled then, closed her eyes, and fell into a deep sleep.

When she awoke, the old man was standing at the foot of the bed staring at her.

'What are you doing there you ugly swine,' Linf asked him politely.

The old man had a serious look on his face as he spoke. 'We need to talk about yesterday.'

Linf lay there silently, waiting for the old man to continue. She had never been much of a talker.

'I have decided to let you in on a little secret.' He paused. Linf smiled inwardly. She already knew the secret.

'I am going to show you how to absorb the power you pulled into yourself yesterday.'

Linf looked at him suspiciously. 'Why would you do that, human?'

'First of all, you need to remember that I am powerful goblin.' The old man stared at her as he spoke. 'I can help make you powerful too, but if I sense you mean me harm I will not hesitate to kill you.'

'Again I ask human garbage, why would you do that?' Linf was getting impatient and she didn't want to talk with this human any longer. She was bored and still tired.

'I am going to make you powerful. Powerful enough to kill most creatures you come across like I have done for countless years now.'

Linf continued to stare at him, just wishing he would leave. She was also picturing her teeth ripping the old man apart. That would be a messy meal she would enjoy.

'The reason I want you powerful is because I need an ally. Someone to come with me when I return to the lands of men.' He tried to gauge what the goblin was thinking, but Linf was giving nothing away.

'I need someone to watch my back and believe it or not, I have chosen you, because you are the only other creature I know of that can do what I do.'

'Why would I want to go where men live?' Linf snarled. 'They would just kill me.' There was no way she was going with the old fool.

'If you are strong enough, you need not fear,' the old man encouraged. 'You can hunt at night, stealing into homes and catching the stray person out and about. Men sustain me so much better than any other creature.' He knew that he had to appeal to the goblin's greedy nature. 'And you can feed on their young.'

Linf tilted her head at that last comment and the look he returned her showed that he knew he had struck a chord. Human young were her ultimate weakness. Linf knew now, thinking about what he had said, that she would probably go with him. She decided to hold off on killing him for now. She would wait a while longer. Let him teach her and then kill him.

Linf didn't say a word to the old man as he stood there waiting for an answer.

Instead, she slowly nodded her head, closed her eyes, and pretended to sleep. When Linf opened her eyes again a short time later, the old man was gone.

The next morning, the old man was again at the foot of the bed when she awoke.

'Is that all you do, you old fool? Quit staring at me,' Linf said to him in an irritated voice.

Brax was in no mood for the goblin's sharp tongue today. 'We start your training today. Now in fact.'

Linf snarled at him. 'When I have eaten, we can start. Where's my food?'

The old man moved to a small table next to the door. He didn't bother trying to argue with her. It would be much quicker just to give her some food.

He came back with a plate of meat. Not as plentiful as the previous meal, but his supply wasn't endless and goblins had ferocious appetites.

After the goblin had finished and thrown her bowl into the wall again, Brax left the room.

When he returned he had with him a small animal. A rodent of sorts, it struggled as he held it up by the skin of its back.

'Do you see this creature here, goblin?' Brax asked Linf in a condescending voice. He wanted to get her attention, and although her temper was under control for the most part, Brax knew she still didn't appreciate him talking to her like she was stupid.

'Yes, human. I'm not as stupid as you are.' Linf probably wasn't all that hungry anymore but would never say no to a snack, especially one freshly killed.

'How do you think that it is feeling right now?' he asked the goblin more seriously this time.

'It is probably disgusted by your smell and your filthy hands.' Linf retorted.

Brax wondered then, not for the first time, and he knew not for the last, how he was going to put up with this goblin for the next few days, let alone weeks. He tried not to think about the long term.

'You think you are a clever little goblin, but you are a fool if you think you will ever taste the flesh of a human child if you are not going to take this seriously.' He shook his head as he finished speaking and narrowed his eyes at the goblin tied to the bed.

'Of course it's afraid you stupid human.' Linf replied. 'Why don't you just get to teaching me and not asking stupid questions from your stupid mouth?'

Brax took in a deep breath and let it out slowly before speaking again.

'Do you know that it is afraid because it struggles or from the fear in its eyes?' Inwardly, he begged that the goblin would learn fast so they could be gone from here. His need to be away had grown increasingly since he had discovered this one's talents.

'I know it's scared, old man, because it knows that I'm going to rip it to shreds very soon and eat its stupid little brain,' Linf said with a half snarl, half smile.

'Its brain is probably about the same size as yours,' she added looking at Brax with an expression of boredom on her face.

'Okay then, my clever goblin,' Brax continued without pause or biting at her comments this time, 'how can you draw that fear out of it and into you?'

They both just sat there and stared at each other for a time until the goblin finally broke the silence.

Linf didn't want to play this word game with him any longer. She was bored and wanted to sleep now that she had eaten. But the chance to have more of the power she had last night was too tempting a chance to pass up. Plus she wanted to eat the rat, so after a while, she answered him. Without the sarcasm.

'Isn't that what you are supposed to be telling me?' Linf asked.

The human just looked at her for a while longer before nodding his head and answering.

'Yes it is,' was all he said.

Linf waited for him to continue, but he didn't.

'Well?' the goblin asked. 'Tell me then.' She was beginning to lose interest again.

'Okay. To begin with, it is easier to do if you are touching the one you wish to drain.' Brax walked over to the side of the bed.

'But before I hand this to you, it is important that you don't kill it.' Brax held it at arm's length as the goblin hungrily tried reaching for it.

'One,' he continued quickly, 'it needs to be alive or it has no fear or anger. Those emotions leave the moment the heart stops beating.'

Linf pulled her arm back and patiently waited for the human to finish his game of tease the goblin. She couldn't wait to rip both of their throats out.

'Two,' Brax spoke in a serious voice now, 'you need to learn how not to kill your prey.' He knew the goblin wouldn't get that part of it but it was only her first real lesson.

Linf stared at him with no expression on her face.

'Just give it to me,' was all she said.

Brax reached out with it in his hand and Linf snatched it from him as soon as it was within reach.

Brax expected her to start eating it straight away. It looked as if that was her intention as she bent her arm and moved the rodent towards her open mouth. Then she stopped.

As her jaws opened and the rodent started to squeal louder, the goblin stopped and just looked at it. Stared at it, in fact.

Brax did well to hide the smile he felt at that moment. Some of what he said must have somehow gotten through.

'I can almost see it,' Linf said. 'It's like the air is moving around it and it's a different colour, but not really a colour.' She was spellbound by it and without further instruction began to pull whatever it was into herself, as anyone else would breathe in the air around them.

Brax stopped the words he was going to say before they came out of his mouth, as he saw the goblin start to absorb the power. He was both delighted and worried at how easily she had worked it out. Her description of it, although primitive, was accurate in its own way.

The 'colours—but not colours' that Linf was describing were to Brax a shimmering wave, dancing around the body of those he drained.

He liked to think of it as their life force.

It was the energy their body released from the emotions they gave off.

As the body absorbed sustenance from food and excreted energy through sweat and steam through physical activity, so the rest of the body also released tiny amounts of itself when it felt angry, stressed, or afraid. None but he, and now the goblin, could both see and draw in those that were released.

He assumed other emotions did the same, but he couldn't see those or draw them in, so they didn't interest him.

However, drawing to him all of the spent emotions was not the greatest aspect to his secret power. It was that these emotions were still connected to the entity expelling them. They very slowly dissipated of their own course over time, but they remained attached to them until they did.

That is why those people in the towns he had grown up in who practised certain arts could describe someone's aura to them. He used to think it was just a parlour trick to fool gullible people.

Later on, he discovered they were simply reading the emotions those people they were fleecing had released from their bodies.

Of course, they weren't able to use those emotions to feed upon.

They were unable to latch on to those expelled emotions and use them to draw out more and more. They couldn't drain them completely as Brax was able to until their life essence was depleted.

Brax was suddenly drawn out of his thoughts by a crunching sound. He focused back on the goblin in time to see Linf put the last part of the rodent in her mouth.

'What are you doing?' he said to her in a harsh voice full of disbelief and disappointment.

The goblin finished chewing the last of it, burped, and looked over at Brax.

'It died so I ate it.' She said matter-of-factly. 'They are nicest when they're fresh.' She smiled her disturbing looking goblin smile. 'Have you got any more of those?'

Brax looked at her and didn't even try to hide the shock on his face.

'Why did you kill it? Wasn't the absorption of its emotions enough for you?' Brax slowly got his temper in check. She had still progressed further than he had originally hoped after all.

'There weren't any left,' the goblin said while picking small bits of flesh from between her teeth. 'That's why it died. Don't you even listen to the things you tell me?'

Linf paused and looked straight at Brax.

'I know I call you stupid all the time, but I think you really are that stupid.'

The shock Brax felt moments before had been replaced by a small amount of fear. This time, he tried very hard to disguise his feelings.

'You completely drained it before you killed it? How can you be sure?' He himself wasn't all that sure about it.

Linf shook her head before answering.

'I'll talk slowly for you . . . I drained it . . . it died . . . so then I ate it.' She lay back down and closed her eyes.

Brax decided to let her be for now and walked out of the room. He needed time to think.

He also needed to find another rodent.

Their day of departure grew nearer.

Brax was still confident that his powers exceeded those of the goblin; however, he intended to take every precaution. He had no doubt when the goblin felt it no longer needed him it wouldn't hesitate to kill him. If he wasn't ready, his life would end that day. He was under no illusions.

Some things he held back when teaching Linf how to use her powers. Small things, but in a life and death tussle, they could be the difference. The goblin was dangerous. Only he knew just how dangerous, but he needed her. Needed her strength if he were to achieve his goal. A goal he had desired for a very long time.

The goblin had no idea, how could she. The fact she was a slave to her basic instincts, to feed and survive, was why Brax had allowed her to live and why he felt he could manipulate her for as long as he needed her services.

Linf sat up as Brax entered the room. Her restraints were still on and had been reinforced, a design made using thin vines weaved over and over again. It had taken Brax a long time to construct them, but they were obviously necessary. Linf had ceased trying to break the bonds long before this day. She now sat with apparent ease, as if she chose to be there strapped to the bed. Brax knew better.

'Soon we leave, Linf'.

The goblin made no move to indicate she cared, but her eyes gave away her emotions, even if Brax wasn't already able to pick up on them.

'Let me make it clear goblin.' Brax spoke slowly in the hope that she would listen to him. 'We have a long way to travel to get where we are going and you could never find it without me.'

Linf sat there looking at him, then down at her bonds and back up at Brax.

He took a deep breath and continued talking.

'I will take the bonds off for a time when you tell me the meaning of what I just told you.'

Without hesitation, Linf responded, 'I won't make it where you want us to go without you so I better not kill you yet.' She concluded with a smile and again looked at her bonds.

Not for the first time Brax thought to himself why he didn't just kill her now.

CHAPTER 19

King Dayhen of the Storm

THE DOORS TO the throne room swung open and the king's chamberlain swept passed the guards inside the door with a swirl of his cloak.

'Always one for the dramatic entrance,' Dayhen thought, as he lifted an eyebrow and glanced quickly at the man standing at his shoulder, then back to his Chamberlain Mellor. An old man, he was nevertheless still spry and at times Dayhen wondered what his secret was. He must be about ninety by now.

Yet as Mellor approached closer to the throne, Dayhen was quick to note the frantic expression on his face, as if the Dark Swell itself was headed for the city.

'What ails thee, Mellor?' Dayhen asked as Mellor knelt before him and then rose, again with a swirl of his cloak. Even in a state of panic, he still remembered to add some flourish.

'Your Majesty. . .' Mellor began in a shaky voice, the first time the king had heard a tremor in his voice. He had just noticed that Mellor's face was a pale white.

'Your Majesty,' he repeated, swallowing before he spoke his next words. 'Glorfiden is destroyed . . . the elves are no more.'

With that, he knelt again and bowed his head. He swung an arm back and signalled to the guards at the door.

Dayhen felt a dread chill course through his body. He looked to the sorcerer standing at his left for confirmation. Derekia stood motionless, his dark eyes wide and the blood draining from his face.

The king stood, trying to regain his composure as the doors opened again.

'How could such a thing come to pass, Mellor? How!' his words betrayed the panic he felt inside.

Mellor looked up. 'Your messenger sire,' was all he said before lowering his head again.

A man walked through the open doorway and stopped next to the kneeling chamberlain.

Dressed in green and still armed with long sword and a longbow, he did not kneel or bow to the king.

The Forest Stalkers gave fealty to none but their own Lord, yet they had been allies to the Kings of Dark Swell for countless years.

'Lord King of the Storm, it is as your man here has informed you.' He spoke matter of fact, with a thick accent. Their first language was not that which other men used. 'Glorfiden was savaged by a lightning strike and is now ashes some three days past. Someone has made a mockery of your name.'

The Forest Stalker did not give his name and Dayhen did not ask for it.

Dayhen ran a hand through his thick brown hair and sighed. The Stalkers were not the kind to embellish or tell anything other than how it is.

'Yet how can you be sure of the fate of the elves? How can you be sure none survived?' Dayhen was still trying to fully grasp what it all meant.

'The morning after the storm, Lord King I ventured into the forest. I didn't go far knowing it was my death to be in there at all, but after some time waiting beneath the trees, no elves came upon me.' He needed to say no more. All knew the elves let none into their forest and knew when any were within its borders. They suffered not even the Forest Stalkers within their realm. 'I therefore braved the journey a little further to where I saw many trees blasted from the ground. Beyond those . . . the trees were no more. The centre of the forest is gone,' was all he said.

'Thank you for your haste in informing us.' The king nodded at the Forest Stalker, who inclined his head in turn and left the throne room with as little fuss as when he walked in.

Dayhen turned to his wizard again. 'The evil that has threatened seems finally to have shown itself.'

Derekia slowly nodded, not looking at his king.

'We must not be surprised as Glendrond was Derekia. We must be ready.' He turned and watched the doors close again after the Forest Stalker.

'Meet me again this evening, Derekia, after you speak with your mages.'

Dayhen rose and left through the main doors, his guards following closely behind him.

Derekia turned and left through a passage behind the throne.

Mellor remained kneeling until one of the guards finally went to him and helped him up.

His daughter and grandson would be fine he thought to himself. But deep down, he knew that if the forest of the elves was no more, there was little likelihood that Corein and Mort could have survived.

It also occurred to him that even if she had survived, without the protection the elves offered through her proximity to their forest, then the evil that had infected the land would soon find its way to their door.

A shudder swept through his body again as he slowly walked out of the throne room.

CHAPTER 20

Save the Princess

VALDOR REACHED THE other side of the clearing and looked across at the trees one more time before continuing along the overgrown track. His last glance had shown him that the Squargrin weren't yet halfway around the clearing, but they were still moving quickly and their numbers seemed to be increasing as they moved along.

Valdor guessed he would have at least another hour before they caught up to him. He knew he needed to find a place to make his stand before then or hope the king had sent a forward party to meet them.

He didn't plan on resting his hopes on that. He would keep moving quickly for the next half hour and if he hadn't found anywhere suitable by then he would branch out in to the forest and try his chances there.

He was still amazed at the condition of the princess. Not long ago he had all but given up hope she would live. Now she looked as if she would at least make it until he got her back to Lakerth. She was unconscious still and appeared very weak, but her heart beat was much stronger.

After another twenty minutes, they came to the Regent River. It wasn't a wide river, but it was deep in the centre and free flowing at present. The bridge across it was a solid one, made of hardy wooden beams. It was strong enough to get a carriage across, so Valdor knew that destroying it was not an option. He wondered how the small creatures would fare in the water and a plan began to form in his mind.

He quickly decided this would be the best place to make his stand. He could leave the princess safely at the far end of the bridge while he fought those that tried to cross. It was wide enough that their arrows would be almost ineffective when shot from the trees on this side of the river. He was counting on them not being able to swim across the water.

The bridge was wide enough for a carriage as long as nothing was at its side. He was confident none would be able to pass him.

Moving to the far side he lay Areana gently on the ground, secreting her body as best he could behind the final support beam. It would protect her from any stray arrows.

Looking down at her, he marvelled yet again at her appearance. He could see that she would mature into a beautiful lady. She had her mother's hair and the same large green eyes. She was still a child and did not have the effect on him Queen Kainet had, but he saw there was so much about her that made him think of her mother. It gave him a strange kind of solace as he thought of his queen's passing. There was a large part of her lying on the ground in front of him. A part that only he could keep safe.

He never regretted all of the ordeals and trials he had been put through his whole life. He believed in his duty and his purpose in life had always been to protect others. To protect those that were not strong enough to fight for themselves.

Yet in all that time fighting against foes from other realms, those within his own and training until he could barely stand upright, he had never felt the same force of purpose he did now as he turned around to face what was coming.

He stood alone against hundreds of the creatures. If he fell or if he stumbled and let even one through, the princess would die today.

He clenched his jaw and stepped forward as a steely calm came over him.

His mind emptied of all thoughts. Except one.

Kill them all.

The trees began to teem with Squargrin as those that reached the last trees before the river stopped in the branches in which they swung.

They saw the man standing alone on the bridge and some of them remembered him from earlier.

They began by firing their arrows at him, but many missed their mark and the missiles clattered harmlessly to either side of him, some even falling into the fast flowing river below.

Those that would have found their mark Valdor caught in his left hand. He didn't bother using his sword to swat them away. He wanted to show the contempt he felt for their efforts to shoot at him with their bows.

It soon worked, as the first of them tentatively dropped on to the ground and moved to the path at the start of the bridge.

Valdor didn't move from his position in the centre. The calm he felt remained.

As their numbers grew on the ground, those in the front gained more confidence and soon began their awkward lope towards him, their chorus of screeches building as they attacked.

As they were almost within reach, Valdor stepped forward and swung his sword in a mighty arc from right to left. Six of the creatures died in that first swing and then five more on his return arc back.

Those behind the ones that died tried to pull up after seeing all those in front of them die so quickly and easily, but there were too many behind them pushing forward now and they had nowhere to retreat to. They were pushed forward as they tried to stop and without any momentum Valdor simply stepped forward one more pace and slew each of them with another one handed swing.

This pattern repeated itself a few more times before the creatures were able to finally move back out of reach of his sword.

As they did, Valdor stepped back to the centre of the bridge. He wouldn't risk getting too close to those still shooting their arrows from the safety of the trees. They lacked any penetration from where he was and he was still able to catch them or swat them aside with his free hand without losing any of his form.

He had time now to assess the whole scene again and noticed movement down at the river to his right. A few of the creatures had made their way to the bank of the river. They stood there squawking among themselves as those on the bridge also looked down at them.

They will have realised that if their fellow Squargrin were able to swim across, then they could come at him from both directions. This would be far more appealing than adding their bodies to those already mounting up on the bridge in front of him.

The first one finally got up the courage to try, as he was pushed in by one of his fellow Squargrin. He began to splash about as he slowly made his way out into the water, yet as soon as he made it to where the river was flowing freely, he made a last gurgled squeal as he was washed downstream and dragged under.

Those others that were standing with him all stepped back from the water and looked up at those on the trail. It was clear to Valdor that there would be no more attempts to swim across to the other side.

He was beginning to turn his attention back to face those on the trail when he noticed one of those down at the water squawk loudly and point under the bridge. His eyes were drawn back to them, and although he didn't understand their language, he understood its meaning straight away.

Their bodies were made to swing through the trees at pace and not to swim through water, especially a fast flowing river.

He was lucky they hadn't thought to do it earlier, but he knew he was now in real trouble. They were going to attempt to swing underneath the bridge to get to the other side.

He was torn as to what he could do. His first instinct was to get back to the princess and stand next to her to stop any coming underneath from approaching her, but he knew if he did that he would be giving up the only position he had to stop them coming across the bridge.

If they got behind him, they were both going to die, yet he couldn't think how he could stop them from accessing the bottom of the bridge and swinging across under it. They would move quickly, he had seen how adept they were in the trees. He wouldn't be able to skewer them through the gaps in the wooden beams and keep those on the bridge at bay at the same time.

If he tried to pick the princess up and run for it, they would get ahead of him in the trees as they had before and he would have them attacking him from every side.

He saw them begin to make their way to the underside of the
bridge and he knew he had run out of time to think. He had to
act now.

Racing back to the princess, he stopped to pick her up and moved
quickly down to the river's edge as those on the bridge began their
pursuit of him.

Putting his sword into his sheath and holding the princess in front
of him with his hand under her chin, he walked backwards into the
water as he looked up and saw the first of them make their way to
his side from under the bridge. The others on the bridge had made
their way to where he had sat the princess down earlier.

He lay down in the water as they came screeching towards the
water's edge, pulling out their small bows as Valdor lay down in the
water. Kicking out with his legs, he let the flow of the water begin
to take him downstream.

None of the arrows found their mark as he found the faster
moving currents. He had time to see them lope back to the trees
and begin to swing their way through them as they followed him
down river.

Valdor struggled to keep them both above the water. The water
tried to swing his body around, but he fought it strongly, keeping
the head of the princess above the increasing force of the current. He
looked across and saw he was moving faster than those in the trees,
but not by much. He didn't want to be in the water any longer than
he had to but he knew that he needed to be a long way in front of
them before he risked swimming for the shore.

There would be all sorts of dangers in the water. Snags, fallen
logs, and other things beneath the surface that made the river their
home, but he had no choice but to let the river take them.

It was deep enough here that he didn't have to worry about
rapids and the rocks that came with those, but further down there
might be.

He was finding it difficult enough to swim with the princess
in this part of the river. Having to deal with rapids would make it
impossible to hold on to her and keep them both safe, especially as
he couldn't see what was in front of them.

After about ten minutes of letting the flow take them and without striking any of the dangers he had feared, he saw movement in the trees again.

They had left the Squargrin behind not long after they began and he knew they could not have caught up to them. The flow was still strong and they had gone a long distance.

The movement he saw was barely perceptible, but he saw a flash of green again and knew he hadn't been mistaken.

Moving his shoulders towards the bank, he began kicking his legs strongly again. Soon he found his way out of the free flowing part and into a pool of calm water where the river swept around to the left.

Finding the bottom of the river with his feet, he lifted the princess into his arms and walked to the shallow bank in front of him.

Walking clear of the water, he lay the princess down on the ground and waited for those within the forest to show themselves. He hoped there was enough of them to fight off the creatures that followed him.

Not as proficient in the forest as elves were, the forest stalkers were still feared in the realm of men by those moving through the outer forests. These were not their forests, and he was surprised to see one of them this close to the capital, but Valdor gave a slight bow of his head in greeting as the man stepped out of the trees.

Behind him were three others, all similarly dressed in light green and brown cloaks, designed to camouflage them amongst the trees.

'Never did I think to see one of the King's Shield swimming in the Darkening River,' said the one who stood in front of the others.

'Nor did I,' Valdor replied, 'but these are strange times and dangerous ones.'

The forest stalker nodded his head in agreement as Valdor continued.

'We are being chased by a large number of tree-swinging creatures not of this realm. They move quickly and won't be far away.'

'There must be quite a few to have you flee from them down the river.' The stalker looked down at the princess and arched an eyebrow at Valdor.

'She is the Princess Areana.' Valdor didn't need to explain his need to keep her alive. Even though they had little to do with the king, they were still considered his allies and had assisted him in the past when called upon. They knew who the princess was.

'Come with us,' he said to Valdor. 'Although we too don't hail from here, we know this part of the forest well.'

He turned then and they began to move off. Valdor quickly checked on the health of Areana and deemed her not much worse than before they got into the river. He picked her up and quickly moved to follow the Forest Stalkers through the trees.

They didn't go further into the forest but instead continued to follow the line of the trees that ran parallel to the water.

After a few minutes, they came to a spit in the river where a thin sandbar had been created from the flow of the river around it.

It was thin enough so that the creatures would be unable to get around them, but it was still close to the trees. They would definitely look to rain arrows down upon them as they had on their first mad dash away from them.

Valdor knew this would leave the princess vulnerable as he looked around for something to shield her from their arrows.

He found a small log washed up against the bank a short distance upstream and walked quickly to retrieve it, after he had lain the princess down on the sand at the end of the spit.

He managed to drag it back with the help of two of the Forest Stalkers and place it in front of the princess. When he was satisfied that it was in a position that would protect her, he turned back to their leader.

'What brings you here?' Valdor asked.

'We wait for one of our people to return. He had a message for your king.' He didn't elaborate and Valdor didn't ask further.

He saw those across the other side of the river first. The trees shook as the huge number of Squargrin swung through them until they came level to where Valdor and his new friends had stopped.

Valdor had expected they would cover both sides of the river and he was right. However, looking across the water, he was glad to see there was a huge number on the wrong side of the river. Many hundreds of them that would be good for nothing more than jumping around and squawking at them on one side of the river. Their small bows wouldn't be able to shoot their arrows close to this side. The princess was safe from them.

He turned his attention back to those he knew would be coming on his side. He heard the shaking of the branches and leaves before he saw them come into sight.

Much like the Squargrin, the Forest Stalkers preferred to shoot with their bows and only used their swords when pressed, but they had limited arrows and the creatures coming through the trees were too many.

They fired off most of what they had when they came into range and even though each shot dropped a Squargrin from the tree, by the time they had finished shooting, there were still well over a hundred of the creatures remaining.

The Squargrin didn't bother leaping from the branches this time. They were well within range of those standing on the river bank and they rained down as many arrows as they were able.

The Forest Stalkers were naturally agile and quick and initially they were able to dodge or swipe away the arrows fired at them. But as the number of Squargrin swelled within the trees, the Forest Men quickly realised they would not be able to evade them any longer.

Valdor was another matter entirely. Without the princess to burden his thoughts and defences, he was a blur of movement, moving faster than the arrows themselves. Some of them came close to penetrating his defence, but none struck him.

'Go,' he said to those standing near him, but the Stalkers were already on the move. The four of them moved quickly downstream along the bank before darting back into the foliage of the tree line.

Some of the Squargrin peeled off to chase after the fleeing men, but most stayed where they were, firing off arrows as quickly as they could.

Valdor continued to bat away their arrows, confident in the knowledge that the Forest Stalkers weren't fleeing and that the creatures in the trees would run out of arrows soon enough.

Which they did.

It was then the Forest Stalkers reappeared from the spot they had gone into, their blades bloodied now. Valdor watched as they briefly sheathed them to fire off their remaining arrows.

Those left in the trees had no choice but to jump down and attack with their swords.

The Forest Stalkers weren't far from Valdor by the time the creatures reached them and they began to deal out swift death to any that came near them. They were adept with their swords as well and with the Squargrin only coming at them from the one direction none of them were troubled in dispatching them.

Valdor hardly broke a sweat dealing with those foolish enough to come towards where he stood in front of the princess and her wooden shield.

Perhaps thirty of the Squargrin fled back into the trees, squawking as they made their way back to meet with those others across the river who had already begun making their own way back towards the bridge.

Valdor knew they would meet up again soon enough. For some reason, they were determined to take the princess down. He knew they would return and in much greater numbers.

While the Forest Stalkers went back to the trees to retrieve their arrows from the bodies they had slain, Valdor walked over to check on the princess.

She was as he had left her and was still breathing steadily. However, this time as he stooped over and put his hands under her legs and shoulders her eyes opened and he stood up in shock. She smiled at the King's Shield leaning above her and Valdor thought he looked upon his queen again.

The shock he felt quickly left him as the princess closed her eyes again and fell back into a deep sleep. He didn't know why she had smiled at him when she opened her eyes, but it was the exact same one his queen had given him when she lifted his chin and looked at him on the day of his official acceptance into the King's Shield.

He was confused all over again at the feelings coursing through his body. Lord Thaiden had told him once to ignore them, that they weren't a component of his duties. He understood that, but as he lifted her up into his arms, he couldn't help but think about them.

She was still only a child, but he could see now the woman that she would grow into. She would look a lot like her mother, but at the same time, she would be her own woman. Looking down at her in his arms, so fragile and weak, he felt that she would be a woman that he would easily lay his life down for. Not just because she would be his queen one day but because she would be someone quite extraordinary.

He realised his emotions were confusing to him because he felt so strongly based only on how she looked and nothing more. How could only her appearance have such a profound impact on him?

He looked up then as the Forest Stalkers returned to where he waited on the sandbar. Valdor tried his best to clear his mind as he knew they weren't out of danger yet.

'Where to now?' Valdor asked them. 'There will be many more of them next time.'

The one in front looked to think for a time before answering him.

'We should go into the forest,' he said. 'There are no better places than this along the river, but if they come in greater numbers it is risky to stay here.'

'They fight better in the trees,' Valdor replied, surprised that he would suggest going into the forest.

'So do we,' he said, 'and the one we are waiting for will be here shortly.' He paused then. 'His skills far exceed ours.'

Valdor was surprised to hear that. He had been impressed with how they fought so far. They used their bows very well and they were more than adept with a blade.

'I don't think one more will turn the odds in our favour within the trees,' he persisted. He didn't intend on taking the princess headlong into an area where it would be too difficult to defend her.

He could see again the Forest Stalker thinking how much he would say before answering.

'He has powers far beyond ours. Powers that will help make light work of those creatures that pursue you.' Again he chose not to elaborate.

Valdor thought quickly through his options. Staying on the bank would make it hard for them to defend themselves against such huge numbers. They would have more arrows this time and would be able to swarm them as when they first attacked and killed so many of the King's Shield.

Valdor didn't know how far off Thaiden, Heridah, and the others were and he couldn't rely on them being here in time. If there was no better place along the river bank and he had no reason not to believe them, then he must trust the Forest Stalkers and their faith in the abilities of this other one to protect them all.

He gave a short nod and followed them into the trees.

CHAPTER 21

Where to Now for the Dwarf?

B RINDEL LOOKED ACROSS at the mountains to his left. He was coming to the Southern tip and knew he would be entering the realm of men soon.

He had managed to scrounge some food earlier in the day from a couple of well-placed traps, but he was still hungry and was looking forward to a warm meal and a soft bed.

The Southern Dwarves had told him there were a couple of sizeable settlements near their borders, but he had no idea exactly where they were. He was hoping he might come upon a well-worn track shortly and be able to follow it until he came across one of them. It wasn't all that hard he thought.

He looked across to his right from the ridge he walked along and could still make out the southernmost part of the elven forest. It had ended halfway through his trek that morning and he was glad to see the end of it. Those trees were a little foreboding even with all of his protections. It was just somewhere Dwarves weren't meant to go. Too many sneaky elves in those trees and some of them would have been powerful enough to take him down in their own environment.

Back when they were alive anyhow.

After a couple more hours of trekking, he finally saw to his left the semblance of a trail. It was mid-afternoon by the time he stepped on to it.

He could see now that although it wasn't used as much anymore, it was far from overgrown and obviously still frequented by the odd traveller coming out of the mountains. He figured this was the trail used by his Southern cousins to move to and from the lands of men.

'Excellent,' he said to himself as he started to move along down it at a slightly quicker pace. He wasn't in a mad hurry to get to wherever it was he was going, but he was a hungry dwarf and he needed to eat soon. He didn't want his growing hunger to affect his mood when he finally found somewhere to eat. A good first impression was probably going to be needed.

It wasn't long until the trail levelled out and trees began to grow on either side of the path he walked. The Mountains were well behind him now and the land he was walking into was much flatter and a lot greener.

He didn't like the trees here either, but they were more spread out than those in the elven forest and there was very little undergrowth. He also knew there wouldn't be any elves in these ones, so he wasn't too concerned with scouring his surroundings as he walked.

After another hour or so, he turned a corner in the track and saw a small wooden building built just back from the dirt track. There was a thin tendril of smoke coming from one of its chimneys and two large horses tied up outside.

'Finally,' he said with a smile and made his way on to the porch and stepped up to the front doors.

They were closed, so he tried the door handle. The doors were locked and barred from the inside.

'Oh you have got to be kidding me!' he said out loud in dwarfish.

He pushed his nose up to the gap between the two doors and inhaled deeply. He could definitely smell something cooking.

He stepped back again and took another quick look around.

He knew this was a place for travellers to stop. There were a few stables just to the side of the building and it was built so close to the track that there was no way this was someone's home.

Plus he had been told by those dwarves that had been this way that there were places like this all along the tracks and trails that led to the human capital. All the way to the northern shores of the Dark Swell.

Brindel walked back up to the front door and as politely as he could banged on it with one of his gauntleted fists. The door splintered a little where he struck it and he stepped back wincing. That's not the kind of thing that would make friends of those inside he thought.

He heard a number of footsteps from inside. One of them went to the closest window and he saw the sheet covering it open a crack. He noticed also the bars behind the glass, which looked to have been freshly done. There were still wood shavings on the porch underneath it.

The footsteps moved from the window to behind the door.

'What do you want, dwarf?' a voice yelled at him.

Charming, Brindel thought. Very hospitable of them.

'I'm hungry and tired,' he yelled back in the common tongue used by men. All dwarves were taught it from a young age. They needed to be able to talk with those they traded with, both in gems and their fighting prowess.

'How many of you are there?' the voice yelled again.

Brindel sighed. He was starting to get irritated.

'Just me. I have plenty to offer in the way of gems and stones, so just open the bloody door and give me something to eat!' he decided that pleasantries were no longer the standard here. He had a large purse containing a variety of gemstones and other stones valued by men, but if they didn't open the door now, he would smash it down and help himself. At least that way he wouldn't have to part with any of his stones.

He heard the beams removed from the inside of the door and the keys turned in the locks. 'Seems like someone isn't too trusting of strangers,' he thought. None of the other dwarves had ever made mention of this. He had been led to believe they were welcome at these waypoints, if not so much in the larger settlements.

The doors both swung open and the man he had been conversing with stepped back, an old sword in his hand pointed straight at him.

Behind him were three other men. One also had a sword, another a pitchfork, and the third a crossbow. The last one was only young, but out of the three of them, his were the only steady hands. The crossbow he held was pointed straight at Brindel's head.

'Where are you from dwarf?' the same man asked him.

'Are you the owner of this fine establishment?' Brindel asked, not having moved yet.

'I am dwarf, now answer my question.' Brindel could see the fear in his eyes and the unsteady way he held his sword.

'Fine,' Brindel said. 'I'll play your little "let's get to know the stranger" game, for all the good it's worth to you. My name is Brindel and I am from the Northern Mountains.'

'The North?' the man said sounding surprised and looking a lot more worried. All men knew which Mountains the warrior clans were in.

'We never see Northern Dwarves on their own. Where is all your fancy armour and jewels?' Brindel realised he was suspicious of something, but if he started on about how much nicer their armour looked, things were going to get real ugly in here.

'Listen,' Brindel began as he walked through the open doors. 'I'm not going to talk with you any more until you have sat me down and brought me some food and ale. That is what you do here isn't it?'

The men had all taken steps backwards as he entered, except for the boy with the crossbow. His arms still hadn't wavered.

Brindel walked over to a table situated near the fireplace, not that there was anything burning. It did enable him to have no one to his back however and he could see them all from where he sat.

Sitting down, he took his helm off and placed it on the stool next to the one he sat on. This was both to make them feel safer about his intentions, but mostly so he could eat and drink that which they were going to bring over for him.

That same food and drink that they had better hurry up and get for him he thought, as none of them had yet moved.

'I don't know what it is that is making you all so nervous and extremely rude,' he barked at them, 'but if you don't hurry up and get me something to eat I'm going to get even grumpier.' He glared now at the man with the shaky sword arm. 'Trust me when I say you don't want to see me when I'm grumpy.' He finished his last sentence by banging down the gauntlets he had just removed on to the stool to his other side.

'These are dangerous times, dwarf,' the man spoke back to him in a voice bordering on panic. 'Most men have moved from the villages and smaller towns and headed to Lakerth. There are creatures about that at first don't seem to be anything other than a friend. Stories have made their way here about other places like ours that welcomed in strangers, even dwarves and later none were found alive.'

Brindel was beginning to understand the fear and distrust, but he really didn't care right now. It looked like he would have to help himself after all.

'If none were left alive,' Brindel asked with very little patience, 'how do you know what happened? And the only reason I can think of as to why a dwarf would get angry enough to hurt anyone not directly threatening him, is if that same person offered food and ale and neglected to serve it to that very same dwarf.'

He looked across at the boy with the crossbow. 'And you!' he said in a quieter voice full of foreboding. 'Either shoot one of those bolts at me or point that thing in another direction. Better still', he continued, 'go and get me something to eat!' The last said in a voice indicating that he was done being polite.

Yet at that same moment, while looking at the boy, it suddenly dawned on him that maybe it had been a bad idea taking his helm from his head. This one still had a steady hand. The crossbow seemed taut and well-built and he knew from that distance he probably wouldn't be able to get out of the way before it embedded itself in his skull. Raising his hand wouldn't even help him without his gauntlets on.

'No more sudden banging noises,' he told himself, as he turned his attention back to the owner of the establishment.

'So why then are you all still here?' Brindel asked, suddenly curious now that he was feeling a little less sure of himself.

'My wife is sick,' the man said, 'plus we don't really have the luxury to be up and leaving. It hasn't been very profitable here of late.'

Brindel noticed the one who had the pitchfork was over at the door, putting the beam back up that had just been taken down to let him in.

'Just so you're not interrupted during your meal,' the man said to him reassuringly, but with a catch to his voice now. 'Like I said, these are dangerous times.'

It dawned on Brindel now where this was going and the real reason this man was so nervous. They were intent on robbing him! The cheek of them he thought, as he ducked his head down to his right and reached out for his helm.

The bolt thudded into the wall exactly where his head had been just before he moved. Quickly putting his helm back on, minus the straps, he pulled his axe from his belt as he stood.

The man with the sword had made no move towards him. He must have expected and hoped, Brindel assumed, that the bolt would be sticking out of his head right at this moment. The fear was back in his eyes again now.

Brindel saw in his peripheral vision that the boy was frantically trying to reload another bolt, while the man at the door had picked up his pitchfork again. He couldn't see where the other one had gone.

'It seems they may be telling another story about how a dwarf walked into one of these places and later none were found alive.' He walked slowly at the man in front of him, raising his axe as he closed in on him.

The man swung his sword wildly at Brindel but it was nonchalantly knocked aside by the dwarf, who then proceeded to sink his axe head deep into the man's chest.

Brindel turned to the one with the pitchfork. A pitchfork! He shook his head at him and didn't even bother trying to deflect it as the man drove it at his stomach. The prods snapped as they struck his armoured chest plate and Brindel swung his axe downwards this time, cutting through his right thigh. As the man fell forward, the dwarf chopped his head clean off. He spun as he did this, finishing in a stance that left him facing the boy with the crossbow.

He had reloaded and it was once more pointed at Brindel's face, his arms still remarkably steady.

'You're a brave one, lad,' Brindel said, 'even though you're using such a cowardly weapon.'

'You can leave now,' the boy said to him in a shaky voice. His arms were steady, but he was obviously a bit upset by what he had just seen. Brindel chuckled at his own thoughts. A bit upset might have been understating it a little. He wouldn't be surprised if he'd wet his pants already.

'Just leave your jewel pouch and I'll let you live.'

'This boy was priceless,' Brindel thought.

'Just leave you my pouch?' Brindel heard one of the horses outside take off at a gallop south along the track as he finished his sentence. So that's what happened to the other brave soul.

'Boy, if you shoot another bolt at me, I'm going to take my hammer out and I'm going to pound both of your arms and legs into a jelly.' He didn't raise his voice this time. 'Then I'm going to leave you there to slowly die. Rather painfully too from what I saw the last time I did it.' Brindel was sure he was wetting himself now, going by the look on his face.

'Then I'm going to sit down and eat. If you make too much noise while you're dying, I'll get up, walk over to where you are bleeding all over the floor, and I'll put my boot right through your face. Are we clear?' he finished, not yet moving towards him.

As quick as the bolt he had shot earlier, the boy fled out of the room and into the back. Brindel heard a door slam and then seconds after that the other of the horses that had been tied up out front started galloping at pace, also south along the track.

Brindel smiled to himself as he walked into the back room to see what food and ale they had for him. His stomach was grumbling so loudly now he could hardly hear himself think.

After he had scrounged all of the mediocre supply they had left there, he went back out into the main room to eat it.

He knew he'd have to stuff himself good and proper. He didn't know when he would be getting his next decent meal.

Going south wasn't really an option now. Those two that had ridden off not only knew what he looked like, but he'd given them his name.

He didn't lie about his name to anyone. It was the one his parents gave him and he was proud of it.

Without his usual good humour, he figured that those further south wouldn't be any more welcoming than this lot had been.

Back to the mountains then, he realised with a sigh.

Yet he didn't really want to head back to any of the Dwarven kingdoms.

No, he decided. He would go into the mountains through the south, but he would take a path he knew that would steer him clear of his brethren and eventually take him into the Eastern Plains.

He knew there was a warrior people that lived out in that god-forsaken wilderness, although he was pretty sure if there was any wealth to be made his Southern cousins would have had at it before now.

Yet he was kind of out of options at this point in time, he thought, as he spooned another mouthful of the stew into his mouth.

'The Plains it is,' he said out loud to himself as he looked down at his bowl and wondered what in the pits of the putrid swamps that meat was that he had just swallowed!

CHAPTER 22

Jarkene and Corein

THEY AROSE EARLY and ate a small breakfast. They were both excited at the prospect of meeting with the elves, although Mort was a little nervous at how he would be received. His father had just destroyed their families and their home after all.

'Do you know the ones that are coming?' he asked her after they had both finished eating.

'I know all of the elves of Glorfiden Mort, but as to who was on this hunting party, no I don't.' Mort noticed that her excitement seemed to have lessened somewhat since last night. He assumed she wasn't feeling all that good about having to tell them the news of what had happened.

'Will you tell them who was responsible?' he asked her as he looked down at the ground in front of her, too ashamed to look at her knowing why he asked it.

She took her time to answer and eventually he looked up at her.

'You are important to me, Mort. You are important to them too, although they may not see it straight away.' She sighed before continuing.

'I don't see that it would help anyone to tell them your father was the one who did it. Not until I am sure of the reception they will give to you first.'

Mort couldn't help letting out a sigh of relief.

'Thank you, Mendina,' was all he said and looked down again at the grass.

Her next question took him completely by surprise.

'Did your mother ever tell you how she met Lord Jarkene?'

Mort stared at her this time, surprised that anything to do with his father interested her still.

'I only ask as I am curious as to how a human woman came to win the heart of an elven lord. I remember saying those words to you not long after we met.'

Mort looked at her and gave a thin smile.

'My mother loves to tell me that story. I used to ask her to tell me again all the time when I was young, especially after he left.'

He paused for a moment in thought before beginning.

'My mother was born and raised in the city of Lakerth, right on the shores of the Dark Swell. Her father worked for the king and she eventually met a young man who took her away to his homeland at Mayfield, where they were to be wed. The town where he lived wasn't too distant from the borders of Glorfiden itself. Not a large town, but it was a prosperous area and he was quite wealthy. Anyway, before they were married, he died in an accident when he was thrown from his horse. Instead of returning to the capital, my mother decided to stay in Mayfield.'

Mort looked at Mendina to gauge her reaction, but she looked content for him to continue, so he did.

'She would tell me often that she felt more alive outside of the walls of the town, which seemed to enclose her spirit. She enjoyed the freedom to travel through the countryside. Although none dared venture into Glorfiden, there were still fell creatures abroad and the town was quite isolated.' Mort smiled as he thought of his mother and all the stories she liked to tell him. It had been his favourite part of growing up.

'Anyway,' he continued, focusing his mind back on the tale of his parents, 'because of her beauty, she was courted by every man in the town that didn't already have a wife, and some that already did, but none ever took her fancy. She told me that the first man she had left Lakerth to marry hadn't stolen her heart. He was kind, she said, and he had offered her an escape from the confines of the city, so she had said yes to his proposal. She told me she mourned his death, but wasn't heartbroken.' He stopped then, trying to think of his name.

'Have you forgotten the story, Mort?' Mendina asked, interrupting his thinking.

'No, I have forgotten the name of the man she was to marry. No matter,' he said hurriedly, 'it was almost fifty years ago since it happened and probably nearly forty since my mother last told me his name, so I shouldn't feel bad for forgetting.'

'Then one day. . .' Mort began, but was again interrupted by Mendina.

'Forty years?' she asked. 'I think you are mistaken, Mort. Your mother looks no more than 40 herself and you are still yet to grow fully into a man.' She tilted her head at him, waiting for his reply.

'I am so a man,' he said defensively.

Mendina raised her eyebrows, possibly as an indication that his response just proved her point.

'Anyway,' Mort continued, 'my mother is almost 70 years old and I am over 40. So you see I am very much a man, Mendina.' As those last words left his mouth, he wished he could take them back. Why did he say such foolish things to her all the time? No wonder she thought him a boy still.

She looked shocked by what he just said and didn't respond.

'I am part elf, remember?' he said to her defensively.

'Yes, I understand that, Mort, although I am still surprised to hear your age, as you are part man as well. I mean that as no insult,' she quickly added.

'What I am most surprised about,' Mendina continued, 'is that your mother is all human and she most certainly does not look to be 70!'

'Oh that,' Mort said, almost as if it were of no consequence. 'She told me that because my father couldn't bear the thought of growing old without her, he would help her live longer, so they could be together for many, many years and her beauty would not fade as others of her kind did.'

Mendina's eyes bulged at that.

'How did he do such a thing?' she asked loudly.

'I don't know,' Mort replied. 'I don't even know if he did anything to me, or whether it is the elf part of me that makes me look so young still.'

Neither spoke again for a short time, both lost in their own thoughts.

'So do you want me to continue?' Mort finally asked.

Mendina took a moment to reply.

'Yes, please do. I am intrigued still.' She seemed to be concentrating on him again, so he continued.

'Ah, where was I?' he asked.

'Your mother wanted no man in her town I believe and then you forgot that man's name.' Mendina said impatiently.

'Right,' Mort said. 'His name isn't important, is it?'

Mendina just looked at him.

'Okay,' Mort said and continued.

'Then one day, riding by herself near the trees that border your forest realm, she was set upon by a small group of Fire Wolves. They came at her from the west I think and at first she looked to outrun them. But they are fast and as they steadily gained distance on her, she knew it was only a matter of time before they caught her. With eyes that glowed a dark red, they were almost as big as the horse she rode. Their eyes were where they got their name from, did you know that?'

'Yes, Mort,' she said in a voice full of patience. 'We call them Blood Wolves.'

'So anyway, as they closed in on her, she turned in the only direction she knew that she might be safe from the beasts. Into the elven forest.'

'Now the Fire Wolves, or Blood Wolves, whichever you want to call them, also would have known the risks in following her into the trees. They had some small intelligence and had probably weighed up the risk with the reward and decided to chase her inside. My mother guessed they believed they wouldn't have to venture too far into the forest before they caught her.'

'Although that part of the forest wasn't dense, it was still not fast going on horseback and it wasn't long before they were close enough to strike.'

'She was knocked from her horse and crashed unceremoniously into the soft undergrowth. Her mount, in a blind panic, kept going deeper into the forest.'

'I don't remember the name of her horse either,' Mort said in a frustrated voice.

'Mort!' Mendina shouted at him. 'I am enjoying your story telling, but the names of men and horses really aren't that important.'

Mort could feel his whole face redden and he continued.

'The creatures, those Blood Wolves, would have been loath to let the horse leave, but they would have tired from chasing her and now with no rider to slow it, her mount shot through the trees even faster. The risk they took was a great one already, so they didn't bother chasing and instead stopped for my mother.'

'She told me she knew she was about to die at that moment. Then just as they moved in for the kill, an elf jumped from the trees and stood between her and the beasts.'

'The Blood Wolves stopped in their tracks and looked nervously around. They appeared to smell the air and she believes that when they could neither see nor smell any others they became more confident.'

'When the elf pulled out a sword instead of blasting them with his magic, they attacked in unison, confident now in their kill.'

'Of course they weren't to know they faced an elven lord.'

'He slew them quickly and with a grace my mother couldn't believe.'

'When he was done with them, he turned to her. He stood there for a moment staring at her before he spoke. She told me she remembers each word from that point exactly as they were spoken, as if some spell were cast upon her.'

'*You know it is death for any to enter this forest, unless they are invited?*'

'My mother was both terrified and in awe of him. She said he was the most striking creature she had ever seen and although he spoke to her in Elfish, she was able to understand every word he spoke.' Mort stopped then.

'How is that done, Mendina?' he asked her.

'A spell that those strongest in magic have Mort. A spell that lets the ears hear the meaning and not the words. I am unable to do it,' she finished with a shrug. 'Please continue?' she asked in a quiet voice.

'After a short time, where she just stared at him,' Mort continued, 'my mother found her voice at last.'

'*I had no choice. It would have been my death anyway if I hadn't come this way. It was my last chance and I would rather die at your hands than at the jaws of those things.*'

'She said that he stood there in front of her for a time, not moving or speaking, but his eyes consumed her with their intensity.'

After a while, she spoke again. '*I have one boon to ask of you if I may?*'

He tilted his head and gave her a thin smile, which she noted didn't reach his eyes. '*A boon? You intrude upon our forest and ask for a favour of me after I have just saved you from those beasts?*'

She lowered her head. '*I ask that my body is returned to my people so that my father may bury me. That is all I ask.*'

'*What is your name?*' he asked.

She looked up at him. '*My name is Corein. My father lives in Lakerth.*'

'*A long and perilous journey, Corein,*' he replied, '*and a trek taken just to return the body of one slain by an elf. Do you think that elf would not also share your fate?*'

My mother said at that moment she knew her life was forfeit, but she still hoped to have her request fulfilled.

'*You would need only take me to the nearby town of Mayfield. They would see me the rest of the way.*'

'*I shall see what I can do. Stand up Corein of Lakerth,*' he said to her in a voice without emotion. She stood in front of him and noticed that he had taken his sword out again.

'*For setting foot within the forest of Glorfiden, the penalty is death. The law for trespassers is absolute.*' He stepped forward and raised his sword.

Corein remained still, raised her chin, and looked him straight in the eye.

'*Perillian. Stop!*'

The elf froze his sword in its arc towards her neck, but didn't lower it.

My mother looked across at where the voice had come from and saw another elf similar in appearance to the one about to end her life step forward.

'*Do we kill defenceless women now without hearing their story first? Are we such a barbaric race, unburdened by compassion?*' She saw he had a large smile on his face as he strode towards them and she said it was beatific.

'The one with the sword, Perillian,' she thought she heard rightly, gave an exaggerated sigh and lowered his sword.

'*Jarkene, why do you intervene?*' He turned to the smiling elf as he spoke. '*You know as well as I that her life is forfeit.*' He spoke in a voice which indicated he had to remind this other elf of the proper way to do things all too regularly.

'*Oh indeed, I know very well our laws and why we have them.*' His smile didn't leave his face, until he got next to the other elf and turned from him to my mother.

Then it disappeared altogether and his face took on a serious look. She didn't know what it meant, but she didn't think it augured well for her.

He looked directly into her eyes when he spoke next and held her transfixed.

'*I don't think this one will taste the cut of your sword this day Perillian.*' His voice was serious now, otherworldly to Corein's ears.

Perillian turned his head sharply to look at his fellow elf.

'*You forget yourself, "little" brother. The laws are clear. There has never been an exception to this and today is no different.*' He turned back to my mother and again raised his sword.

Jarkene put his hand out and rested it on the shoulder of his brother.

'*It has been quite some time since we have tested our skills against one another, Perillian.*'

Once again, his sword froze before it struck.

'*You would contest me for the sake of a human female? I know you have always had peculiar interests, Jarkene, but are you mad?!*' Perillian shrugged the hand from his shoulder and turned to face his brother, his sword still in his hand but now lowered and pointed at the ground.

Jarkene's smile had returned as he faced his brother.

'*Why is she in our forest?*' he asked.

'*It matters not why she is here Jarkene and you know that! Your "Lord Protector" has made it clear to you before that this law will not be debated.*' Corein heard the strange emphasis Perillian put on the title of the one she assumed was their leader.

Jarkene's smile didn't waver.

'*Tell me anyway. How did she come to be here?*'

Perillian seemed to take a moment to compose himself.

'*You know as well as I do she was chased in here by those fell beasts. Why do you play this game with me, Jarkene? What do you hope to achieve? Have you taken a fancy to this one? Will you take a human bride back to our father?*' This time Perillian smiled but it still didn't seem natural to his face. Unlike that of his brother, whose smile touched his eyes as well, Perillian's looked forced.

'*A human bride?*' he responded in a bright tone, cupping his chin with one hand in a thoughtful pose. '*Is that also forbidden brother?*'

Perillian looked at him with a stony expression on his face.

'*Have you had your fun yet?*' Perillian finally spoke. '*I think it cruel to play with the human's emotions this way.*' Jarkene continued to stand there, apparently deep in thought. '*I intend to give her a quick death and then return her body to her people.*'

Jarkene turned to my mother.

'*Would you like that quick death, Lady Corein? A painless death so valiantly offered you by my brother.*'

My mother said she took some time to answer. She was fairly sure now that this one was just mocking her. He was sporting with his brother and had no real interest in saving her life at the expense of battling with his sibling.

'*I would be grateful,*' she managed to speak in a soft voice, '*if my death were quick and my body returned to my father.*'

'*And what about your husband, fair lady. Surely one as beautiful as you is not alone in this cold world.*' Jarkene again looked at her with an intensity that left her confused about his motives.

'*My betrothed died shortly after we arrived here from the capital and I have not found anyone since then.*' Her fear was beginning to lessen a little the more Jarkene spoke to her. Partly due to his confident air putting her at ease and partly due to the anger that was building when she thought he mocked her.

My mother saw now that although these two brothers were alike in appearance, they were different beings entirely. She saw the seriousness in Perillian, the duty to protect his home as being absolute.

But his brother was a mystery to her. He was defending her right to live, but she had no idea of his motives. That held almost as much fear for her as the death awaiting her at the edge of Perillian's sword.

Jarkene turned back to his brother.

'*Well she is without bond, big brother, so I guess the idea of marriage is not out of the question.*' His smile returned as he looked at Perillian.

Perillian's smile disappeared as quickly as it had appeared.

'*Enough of this.*' He turned again and began to raise his sword as Jarkene spoke once more.

'*Lady Corein,*' he spoke quickly as his brother began to strike. '*You are welcomed into the forest of Glorfiden.*'

Inches from her throat, Perillian's sword stopped. My mother had readied herself for the blow and she told me she had felt a calm overcome her.

As the sword stopped its killing blow yet again, her shoulders slumped and she fell to her knees on the ground.

Before she could say anything, Perillian turned to his brother, this time his sword pointed towards him.

'*You have gone too far this time, Jarkene!*' he spoke in a voice full of contempt and anger.

Jarkene ignored him. Pushing the tip of the sword out of his path, he walked over to my mother and lifted her from the ground. She immediately rained blows with her fists into his chest before he grabbed her wrists and held them to the side.

He waited for her to stop her struggling. When she did, she looked up at him and into his eyes. From this close, she said all of her anger melted away and was replaced by something else. She was mesmerised for a short time before coming back to herself.

'*Why do you play with me?*' she asked in a voice full of anguish. '*Are your people so cruel?*'

Jarkene let go her wrists and stepped back from her.

'*There are no more games,*' he said to her in a melodic voice. '*You are indeed welcomed into my home. None may now lay hand on you, for you are my guest.*' He inclined his head slightly in what she assumed was a gesture of his sincerity.

'*Glendrond will not let her stay, Jarkene, you know this as well as I. You have prolonged her life for but a short time longer.*' With that the Lord Perillian turned from them and shortly disappeared amongst the trees. My mother had watched him leave. One moment he was there and the next he was gone.

Then her attention was drawn back to Jarkene.

'*Is what your brother says true?*' She had hold of herself again, but Perillian's words had killed off again what small hope she had gained when told she was now a guest.

Jarkene stared at her now. He looked her over as one would a beast at market.

'*I have told you that none shall harm you. I intend to keep my word on that.*'

She said he smiled at her again and her worries were washed away as he extended his hand to hers.

She told me she didn't hesitate in taking it and they walked into the forest to meet his father.

Mort realised he had been looking up at the trees for the last section of his story, reaching back into his memory so that he could tell it exactly as his mother had told him.

He looked across at Mendina again and saw she had tears streaming down her cheeks.

He didn't know why she cried and he didn't know what to do, so he just sat there and looked at her.

He figured he would wait and see what she did or said first.

Otherwise, he knew he would say or do something stupid.

Mendina didn't know why she cried. For all his immaturity Mort still told a compelling tale. She thought it was probably because it was a tale told about two of her Lords and a story she had never heard before.

It also brought home to her again the realisation that Jarkene had ended up killing his brother, the Lord Perillian, who everyone had loved and trusted.

It was an especially sad story though, because it was the very beginning of the tale which had ended above the forest of her home only a few days earlier.

It opened up to her a whole new perspective as to why Jarkene had done what he did and why the Protector and Nurturer had condemned him for it.

The fact that she had also met Mort's mother added to the emotion of it all and the tears had just flowed.

'That is a fascinating tale, Mort,' she eventually said to him, wiping the tears from her eyes. 'Thank you for telling it to me.'

'It doesn't explain why he did it, Mendina.' Mort said to her, seemingly absorbed back into his own thoughts again.

'No, it doesn't,' she said, the sadness again replaced by anger. She was beginning to slowly put the pieces together, but regardless of whether she ever found out what was in his mind when he sent the storm, there was nothing that could convince her that Jarkene was nothing but evil now and had to die for what he had done.

She wasn't yet ready to talk to Mort about why she thought he had attacked his own home. She knew his own feelings about his father were still raw and he would also never understand, but she thought it best for now that he worked through his own thoughts and emotions. She didn't want to get between him and Jarkene. She wanted Mortinan firmly by her side.

CHAPTER 23

Mortinan and Mendina
A Stranger Appears

T HEY REMAINED SEATED under the trees of the forest for the
next few hours with little conversation, each absorbed in
their own thoughts.

Just as Mort thought again that the elves should be arriving very
soon, he was grabbed roughly from behind and forced down face
first into the grass he sat on. His arms were held behind his back and
a knee driven into his kidney before he was even able to let out a
groan of surprise and pain.

'You should keep better watch, Mendina,' a male voice spoke in
Elfish from a standing position above him.

'Get off him,' he heard Mendina say in an alarmed voice. 'He is
not our enemy, Palir.'

'Do not speak to me about the defence of this forest, elfling.'
The voice was angry and Mort didn't like the tone he used.
'He is a stranger and his life is forfeit. Why are you travelling
with him?'

'His life is not forfeit,' Mendina replied in a timid voice. Mort
had never heard her speak in such a way before. 'I have welcomed
him to Glorfiden.' Her voice trailed off as she finished.

The elf laughed sharply at her words.

'We will see what the Protector and Nurturer says about that,' he replied. His tone spoke volumes to Mort. He knew it wouldn't end well for him. 'That is if he deems it worth his time.'

'Turn him over,' Mendina said, the confidence back in her voice. 'I'm sure that if the Protector and Nurturer were still alive he would have welcomed his Grandson.'

. Mort heard a gasp from the one that held him down. He realised it was a female elf.

Mendina continued before any could respond to her dreadful announcement.

'We have come from the centre of the forest.' She spoke with a voice full of dread, but the strength Mort had so quickly fallen in love with remained. 'Our home is destroyed,' she said. 'There are none that remain alive.'

The entire forest seemed to go silent in that moment. Mortinan could hear only the sound of his own breath, as he struggled to get air into his lungs. The knee of his captor pushed harder into the centre of his back as Mendina's words impacted upon her. She must have forgotten how much force she was using.

The silence stretched on for what seemed like minutes before the knee was taken off his back. A hand grabbed his arm in a fierce grip and he was swung over onto his back.

He stared into the face of a male elf who looked ready to kill.

'Jarkene's bastard, are you?' he snarled at him. It wasn't put as a question, but Mort chose to answer anyway, against the murmur in his brain that was telling him to keep quiet.

'Jarkene sired me, which makes me a part of this forest also,' was all he said.

The elf leaned down, grabbed him by his shirt, and lifted him to his feet, still with his hand fisted in Mort's top.

'Jarkene was a traitor and a fool.' He looked deep into Mort's eyes. 'You will get no favours from me being his son.'

Mort was truly concerned now. This was not how he had seen this playing out. Yet he also hadn't anticipated Mendina blurting out straight away that their leader, families, and home were all no more.

Mort bit his tongue this time and stayed silent.

He could see tiny flames in the eyes of the elf that he faced.

He knew very well where his blind anger would be directed.

Mendina saw them too.

'There has been enough killing already, Palir,' Mendina said in a voice still confident but quietly and with a tone of respect. 'Enough elves have died.' She had seen the stretcher with an elf's body covered by his cloak.

'He is not an elf!' Palir turned to Mendina. 'He should not have come in to our forest. Not before all this happened and not now.'

He turned back to Mort.

'If what Mendina says is true, then I am now the oldest elf left in Glorfiden and there is no need to take you to the centre of the forest to pass judgement.' The flames were slowly growing in size.

'The penalty for entry into Glorfiden is death.' He spoke with no emotion in his voice.

Mendina knew she had to choose. She knew Mort well enough that he wouldn't willingly fight against an elf, perhaps even to save his own life. He would probably try to defend himself, but without the passion he needed to truly fight back, he would be no match for Palir. Let alone the other four.

He also had not an inkling of how to use his powers in battle.

Mendina quickly came to the realisation that to save Mort she may have to get him to fight and perhaps kill. The thought was abhorrent, but so was the thought of him being executed right in front of her eyes for no other reason than being born who he was.

'Palir,' she said in a quiet voice, which she hoped would have more impact. 'I won't let you kill him.'

Palir turned to her again and she saw the flames were still growing. Soon he would be well beyond all reason.

'You have no say in this Mendina. I have passed sentence already.' Yet he continued to look at her. He must have seen something in the way she looked at him.

'You misunderstand me,' she said, holding his gaze and continuing to talk in a soft voice. 'If you don't stop, then you are going to get everyone here killed. Then there will be no more elves left in all of the land.'

She knew he wouldn't change his mind that easily, so she hoped her next words would impact on him the same way they had her.

'He is the son of an elven lord Palir. He can see the magic!' She spoke the last sentence fervently, hoping to get through to him.

His eyes narrowed and he looked at her more intently, but the flames steadied.

'He is a half-breed elfling and how would you even know such a thing?' Mendina had hoped he would be aware of it. She had seen him often with Quaneillan.

'The question is how he would know it?' she replied.

'That makes no difference,' he answered, but she knew he was listening to her now.

'It makes all the difference,' she pleaded. 'He is powerful Palir, more powerful than any of you here realise. We are going to need him.'

'We don't need this Halfling. He is not one of us. He will never be one of us.' Palir was determined but she knew she had to get him to see reason. If she couldn't, Mort would probably die in the next few moments.

'We may be the last six left alive, Palir.' Her voice choked a little as she spoke the words, but she continued on. 'How long before all others in this land learn that the elves are all but destroyed and come searching to make their homes in our forest.'

'We will never let that happen!' he spat back at her. 'We will continue to kill anything that sets foot within the trees, as we have always done.' He pointed an arm at Mort while keeping his eyes on Mendina. 'Including this one.'

'Brave words, Palir,' she replied quietly. 'And I will die with you in the attempt, until there are none of us left. Yet, something sent the storm that destroyed our home and murdered our families. Will you kill whatever that is too?' She paused and lowered her voice further. 'Glendrond couldn't even stop it.'

'And you think this bastard child of a disgraced elf could succeed where Glendrond could not?' The flames started to grow again.

'I don't know,' she answered in all honesty. 'But I do know he is our best chance.'

She didn't know what else to say. She had laid it all out for Palir. It was his decision now. She hoped that she had somehow gotten through to him.

Palir turned back towards Mort as she finished speaking. She knew what came next.

'Let me prove to you all what he can do.' She heard the desperate plea in her own voice as she turned and looked around at the others. None of them looked at her and she turned her attention back to Palir.

He also didn't bother to respond. She could see that his eyes were almost completely consumed by the flames now. She wasn't even sure if he had heard her.

Still none of the others moved or spoke. They simply waited for Palir to dispense his justice.

Mendina walked slowly over to where Palir and Mort stood. Palir still had Mort's shirt in his grasp, his fist bunched at the top with his knuckles on Mort's chest.

Mendina moved slowly, careful not to alarm the elf holding him and put her hand on Mort's arm. None moved to stop her. She softly spoke a few words.

Mort felt the same sensation pass through his body as he had when his mother stopped the flames in Mendina's eyes.

Only this time he was able to see the magic pass out of him and into Palir. He surmised it was because he was in the forest now and all of his senses were more attuned to the magic.

As soon as it finished leaving his body, he looked up and into the eyes of the elf that had hold of him.

Palir's eyes had returned to their natural look and colour, but his face held a terrible sadness within it. He dropped his head and let go of Mort's chest.

Mendina looked around at the others.

'He is not a threat to any of us. At least take the time to give him a chance to prove himself.' She looked at each one of them. She knew them all, but hadn't been close to any of them.

'We are going back now, Mendina.' It was Palir who spoke now. He was looking at her again and at Mort as well.

'We will look for others and we will rebuild what we can.' He paused for a moment. 'But he must leave.' He was looking directly at Mendina now and although there were no longer flames in his eyes, she knew his mind would not be swayed any further.

It was more than she had hoped for moments before, but it still gave her a sinking feeling in her stomach.

'I was hoping you might be able to work with him Palir. To teach him how he can use his magic.' She realised she was pleading still, but she was desperate. Desperate not to be separated from her own kind again.

'Never,' was all he said as he began to walk towards the river and the boat that they had come across in. The others quickly joined him, two of them carrying the stretcher of their fallen companion. Before Mendina could think of anything else to say they had already pushed off from the shore and started their way back across the river.

She looked over at Mort and still no words came to her.

Mort just shrugged at her and picked up his pack. Without further delay they set off again in the direction the elves had come from.

Neither of them knew where they were going, but they had nowhere else to go.

They continued travelling southeast through the forest, still with no destination in mind. Each of them was absorbed in their own thoughts and both felt they needed to keep moving.

Mort's thoughts were of his encounter with the elves. He hadn't necessarily expected a warm welcome, but being shoved face first into the ground and then called Jarkene's bastard was not what he had imagined.

Palir had looked at him with such contempt and loathing that he doubted he would ever be welcomed back to Glorfiden again.

That was something he didn't want to dwell on, but it consumed his thoughts.

Mendina similarly was thinking of their encounter with the elves, but not for the same reasons as Mort. She saw it from a whole different perspective. She was still trembling slightly as they set off again. What had her rattled was the way they had just left her.

There were no 'goodbyes'. No 'stay safe'. There was only animosity and a lack of any care at all for how she was and what she had been through.

She understood they would all have been rattled by the news their home and families were destroyed, as she had been. Yet they had treated her like she was an outcast now. There were very few elves left in the land and they didn't want anything to do with her. She couldn't understand it and she couldn't stop thinking about it.

After a couple more hours of slow, monotonous walking, they came to a shallow creek, the water trickling through the smooth stones which littered its bottom. The water rose to their calves as they stepped in from the bank. As they began to cross, both suddenly stopped in their tracks, quickly drawn from their individual thoughts.

Mort tried to think quickly of what spell he should cast, but his mind was still foggy from their last encounter and the man in front of them spoke before he had focused his thoughts.

'I have only a message for the two of you. Nothing more.' He was an old man, very unremarkable looking on the surface, but Mort sensed much more about him. In so far as he could sense absolutely nothing about him. He surmised it was that nothingness that gave him the impression this man was not as he appeared.

'You both seek something but have no idea what it is you are looking for.' He smiled at them. 'I am here to offer you a purpose and a clue to reach it.'

'A clue to what?' Mort asked. Embarrassed by his inability to form any kind of spell within his mind, he jumped in with his question.

'You must find an idol of mud. Without the idol there is nothing else for you to find.' He stopped talking and just stood there, as if he were waiting for something.

Mort's mind drew a blank again, so Mendina stepped forward.

'Who are you and where do we find this idol?' Mendina had the same non-feeling about the man in front of them, but for whatever reason she didn't feel threatened by him.

'You must travel east,' was all he said, before turning and vanishing into the trees behind him.

The two of them stayed standing where they were and looked at each other.

Mort was the first to speak.

'Didn't you say that east would be a very bad idea?' For some reason, he knew if they were to chase after the man they would never catch up with him.

'Yes, Mort,' Mendina replied. She also sensed there was no point going after him. 'There are only mountains to the east of here and I told you already who dwells in those mountains.'

The dwarves. Mendina had spoken to Mort in length of the dwarves when they had discussed where they might go. She had made it clear, despite how powerful he became, that it would be their deaths to go near those mountains.

As it stood now, he still wasn't close to coming into that promised power.

'I don't know who he was,' Mort continued, 'but I believe the words he spoke.'

Mendina agreed. They needed to find that idol. But there was no way they could go into the mountains.

A thought occurred to Mort.

'What is on the other side of the mountains?' he asked.

Mendina slowly shook her head.

'I don't know, Mort. But unless the idol is there I fear we won't find it. If it is in those mountains, then it is lost to us.' She felt a sinking feeling in the pit of her stomach at the thought of not being able to get the idol.

'How far south do the mountains go?' Mort asked next. He wished he knew more of the land in which they lived, but his had been a sheltered existence.

'They stretch not much farther south than the forest.' Mendina replied.

Mort's hopes lifted at hearing that. They could continue to walk under the protection of the forest trees almost to the end of the mountain range.

'Then it seems we have no choice but to go around them.'

Mendina nodded her head in agreement. The thought of travelling so far on foot went against the urgency that suddenly overwhelmed her senses. She would like to get there quicker, but she knew they had no choice.

'We were going to the land of men anyway,' she said. 'This just means we won't be staying there very long.'

CHAPTER 24

Kabir
A Stranger Appears

THE FOLLOWING FEW days were intense for all of those involved in the training. Kabir knew he needed to impress their leader, but more importantly was the responsibility he felt for the men he was beginning to respect more and more each day. Their lives would depend on how well he taught them the skills he knew they would need.

He saw the commitment and determination within each one of them and he liked what he saw. He had never doubted their skills, but their efforts and ability to adapt surprised him. He was more hopeful each day that not only would Crenshen give him the extra men he knew they would need, but they would be ready to fight and fight well when the time came to move on the insect lair.

There were also times when some of the plainsmen he was working with even let their guards down a little while he was talking with them. It showed him they did have a sense of humour. It was only when they were resting from their exertions or after the days training, but they were no longer shy at letting him brag about his skills and exploits without sharing a comment or two.

His first taste of that was two nights before, as he sat talking to a few of the men that had their tents spaced around his own. They were eating their dinner and Kabir was regaling them with stories about his people and his own adventures growing up in the highlands.

'Where did you get that hulking sword of yours, barbarian?' A man named Festen had asked him. 'Do all of your people carry around such huge pieces of iron?'

'Do they also sleep with them?' The plainsman who chimed in before Kabir could reply was called Gregg. He was the youngest of those seated around him. Kabir guessed he was maybe 20 years old and he reminded him a lot of his brother in both his wit and his fighting skills. Kabir recognised talent when he saw it and young Gregg had plenty of it.

Kabir chuckled at their questions. The competitiveness within him made him want to beat them not only in the arena but in a battle of wits too. All of those seated around him trained with him.

'My father gave me this sword before I left,' Kabir answered 'and there aren't many like it in my village Festen.' He looked then at the youngest one. 'To your question, Gregg, I am indeed the only one I know of that sleeps with his sword. It is the mightiest gift any in my village could have been given and I would never risk losing it.'

His tone grew serious and he spoke in a much quieter voice, but loud enough that they could all hear.

'I am told it is old Plainsman.' He leaned forward towards Gregg as he spoke. 'As old as anything in our highlands. It is said that it was forged before your people left our lands to start their lives in the lowlands. To a life in the plains where life is easier and you are able to go everywhere on the four legs of another rather than using your own two legs.'

Kabir's jibe was met with silence and he thought he may have overstepped the line. He knew their lives weren't easy, but he had become more confident that they had finally accepted his sense of humour.

He looked at the faces surrounding him, faces that had suddenly turned serious. He was about to apologise when they all burst into laughter, none laughing harder than the youngest plainsman.

'We tell that story a little differently to yours highlander,' Festen said, in between trying to stop himself laughing.

Kabir was less than amused at their response. He would have preferred their animosity than their ridicule. In the back of his mind, he knew he had started it, but his ego didn't appreciate the level of mirth they were showing.

'In our tales of old,' Gregg said with a large smile on his face, 'which are the truth of what really happened, it was your people that were too heavy and slow to learn how to ride the magnificent horses gifted to us. Instead, they left for a simpler and less humiliating existence in the hills and took with them only the smallest and slowest of those horses that didn't throw them from their proud and mighty backs.' The laughter had stopped, but they all now sat there with huge, stupid grins on their faces.

As he thought back on it, Kabir could still feel how his jaw had begun to clench and his breathing grow heavier. He knew he would need to teach these men some manners come the following day. It was only the thought of the satisfaction he would get then that had kept him seated instead of throwing those smug plainsmen head first into their tents.

Kabir had also begun to meet more of those within the settlement not involved with training. He still didn't have free rein to wander around as he pleased, but he understood their reticence. Denizen would always be by his side when they walked amongst the tents, stopping to chat to cooks, smiths, and weavers. Denizen and those plainsmen he spoke to seemed happy to tell him about how they lived. He was a stranger among them and there remained some natural suspicion towards him, but he began to relax more and more each day.

He was enjoying his time with them and although his thirst for action and adventure still burned within him, this urge was sated by the things he was learning about these fascinating people. He was told about how they hunted and what knowledge they had acquired living in the plains. There were dangers throughout their homelands and he had no doubt he would get to see the action he craved soon enough. With that would come the glory.

He didn't see much of the younger ones though. Denizen would tell him they trained elsewhere, that they were taken to another settlement further west where their horse masters lived and bred the steeds that were the life blood of Denizen's people.

Kabir would have enjoyed seeing how they learnt the skills on horseback that he had seen and tried to emulate. Learning since an early age, he realised those skills would always be beyond one such as he, yet Denizen was happy to impart snippets of teaching as they wandered around.

'What about your women?' Kabir asked one evening as they waited for a meal near to the arena they trained on. It was the first time they had eaten here and most of the settlement seemed to be making their way there. 'I have yet to see any of them amongst those of your people who fight on horseback.'

Denizen looked at Kabir for a moment before answering.

'Those that show greater skills as they mature remain at the riding grounds. Most of those are women and are responsible for training our young hunters and warriors. Their skills on horseback often exceed those of the men.'

Kabir thought on this as he looked across at a few men bringing in frames for what looked like large spits. They placed three of them next to some hot rocks they had started heating earlier in the day. They looked hot now and Kabir wondered what they would be eating tonight. He was very hungry from the day's efforts. Meals during the day were more like snacks to his giant frame and he was salivating at the thought of freshly cooked meat.

Yet he was intrigued to hear more about the women of the plains. He continued the conversation as he waited for the beasts to appear that they would be putting on the spits.

'How far away are these training grounds?' Kabir asked, looking at Denizen as he asked. The plainsman appeared to be suffering some sort of discomfort as he looked directly at the barbarian.

'They are quite a few days solid riding from here.' He continued to stare at Kabir as if thinking about whether he should say further.

'I have heard that those of your people who seek adventure often look for more than just glory in battle.' Kabir could tell straight away that Denizen had taken on a very serious tone. 'It is told that before my time, there was one such adventurer who came across the grounds where our young ones are taught their skills.'

Kabir raised his eyebrows in surprise.

'I have heard very little of any adventurer making his way here before myself.' Kabir replied, suddenly very interested in Denizen's tale.

'There is a reason for that my friend.' Kabir definitely heard the emphasis on the 'my friend'. 'This adventurer I told you about was found wandering near to our training grounds and was offered shelter there, if not friendship straight away. Eventually, he was accepted among our people and his fighting skills, as yours are, were well received and admired.'

Kabir could believe that part. Those that chose adventuring were usually the best amongst them.

'After a time though, he became interested in one of those who teach our young their riding skills. She didn't return his attentions and he became more persistent, even after being warned to stop.'

Kabir thought he knew where this story was going and why he hadn't heard it before.

'One day, he went to her quarters uninvited and was rough with her in his advances. She ended up cutting him with her knife and he responded by beating her.' Denizen was still looking at him as he finished his tale.

'Those others that heard the commotion went to her tent to see what was going on. The barbarian was carried out a short time later and buried in an unmarked grave some distance away.'

Kabir nodded his head and when Denizen continued to stare at him it finally occurred to him why the Plainsman was telling him this story.

'You think I have intentions for your women?' he made no effort to try and hide his surprise and disappointment.

'I am merely telling you, Kabir, that if the idea were ever to enter your mind, then it would be best if you didn't go there.' He offered no apology for his words. 'Our women are considered to be the most beautiful in the land.'

Kabir's initial disappointment quickly faded at those last words. Instead, his interest was suddenly piqued.

'Are you suggesting that the women of my home are far too homely and unattractive for your taste?' He wasn't upset, but he thought he might be able to teach Denizen a lesson for his callous remarks.

'I have never seen any of your women, as well you know. I was simply saying that our women are both graceful and deadly, so it would be in your best interests not to go there.' Denizen wasn't backing down. Kabir was inwardly smiling.

'So then you are saying that I am too homely and unattractive for your women?' Kabir continued, waiting for Denizen for bite.

'That is exactly what I'm saying.' Denizen said suddenly smiling. The others sitting near to them burst into laughter as Denizen smiled.

Kabir looked around at them and then back at Denizen's smiling face. He had been the one getting played the whole time.

If this had happened in his own village, it would have been on now. He would have started throwing bodies around, which would have finished in a lot of bruises and swollen faces but plenty of laughs as well. He didn't think it would be a good idea to do the same here, so after his initial shock, he joined in with the laughter.

They all eventually stopped their laughter and several of the men began setting up the large carcasses of some beast Kabir had never seen before.

'Very good, Plainsman.' Kabir said, a smile still on his face.

'I'm glad I didn't upset you too much, my friend.' Denizen replied, still with a small grin on his face. 'We wouldn't dare tell our women who they could or couldn't have court them. I did mean what I said though, Kabir. Don't go near our women.'

Kabir was confused now as he let out a small laugh, followed by a confused look, as Denizen turned his attention and conversation to the man seated next to him.

The next day, after Kabir had finished another gruelling practice session with his select band of plainsmen, he returned to his small tent hoping to collapse into his bunk for a nap. Instead, he stopped short just inside the doorway, as he pulled back the flap and stepped in.

A male stood in the centre of his tent only a few feet in front of him.

Kabir's first instinct was to draw his sword, but the thought died in his head as his hand touched the handle and the man began to speak.

'I am here to give you a message, Kabir, nothing more.' The man smiled at him.

Kabir remained wary, but he didn't feel threatened by the man.

'I will hear your message?' Kabir responded politely. He knew this man was more than just a messenger.

'You need to find an idol of mud, barbarian. That is my message.' He inclined his head to indicate he had finished.

'What do I need with an idol of mud?' Kabir asked, thinking straight away there was more to this idol than its description entailed.

'Of that I cannot say, but you need to find it.' He then turned as if to leave, even though there was no flap at the rear of his tent.

'Where is it?' Kabir said quickly before the man left.

'You don't need to look far' he said over his shoulder as he walked straight through the fabric of the tent.

Kabir was struck dumb for a moment before he raced out the front of his tent and around to the back.

He hadn't expected to see him there but he had to look anyway. There was a tent to the rear of his and two plainsmen stood out the front of it deep in conversation.

Kabir strode up to them both and interrupted their discussion.

'Did you just see a man walk past here?' He was still a bit shocked by what had just happened and spoke urgently to them.

The two men looked at him and quickly scanned their surroundings.

One of them turned back to Kabir and spoke.

'We have seen no one, barbarian.' He furrowed his brow at Kabir, a look of concern on his face. 'Was he friend or foe?'

The other plainsman nudged his companion with an elbow.

'I think the barbarian may have copped a couple of hard blows during practice today.' He chuckled at his words and the other one smiled.

Kabir smiled back, gave a curt nod, and returned to the front of his tent.

An idol of mud, he pondered. Where would he find an idol of mud in these parts?

He also wondered why the old man's words had impacted so strongly upon him.

He believed there was nothing more important to him than finding this idol.

The fatigue he felt moments ago was now gone. His mind was racing and he stalked back into his tent.

You don't have to look far. Was there an idol here in the camp of the plainsmen? He had never heard any speak of it, nor did he think that it would be the kind of thing they would have here. An idol made of mud? It made no sense.

He lay down on his blankets and as quickly as his fatigue had disappeared, it returned as his head touched his makeshift pillow.

His thoughts were of the idol as his eyes closed and he drifted off to sleep.

CHAPTER 25

Linf
A Stranger Appears

B RAX HAD ALMOST finished his preparations for their departure. He had accumulated quite an array of belongings over his time in the forest and also before he arrived here. That happens when you've been alive for over 200 years.

He was loathe to leave too much of it behind, but he was not going to be able to take it all. He frowned again as he looked at what he couldn't take. It hurt that it would all be taken by scavengers eventually.

He didn't plan on ever returning.

He had a small cart which he had already loaded with a large selection of those items he refused to abandon. Some were of substantial value that he would be able to trade, others were of even greater value which he would never sell to anyone. His cloak was just one of a number of magical items that augmented his already considerable powers. This he had stashed within a large chest. A chest that held many other treasures that he had needed to secure in a way that would prevent the goblin 'accidently' finding.

He was confident that the lock and booby trap within would be enough to turn any prying eyes and hands away. If something were able to somehow open it, they would probably no longer have hands and eyes anyway.

He grinned at the deviously wrought mechanism he had constructed and the barbed, razor-edged projectiles that would shoot forth from the small charge of explosive. If the right combination of moves wasn't completed when opening the chest, there would be no getting out of the way.

His smile turned to a grimace yet again as he looked once more at all of those items he had to leave behind.

The cart still had room on it, but he didn't fancy travelling with the goblin sitting next to him up front. He had instead set up a space at the back of the cart where he could keep Linf bound. He didn't know what her reaction would be when she found out she would be trapped again so soon after having her bonds removed.

'I don't care what she thinks,' he said out loud to himself. 'The goblin should be happy that I even let her live.' He liked to believe this was true, but he knew Linf's mind didn't work that way.

She was a selfish goblin who thought only of her own survival and needs. She would want to be free; however, there was no way Brax was going to let that happen. They would be moving through inhabited lands again, the lands of men, and he needed to be wary, for his own welfare. He didn't need to be second guessing what the goblin would be doing if he got into trouble.

He surmised it would be a good first test of his strength against that of Linf.

It would also be a good ruse having a goblin shackled in his cart. He could say that he was taking a prisoner to the capital and hopefully none would question him too deeply.

His gaze moved to the two steeds he had to pull his cart. They were the finest horses around these parts. There were quite a few that ran wild throughout the forest where he lived and he had been able to capture the best of them. Horses were a flighty beast, and because of this, they were always easy for him to catch.

Using the large amount of fear they exuded to weaken them, he would steadily nurse them back to health and then drain them again until they finally came to trust him. The two he had now were completely loyal to him. They trusted him implicitly after the 'special' care he had given them. They were his only family and the only other living things he truly cared about. They looked as regal as they were strong. One was a dark grey with streaks of white through his mane and tail. He was called Storm Cloud. The mare next to him was completely black except for the white star-shaped colour on the front of her head. She was almost as large as the male beside her and was named Dark Star.

After a very in-depth conversation with Linf earlier, she was now acutely aware of the consequences should she harm either of his two horses. Brax got the same reaction as he always did, which was a blank stare and smart comment. The threat of cutting her legs off and dropping her on the outskirts of her goblin settlement didn't seem to worry Linf, but Brax had no doubt she understood that it would happen.

He walked over to where Storm Cloud stood next to the cart. He was curiously sniffing the contents as Brax took his head between his hands. Dark Star stood next to him doing the same. The two horses were not just his only two friends in the world, they were also inseparable from each other. Neither of them suspected it was he that had caused them such pain and distress when he first caught them and then trained them. They trusted him completely and he no longer had need to cause them any discomfort.

He rested his head against that of the mighty stallion.

'We leave tomorrow,' he said to him in a quiet voice. He reached over to stroke the face of Dark Star as his head rested against that of Storm Cloud. They seemed to sense his excitement as both whinnied softly to each other.

Patting them both gently, he stepped away and turned back to his house. He would have one more conversation with the goblin before retiring for the night. He would try not to let it ruin his mood too much.

Linf awoke and opened her eyes. She looked at the rug of the horse on the wall and imagined eating it, the same thing she had done nearly every time she awoke since being held prisoner in the old man's dwelling.

This time, however, her attention quickly turned to the man standing in the doorway. It wasn't the same ugly face she had been looking at every day since Brax had brought her there, but it was still ugly.

She looked at its eyes and grew wary. They were black, a black darker than anything she had ever seen.

'What the hell are you?' she growled, testing the bonds that held her wrists. She had been practising her skills a lot in the last few days and her strength had grown a little each time, yet the small amount of power she was able to absorb had all but deserted her while she slept. She wouldn't be breaking the bonds this time.

'I have a message for you, goblin child.' It also spoke to her in the native goblin tongue and she grew even more suspicious.

'You need to find an idol made of mud,' the man said, and then just stared at her.

'An idol of mud?' Linf snarled. 'Why the hell would I want an idol of mud?' This human was as stupid as the one trying to teach her.

Then it smiled at her and said one more thing before turning away and walking out the door.

'It won't be found west in the lands of men. You must go north instead. You will not find what you are after until it has been discovered.'

Linf watched him leave and then a few moments later Brax walked into the room.

'Are you ready for another lesson goblin, before we leave?' he asked, as if nothing out of the ordinary had just happened.

'Who was your idiot friend?' Linf asked him.

'What friend?' Brax asked, wondering what the goblin was up to. He reached out with his powers but sensed nothing to alarm him.

'The one that was just here in the room. Don't play stupid with me, as hard as that is for you to do.' Linf had just awoken. She was hungry and in no mood to bandy words with him this morning.

'There is no one else here, Linf. Nor has there been another human in this place for years.' He still didn't understand what the goblin was hoping to achieve with this conversation.

Linf just stared at him.

'Whatever,' she finally said. 'Where's my food?' She sunk back into the pillow and waited to be fed.

CHAPTER 26

Valdor
A Stranger Appears

THEY HAD TRAVELLED only minutes before Valdor heard a keen whistle come from a place not far in front of them. One of those with him gave a similar call and he knew straight away the one they were looking for was nearby.

They kept moving swiftly through the forest until they came upon the leader of this small party of men. He was waiting in clear sight between two large beech trees, the shimmering green leaves reaching nearly to his head, an almost perfect match to his garments.

He looked and dressed no differently to the other Forest Stalkers. Dressed in the same colours and light materials, he also carried a bow and sword.

The others greeted him with a simple nod of their heads and he returned the gesture before turning his attention to Valdor. The monk still had the princess in his arms.

'You may rest the Lady Areana somewhere comfortable now, Valdor. We will fight them here.' It was all he said in greeting before turning his attention back to the trees.

Valdor was about to say something but decided to heed his advice. If they were going to make their stand here, then he wanted to find a place for her where she would be hidden from sight, yet still in a place where he could watch over her while fighting the Squargrin effectively.

He found a spot secreted amongst two fallen logs side by side to one another. They would keep her safe from sight and from any stray or deliberate arrows.

He remained standing guard in front of them as he turned to see what the Forest Stalkers were doing.

The four he had arrived with were still standing in the same spot they had been when they arrived at this place, only now they were munching on some kind of flat bread. It was obviously dry, as it crunched when they bit into it.

He was barely able to make out their leader in the lower branches of the tree in front of him. He seemed to be doing something up there, but Valdor had no idea what. He rubbed one branch and then gracefully moved to the next one. He did it fast and before long had made his way around all of those trees that encircled the spot where they stood.

Jumping lightly back on to the ground, he went and stood with his fellow Forest Stalkers. One of them handed him some of the crunchy bread and he stood there with them and ate.

Valdor wanted to know what he had just done, but he guessed if he wanted to tell him then he would have.

The others had shown themselves to be very minimalistic conversationalists and he was satisfied to simply wait by the princess and see what would happen. They all seemed very relaxed.

Valdor didn't have to wait long before he heard the trees begin to rustle loudly in the distance. They were making no effort at trying to approach quietly.

They were coming from the same direction Valdor and his companions had taken from the river. They were apparently quite adept at tracking.

The leader of the Forest Stalkers turned to Valdor.

'They will be here shortly,' he said in the same monotone voice they all spoke with. 'You needn't worry about them firing their arrows at you from the trees Valdor. You need only be mindful of your sword swings on the ground.'

He turned back towards the sounds of the oncoming Squargrin and raised his hands in a grand gesture, as if he were addressing a large crowd.

The first of them reached the branches surrounding their group and stopped. Unlike the previous encounters, they didn't start firing their arrows straight away.

They have learnt from before Valdor thought. He looked across at the Forest Stalkers and was surprised to see that none of them had their bows out. Apart from their leader, who just stood there with his arms raised upwards and forward, they stood only with their swords at the ready.

The Squargrin began to quickly bunch up and then spread out amongst the branches of the trees surrounding them. Valdor was beginning to get concerned they would be able to come at him from behind as well. He would have to fight from the other side of the fallen logs that housed the unconscious form of the princess. He would then have to rely on the Forest Stalkers stopping too many attacking from their side, which he didn't like.

When finally the branches were thick with the small creatures and Valdor saw many of them draw their small bows and place arrows at the ready, the leader of the Forest Stalkers spoke a few words loudly into the air in a language Valdor had never heard.

The moment he stopped speaking, the Squargrin began falling from the branches. Valdor hadn't seen the trees move. To his eyes, they all simply lost their grip on the branches they were holding or standing on. Every last one of them fell to the ground.

Valdor didn't hesitate. Before many had even found their feet, he began slicing off limbs and heads.

Many of the Squargrin had drawn their short swords and were ready to fight as the monk moved amongst them, but he was a whirlwind now.

Many tried desperately to scuttle back into the trees, which they achieved with deft skill, yet as soon as they stepped out or swung on to a branch, their grip again gave way and they crashed to the ground.

This repeated itself a couple more times before those Squargrin that remained began to flee back the way they had come.

Valdor looked around at the Forest Stalkers and saw they had dealt out just as much death as he. The bodies of the creatures were sprawled everywhere in a bloodied mess and those they fought had also begun to flee.

The leader looked at Valdor. 'Farewell monk. We will take care of the rest of these. You needn't look over your shoulder for them again this day.' He pointed in a direction to his right and without waiting for Valdor's own farewell they took off at a run in pursuit of those Squargrin that were still left alive.

Valdor walked over to where the princess lay and picked her up gently in his arms. This time she didn't awaken.

He had barely begun to warm up before the cowardly creatures had fled and he was still breathing easy as he started making his way through the forest in the direction the Forest Stalker had pointed.

It didn't take him long to find himself back on the path to the capital.

He didn't know how much farther along he was than when he had left it at the bridge.

The princess still hadn't woken but her breathing remained steady. Now that the creatures which had been stalking them had been dispatched, he would be able to move faster.

Before he began the last part of his journey, Valdor lay Areana down on some grass next to the track so he could check on her properly.

Her hurts were still as he had last seen them. Not mended, but no worse.

He looked up in the direction they needed to go. He guessed they should be at the capital midway through the next day.

He was about to pick her up again and continue on when he noticed a man standing on the path, less than ten strides from them. He was initially shocked that he had appeared without Valdor noticing, but for some reason, he didn't consider him a threat.

'Greetings Valdor,' the man spoke eloquently. 'I bring you a message.'

He stopped and waited for Valdor to respond.

Valdor quickly checked his surroundings before turning back to the man.

'I am in a hurry good man, please be quick.' Valdor wasn't going to wait long.

The man gave a tiny bow of his head and continued.

'You are tasked now with finding an idol of mud. This needs to be found before anything can be revealed.' His expression remained serious.

Valdor was in no mood for riddles. He stooped down to pick the princess up in his arms and began to walk towards the man.

'Look beyond the mountains brave warrior. You must look to the east. Do not delay.' The last was barely a whisper as the man disappeared before his eyes, but his words remained clear in his mind.

For a moment, Valdor was torn. He knew without question that he would not abandon the princess here to embark upon some vague quest just given to him by someone he didn't even know. Yet something had taken root within him and it had started to nag already.

He was a king's man. His commander had ordered him to take the princess to safety, to somewhere that she could be healed.

Looking down at her, he knew that he hadn't needed Thaiden's order to fulfil that task.

Yet something about the old man bothered him.

He was a pious man and as foolish as it seemed, he wasn't sure that he hadn't just been given an order from his god.

Without putting the princess at any greater risk of injury, he picked up his already extraordinary pace.

He intended to be at the city by early morning now.

CHAPTER 27

Brindel
A Stranger Appears

BRINDEL DECIDED TO spend the night in the tavern.

He had nowhere urgent he needed to be and he had been looking forward to a nice bed for days now. Even though it was fairly soiled and well worn, after he had lain his own blanket over the top, it was considerably more comfortable than the ground he had been sleeping on.

Going on what the old man had said about most people having already fled towards the capital, he wasn't fearful of those that escaped returning with any family or friends in sufficient numbers to cause him any real concern.

He slept soundly and awoke feeling somewhat more refreshed.

He walked back into the kitchen and scrounged again for something to eat.

After the way his stomach had sounded the evening before as a result of last night's cooked meal, he decided he would have a light breakfast. He felt it would be better if he knew what it was that he was putting into his mouth.

He found some salted meats wrapped up in the pantry of which he ate a few and packed the rest. They smelt of beef so he was okay with eating them. There were also a couple of loaves of stale bread.

They weren't yet mouldy, so he washed some down with water and found it wasn't too bad. He packed that which he didn't eat. If they went a little mouldy on his travels, he could just pick off the green bits.

Once his travel bag was packed and he had put on all of his armour and other talismans, he looked around to see if there was anything else he might need. He wasn't surprised when he saw nothing that took his fancy and so walked to the front door.

He had left it barred. He hadn't wanted any surprises during the night.

He unbolted it and removed the bars. He opened the door and waited a moment for his eyes to accustom themselves to the bright sunshine outside. It had been rather gloomy inside with all the windows covered.

He eventually stepped out with his right hand keeping the greater part of the glare out of his eyes and stopped in his tracks.

Six men in full armour sat perched on top of their mounts, in a half circle on the path in front of him. They had obviously been waiting for him to come out. Two held crossbows in their hands and apart from the one directly in front of him, the others held long swords.

Brindel squinted through the eye slits of his helm and let out a long sigh.

'Stay where you are dwarf!' The one without a sword in his hand spoke to him in a loud and serious voice.

After such a good start to the day, Brindel was very disappointed with this turn of events. These men had made it here quickly. They can't have been far off when whoever it was had told them about what happened here. No doubt they would have left out the part about them trying to kill him first.

'Greetings to you,' Brindel replied. He thought he would have sounded polite enough. He really wasn't in the mood to fight these men this morning.

He saw a movement behind them further down the track and spied the young one with the crossbow from last night.

'If that little coward down there told you I was responsible for the death of those inside, you should know they tried to rob me first.'

'I am Captain Forsythe of the king's army dwarf and we are not here to pass judgement on you.' He still sounded very official. 'We are here to ensure the safety of all those still remaining in the outer reaches of the King's Realm and to order them south to the capital. For their own safety.' He added.

'That is well,' Brindel replied. 'This was going to be a good morning after all,' he thought. 'But there are none north of here all the way to the mountains. I guess you boys are good to return yourselves now.' He smiled at them in a gesture of good will and safe travels.

'Yes, this was to be our last stop,' the captain continued. 'You are free to continue your travels south dwarf Brindel and we will ride with you.'

'Alas, I have decided to end my journey into your fascinating lands here. Even after the incredible welcome I received yesterday evening, I feel that I miss the mountains more than I thought I would.' He shrugged his shoulders and made to move off the steps.

'Dwarf, I'm afraid it's not safe for you to go that way. I must insist that you continue southwards. I'm sure the welcome you receive in the larger settlements will be much more to your liking.' This captain was far too serious for Brindel's liking and he was beginning to think that perhaps they weren't as forgiving as his words suggested.

Dwarves were sarcastic, ruthless, and honest to a point, yet at least they spoke their mind and didn't try to be tricky. They didn't speak with honey in their mouths while holding a knife hidden behind their backs.

He realised this probably wasn't going to end well after all. They looked to be seasoned fighters. If what the old man said last night about evil running rampant in this realm, then soldiers that made it this far north could obviously look after themselves. He wasn't worried for himself, but he knew that these men probably underestimated him and overestimated their own capabilities in fighting him.

Also, they were just honest soldiers executing their duty to their king. They weren't men trying to kill and rob him and they weren't filthy elves.

He really didn't want to have to kill them.

He knew that word would eventually find its way to the Dwarven Kingdoms if he killed these king's men. His brethren would be very unhappy about that. Much of the wealth and mercenary work they received across the land was paid for by King Dayhen. Such a feat would certainly put a dampener on that. It may even endanger those dwarves who next made their way south to the capital.

He would have to stop by the Southern Kingdom and warn them. He really hadn't wanted to stop by there again.

'I appreciate your concern, captain, but I really must head back to the mountains. My skills and expertise are needed there. My short legs would also make any trip south far too slow for your liking, although I do appreciate the offer of an "escort".' He emphasised the word escort so that the captain would hopefully cease his cute roundabout way of trying to say he was coming with them.

'Maybe he might be able to have them second guess themselves,' he thought. They were obviously loathe to fight him themselves or else they wouldn't have tried to trick him into going south. A voluntary prisoner indeed. They would have been planning to wait until they had greater numbers or a wizard and they would have tried to grab him then with far less risk. He could kind of understand why they tried to trick him, but it was still pretty cowardly.

'I'm afraid. . .' the captain began again, but Brindel cut him short.

'Yes, you're afraid you must insist. I get it.' Brindel was through with the niceties. 'Listen to me, Captain Forsythe. My name is Brindel, as you've already been told, and I am a dwarf from the Northern Mountains. I am a very skilled fighter, as are all of those who come from the mountains where I live. You and your men look as if you already know this, else you wouldn't be trying to get me to voluntarily walk with you, until you think it safer to try and grab me.' He wasn't finished but he stopped to make sure they understood that he knew what they were doing.

'We would prefer to avoid bloodshed Dwarf Brindel, on that we are agreed,' Captain Forsythe replied, still in that gratingly serious tone.

'Good,' Brindel said. 'Then I should also tell you that I am a smith among my people as well and the pieces I make are far more powerful than those my southern cousins are able to craft.' He saw the captain's eyebrows rise at the last part.

'We know of your fighting prowess in the North dwarf, but I must confess I have never heard of a Northern smith.' He was still serious but he seemed to have relaxed a little hearing Brindel's last comment.

'Then hopefully you also know of the honesty of my people. We never hide behind lies and deceit.' He took a deep breath before continuing. This would tell him whether it was going to be a fight or not. 'I tell you now captain, if you try to take me by force I will resist and all of these men here with you will die this morning and it is far too nice a day for that.' He quickly raised his left hand as the captain drew his sword and the two with the crossbows lifted their arms and took aim at him.

'Please stop,' he said in a loud voice, but not with any alarm in his voice. 'I only say this because I don't want to fight you. Think for a moment,' he said as his hand tightened on his axe hilt. 'You will fight me today because that boy tells you I killed those inside. Is it worth the lives of any of your men to try and arrest a dwarf who was only trying to defend himself from being robbed?'

The captain jumped from his horse, as did those of his men without crossbows. They all stepped a pace in front of their mounts, but none yet moved any closer as the captain replied.

'Then you will be tried, dwarf, and our Lord will decide your guilt or otherwise.' He didn't look like he was going to budge on this. Brindel felt sorry for his men, but not for this one. There was something that annoyed him about the way he spoke and now he knew what it was. He was an idiot.

'That isn't going to happen,' Brindel said, 'but because your men are only following your ridiculous orders I will not kill any of them. Let's get this over with shall we?' Brindel drew his axe from his belt and held it up in front of him.

Two crossbow bolts flew through the air and bounced harmlessly from the thigh guards he wore.

So they were going to try and take him alive. He decided he would still let the others live.

'Take him now,' the captain said, yet none of them moved. He wondered who he was talking to when he caught a flash of light to his right and the gems on his right shoulder lit up before absorbing the bolt of power that had been cast at him from thin air.

So they had a wizard with them. It made sense now how this fool had made it this far alive with only five other men. And the wizard was somehow invisible. Brindel would love to know how he did that or what item of power he possessed. He had heard such items existed but he had never before seen one.

Brindel turned away from where the bolt of power had come from and looked back at the captain, who was looking much less sure of himself now.

He would deal with the wizard shortly, but for now, he wanted to be rid of this Captain Forsythe.

He jumped from the top step of the porch surrounding the tavern and landed only a few feet from where the captain stood.

Another bolt of energy struck his helm this time. It was more forceful than the last and he knew it was intended to kill and not stun, but the embedded jewels did their job and he hardly felt the impact. The captain's men were slow to move to defend their leader. They had obviously known there was a wizard with them and would have seen him in action before. They were stunned to see this dwarf struck twice with bolts of energy and not miss a step.

The captain was left alone to defend himself against Brindel for the first few strokes. The dwarf didn't need more to breach his panicked defences.

The captain screamed in pain and shock before his men could get to him, Brindel's axe head sliding off his defensive stroke and into his shoulder blade. The dwarf quickly turned the blade sideways and pushed it into his neck cutting the scream off prematurely as their leader fell to the ground.

Brindel quickly jumped back and yelled out 'Stop!' before any of the others came at him. They were still hesitant as another bolt of power smashed into his breast plate.

Brindel looked over at where the wizard was shooting the bolts from.

'If you stop firing now and show yourself, I'll let the rest of you leave. This is my final offer,' he growled at them. Although their impacts were quickly absorbed he was getting very annoyed at the wizard continuing to cast them at him. He had never liked the cowardly elves and their spells. He was beginning to feel the same way about the human wizards as well. His talismans could be broken or worn down if they absorbed too much and he didn't have anything to replace them with anymore.

Neither of the men with the crossbows had fired again since their first shots and none of the other men moved forward to attack.

The bolts also stopped, although the wizard still hadn't shown himself.

Those with the swords now turned, sheathed their weapons, and climbed back on their horses. Without their captain to order them to attack, they had obviously seen enough of what this dwarf could do. The fact their wizard was also unable to do anything other than annoy him probably made their decision even easier.

Brindel was satisfied. At least not all humans were as brain dead as their captain had been. He was a little proud of himself that he hadn't tried to kill any of the others.

'We have evil aplenty walking the lands at the moment, dwarf. We really don't need to throw our lives away against one such as you.' One of the men on horseback who had fired a crossbow bolt at him was the one who spoke.

'Good,' was all Brindel said in response. 'I'll be on my way now then.' He tucked his axe back into his belt and moved down off the porch again. Without making it too obvious, he scoured the track and surrounding trees for the wizard. He would have a horse nearby, but Brindel didn't catch sight of him as the soldiers all began to ride away. None of them made any effort to retrieve the body of their fallen captain, to which he was a little surprised.

Suddenly, a ball of fire shot out of the air from just behind the last of the departing soldiers. Brindel flinched momentarily before the fireball struck the body of their recently departed leader and it burst into flames.

Brindel's only regret as he walked away was not getting his hands on that invisibility item. It would have made him almost unbeatable, but more importantly, it would have saved him having to speak to so many of those he came in contact with.

He had yet to find anyone on his journey who changed his mind to the fact that he was so much better off on his own.

The land he lived in was a crazy place and he feared it was only going to get worse.

Brindel made his way back into the Southern Mountain range the following evening. He hadn't been in a hurry, but he still didn't dawdle. The weather was pleasant enough at the moment, but he didn't want to get stuck out in the cold of the mountains if it were to suddenly turn on him.

He was lucky enough to find a small cave not far from the faint animal track he had been walking along. He knew the nights were freezing in this part of the world regardless of the weather during the days.

It was currently uninhabited and he had another restful night's sleep, as uncomfortable as it was sleeping with his armour on. Without protection or companionship, he wouldn't risk falling asleep on his own in the wild and have some creature stumble upon him while he snored.

He was up early the next day and had been walking for hours when a man, unlike any he had seen, appeared from around the corner of the mountain track.

Brindel held forward his axe.

'I am no threat to you dwarf,' he said to him flawlessly in his own Dwarfish tongue.

Brindel didn't move his stance.

The man smiled a little and continued talking.

'I only bring you a message.'

Brindel waited for him to say more. He noticed almost immediately that he wasn't armed. A user of magic he surmised. This one will be in for a surprise if he tries to attack me he thought to himself, readying himself to move the moment a spell was cast his way.

'You seek something but know not what it is. A calling you have felt for days now. I bring the first clue to that destination.'

Brindel's interest was definitely piqued now. He saw this man in a different light altogether.

'You must find a rod with an idol of mud. Be aware that the idol may not be what you expect it to be. Until this is found, there is nowhere else for you to search.'

The man stayed where he was and said no more for a time, so Brindel spoke.

'Where do I find it?' he asked, but wasn't hopeful of an answer. He had the feeling that the purpose for which this one had found him had been served.

The man said four more words before he smiled once more and disappeared back around the corner of the track.

'Underground. To the east,' was all he offered.

Brindel took one hand off his axe and raised it towards where the man had been standing.

'Wait, that doesn't help. Are you serious?' He walked around the corner but the man had gone. He had literally vanished into thin air. Brindel could see for miles from this point and there was nowhere he could have gone other than into the thin air off the side of the track he walked on.

Brindel stood there and thought about the words the man had said to him.

An idol of mud. Not in the dwarven Mountains, he realised. No dwarf would ever make an idol out of mud. Ludicrous.

The second part about it being not what it seemed could wait until he discovered where it was and who held it, so he put that out of his mind for now.

Underground. That was the key. An idol of mud underground. He had no idea where it could be but he realised that he needed to keep going the way he was. He was at least on the right track in leaving the mountains again. There was none to help him here. He had been laughed at enough by other dwarves without asking them about an idol of mud. He could hear their responses now.

'*Such a place would be somewhere you might be able to find someone to buy one of your pieces.*'

'*You could start making weapons and armour with mud. Very prosperous.*'

Dwarves were so funny.

CHAPTER 28

A Decision To Be Made

JARKENE MOVED THROUGH the forest at a run, with a grace few anywhere could match. He moved through the trees at an incredible pace and also along the ground when he had to, without losing much speed.

Bunched close together for most of the way, the trees made it easy for the elven lord to bound from one sturdy tree branch to the next. Only when the ground was reasonably flat and free of too many obstacles did he make his way down from the branches.

Although he had stopped at the fringe and savoured the moment of his re-entering the forest, the magic source at the centre beckoned him. He was in a hurry to engorge himself on it and to recharge his staff once more.

Jarkene was also aware that if he happened to run into his brother before he got to the centre, then he may not have the strength within him at present to best him. He had tested the weather rod he possessed, but it would be some time yet before it was ready to be used as a weapon again.

He knew also that even though his skills with sword and bow were impressive, he could not defeat his brother that way. In a battle with weapons, Perillian was the equal of none, bar their father.

Jarkene's strength lay in his magic and he knew now his father had been vanquished he was without peer.

He sent his senses ahead of him as he ran. He had missed the trees almost as much as he had the magic. He knew he would be able to sense from them if any other was approaching him well before they got near. That had always been the reason why the elves were so ruthless in the protection of their home. Each and every tree was an alarm beacon against anything that moved within Glorfiden.

So far they hadn't registered another living soul for a long way ahead of him. His confidence grew the further into the forest he ran.

As he reached the first of the blackened trees, his pace slowed and the true realisation of what he had done seeped into him for the very first time. He had sensed the anguish of those healthy trees that bordered the area of destruction, but until he saw the devastation, it hadn't completely registered.

Deep down, Jarkene had known what havoc his actions would have wrought, but his desire for revenge and his hunger to return to his home had worked to push such thoughts aside.

It wasn't until he stopped and looked upon those trees—trees that were now no more than ash and smouldering wrecks—that the impact of what he had done finally found its mark.

However, there were no tears from the new Lord of this Forest.

He simply collapsed to his knees and slumped there with his mouth open and his eyes staring vacantly in front of him.

If his brother had come upon him now he knew he would not sense him. The trees for as far as he could see would not let him know of the approach of anyone. They no longer sensed anything.

He was so close to the pool of power, but he was helpless to move.

He could feel it, reaching deep into the soil of this once proud and mighty forest, but he still couldn't stand.

He didn't know whether the madness that had ruled him and brought him to do this was still there in his mind, but he knew the hate he had felt coursing through him all those years melted away in those moments, as he looked out at the field of death and destruction before him.

Finally, he found the strength to stand.

Steeling himself to the task ahead, he began to walk across the wide stream flowing strongly in front of him.

Still no tears came as he walked among those trees whose lives he had taken, but his heart was heavy and he no longer felt a need for haste. He wasn't even sure that he would have the mental strength to want to fight his brother if he came upon him now, or any other elf for that matter.

He dreaded the thought of looking into the eyes of another elf, standing amidst the destruction in the once proud heart of Glorfiden.

When he finally came to the edge of the pool of magic, his mind was numb and his body fatigued from the mental strain.

He fell to his knees once more and began to drink from it. He drew in as much as he ever had before. There were no restrictions on him now and he drank from it like a man dying of thirst.

All thoughts were banished from his mind as he let the magic transform him.

When he could take no more he reached over to the staff he had left on the ground, placed the end on to the ash-covered dirt and pulled more of the magic into it. The staff soon began to pulse with it.

When finally both he and his staff were topped to overflowing, he stopped and stood once more.

He put forth his senses, beginning to reach out to all corners of the forest. He needed to know if any lived and he needed to know where his brother was.

Without the use of the trees within the centre of the forest he was limited to sensing only those that had magic within them.

He was surprised to sense there were at least three elves not far from where he stood and heading slowly in this direction. He didn't know who they were, but one of them had considerable magic prowess. They were still half a day from reaching him so he sent his senses further out.

There were no more within the blackened area with magic, so he sent his reach out to the trees and found him almost straight away.

His brother was heading south, away from the centre, and he had with him another elf. Weak in magic, he presumed it was probably an elfling.

They moved slowly and he knew it wouldn't take him long to catch them. Especially now that he was as strong as he had ever been.

After finding Perillian's location, he wanted to look at him in the physical sense, but he stopped himself. His mind was still fragile and he knew if he looked upon his brother, it may be his undoing.

Although the feel of energy and power flowing through him had taken away a lot of the horror and self-loathing that had consumed him on his walk through the trees, he was still feeling unsure as to whether he could battle his brother and ultimately kill him.

He knew he wouldn't be able to avoid him forever, but he realised now that he was in no hurry to see him.

He withdrew from the trees and thought about what his next move was going to be.

He didn't want to face those elves making their way towards him. They may be all that were left of his people and he wouldn't risk their welfare in a confrontation.

He would go directly south instead and decide as he went whether he would turn west and seek out his brother, or turn east and visit the graves of his wife and son.

The barrier that Glendrond had put up had stopped him from not only going into the forest, but had reached as far as the home those he had cherished most in the world had lived. He had seen through the barrier from a distance the headstones his people had put up for them and the burnt out husk of the home he had helped create.

He would finally be able to kneel at their graves and say his long overdue goodbyes.

CHAPTER 29

A Long Time Coming

Mort and Mendina continued their journey out of the forest.

Although Mendina had a fairly good idea how far they had to travel, she had never been to this part of the forest before. Glorfiden covered a very large area and apart from the place where Mort had come upon her, she didn't generally forage too far from the centre. Reaching out to the trees before her, she saw they weren't far from the boundary.

'Have any of the elves ventured outside of the forest before, Mendina?' Mort asked. They had been travelling in silence for the most part since the old man had appeared. 'I mean into the land of men?' he added.

'Not that I am aware of Mort,' she answered. 'There has never really been a need to do so. We are happiest amongst the trees as you know and those older than me have said that being outside of the forest is painful for an elf.'

She stopped and looked at Mort.

'The trees outside of Glorfiden and other regions are said to be painful to our senses. I'm not sure if they were just trying to scare us so that we wouldn't venture outside, but I'm not looking forward to it.'

Mort nodded but had no reply. He kind of knew what she meant. He had always felt uncomfortable when he had ventured with his mother into the town of Mayfield. It had never felt right and people always stared at him.

Mendina shrugged and started walking again.

After a couple more hours of walking, they both sensed something at the same time. The trees far ahead of them, but in the direction they were walking, had sent forth an alarm to those around them. Those images had now reached the trees where Mort and Mendina both stood, frozen in their tracks.

Something not of Glorfiden had crossed its borders and was making its way in their direction.

They looked at each other.

'You are ready?' Mendina asked him, but it was as much a statement as it was a question.

'Did I get that right?' Mort asked her, unable to disguise the concern in his voice. 'Are they wolves?'

Mendina nodded. The images she got from the trees were of large, dark-coloured beasts, moving quickly through the trees. Of course the trees couldn't see, but they could pick up shapes and forms from the breeze that creatures left in their wake. Mendina was still fascinated at how they did it, but for now, she was more concerned by the images she saw.

Surely, they were mistaken. There couldn't be more than ten of them!

'I count twelve, Mort, and they are moving fast.' Her voice was low and she was starting to panic.

Mendina saw Mort nod his head in agreement. She knew he would be able to see the fear in her eyes and she was shamed. Looking back in the direction they had come she tried to push the fear aside. She was determined to fight as fiercely as she could.

Even still, she knew they would not prevail against twelve of the beasts.

'I want you to get into the trees, Mendina.' Mort's voice was even as he spoke, without emotion.

She nodded. 'They will know we are there Mort and I don't think they will leave once they have found us.'

'I know,' Mort replied, 'but we will be able to pick them off at our leisure from up there.'

Mendina suddenly felt calmer. Why hadn't she thought of that from the beginning? She was an elf and she was in her own forest and still she had needed a half-elf to explain to her that she would be safe in the trees.

Pulling herself up into the nearest one, Mendina began to climb but stopped as she looked down to see Mort still standing on the ground, staring at nothing in front of him.

'What are you doing?!' she yelled down at him.

'I sense something else. . .' He looked up at her then. 'I don't know what it is, but it is beyond the wolves. Can you see what it is?' he asked.

Mendina reached out to the trees again, but she couldn't see past the wolves that were racing towards them. They would be here shortly.

'I can't, Mort. I only sense the wolves.' She paused before yelling to him. 'Get into the tree, they are nearly here!'

Mort seemed to come out of his trance as he reached up and hoisted himself up into the same tree Mendina was in.

When both were satisfied they were high enough off the ground they stopped on a large bough and looked down.

Within seconds the giant canines arrived and as one they began circling the tree the elf and her companion were standing in.

They made no effort to jump up. They just continued circling it when suddenly, as one unit, they all looked up.

Mendina couldn't help the panic she felt as those baleful, blood-red eyes turned at the same time to look up at them.

She had never actually seen one of the Blood Wolves before. They very rarely came into the forest. Mort's story of how his mother met Jarkene was the reason for that. They were always quickly dispatched if they had dared trespass into Glorfiden.

Mendina was both horrified and angry that they now did so with such contempt and in such numbers.

As she looked down she saw one of them suddenly rise into the air, as if it were flying towards her. Her eyes bulged and she involuntarily stepped back along the bough she was on. It seemed to struggle momentarily, before its whole body froze, as it lifted higher into the air.

Just as suddenly it crashed back on to the ground below it with a thud. It didn't actually fall, she realised after she heard the impact. She heard bones snap as if it had been thrown at speed. It tried to rise from the ground, but was unable to, flopping back on to its side.

Mendina looked to Mort and saw he was looking at her with a smile on his face.

'One down,' he said and turned his attention back to the wolves on the ground.

They had moved back and away from the tree the moment they saw their fellow pack member slam into the ground.

They began to growl, a low guttural sound that made the hairs on Mendina's arms stand on end.

'They think they can hide from me do they?' Mort said in a voice that showed Mendina he was as outraged as she that these monsters had come into the forest.

She didn't know how he did it, but she saw another of the beasts come back into view, again frozen in place and rising still into the air. It also crashed into the earth below, right next to where its fellow wolf lay twitching.

This one made no effort to get up. It had hit with a force greater than that of the other and she knew it was dead.

The growls grew louder for a short time and then stopped.

'They're here,' Mort said and Mendina reached out again to the trees. He was right. The wolves were no longer the only creatures below them.

There were three others there now. Each of them in the shape of a man, two larger than the other one.

Mendina could feel that Mort was no longer attacking the wolves but was instead putting up a shield of air between them and those on the ground.

'One of them has magic, Mendina,' he said to her in a voice no longer as confident as it had been moments before.

She could sense it thickening still as the first bolt of power slammed into it, knocking Mort backwards and into her. He hit her hard on the bridge of the nose with his shoulder. She reached out to grab hold of something as she fell, but her hand grabbed only air as she crashed into a couple of branches, before falling in a heap on the ground below. Sucking in a deep breath, she rolled over in time to see a fireball screaming through the air towards her.

She began to draw the moisture in the air to her, knowing as she did that she didn't have time to stop it.

Mort put out a despairing hand towards Mendina as she fell. He saw her descent slowed by the limbs and branches below her, but she still hit the ground hard and his heart stopped.

Quickly regaining his senses, he reached out with his magic, enclosing her form by thickening the air around her as he had done with the wolves. A fireball crashed into the barrier around her, but this time he had filled it with moisture as well from the air surrounding her and the fireball sizzled and died.

Unlike his previous efforts with the wolves, he had put all of his strength, power, and passion into this shield as the anger boiled within him.

He began to lift her towards the safety of the tree when he felt another fireball released, but instead of impacting into his shield this time, whoever had cast it threw it instead at the line of magic Mort fed into the shield from where he stood in the trees. It sliced through it like a knife through rope and she fell to the ground again.

Mort reached out once more to enclose her as she struck the ground and at the same time he leaped down to the next bough.

He waited for the next attack, but when nothing came he climbed further down.

Soon he had made his way to the ground, standing between Mendina and those in front of him.

Releasing the air from around her, Mendina was able to push herself up into a sitting position as Mort faced down the three men and ten wolves that stood only fifteen paces in front of him.

Mort knew immediately that the one in the middle was the magic user. He was light skinned but had tattoos on his bald skull and on each of his cheeks. He was dressed in a black flowing outfit, tied at the waist with pouches hanging from it. He smiled at Mort as he spoke.

'This one is not even an elf.' Mort knew he was speaking to those next to him and he noticed that the smile didn't leave his face.

'I think we shall have some sport before we let the wolves have their fill.'

Mort had never been filled with such anger before. He could feel his limbs shaking with the effort to remain calm so he could think what his next move would be. So far, his air attacks had been successful against one wolf at a time. Now he faced a man who was strong in the use of magic, two fierce looking warriors and ten huge, angry Blood Wolves.

He was at a loss as to how he could beat them all back at once and he knew what would happen if even one of them got within reach, let alone what one of those spells would do to them.

He feared at that moment that all of the faith Mendina had put in him, that all of her talk about how powerful he was, was nothing more than that. Talk.

'Don't you know what to do?' the tattooed one said to him. 'Is that little air spell the only one you know?' He mocked Mort, which only made him angrier and more frantic.

Mort heard Mendina's soft voice at his shoulder. He knew she was back on her feet and it bolstered his courage and determination, knowing she was standing at his side.

'Think of all the elements, Mort. You have the earth, wind, and water at your disposal. They are powerful and you are in the forest.'

Mort wondered how he could use the earth as a weapon, but his mind was blank. He knew how to pull the moisture out of the air as he had just done to help stop the fireball, but he didn't know how to attack with it unless there was a body of water.

He had only air, so without further thought, he pushed out with his magic and flung it at those in front of him.

It sent all of the wolves tumbling backwards into the trees behind them, but he had time enough to see them slowly get back on their feet. They were stunned, but they were very much still alive.

The mage simply waved his hand in front of himself and the wind stopped before it reached him. The two warriors held up their swords and Mort saw the magic swept to either side of them.

He knew at that moment he couldn't beat them. He also knew they couldn't outrun them, or at least he couldn't.

'Mendina, I'm serious when I say this, but you need to run.' He hoped she would listen. 'I will do what I can to hold them back, but you need to go.'

'I'm not going anywhere,' she said. 'I know you can beat them. You just have to believe in yourself. You can see the magic, you can see what he is doing.' Her voice was steady but he knew she probably felt as he did.

'I don't know what I'm doing, Mendina.' His voice betrayed the panic he felt.

The two swordsmen started to move towards them. They were also dressed in black but without the same tattoos as the mage. They still looked powerful and dangerous.

Mort was at a loss. Even knowing they would kill Mendina, he was frozen in indecision and hopelessness.

Mendina flung a spell at them, a shield of moisture that made their efforts to move forward sluggish, but the magic user behind them waved his hand once more and the wall of mist fell away.

The swordsmen spread one to either side then as they moved forward. Even if Mort was able to think of something to do, he would struggle to attack them both at the same time.

They raised their swords as they halved the distance and then suddenly stopped. Mort saw a thick tendril of magic come from somewhere behind him and pass his right shoulder. The magic split and struck out at both of the swordsmen as they moved in for the kill. He saw the magic force its way into their bodies and freeze them where they stood. Mort watched on fascinated, as they collapsed to the ground, encased in a shroud of magic. He didn't know exactly what was happening to them, but he could see that they were dying. He could also see that the magic had somehow been 'tied off'. He didn't know of a better way to describe it to himself, but the tendril had gone while the magic still surrounded them.

His attention was then drawn to the magician with the tattoos. He looked to Mort's right and sent forth a fireball. It hadn't travelled more than two strides from its caster when it was struck by a bolt of something sent from the same direction as before and shattered mid-air.

He couldn't look away as the magician was also struck by another large tendril of magic. This one seemed to encircle his head. The tattooed mage grabbed his head in a feeble attempt to shake it off him, but moments later his skull exploded.

Mort was stunned. Both by what had happened and how quickly and ruthlessly they had been dispatched. He managed to tear his vision away from the dead magic user in time to see the wolves attack.

A chorus of cracking sounds rang through the forest as the wolves were each struck by small horizontal bolts of lightning. It had the unpleasant effect of reminding him instantly of the destruction of Glorfiden only days ago. As he was then, he stood transfixed, as each of the wolves fell in a smouldering heap in quick succession.

Mort could smell only burning flesh and hair when Mendina grabbed hold of his arm. As the last wolf fell to the ground, Mort heard her moan in anguish.

'Oh no,' was all she said as he turned to look at her. She was facing behind him and her pale skin had gone white, as if she had seen a ghost or a demon from the depths.

Mort had assumed it was those elves he had met earlier, come to their rescue just in time, but the moment he saw Mendina's face, he knew exactly who it was that had saved them. He knew before he turned to look at him.

Jarkene was aware of them all the moment they entered the forest. A dozen Blood Wolves was a surprise. The creatures didn't generally hunt in such large packs and they never came storming into the forest unless they were chasing someone or something. He hadn't sensed anything come in before them.

He started moving quickly in that direction. He wasn't far from them and he noticed the direction they were heading would bring them to his brother and the elfling within minutes, if not sooner.

Jarkene knew that Perillian would enjoy the sport. He remembered fondly going out with his brother just to watch him combat creatures and men that had been foolish or desperate enough to enter the forest. His brother was a fierce sight with sword in hand. His magic was strong of course, but his swordplay was a magic all of its own.

He was confident that if he moved quickly enough he should get there in time to see.

Then he felt the others enter the forest.

There were two Ve-Karn warriors and a Dark-Mage from the Northern Lands. Their home was to the far west of Glorfiden and they sometimes travelled south to the lands of men to wreak havoc among the smaller settlements.

Some more sport for his brother. With those others coming through, it would make it easier for Jarkene to remain undetected until his brother had finished with the trespassers.

He thought, as he ran through the trees, that although the elves had been all but destroyed, it still surprised him that these creatures would be brave enough to enter the forest already. They wouldn't know for sure how many elves still remained alive in Glorfiden and to risk it still seemed like folly to him.

At the same time, he hoped that more would continue to do so in the days to come. He knew he would need to keep himself busy as he tried to come to terms with what he had done.

He prayed his brother would at least hear him out before trying to kill him.

It didn't take him long before he came to where the wolves and men had surrounded the tree his brother and the elfling were in. They had just knocked the elven girl from the tree when they came into sight. He knew that none there would see him; not even his brother would be able to penetrate his glamour unless he was consciously looking for him.

As he stepped out for a better view, he saw the Dark-Mage about to shoot a fireball at the girl on the ground. She looked like she had the wind knocked out of her and was in no state to defend herself.

Jarkene was almost too late with his efforts to save her. He was confused and startled to sense his brother hiding in a tree. Hiding? In a tree?

He was further thrown off by the barrier of air Perillian had cast to protect the elfling from the fireball.

He must have known what would happen when that fireball struck the air surrounding her? She would die quickly in an inferno, probably without the fireball even impacting her body.

He sucked moisture from the air and put a strong barrier in front of her. The fireball sizzled and died just before it struck her.

As the one in the tree finally jumped to the ground and stood in front of the elfling, Jarkene knew straight away it wasn't his brother.

He wasn't sure whether he was relieved or saddened.

He hadn't been looking forward to fighting him, but he genuinely loved his brother and had been looking forward to seeing him.

In the same instant, he saw that he wasn't even an elf! He was confused and angered that this interloper had made him think it was his brother.

He couldn't think why an elfling would be travelling with a human through the forest of Glorfiden.

The sudden impulse to kill him where he stood dissipated almost straight away when he realised that he had done the same thing many years before.

He decided he would kill the intruders first and then deal with the human. He still had an elfling to save.

He could see that the human was strong, that he had within him a depth of magic that he had never seen in a man before. Yet he looked to have had no training before today.

This was reinforced to him as he saw his next feeble effort, which resulted in pushing the wolves back only a short distance, hardly hurting them at all.

He shook his head. To think this was the same one that had followed his magic back to the mountain.

His attention was drawn now to the two Ve-Karn warriors as they began to move towards the man and the elfling.

He reached forth with his magic and drew the air from their lungs. They stopped in their tracks as they tried to draw breath, but Jarkene had already sucked the air from their immediate environment as well, before encasing them in a barrier that let no more inside of it.

For a moment, they tried feebly to use their weapons to slice through it, but Jarkene's magic was much stronger than that of the human and they both collapsed to the ground.

He left them there wrapped up in their airless cocoons knowing they would be dead soon.

He then turned his attention to the mage. This one had finally worked out that he was there and Jarkene saw the fireball leave his hand. He knew it was coming before it had even been cast, and with a small amount of effort, he blasted it from the air with an electrical charge of his own.

Reaching out with his magic again, he compressed the air around the skull of his opponent. The pressure he exerted squashed it like a ripe melon, sending parts of his skull and brain flying through the air.

The wolves attacked, as what was left of the mage fell to the ground. He rapidly fired off bolts of lightning at each one of them in quick succession.

As the last one died, he turned his attention back to the two whose lives he had just saved. The elfling turned first and he thought he recognised her. Mendina, if he remembered correctly. She was only young when he had been banished, but her features were the same.

He saw the look of shock and horror on her face as she grabbed the arm of the human standing next to her.

He saw her mouth the words 'oh no' and knew she was aware he was responsible for the destruction. He hoped she didn't do anything stupid, but still he knew he would be able to control her without causing any harm.

As her companion turned around, Jarkene sent forth his magic to entrap him. He wanted to have some time to speak with Mendina.

When he saw the man's face, the tendrils fell from the air and his whole world stopped moving.

He recognised him straight away. How could he not? He was half of the reason he had destroyed the elves and his home.

He couldn't think of any words to say. His mind was numb and he was incapable of moving as Mortinan cast his spell.

CHAPTER 30

To the Nest

KABIR DIDN'T SLEEP well that night. He tossed and turned in his cot, his mind going over and over what the old man had said to him.

He was no closer to an answer when the sun finally came up and he began to prepare himself for the day's training.

He had thought a number of times during his restlessness the night before of going straight to Denizen's tent and asking him about the idol of mud. But the plainsman had been pushing himself very hard during their lessons and he had decided not to disturb his rest. He showed little discomfort from his injured arm, but Kabir knew it must be taking its toll on him.

The morning was a different matter, and although it was still early, he immediately went in search of his friend.

He wasn't all that surprised to find Denizen awake when he hollered to him from outside his tent.

After a short wait, the plainsman pushed aside his tent flap and stepped outside.

'To what do I owe the pleasure of your company so early in the morning, Kabir?' he asked cheerily. At least he'd obviously slept well the barbarian thought.

'I come to ask you a question, Denizen,' he began, 'and though it may seem an odd one, it is important to me.'

'Ask your question,' Denizen said seriously. Kabir knew he could count on his new friend not to mock when he asked.

'Have you ever heard of an idol of mud?' Kabir asked. He didn't embellish on why he wanted to know.

Denizen looked at him for a time. Kabir could sense he wanted to ask more, but he kept his answer short.

'No,' he replied simply.

Kabir knew the disappointment would be showing on his face.

'I won't ask why you want to know,' his friend said to him.

'I was told there was one not far from here.' Kabir said to him, hoping for something, anything really.

'I can tell you we have been riding these plains for a very long time my friend and I have never heard talk of such an item,' Denizen replied. He looked seriously at the barbarian as he continued.

'Yet there is one place that we have never been. A place where I know the occupants are well known for their use of mud.' A smirk reached his face then. 'Somewhere that we hope to visit sooner rather than later.'

Of course Kabir thought to himself. The insect lair!

'I need to see it, Denizen.' The need for him to get his hands on this idol seemed greater now that he knew its location.

'We aren't ready yet, my barbarian friend,' he still spoke seriously. 'But we will get there soon enough I hope.'

Kabir's mind was racing. He was aware they weren't ready and may not be for some time, yet he needed to get there much sooner.

He knew also there was no way Crenshen would let his men attack the nest until he was sure they had a fighting chance.

Their leader had been pleased with their progress after he came for his inspection at the end of their first week of training. He had given him double the men to train but had made it clear that he still wasn't sure if they would be ready any time soon.

'Then can you take me there to look at it. I need to see it for myself.' he said and then added, 'to help plan for the assault when it comes.'

Denizen recognised the last part had been an afterthought.

'I won't let you throw your life away, barbarian,' he said in a tone that didn't invite discussion.

Kabir thought for a moment before his next question.

'If I give you my word that I will not charge the lair on my own, but will simply look at it from a distance, will you take me there?' He guessed this would be the best he could hope for.

'It is a two-day ride just to get there, Kabir,' he answered. 'That's at least four days where you will not be here to train the men.'

Kabir began to weigh up his need to see the lair against the possibility of extending the time needed to school the plainsmen. It would certainly extend it considerably.

'Also,' Denizen continued after Kabir made no reply, 'the group that attacked us may be only the start of whatever it is they have planned. They may be out there in larger groups still. I think it too dangerous a journey just so that you can look at it. We have men that have seen it that will be able to describe it to you.'

Kabir scowled. He knew it was a terrible idea to go and look at it but he couldn't shake the need within him to start heading there now.

His mind raced. He needed to come up with a reason to ride there that would allow him to get close enough, but would not put anyone else in danger. He knew he also had to convince first Denizen and then Crenshen.

He knew Denizen would be the easier of the two and that with his help he could talk his leader into allowing it.

What was it that the plainsmen could gain by him riding to their lair?

Crenshen was worried about how the insect creatures had been roaming in greater numbers of late and what their intentions were in regards to his people. He smiled inwardly to himself as he put forth his idea to Denizen.

'What if we were to take with us half those that I have been training?' he was suddenly excited by his idea. 'Your leader needs information on what they are up to and it could give us opportunity to practice some of the skills they have learnt.'

He saw Denizen consider it. He knew he must realise the importance of both suggestions he put forth. It would be something they could benefit from, both in intelligence gathered and practice against their foes before any concerted attack began.

'I know that what you suggest is to get you near to their lair. For what reason I know not, but your words still hold merit. I fear for you in that this idea stems from something other than how it sounds, yet I will speak with Crenshen for you.' He then added. 'But that is all I can do.'

Kabir smiled. He was hopeful that with Denizen's backing, his leader would say yes.

Kabir had formed the men up for the day's training when Denizen returned from his leader's tent. He strode casually up to the barbarian with a serious look on his face. Kabir couldn't tell if he'd been successful in talking Crenshen into allowing their expedition or not.

The plainsman rarely wasted words and this was no exception.

'He has allowed it.' Denizen said with little emotion. Kabir didn't know whether Denizen was happy with the news, but he knew that he was very excited by it. 'Initially, he said no, but I managed to convince him of the merits for such an outing.'

'My thanks,' Kabir said solemnly. 'We should leave now,' he added in an excited voice. 'Have you chosen those we will take with us?'

Denizen looked at him and raised his eyebrows.

'Kabir I have just returned with the news it has been allowed. How would I have had time to select which men are to come with us?' He shook his head at him and turned to his men.

'It has been decided that we need to find out more about what the insects are up to.' He spoke loudly so all could hear his words. 'We will be riding towards their lair. Half of you here will come with Kabir and myself. The other half will remain and continue their training under Tremill's guidance.'

Tremill stepped forward and looked to speak, but Denizen continued quickly before he could get the words out.

'It will be dangerous, but those that I choose will be ready. We will fight them as we always have, but if the opportunity presents, we will fight them on the ground as well.' He looked at Tremill. 'You I am leaving here as there are no others I trust enough to get the rest of the men here up to speed. You know this is true.'

Kabir could see that Tremill wanted to say something. He looked ready to burst with the effort of remaining silent, yet in this matter, his respect for his captain was greater than his own ego and he remained silent. Bowing his head, he walked up next to Denizen and turned to face the men.

Denizen turned to Kabir and gave him a wry look.

'Those of you who began their training first are coming with us.' Denizen continued. 'Go and get your swords and make preparations for leaving. We depart in one hour.'

Speaking quietly to his next in command, he said, 'I would rather you came with us, but this is too important. They have to be ready.'

Tremill again just nodded to Denizen. He waited for those that were going with Denizen to leave the arena and then started barking instructions at those that remained.

Tremill's captain didn't envy those men he had left behind. He knew that Tremill wouldn't seriously injure any of them, but they were all going to sleep very well for the next few nights.

As he went to turn away to get himself readied, Denizen stopped and turned back to look at the barbarian. Kabir knew he wanted to ask him something, but it was obviously difficult for him, going by the uncomfortable look on his face.

'I am not one to ever pry into the heart of a man that I have given my trust to Kabir. Yet in this I feel I must ask. The lives of my men are mine to protect.' He continued to stare at Kabir.

Kabir himself began to feel a little uncomfortable. He needed the respect of this man and he didn't know if his reason for going there would lose him some or all of it.

Kabir decided to save him the anguish of asking and decided to just tell him.

'I had a visitor, Denizen. He came to my tent and told me I needed to find the idol.' He could see the disbelief in the Plainsman's face. 'He disappeared after giving me the message and I have felt a compulsion ever since to find it.'

Denizen continued to stare at him without saying anything.

'I wouldn't believe it either,' Kabir said in a defensive voice. 'It happened though and I need to see where it is.'

Eventually Denizen spoke.

'I believe that you are convinced of the truth of this,' he said in a conciliatory tone. 'So long as it doesn't put the lives of my men at risk.'

Kabir nodded.

'If you decide to charge inside the lair, barbarian, we will not follow you. I give you fair warning,' Denizen finished bluntly.

Kabir didn't blame him for his doubt and wouldn't blame them if they left him to his fate.

'I wouldn't let you come with me anyway,' Kabir said. He tried for bravado but Denizen didn't seem to see the humour in it.

'You have already given me your word, Kabir, that you have no intention of going inside when we get to the lair.' He looked at him intently then. 'You seem to be a man that is true to his word.'

Kabir puffed his chest out at that comment. He was offended that Denizen could say such a thing, yet he knew why he would. It was clear to him that Kabir was desperate for the idol and desperate men did strange things. Things they wouldn't normally do.

'Enough said,' Denizen said, his voice returning to one of calmness and friendliness. 'We need to get ready to go and I don't mean to insult you.'

'Agreed,' Kabir said in a tight voice and both men left to get ready.

In less than an hour, all of those heading out for the insect lair were ready. Their horses had been checked and prepared for the ride ahead. Their meagre supplies had been packed and they had said their farewells to loved ones. It was part of their everyday life to be on horseback riding the plains, but of late they had gotten into the habit of saying good-bye before they left.

Kabir rode the same horse he had ridden into camp on the day he arrived. Crenshen had gifted him with it not long after he began training the men. He had deemed him worthy of the honour after his exploits in the plains.

Kabir couldn't help but feel guilty, remembering the conversation he had with the boy who had taken the horse from him when he arrived. It had belonged to his father, who had been killed by the insect creatures. He had told Kabir the horse would be given to his son or to one deemed more worthy of it.

Kabir had spoken to Denizen about it in length, not wanting to part the horse from the man's son. Denizen had convinced him it would be a greater embarrassment were he to offer it back to him. Their leader had given the horse to Kabir and that was the end of it.

He let it go for now, but he intended to revisit it sometime in the future when the opportunity presented. How a man's son could be considered less worthy of his father's horse was something he couldn't understand. He knew the Plainsmen lived with different beliefs and Kabir accepted and respected most of them, but this one he could not fathom.

Throughout the first day of travel, Kabir rode up front with Denizen. The Plainsman spent a lot of his time explaining to the barbarian how they moved and fought on horseback. He tried his best to get the barbarian to understand the formations they used and how they attacked as a unit.

When he began his tutorials, Kabir explained that he understood a little of what he was saying, but he was the first to admit he would be more of a hindrance than a help if he stayed on horseback when they had to fight.

'I understand that,' Denizen said in response to Kabir's continued assertion that he wouldn't be able to fight on horseback.

'I mean no insult,' Kabir said yet again, 'but there isn't much point in telling me in too much detail how you fight, as the first thing I'll be doing is jumping off my horse.'

'You misunderstand, barbarian,' Denizen said in an affable voice. He seemed to be in good spirits throughout the ride so far. Kabir noticed how the mood of every one of them changed whenever they were riding. They were serious still, but there was a lighter air about them. Horseback seemed to be where they were happiest.

'I tell you these things so you don't get in our way,' Denizen continued. 'So you are able to fight in such a position that we can keep watch on your back and assist you when required.'

Kabir thought about the merits of Denizen's words and nodded his head in acceptance.

'You should know also that the insect creatures aren't the only dangers that call these plains their home.' Denizen said.

'The others back in your camp spoke briefly of the other monsters that inhabit your lands,' Kabir replied, 'but none ever spoke to me about how they fight,' he finished. He had been so obsessed with the insect lair that he hadn't bothered asking too much about the other dangers they may come across.

'Then now might be a good time to do so,' Denizen replied. 'As a group, the insects are now the most feared, but they have only recently hunted in such numbers. Before this began, there are certain creatures that roam our lands which are more deadly and have been the cause of many deaths among our people. Too many deaths,' he said, looking forlornly at the Barbarian.

'The worst of these are the Death Spikes.'

Kabir listened avidly to his every word. He wanted and needed to learn about all the things dreaded by those around him. It was through such challenges that he would obtain the greatest glory. He heard the sadness in the words of his friend, but he couldn't help feeling excited at the prospect of meeting whatever these Death Spikes were.

'They are trees and are rooted to the ground,' Denizen continued, a little confused by the look the Barbarian was giving him. Was he excited by his tale? 'They look no different to any other tree growing in that part of the plains. Their branches are sharp and they strike quickly and without warning. We have tried to mark the locations of those that we have encountered, but more grow and I am certain there are many we have yet to come across. The plains are vast, Kabir, and there are horrors everywhere.'

'What are they?' Kabir asked. 'Do they have a mind, and what do they do with those they kill?' If they were trees, he wondered how they would consume their prey.

'We don't know what they are, but they draw the bodies of their prey into the centre of their trunks through a hollow at the top. We assume the bodies somehow find their way to the roots. We have tried burning them, but they have an immunity to flames. The bark is extremely strong and our arrows bounce off them. If you are lucky enough to recognise one before it attacks or are aware of the location of one, then I strongly suggest you avoid going near it.'

Kabir had already begun thinking of ways he could kill it before Denizen had even finished his description of it. He just nodded his head as the plainsman stared at him.

They continued their journey through the plains while Denizen continued with Kabir's education in relation to all things good and bad throughout his homeland. Kabir continued to listen with interest.

Unfortunately, for the barbarian, they met none of the fierce creatures Denizen spoke of throughout the whole of that first day of travel.

Perhaps their numbers kept some of them away. Maybe Denizen's scouts were responsible for killing some of them. Either way, he was more than a little disappointed. It had been many days since he had wiped blood from his blade.

He supposed that he may have ridden past Death Spikes, but none of them rode too close to any of the trees. Trees of any description were scarce in this part of the plains and easily avoided.

When Denizen finally called a halt to the day's ride, Kabir was weary and sore. He wasn't used to riding all day in one of their saddles. His saddle would have been too small to use on one of their horses, even if he hadn't left it in the plains. His calves were rubbed raw and his buttocks ached.

He gingerly got down from his mount and waited to see what the others would do with their horses.

Denizen handed his to one of his men, who walked a short distance before driving a long stake into the ground. Another of his men stuck another stake up from that one as yet another ran a small piece of wood from one to the other. He used some form of thin rope to fix them together. To this, he tied the horses. He looked around and saw others doing the same thing. He figured there would be room to tie up four or five horses on either side of the makeshift hitching posts.

'They are not strong enough to hold them if they are spooked,' Denizen said to Kabir. Kabir realised he had been staring. 'We don't like them wandering, though, so it is enough to keep them in the one spot through the night.'

Kabir nodded. He had learnt so much from Denizen today. He knew he wouldn't be able to remember it all, but hopefully he would remember the important parts.

Kabir walked his horse up to the posts and tied it. He saw one of the men watching him, as he used a knot that would hold his horse there, but allow his mount to slip free if he pulled back hard on it. The plainsman nodded in approval and went back to his own chores.

Kabir took the saddle from his horse and walked back to where Denizen had sat down. One of his men had already brought his saddle back for him and he was removing his blankets from the bag at the side.

They all had a quick meal before lying down to rest. They didn't waste energy talking before sleep. Many of them would be woken for their turn at watch in a few hours' time. Kabir was not one of those. He was fortunate enough to be able to sleep right through to first light.

He protested at first, before Denizen explained to him that he didn't know the different sounds certain creatures made, or the way others smelled or attacked. He wasn't competent enough to stand watch at night in the plains. 'I don't want you getting any of us killed this night, barbarian,' was all he said.

Kabir felt more than a little insulted, but after searching for something poignant to say in reply, he realised he had nothing.

Eventually his ego subsided enough for him to lay down and drift off into a deep sleep.

He awoke to the dim light of a new day. The sun, although not yet visible, had already chased away the dark of the night as it heralded its imminent arrival.

Kabir stretched his legs and arms. He was still sore in a few select spots. He sat up and looked around. All of the plainsmen were already up and moving around. He wasn't looking forward to the day's ride.

He stood and walked away from where the others were packing up their things and relieved himself before going to check on his horse.

It wasn't long before they were on their way again.

Denizen told him as they packed up that they should be in a position to see the nest before the sun had disappeared for the day.

Hopefully, they would come across a few of the insect warriors before they got there, Kabir thought. Practising their ground skills had been a large part of selling this journey to Crenshen and he knew they needed the practice before any onslaught against the insects' home should begin.

It was around midday when one of Denizen's scouts returned to the main group. He pulled up in front of his commander.

'A group of about twenty or so are fanned out not far ahead of us, Denizen.' He paused before continuing. 'They are simply standing there, spread out evenly and facing in our direction.'

Denizen looked genuinely confused.

'How far away are they, Hallor?' he asked.

'A hard five-minute ride,' his man answered.

Kabir remembered enough of what Denizen had told him about how the insect creatures fought. He had seen some of it himself. Standing still to keep watch or keep guard or whatever it was they were doing was way out of character for them. It showed more of a human mindset than that of an insect. Everything they had done previously had him believing they thought more as insects than intelligent creatures.

'Thoughts, barbarian?' Denizen asked as he turned his focus to Kabir.

'It may work out well for us. This could be the perfect way for your men to practice the techniques they have been learning.' Kabir was excited by the prospect, but he was worried by their behaviour as well. He knew Denizen wasn't pleased about it.

'How is that?' The plainsman asked him.

'If they are spread out then your men can practice fighting only one or two of them at a time, as it would be within their tunnels. Your men can spread out in twos. One can dismount when they come at them, while the other provides cover from a short distance away on his horse.' The more Kabir thought about it and said his thoughts out loud, the more he liked the opportunity that now presented itself to them.

Denizen didn't look so convinced.

'How far apart are they?' He spoke to his scout again. The scout wouldn't go anywhere until dismissed.

'Fifty paces Denizen. The distance looks to be consistent all the way along.'

Denizen shook his head and swore.

'It doesn't feel right, Kabir.' Kabir began to reply but Denizen held up a hand. Usually, Kabir would talk right over the top of someone telling him to keep quiet in such a way, but these were Denizen's men. Their lives were in his hands.

'I agree that it *seems* the perfect opportunity to do what we came here to try, but there is something we are missing. Something we aren't seeing.' He turned his attention back to his scout.

'Tell me in detail everything you saw. Leave nothing out!' he sounded angry, but Kabir knew it was just frustration.

'We were scouting ahead, looking for any signs of movement in the grass. It wasn't until we were within a hundred paces that we saw the first one. We didn't see it sooner as it wasn't moving. When we got within fifty paces, we saw the next one further along. This one also was simply standing there, not moving.' Kabir could see that Hallor was thinking hard as he spoke. He wouldn't want to inadvertently leave anything out and let his leader down.

'I fired an arrow next to it and saw it flinch, but it still didn't attack and nor did it flee. I can assure you they are alive, Denizen, but they stand there with a purpose. We split up to see how wide they spread before meeting back at where we first saw them. There are twenty of them. Fentin remained to keep watch while I rode back here.' It seemed he had nothing more to add.

'Describe the ground around where they stood.' Denizen was trying to work out what their purpose was. Kabir respected his caution, but he would prefer to just go and attack them. Make plans for retreat if needed, but Denizen must know they had no choice here but to fight them.

'The grass was cleared around them,' the scout answered. 'In front of them, but not behind. We assumed it was so they have a clear sight of any that approached.'

'So you could not see whether there were more behind them, waiting in the grass?' Denizen asked.

'We couldn't make out any others, but I couldn't say with certainty that there were no more hidden from our sight.' Denizen must have motioned to him as he turned his horse and rode back out the way he had come.

'It is a trap, Kabir.' Denizen spoke with more certainty now. 'There is no other explanation why they would just stand there in plain sight. I will not be sending just two men to fight each one.'

Kabir understood his reasoning, but he wasn't sure he agreed with him.

'I guess you can send two to fight one of them, with the rest of your men just back from the one with the bow on horseback.' Kabir agreed that something strange was going on, but he believed the insect creatures were more likely a defensive wall, rather than the bait for a trap. 'If it is a trap, he will have all of your men there to defend him.'

'Agreed,' Denizen said. 'We will move at the one that marks the end of their line. We will flank the one that has no other to one side of him.'

He began to bark orders to his men so they could pass on to the others what the situation was.

It didn't take long before they were ready to move off.

Kabir would make sure he was at the front should anything happen.

Denizen and the rest of his men stopped about 100 paces from where the insect creature was standing. They had flanked his position as planned and the moment they had stopped the insect creature turned so that it was now facing their current position.

Denizen scoured the grasses surrounding it, but saw nothing that indicated anything else moving out there. Now that he saw it for himself, he was even more unnerved and certain this was a trap.

His men had fanned out behind him and his scouts still watched the next two 'sentry' insect creatures. They had given no signal that any of the others had moved.

Denizen had already spoken to the two men that he had chosen to approach this one and kill it.

Kabir looked across at his friend. He was watching his men intently as they moved off. He would prefer it to be him riding to fight it.

When they were fifty paces from their main force and the same distance from the insect creature, one of them slid from his horse. He took out his sword and continued on foot. His companion took out his bow, notched an arrow, and trained it on the 'sentry'.

Kabir held his breath as the plainsman moved within thirty paces, then twenty paces. Kabir thought he saw the insect creature lift its head as if it were listening to something.

When the plainsman got within ten paces, the creature moved. It leapt through the air at him, more than halving the distance between them in one bound.

Kabir half expected to see the plainsman panic at the sudden attack, until he remembered the man that Denizen had selected. He knew Krithel as a level-headed and very skilful fighter who seemed to enjoy the challenge almost as much as he did. Denizen had chosen wisely.

The creature landed gracefully in front of Krithel, but instead of following through with its momentum, as Kabir had expected, it stopped where it landed. Still Krithel didn't panic. Kabir saw that his balance remained solid as the creature circled him. His sword was steady as he followed the movements of the insect creature.

The 'sentry' stopped when its back was to Kabir and froze once more. Krithel made no move towards it, as they had practised. They were easier to fight using their own momentum against them.

It took a little while for them to see what its ploy was, as the grass behind Krithel erupted in a ball of dust. Another of the creatures burst from the ground and leapt at his back.

Denizen had sent Peteir to watch over his best friend Krithel. He was one of their best with bow and arrow and Denizen knew his arrow would find its mark if he was needed.

Peteir watched with interest as the insect creature moved. It was his task to check the immediate surrounds, not to watch his friend, but he wanted to make sure his friend was okay. He crept closer on his horse as Krithel had moved forward. He stopped when the creature had moved and began circling Krithel.

It was fortunate that he had moved. If he had stayed where he was, then the insect creature would have blocked his view when it stopped again.

He knew when he had crept forward that he would be reprimanded by Denizen quite severely when he returned, but he wanted to be able to help if Krithel got in any trouble.

It was because he was better able to see his surroundings that he saw the grass move when the insect creature had its back to him. It wasn't much of an indication, but he had been hunting in these plains for years and his eyes very rarely lied to him.

He already had his arrow cocked and his right hand next to his ear when the other one burst forth from the ground behind Krithel.

The arrow flew through the air and found its mark, piercing the front of its face, the arrow tip sinking into the brain of the insect creature. It dropped dead a couple of paces behind Krithel as he stood facing the other one.

Peteir looked on in horror as Krithel turned his head to see what was behind him. He must have seen the arrow fly over his head. Why was he turning around?

The time it took him to turn his head back to the creature he faced was all the time it needed to strike at him. It had started its move as Krithel turned his head to look back and its front paw struck out at the belly of the plainsman.

Krithel turned his body in a belated attempt to move out of the way and swung his sword down in an arc, as they had trained so many times in the last few weeks. His sword sliced into its outstretched limb as an arrow struck it from behind. The insect creature collapsed to the ground, dead from the arrow in the back of its head.

Krithel was surprised and angry at seeing the arrow sticking out of the back of its head. Peteir knew they were here to practice and yet he had taken his kill from him.

He was about to shoot a volley of angry words at his friend when his legs buckled suddenly and he collapsed to his knees. He looked down in disbelief at the gaping wound in his side. Strangely, he felt no pain as his stunned gaze took in the sight of his innards hanging outside of his belly. He was initially more shocked the creature had managed to strike him, than the knowledge his life was fading from him.

He barely registered the horse that came to a sudden stop in front of him and the man riding it jump from its back.

Peteir jumped from his horse, all concerns forgotten as to whether there might be any more of the creatures nearby. His attention was focused on the horrific sight of his friend's life leaving him through the wound in his stomach.

He moved quickly to Krithel's side as his friend toppled sideways and then onto his back. Peteir began to frantically try and push Krithel's insides back into his stomach. He managed to push most of it in before moving his attention to his friend's face. He looked into Krithel's eyes as he held the wound in an effort to stop the bleeding.

When the blood began bubbling up through his lips, he knew there was nothing more he could do for him.

His passing was quick. He looked to say something before his eyes closed and his heart stopped beating, but he never had time.

Peteir stood up from his friend's body but couldn't take his eyes from his face. A hand grabbed his shoulder and turned him gently around.

'We need to go,' Denizen said to him.

Peteir couldn't focus properly, although he had registered that it was his commander who spoke to him.

'Peteir!' Denizen spoke louder and shook his shoulder gently.

Peteir came out of his trance, shaking his head.

'My apologies, Denizen,' he said, coming back to himself quickly. He had no idea what had just happened to him. He had seen death before.

He was embarrassed as he turned from Denizen and jumped into the saddle of his horse.

'We will come back for him,' Denizen said loudly to all those around him. 'Firstly, we need to move to the next one of these creatures. I intend to kill them all before we return home.'

Peteir looked down at the body of his friend one more time before they moved off towards the next insect creature.

Denizen looked at his man as he got back on to his horse. He had seen men lose it before, but Peteir had seemed to come back to himself fairly quickly. He would try and keep him away from the next battles, but he needed to trust that he would be okay. He didn't have the luxury to be too concerned with individuals. He was their leader and he had already lost one too many today.

He looked at the next insect creature standing fifty paces away. It stood as it had before; however, it no longer stood alone. The insect creature that was hidden under the dirt behind it no longer saw the need to remain hidden.

Denizen wasn't surprised when they both turned and fled. They must have known it would be their deaths if they stayed where they were.

He was surprised when they both stopped and took up position as they had before, this time a hundred paces away.

The feeling that he was missing something very important grew stronger when he saw them stop. Yet he knew that all he could do for now was go from creature to creature until no more of them remained. Then he could show the Barbarian their nest and they could return home.

They approached the next two and he was surprised yet again. This time they remained where they were. Denizen was wary now of a further trap so he sent in four of his men on foot and the rest all within range to fire arrows if required. They lost no more men this time and no more of the insects appeared.

The insect creatures fought fiercely to the end, but they were outnumbered and doomed from the beginning. Still Denizen saw no sign of any of the others fleeing. He noted that those within sight had all retreated to the same distance away as the first two that fled.

He ordered several of his men to ride along the entire length of their line and report back to him if anything else changed.

The next four pairs did as those before them did. As each pair was slain, the next ones along would fall back to just within sight and wait for the plainsmen to attack them.

As Denizen and his men approached the sixth pair, the commander saw one of his men galloping towards his position. He called out to those on foot that were moving towards the next pair to stop, as he saw the look of concern on the face of the plainsman as he pulled his horse up sharply in front of him. Denizen had feared this moment would come, but he still had no idea what would put such a startled look on his man's face. He suspected they were being led to a large force, that maybe they were circling around them and would cut them off from any escape.

He could feel his heart rate increase and the sweat beading on his forehead.

'Denizen, both creatures that were five from the end suddenly turned and started running back towards the direction of their nest. These ones didn't stop at the end of our vision, but continued to run.

We rode further along and as we approached each one they turned and fled, until we got to the last one.' It was then his voice changed from that of giving a report to that of delivering very bad news about a loved one.

Denizen didn't interrupt him.

'The last ones took off north instead, so we followed them for a short distance until we came upon their trail and the trail of many others that had already gone before them.'

Denizen's heart sank into his stomach as his greatest fear was realised. They were indeed circling around them. He thought he knew the answer to his question before he asked it.

'How many would you estimate went before them?' he asked in a quiet voice.

The plainsman stared at him and swallowed before he answered.

'If I had to guess, Denizen, I'd say every last one of them!'

Denizen looked across at his Barbarian friend and saw his brow crinkle in confusion. He knew his expression was probably the same.

'All of them?' he asked, but the question was for himself.

'Why would they need to circle us if they had that many?'

The answer came to him as soon as the words had left his lips.

'Get everyone back here now!' Denizen roared.

He turned to Kabir, who still had a look of confusion on his face.

'They head north,' he repeated. 'When they have travelled for a day, they will turn right and head for our home, or they will turn left and head towards our children and women.' He saw the impact of his words hit the barbarian as his eyes widened. 'Either way, they will kill many. If there are enough of them, they will split their force and attack both.'

The ones they had left here were there to slow them down and nothing more. He cursed himself for being outsmarted by insects. He wasn't fit to lead these men.

The pair at the end that had gone north would catch up to their main force to inform them how far behind Denizen and his men were.

He prayed they wouldn't be too late to help his people.

'Let's move,' he said to his men as they began to form up around him. 'The insect scum think they can attack our homes. We will show them we aren't that easy to kill.'

His men responded with nothing more than steely looks in their eyes. They weren't big on showing their emotion, but each man there knew what was now required of them.

'Hallor, I need you to ride straight to our home and warn them before the insect creatures get there.' Denizen turned as Kabir coughed. The barbarian had something he wanted to say.

'Denizen', he said in a quiet voice. 'If the creatures are smart enough to set up this ruse, they will anticipate you trying to warn everyone. I fear they would have sent a number of their warriors to intercept any you send in that direction.'

'I am not afraid of those stinking insects,' Hallor said in response to Kabir's comment.

Denizen looked at his man. He needed to start thinking smarter and the barbarian made sense. He didn't want to send another man to his death when it served no purpose.

'No, he's right Hallor.' Denizen said.

'We need to get word to them, Denizen,' Hallor persisted.

'I know that,' Denizen replied in a voice that strongly suggested to Hallor that he didn't question him again. 'We don't know how far in front of us they are. They may nearly be there or they may be a long way off yet. We just don't know.'

He raised his voice so that all his men could hear him.

'I know this though,' he said. 'We have maybe four or five hours of light left in this day and I intend to use every minute of it chasing down those insect bastards. Hopefully, we will catch them this day and send them all back to their maker. If we do not, then we continue our pursuit until we find them. Now we ride,' he said without further fanfare and their hunt began.

Kabir rode out front with Denizen as they took off at a gallop. It wasn't long before the pull of the idol began to impact on him as he moved in the opposite direction.

Denizen must have seen how uncomfortable he looked.

'There may not be many of them left guarding the lair, barbarian,' he said to him.

Kabir looked at Denizen. He knew the plainsman wouldn't try to stop him if he chose to leave them and journey to the nest. He knew he wouldn't even judge him.

The pull would get stronger the further north he went. The choice wasn't as easy as he thought it would be. Denizen was right about it being a great opportunity for him, yet none of them were sure just how many were left at the nest. He didn't think it would be left totally unguarded. He suspected they would still have a sizeable number there. His chances would be better if he could go there with his allies. With his friends.

'There isn't much glory if no one is there to see your accomplishments, Denizen. You should know by now that I prefer a crowd.' He smiled at the plainsman. 'There will be many more of them to kill if I go with you and your men.'

Denizen nodded and looked in front as he replied.

'That there will, barbarian. You will get to kill a great many of them.'

He spurred his horse to greater speed, which in turn was matched by each of his men. Kabir held on for his life as his horse looked to match that of their leader.

He hoped the idol would still be there by the time he returned for it.

CHAPTER 31

The Goblin's First Kill

'IT IS TIME for you to try out that leg of yours, goblin,' Brax said to Linf as he removed the restraints from her arms.

Brax had been careful to keep her well fed so she would have the strength to travel. He had been just as careful not to give her more test subjects to drain. He didn't want her too strong until he had convinced the goblin of his own strength and powers. He wanted Linf to fear him enough that she wouldn't try anything stupid before they reached his destination.

He also needed the goblin to know that she was dependent on him if she was to reap the rewards she so desperately wanted.

Basically, he needed Linf to want those rewards more than she wanted to try and kill him.

'Are we leaving at last?' the goblin snarled at him.

'We are,' Brax said. 'So it is time for you to stand up and walk out of here.'

The goblin had smiled as Brax walked to the side of the bed and began to remove the restraints. He left them attached to Linf's arms and instead undid them from the end that was attached to the bed.

He felt the goblin tense after he removed the first one.

He moved to the other side, and before undoing it, he leaned in close and spoke in a soft voice. 'Don't forget what I have told you, goblin. I am much stronger than you still.'

He undid the second restraint from the wall and let it fall.

The goblin sat up straight away and began to remove the restraint from her left forearm.

Brax put his hand on the goblin and immediately began to drain her. The goblin looked alarmed, but she was too weak still to fight back against him.

Brax was relieved and smiled inwardly.

'Those stay on,' was all he said, as he stepped back and stopped the drain.

Brax wasn't surprised at the outburst from the goblin and waited for her to finish. He was too excited and more confident than ever. The threats and insults just washed right over him.

After a couple of minutes venting, the goblin stopped and Brax got the opportunity to speak again.

'Stand up,' he said in a voice with as much authority as he could muster.

The goblin looked at him. Brax thought she was going to start up again, but seemed to stop herself and instead swung her legs over the bed.

She put her good leg down first to support her weight and then gently placed the other leg down on to the floor.

Brax was confident she was healed enough to travel. He knew that each time she had taken some of the power within herself, it would have sped up the healing process. Other than muscle fatigue from not having used them for quite some time, she should be okay.

The goblin stood gingerly, still putting most of her weight on the one leg. Slowly Brax saw her exert more weight onto the other leg as she tested it out.

There was no buckling as she took her first few steps.

Linf's leg felt good as she walked out of the room. She knew she wasn't ready to try running yet, but it felt much stronger than she thought it would. It would never be as strong as it was, as many of the muscles in the calf had been too severely damaged when the goblin cow had torn at it with her teeth. Yet she was confident that the powers she would gain should reduce the chance of the leg troubling her so much in the future.

She walked outside of the house and looked around at her surroundings for the first time.

The trees had been cleared for a short distance and there was a cart in front of the house with two large horses tied to it. These were obviously the beasts she had been warned to stay clear of. Her hunger returned as she looked at them and she could feel herself salivating at the thought of tearing into them. She sensed the fear as she walked towards them and without thinking began to draw it into herself.

Linf felt a hand on her shoulder and fingers dig into her flesh.

'I warned you not to do anything to my horses, goblin.'

Linf's drain stopped as Brax's grip tightened and both of her knees buckled as she was forced to the ground.

'There will be no more warnings. They are more important to me than any help you might offer.' Linf believed him. Every now and again, the human spoke in a way that Linf knew indicated it was time for her to stop. For the time being anyway. She liked to think of it as her survival instinct.

She said nothing in response, which she knew the human would take as some kind of an apology. She wasn't sorry for the need to eat and survive, but she wanted to live now, more than she ever had in the past.

Brax kept hold of her shoulder and lifted Linf back to her feet. He didn't let go of his grip as he walked the goblin around to the back of the cart.

Linf saw the space that had been left for her and at the same time saw the shackles on each side of where she would be sitting.

'You are going to tie me up again?' Linf asked. She was furious but knew that showing that anger now would only cause her more pain and increase the strength of her captor.

'Of course I'm going to tie you up,' was all Brax said to her as he pushed the goblin roughly onto the cart and grabbed hold of each wrist in turn.

Linf continued to stay silent until both hands had been bound once again. She tried to get into a comfortable position and then sat still.

'When will you let me out of this?' she asked, still keeping her temper in check.

'When it is time to hunt,' Brax said, with what she now knew to be a smile. 'When it is time to show you how to drain a man.'

Brax walked to the front of the cart, hopped on to the seat, and grabbed the reins. Storm Cloud and Dark Star started walking forward as they began their journey through the forest and out of the goblin realm.

Linf's thoughts quickly turned from her shackles to sucking the life from her first human victim. She hoped it wouldn't be long.

Their journey through the forest was very slow going, but was still more than a little uncomfortable for Linf.

One of the first things she had noticed while being escorted to the back of the cart was that there was no track leading out of the clearing that surrounded Brax' house. The ground wasn't too uneven underneath the trees, but she knew it wouldn't be a smooth ride.

After the first couple of hours, her leg had started to hurt again. They still hadn't come upon a trail of any kind and she was tired of having her leg bounced as the cart was taken over tree roots and across rocky streams. The uneven ground alone was enough to make the journey increasingly arduous, let alone negotiating all of the other obstacles in their way. Linf suspected early on that the human was doing much of it to deliberately keep her weak.

'When do I eat?' she yelled at the back of the human driving the cart. She couldn't see him over the boxes and other belongings on the cart, but she knew that he could hear her.

Brax had ignored everything she said to him so far on their trip and he continued to do so. Linf's temper was growing, which she knew would leave her vulnerable to the powers of the old man, but she didn't care.

'Where . . . is . . . my . . . food!' she yelled at him again.

The cart shuddered to a halt, which sent a new wave of pain through her leg.

The old man came to the back of the cart and Linf glared at him as she gritted her teeth at the pain.

'We will be through the forest in another hour or so. From there, we will be travelling through the dry lands. The ride will be a little easier for you when we get there.' Brax smiled as if everything was good in the world. Linf didn't share his pleasure.

'My food,' Linf said.

Brax pulled out some dried meat and some bread. Linf couldn't believe what she was seeing. Was he back to torturing her by eating his own food in front of her?

'Where's my food dung heap?' Linf asked, any pretence at being nice had left her an hour ago.

'This is your food, goblin, for the duration of our trip, until we get to the land of men.' He tossed the food into Linf's lap and walked back to the front of the cart while Linf sat there staring disbelievingly at what he had thrown at her.

She had become used to eating fresh meat of late and she didn't like the idea of going back to eating scraps.

The cart took off again and she grabbed hold of the meat and bread before it tumbled from her lap and off the cart. Linf didn't like it, but some food was better than no food.

True to his word, they came to the end of the forest after another hour or so and then changed direction.

Immediately something inside of her told Linf they were going in the wrong direction. She didn't know why but whatever it was pulled at her and she couldn't shake it.

Yelling out to Brax, she was ignored once more. So she kept yelling until the cart finally came to a halt again, still inside the outermost part of the trees.

'Before you say anything, goblin, if this is about food, then I am going to drain you within an inch of your life. You've been warned,' he finished.

'Why aren't we still going the way we were before?' she asked. She wasn't worried about the threat, but she needed to convince Brax to go back in that direction. She didn't want him to just walk away again.

'We go this way because this will take us into the lands of men. North there is only hills and then grass.' He went to move off again but Linf wasn't finished.

'There will be men in the hills and grass, too.' Linf said. It was more hopeful than anything else. She had never been far from the goblin settlement that she had grown up in and didn't know which stories to believe that the other whelps had told to her.

Brax turned back with a sigh.

'Why the need to go north, goblin?' He was only mildly curious but he wanted her to shut up without upsetting her too much. They had a long way to go and a quiet goblin was a good goblin. Draining wouldn't help with her training and wouldn't help if they ran into something he might need her help with.

Before Linf could answer, she heard a low roar some distance into the trees, coming from the same direction in which they had just travelled.

'What was that?' Linf asked. Brax assumed she had never heard a beast that sounded like that before. He smiled.

This will be perfect, he thought.

Before answering, he held up his hand for her to be quiet and listened again to the sounds of the forest.

After a short time the roar came again. This time it was closer.

Brax walked over to Linf and undid her restraints.

'It is time to see just how far you've come, goblin.' He said with a grin.

'What the hell is it?' Linf asked again. Brax could see the fear coming from her.

'Something you don't see or hear too often. They are rare and only come out of their lairs to feed for a short time during the changing of the seasons.' He paused to listen again. 'It definitely has our scent.'

There were lights of anger now amongst the fear emanating from the goblin.

'It is a green bear,' Brax finally answered. 'I am going to need your help with this one.'

'What can I do against a bear?' Linf asked him, shock and fear making her voice sound angry.

'The same thing you did when you drained the rodent, Linf. Only this one will not have any fear.' Brax was going to enjoy this.

'Do you wish you had listened more now?' he asked her.

The anger was equal to the fear coming from her now.

'A bear is a lot different to a rodent you crap pit!' Linf yelled at him.

The roar was much closer now. 'The beast was moving fast,' Brax thought. 'It mustn't have fed yet. It would definitely be angry.'

'No it isn't,' Brax said as the giant bear crashed through the last of the undergrowth and revealed itself to them.

It was bigger than anything Linf had ever seen. It was the size of their horses and then half again as big, as it bounded towards them on all fours.

The fur was a dull green, camouflaging it well against the dark green foliage of the trees and bushes. Linf wondered why it needed to be camouflaged when it could be heard coming from such a long way off.

It was fast too. It was less than fifty paces away when it had come into sight and the time it took Linf to take in its size and colour it had already covered nearly half the ground.

Brax moved in front of her and raised his hands towards it.

The bear slowed its run and then stopped only paces in front of them, rearing up onto its hind legs. It would have been more than twice Linf's height now and goblins weren't short.

Linf knew she was going to die and so she turned to run.

'Linf,' she heard Brax say through gritted teeth. 'This one is stronger than I thought it would be.'

Linf hesitated.

'We can stop it, but I need your help.'

Linf turned back and saw that the bear was still standing on its hind legs, but it wasn't attacking the old man. He had stopped it. For now.

The flight instinct was strong in Linf, but at that moment she realised she needed the old man. Her leg hurt and she was in a place she didn't know. Linf knew that without the human, she wouldn't be able to survive for very long. Not yet anyhow.

'It's too strong for me, human,' she replied. She still didn't move towards it. 'You kill it!'

Brax slowly turned his head to look at the goblin.

'You can see the anger coming from it, can't you?' Linf saw that the old man's breathing was heavy and he looked to be struggling. She could see he was drawing some of it into himself, but the bear looked to be fighting him.

His head would fit inside that jaw and those teeth were the size of his fingers.

'If you can't draw it to you from there you need to get closer.' Brax had turned back to the bear but Linf could hear him clearly still. 'It would be better still if you could touch it.'

Linf was surprised she was still standing this close. There was no way she was getting any closer to it. While the old man was between them, Linf knew she would have time to flee while it fed on his stinking old carcass.

'I'm not going near that,' Linf said, more calmly this time, as she tried to do what she had with the rodent.

She reached out towards the myriad of lights surrounding the beast and began to draw it towards her. The bear roared even louder as she did and she lost all concentration. The bond she had started stopped and the bear began making slow movements towards the human. It would be within reach very soon.

Linf looked around at the horses. She could see they were panicked but for some reason stayed where they were. Linf could see the whites in their eyes as they turned their heads to look back over their shoulders and she could see the fear expelling itself from their bodies.

Maybe if she took some of that she would be strong enough to fight the bear. If not, the old man would die and she would flee on the cart with the horses.

She stepped towards them and began to draw the fear from Dark Star. It was much easier than the bear and she began to feel herself gain strength straight away. It was so much more intoxicating than what she had gotten from the rodent. The mare didn't fight her, instead she just released more fear and panic as Linf drew her in to her own body.

She gave a panicked sound as she began to feel the effects of the drain take hold.

Linf heard the old man say something behind her, but she was too absorbed in the power she was feeling to hear him. It consumed her senses as she drew more and more of Dark Star's fear. She knew the horse was growing weaker, but she couldn't stop. It was like nothing she had ever felt before. Somewhere deep inside, she knew that she had to stop. She knew that she was now strong enough to help, yet she was unable to switch it off.

Linf could no longer feel any pain in her leg.

Suddenly, she felt a sharp blow to the back of her head and everything went black.

Brax was surprised at the size of the beast as it came into sight, but he still didn't consider it a threat.

As it came close, he was already drawing the anger from it and started to weaken it almost immediately. It had reared in surprise and then Brax had pushed his power at it to stop it coming any closer.

It was time to see what the goblin was made of.

He expected her to flee and he could see in her eyes when he turned around that she had every intention of doing it.

He told her to get closer and was surprised that instead of swearing at him or turning tail, she concentrated instead of trying to draw some of the anger from the giant beast.

When the bear roared in pain and anguish, Brax let it come closer to him so that it would easier for the goblin to draw it in, but instead Linf panicked and he saw the bond she had created fall away.

He was both satisfied with the effort but annoyed she had given up so easily. She had been at a point where she should have kept going.

He stopped the bear when it was almost within reach of him, hoping that the goblin would try again now that it was closer.

Then he heard Dark Star whinny. Turning his head, he was horrified to see that the goblin was drawing the fear from her instead.

'Let her go!' he roared, but he could see the amount of power the goblin was absorbing and knew she couldn't hear him.

Taking in as much of the bear's emotions as he could, he sent a huge wave of power at it, knocking the beast back several paces. He knew it wouldn't be getting up in a hurry.

He then turned back to Linf, walked up behind her, and struck the goblin in the back of the head. He hit her hard and for a moment felt a pang of regret. In his fury and concern for Dark Star, he had lost control and hit her hard enough to kill.

It was a shame the goblin would be no help to him now. He was on his own yet again.

Stepping over Linf's body, he walked over to Dark Star. He could see that she had been drained close to death, but she would survive. Storm Cloud was rearing, trying to break free of his restraints. He could sense the pain his companion had gone through and how weak she was. Now that her pain had stopped and Brax was by her side, he stopped rearing and pushed his head towards her instead.

Brax stepped in front of them both and put a hand on both of their heads in an effort to comfort them.

'She will be okay,' he said to the concerned stallion. He knew it would take some time, but she would regain her full strength. Even when he had captured them and was training them, he had never drawn so much from either of them.

He was shocked at how quickly the goblin had been able to draw it from her. If he had waited much longer, she would have been beyond any help.

She was struggling to stand so he removed the harness and other straps from her so that she could rest on the ground. He did the same for Storm Cloud so he could go to her instead of tearing himself free. He went straight over to where she was already seated on the grass.

Brax walked to the cart and took some feed and their water container and placed it in front of her. She would be too weak to eat yet but it would be there when she wanted it.

After he was satisfied that he had done all he could for her, he walked back over to where the goblin lay unmoving on the ground next to the cart.

He saw her chest was still moving. This goblin was hard to kill.

The power she had absorbed from Dark Star had obviously strengthened her enough to survive the blow Brax had dealt her.

He stopped to consider his next move as he looked down at Linf.

He had warned her that if she touched either Storm Cloud or Dark Star, then he would kill her. He had meant it and had very nearly done it already.

Yet the goblin had probably not intended to kill or harm her. She was panicked from Brax's own ruse that the bear was too strong for him. He hadn't thought it through enough and he realised now that he was probably partly to blame. He knew if Dark Star had died then he wouldn't have this dilemma. The goblin would be dead now.

Yet he still needed her and she had tried to help him. Brax realised the goblin may have finally reached the conclusion that she needed him. That he was much more valuable to her to get them through to the lands they were heading towards.

It was that realisation that ultimately saved the goblins life.

He leaned down, picked her up, and threw her back into the rear of the cart. He secured her wrists again and went over to check on Dark Star. They wouldn't be going anywhere now until her strength was back.

Linf awoke to blinding light and a searing pain in her head. It felt like something had been driven into her skull and was still there.

There were tree branches above her and the blue sky of day beyond those. Linf very slowly and gingerly lifted herself up on to her elbows to look around.

She was back in the cart and they were still in the same place when they were attacked by the giant green bear. She could see a pile of innards and the skull of the great beast next to them at the spot where the human had fought with it. He had obviously won, Linf realised, surprised by the fortitude of the old man.

She sat all the way up and waited for the dizziness to stop before turning her body to look towards the front of the cart. She couldn't see the old man, but she saw that the female horse he called Dark Star was sitting on the ground not far away and the male standing near her eating grass.

She remembered what had happened now, before everything went dark.

Linf remembered the power she had taken within her from the horse and how she couldn't stop. She also remembered the words the old man said to her about what would happen if she ever touched either of his horses.

She looked around frantically. Brax was going to kill her. He must have been waiting for her to wake so he could make her suffer first.

She pulled on the restraints but they held. She had lost much of her strength while she lay unconscious, but her leg no longer pained her.

That coward was going to finish her off while she was tied to this god-forsaken cart. It was so unfair. She hadn't wanted to hurt the horse, she just needed the power it gave her. It was just a stupid horse anyway.

The old man must have heard her pulling at the restraints as he walked back around to the rear of the cart and stood there looking at her. Linf noticed he was covered in blood.

Then she noticed the large piece of meat in his hand.

'I thought about killing you, goblin,' he said to her in a voice without emotion. 'I thought about it a lot.'

Linf wasn't sure whether to believe him or not. He had been sneaky plenty of times before. Maybe he was worried that he would get knocked back again, like that time he tried to drain too much of Linf's hate from her.

Linf tried to get angry again, but her mind wouldn't focus. It wasn't something she could just turn on anyway. Instead, she waited to see what would happen next.

'I know that you didn't try to kill Dark Star. If I did think that, you would already be dead.' He still spoke in a way that made Linf wary.

'You tried to help with the bear, which is what I was after.'

Linf was paying attention to his words for the first time in a long time and it quickly dawned on her that the old man had been testing her with the bear. He had killed it in the end. He probably could have done it sooner but he wanted to see what Linf would do. She didn't let the food in Brax's hand distract her this time.

'Why you sneaky son of a stinking rat.' Linf had no trouble building her anger up now.

'Before you continue, goblin, know that you brought it on yourself.' He spoke softly still, but his next sentence was said with venom and much louder. 'Also don't forget that you nearly killed my horse!'

Linf bit down on the words that were about to fly out of her mouth. She was a little more focused now that the pain from her leg was gone.

Also because she was still alive and wanted to stay that way.

'If you had ran, then you would be no use to me, and for that you also would have died.' Brax spoke in his quiet voice once more and Linf further relaxed.

Her attention was able to focus again now on the piece of meat in his hand.

'Is that for me?' she asked.

Brax continued to look at her for a time before finally throwing the meat at her. Linf caught it in her hand. She had been given some slack with her bonds.

She didn't put it in her mouth straight away though.

'When are we leaving?' she asked first.

'When Dark Star is recovered,' Brax said. 'Not a second before.'

Linf knew better than to push him on that topic.

'Which direction are we going? I still think we should keep going the way we were going.' Linf couldn't figure out why she was so hell bent on going to the plains, but she couldn't shake the need.

'I can knock you out again, goblin, if it bothers you that much.' Linf didn't respond. She didn't know if he was serious or not.

'We go east,' Brax finished and left the goblin to her meal.

It wasn't until the sun was straight overhead the next day that Brax decided Dark Star had recuperated enough for them to continue with their journey.

He had kept himself busy with the carcass of the green bear. There was enough meat to keep the goblin satisfied for many days to come. He didn't bother salting her share as he doubted whether the goblin would care if the meat went bad. He had also carefully skinned the mighty beast.

The skin and fur would make a majestic coat, which he would be able to sell. He was confident it would net him a small fortune.

Now they were out of the forest the travelling would indeed be easier and they would move faster. Not as fast as he had hoped, due to Dark Star not being at full strength, but the ground was easier and they could go straight at least.

His mind now turned to the lands ahead.

They would come across the homes of men well before they reached the border of what used to be the King's Realm. The ground between here and the border was fertile land and men had made it their own many years ago, tilling the soil for all sorts of crops. There was even a large settlement they would reach within a few days' travel. Shadow Hill was its name. It was reasonably well fortified and the last time he had been there it was home to hundreds of people. There would be soldiers, but there was no wizard in residence last time he was there.

The lands that were farmed here produced a lot of food for the capital. It needed to be well-guarded this close to where the goblins roamed. It would not be easy pickings for Brax and his new friend.

He intended to further Linf's training by visiting a few farmsteads instead, before they finally made their way to Shadow Hill.

It was another full day before Brax finally saw the first of the tilled fields come into view.

Their journey since they had met the green bear had been rather uneventful. There had been a few smaller pack predators that had fancied themselves against one man on a cart, but after the first couple had been drained and killed, the rest kept their distance.

Now that they were approaching the lands of men, Brax became more wary and more excited at the same time.

The first farmhouse they approached was deserted. The fields looked as if they hadn't been tended to for months. They were overgrown and there was no sign of people or animals. Brax looked through the house and found it had been ransacked. There definitely hadn't been anyone here for some time. Still, it looked as if they had time to pack up most of their things before they left.

He wondered why they had gone. The fields were mature and the harvest looked like it was a plentiful one. They didn't leave because the land was infertile, so that meant something must have scared them away. He knew how brave those who made this their home would have been, to set up here in the first instance. Their farm was on the furthest outskirts of the realm. There was nothing between them and the wild animals, creatures and goblins that lived further west to where they were.

Something dreadful must be walking these parts. Something scary enough to have sent them packing.

The next farm they arrived at was the same. Mature crops and a sturdy, well-built house, but no people or animals remained. There were no signs at either farm that violence had occurred. Brax was convinced they had simply up and left.

It was the same for the next three they came across. The fourth one, however, was a different scene altogether.

These poor souls had left it too late and discovered first-hand what it was that had frightened off the other farmers.

The carcasses had been picked clean, but the skeletons and bones scattered around the front of their farmhouse told him they had been torn apart. There was a lot of blood that had soaked into the ground and sprayed on to objects scattered about. It looked to be only days old and it wasn't the kind of damage scavengers did.

Some of the bones were broken in a grotesque manner. He saw one of the leg bones with holes in it from what looked like teeth marks. Other bones were broken in pieces. They weren't the clean cuts of something sharp. It looked like something had broken them like a child would a twig.

He was really on edge now. The few scavengers he had killed hadn't given him a lot of sustenance. He still felt strong from the bear, but he had been relying on those that lived in these farms to give him the strength he would need before they got to Shadow Hill.

He walked back to the cart, which he had left on the trail with Linf still tied in the back. The goblin had been in a much better mood since yesterday. Brax knew it was because of the regular meat supply she was getting once more. He had been right about the state of the meat not worrying her stomach.

He had given her a coat from his own belongings to make the journey more comfortable. Now that he had the green bear skin he could afford to give one to the goblin to ruin.

He patted Dark Star's neck as he walked back to the front of the cart and hoisted himself up in to the driver's seat. She had regained most of her strength already. He marvelled at her as they set off from the farm.

Morkin had moved to the countryside on the outskirts of the King's Realm many years ago with his wife and three young children. He had shown some promise as an apprentice wizard but had chosen to have a family instead when he met the woman that stole his heart. Studying wizardry and raising a family were not compatible, so he had been forced to forsake his studies. He had never regretted his decision.

Wizards didn't have the time and luxury to raise a family or be a doting husband. The pursuit of magic was all consuming.

He had grown up on a farm where his father had cropped wheat on a small patch of land on the outskirts of Lakerth.

Unfortunately, for Morkin, by the time he had given up his dream to be a wizard, there was no spare land anywhere near the capital and certainly nothing he could afford to purchase.

He had decided then to pack up their things and move his new family east. He faced disappointment after disappointment while looking for suitable land to buy so they could make a home of their own.

Eventually, word reached him of the availability of land at the outskirts of the realm. It would cost him nothing, but he would have to start from scratch.

The land that he had chosen as his own, had turned out to be incredibly fertile and the crops he planted in the first few years flourished.

The home they had dreamed of was finally theirs and they had spent many satisfying years here.

Until several months ago, when farms had suddenly begun to be attacked. Not by the usual sporadic goblin raids, where they sometimes lost livestock and occasionally loved ones. This time, they were beset by monsters come to life out of the nightmares of children. With the regular patrols of guardsmen from Shadow Hill and Morkin's limited skills as an apprentice wizard, they had been able to weather the attacks.

In response, the Lord of Shadow Hill had sent out more guardsmen to patrol and protect all of their livelihoods.

When some of these patrols failed to return, the next lot of guardsmen sent forth came with only a message instead. The farmers had been told to leave their homes and take shelter in Shadow Hill, until the king could send some of his Shield to look into it.

Most had heeded the call to leave, but a few had remained, Morkin amongst them. Morkin had been confident in his ability to protect his family.

He had two grown sons that were very good with the sword. His youngest was still at Shadow Hill doing his one year of training with the guard.

Thankfully, he hadn't been on one of the patrols that didn't return.

Only two days ago, he had heard the screams in the distance. They had come from Crichton's farm.

By the time he got his sons from the fields, collected their swords, and made his way to Crichton's farm, it was much too late to help them.

Whatever had torn the farmer and his family apart had also gone.

For the last two days, they had been packing their own things together in preparation to leave.

Morkin realised it was now far too dangerous to stay. Those in Shadow Hill had bunkered down. Those that had remained anyway.

Many of them had left to the larger town of Havern, not trusting the walls of Shadow Hill to keep this new evil at bay.

Morkin had initially scoffed at the proclamations that there was a vast evil abroad in the land and the whole realm was under threat. His magic had kept the lesser predators and scavengers away so far, but whatever had killed Crichton was nothing like what he had fought or seen in these parts before.

He was packing more of their things into the wagon, when he saw a cart being drawn by two horses, pull up on the trail at the end of the track leading to his house.

He could see only the one man on the front and wasn't overly alarmed, but he had come from the direction of Crichton's farm and not from that of Shadow Hill. What kind of a man would come from that direction all by himself?

'Melkor. Fetch your brother,' he said to his eldest son.

Melkor went into the house and returned with his brother. His wife also came outside to see who the man on the cart was.

'Just a stranger, Harriet. There shouldn't be anything to worry about. He probably just wants directions or information.' He knew he didn't sound too sure of himself, but the scene at Crichton's farm had put him on edge.

Morkin watched the man on the trail walk to the back of his cart. He saw him reach inside, but he couldn't make out what he was doing.

As they walked within ten paces, Morkin stopped and the old man walked to the side of his cart to greet them. He had nothing in his hands.

'Greetings sir. I'm surprised to see anyone still here.' He spoke well and didn't look dangerous. Morkin knew appearances could be deceptive.

'We are just leaving. I fear we have stayed long enough.' The old man just smiled at him.

'So how is it you have been able to survive out here for so long? I hear there are some fell monsters roaming the lands these days.' Morkin wasn't sure if he said it as a warning or as small talk.

'I have skills that have helped so far.' He was going to say more, but something was not right with this one and the hairs on his arms and back were standing up. 'Where do you come from? What is there in the east but Goblins and other less friendly creatures?'

'I don't come from the east good sir. I went there looking for information. I am a servant of the king and I return with a valuable prisoner.' He indicated the rear of the cart, but Morkin couldn't see what he was referring to. The cart was stacked high with all sorts of things.

'You travel heavy for someone who doesn't live in the east.' Morkin didn't like it. There was something very wrong about this man. He decided he would have a quick look at the rear of the cart and then wrap him up in strands of air to question him further.

'I have been away for a long time and collected a lot of valuable items to present to our king.' He continued to smile.

Morkin didn't believe him and his senses remained on edge, but he wanted to see what he had in the cart. With his sons behind him, he walked around and looked inside.

He was shocked to the core when he saw Linf tied up in the back.

He turned to the man. 'Are you crazy? A goblin is your prisoner?'

He quickly wrapped the man in air, thin tendrils of magic that held his arms to his side. Morkin couldn't help noticing the old man didn't flinch or look at all concerned or surprised.

He turned to his sons.

'Melkor, kill the goblin,' he said quickly. 'That abomination shouldn't be allowed to live.'

Brax shook his head at Morkin's instruction to his son.

'The king will be most displeased,' was all he said. He was enjoying the charade, even though this one obviously was not fooled by it. He was just a simple farmer now, but he obviously had some wizard training. Where was his intrigue? Where was his curiosity as to why the king would want a live goblin?

He waited until the man's son raised his sword to Linf.

'Now, goblin,' Brax said in a voice loud enough for the goblin to hear.

Morkin's sword froze where he stood as the young goblin began to drain the fear from him. There was a lot of fear within him and Linf looked to be having no trouble this time pulling it towards her. She no longer had her restraints on and her hand reached out, greedily draining the young man.

The wizard holding him released his hold on Brax the moment he saw his son in trouble, as Brax knew he would. The air around him still held, but the farmer was no longer connected with it and so its strength was lessened considerably.

Not that it would have mattered anyway, Brax thought to himself, as he flexed his arms and puffed out his chest. The strands snapped and faded away with the breeze.

He took two steps towards the trainee wizard and grasped hold of his shoulder as Morkin prepared to cast a spell at Linf.

Morkin's body went rigid as Brax began to drain him. Then Brax paused. This one would be too dangerous to keep alive and there were three others for them to play with. He looked over at the woman heading in their direction with a knife in her hand.

He grabbed hold of Morkin's neck and squeezed it, quickly cutting off the air to his lungs and the blood flow to his head. The farmer collapsed to the ground and Brax put his foot through his head, splattering bone and brains over the ground.

The fear and pain from the younger son was palpable as Brax turned to him. It was easy to begin draining him, until his attention was drawn to the one Linf held. Brax could see he wasn't far from death already. Linf was beyond hearing him, as she had been with Dark Star, so he sent a small pulse of energy at the goblin, knocking her back and severing her hold.

Melkor collapsed to the ground unconscious.

'We don't kill them straight away, remember!' he said to the goblin, as Linf turned a ferocious glare his way.

'That one is yours,' Brax said to the goblin, indicating the woman standing twenty paces away. She had stopped and was staring in horror at her husband on the ground, the knife now limp in her hand.

Linf jumped off the back of the cart and began to walk casually towards her. She looked up and saw the goblin coming towards her and screamed.

Brax saw Linf smile as she went past him, continuing her slow walk towards Morkin's wife.

Brax also smiled as he turned to the youngest son, still rigid with fear as his life force steadily seeped into the old man standing in front of him.

Brax hadn't felt so alive for many, many years, and he started to laugh as he walked up to him and grabbed him on the shoulder.

Linf sat with the old man inside the farmhouse. It was dark outside now and they had already eaten.

The house itself was almost bare. The farmer and his family looked like they had been just about ready to leave.

Brax had her grab a few chairs and a table off the wagon before they came inside for the night, while he tended to his horses.

Linf smiled at how unlucky the humans had been. If they had left hours earlier, they would all still be alive.

Instead, she looked over at the three bound to each other in the middle of the main room. Seated on the floor and tied to the main beam of the house, they all had their heads bowed and made no sound. Linf and the old man had drained them again twice since they had bound them.

The goblin was grateful she had listened to the old man and not tried to kill him. She knew now just how powerful he was. He would have been able to kill her very easily.

When she asked him why he had stopped her killing the boy and then killed the other one, Brax told her the man had been a wizard and had tied him up with ropes of air.

He explained to Linf he would have been too dangerous to keep alive. Linf accepted what he told her. She remembered glancing across and seeing Brax crush his skull with a light stomp.

Ever since she had first drawn in the fear of the younger human, Linf had been buzzing. The amount of life force she held now was incredible. The anguish they had radiated, especially the female cow, was so different to the animals she had fed upon before. Linf remembered when she accidently took some of the power from Brax, but that had been only a morsel compared to the feast she'd had today.

'How do you feel, goblin?' Brax asked her.

Turning her attention from the three bound humans, Linf looked at the old man.

For the first time, she didn't think about how she would kill him. She had never felt so exalted, so powerful. She wanted more and she knew the human could help her with that.

'You didn't lie about how good it is to drain the humans,' Linf drawled.

Brax nodded his head in satisfaction.

'I have a question for you, old man.' Linf continued.

'Ask,' was all he said, but Linf saw he was staring at her now.

'I can draw their fear and anger into me. I know it stops them fighting and makes me very strong.' She was hopeful that the old man wasn't fearful and would answer her.

'How do you push the power back at them? I did it to you once, but I don't know how I did it. Tell me how.' She tried to make it sound polite, but goblins weren't a race of people that were born to pleasantries.

Brax smiled at her and chuckled.

'You just keep wanting more don't you?' He spread his arms wide and looked intensely at the goblin in front of him. 'Is this which you are feeling now not enough for you?' Linf couldn't tell if he was angry or not.

'You said you brought me because you need me to help fight those with real power, not scrawny farmers.' Linf wasn't going to let this go. 'Show me how I can fight better . . . if you're not too afraid of me already.'

Brax sat back and continued to stare at the goblin. Linf wasn't sure if she had gone too far, but it wasn't as if it was something they both hadn't already spoken about.

'Tell me what you remember about how it all works?' Brax said.

Linf was about to abuse him, but quickly realised he hadn't refused her yet. She knew the old man liked to play games. Maybe it was time she learnt to play as well.

'I pull the colours from around them into me and it makes me stronger. The harder I pull, the more of the colours come to me.' Linf didn't have a better way to describe it.

'That's right,' Brax said. 'The colours on the outside are joined to ones on the inside and the ones that come from inside are the ones that weaken them so much, so quickly. It hurts them and makes us powerful.'

Linf nodded and waited for the old man to continue.

'It is that power which you use as an energy force to throw back at them and knock them down. Or you can use it to wrap them up and hold them where they stand.'

Linf still didn't know how to control the colours though.

'Yes you. . .' Linf again managed to hold her frustration in check, although it still took some effort. 'How do you do that!?'

'You can direct the flow goblin.' Brax said simply. 'Instead of pulling it into yourself, you can send it around them and tighten it. Or you can fling it back at them like a punch. Bunch the colours together, squeeze them as tightly as you have time to, and then send it towards them. The tighter it is, the greater the impact.'

Linf tried to picture in her mind how she would do it. After a time she thought she may have worked it out. Now she needed to practice it on someone. In a moment she would, but there were still more questions to ask.

'Won't they just absorb it back into themselves?' It was their own colours after all.

'They cannot. That I know of, only the two of us can do such a thing. Their body has already expelled it. There is no taking it back in.' He continued to look at the goblin. 'You need to practice. I can talk about it all night, but until you do it, you won't really understand.'

'Are you calling me stupid human? You're the stupid one that let the wizard catch you in the first place.' Linf knew she had been thinking the same thing about practising it, but she still didn't like the old man talking down to her. 'I was going to practice anyway,' she finished.

Linf walked over to where the three humans were tied and took the ropes from around them. The two males tried to leap at her, but she began a drain on them both and they fell back down against the beam. She had been thrilled to learn she could take it from more than one person at once. These two being so close together made it easy, but Brax told her she could do it when they weren't even near each other. She still had so much to learn.

Linf picked the woman up and sat her in a chair. She slumped over but managed to keep herself seated.

Linf could see she was very weak still and probably wouldn't survive many more sessions of draining. She looked over at Brax.

'Do we need to keep this one alive still? The others are much stronger than her.' She didn't want the old man getting angry if she accidently killed her.

Brax seemed to think for a bit and then shook his head. 'It's more important that you learn how to do this. If she dies, I won't be angry.'

Linf heard whimpers come from the two human men as she secured them to the beam again. She knew they wouldn't have understood what she said, but they would know that nothing good was about to happen to their mother.

They cared about her. That was good, Linf thought. Their anger and sadness at seeing her kill their mother would give her more strength. Brax said they could stay another day to continue building their powers if these ones held out long enough.

Linf turned back to the woman on the seat. Her head was still down on her chest and she had few of the colours coming from her. Linf needed more from her.

'Old man. Tell her to wake up,' she said.

She heard Brax say something to the human in her own language, but she still didn't move.

Linf turned and looked back at him. 'I thought you were good at this.'

She turned back to the woman as the old man spoke to her again.

This time she lifted her head and the emotions started to flow.

Linf began to draw them towards her and absorbed them almost without trying. It felt wonderful, but it was not what she wanted right now.

'Just hold them in front of you, goblin,' Brax said.

Linf grunted in frustration and annoyance. She tried to push at them with her hands but her body kept absorbing them.

The goblin was glad Brax stayed silent this time.

Linf stopped what she was doing, looked at the floor, and tried to get her concentration back again. She thought about how it felt as the colours went into her body and focused her thoughts on that feeling.

She looked back to the woman and started again. This time when they started to come into her, Linf thought she could feel them. She had her hands held out, as the old man did when he drew the power in. This time she turned her hands back towards herself and clenched her fists. It helped her to focus and she was delighted to see those colours that were about to go into her body stop and return to her hands instead.

Linf faced her hands back towards the woman and opened them. She was able to gently push the colours back towards the human seated on the chair. Smiling, she drew them back into her hands and then back towards the woman again. She repeated it a few times, on each effort increasing her confidence and control. Her speed increased as her control steadied even further.

Sucking even more from the human woman, she held it all within the space between her hands.

Her hands didn't touch the colours, but they pushed them closer together, as Brax had described.

Finally, she was happy with what she had in front of her.

Drawing her arms back, Linf flung her hands forward. The bunched colours flew away from her in a rush.

It struck the wavering female in the chest. Linf saw her torso cave in before the force of it knocked her flying through the air. The female human slammed against the wall, four paces behind where she had been sitting. Her lifeless corpse crumpled to the floor as Linf turned to Brax with a huge grin on her face.

She wasn't surprised to see that the human didn't return her smile.

CHAPTER 32

Time for War

H E HAD BEEN running at a steady pace for a couple of hours when he came across the first scouts on horseback.

The king's soldiers recognised Valdor as one of the King's Shield immediately and the monk saw their faces drain of colour the moment they saw who he was carrying.

'Your fastest horse, captain,' Valdor began and one of the men immediately jumped from his steed.

'No,' Valdor said and turned to him. 'The princess is in no condition to be on horseback. Get back on your horse and get a carriage here as quick as you can!'

The man looked abashed but didn't hesitate in getting back on his horse. He looked to his captain for confirmation, but had already kicked his heels into his mount before his captain had even nodded.

'How far are we?' Valdor asked, not breaking stride.

The captain rode next to the King's Shield, his horse having to slow canter to keep pace with him. His men rode two abreast behind them to keep the dust from their horses' wake out of Valdor's face.

'Two hours at a fast gallop, Valdor.' The Captain, along with most soldiers from the capital, knew this man's legend.

'I expected to see you hours before now, perhaps even days,' Valdor commented to him.

The captain marvelled at not only the pace Valdor was moving at but his ability to do it and keep the princess steady in his arms. He was astonished.

'With everything happening in the realm of late, the king has deemed it wise not to have his soldiers spread so thin throughout his kingdom. Many of his people have already made their way closer to the Capitol.' He couldn't help staring at him. 'We only came because the party sent to escort you yesterday hadn't returned.'

'I have seen no one before you.' Valdor replied. He hadn't noted any signs of a disturbance on the track he now ran on either. 'They didn't make it this far, captain. Have your men stay alert.'

The captain turned in his saddle and barked several orders, before turning back to Valdor.

'How many men were in the first party?' Valdor asked.

'Six Valdor. Six good men.' The captain had known them all well, which was why he had volunteered to come.

'Your numbers may have deterred them, assuming also that they lost some of their own.' He looked now at the captain for the first time as he ran. 'When they see the princess, they will attack regardless. I want none of your men in my way when it happens. Instruct them again if you would. They are all to defend one side of the path, I will look to the other.'

The captain hesitated a moment before turning again to bark his new orders.

They kept the same pace for the next few hours and the men's vigilance began to wane a little as their confidence grew so near to Lakerth.

Valdor expected to see the carriage at any time now, but his pace did not falter.

The captain began to think the horses would tire before he did.

At one point, while he rode beside Valdor, he had broached the subject of what had happened to the rest of the princess' escort.

'Bad things happened,' was all Valdor would say.

In the distance, Valdor saw the dust from a large group of riders heading in their direction. He had assumed they would send many soldiers to escort the carriage that was now heading to them at speed.

They should meet with them soon.

It was at that moment they were attacked.

This part of the track had trees on both sides and a dense undergrowth. Valdor would have chosen it for an ambush and at the first movement to his right he lay the princess down at his feet and drew his sword, not moving from her side.

'Guard the princess!' he yelled, as their attackers burst from the foliage, all of them on the same side Valdor now faced. They were not monsters, but men and he had fought Ve-Karn before in battle.

They were from the far north-western reaches of the land and they were similar in appearance to the Forest Stalkers of this realm. However, that is where the similarities ended. They were no friends of the creatures of the land and certainly not allies with men.

They practised arcane arts, but they weren't spell casters. If they had been, then Valdor might have died in that moment. Four of them at once may have been too many for him to kill quickly enough.

Instead, it was the blades and spears they used that had charms and other mystical elements within them that enabled their wielders to do untold damage to their enemies.

The king's soldiers in the first party sent to meet him would have put up a valiant stand on their own, but they would not have been a match for them. Their martial skills were elite and their opponents would have needed to find the weaknesses in their armours in order to kill them. This was not something the ordinary soldier was able to do when facing four of them at once and with only six of their own.

Two of them went straight for Valdor. He was bloodied still from his earlier battles with the Squargrin and his deeper cuts hadn't had time to heal properly yet. The Ve-Karn knew a King's Shield when they saw one, which is why two of them had concentrated their efforts on Valdor, even though he appeared wounded.

It was too late before they realised the mistake of not having all four attack him.

The closest one thrust a spear at Valdor's throat. Impossibly quick, it would have skewered any other. Valdor moved his body only slightly, barely enough for it to pass by him. As it did, he grabbed the shaft, yanking it forward so that the one holding it was within reach of his sword. As quick as a striking serpent, Valdor's sword pierced the mail at his neck clean through to the other side. Before

his body had even hit the ground Valdor had pulled his sword free
and stepped forward to meet the other one, whose sword was arcing
for his head. He lifted his own blade to meet it and it jarred a little.
He hadn't had time to deflect the blow but instead met the stroke
with a straight blade.

It didn't slow him though, nor the one he fought. The Ve-Karn
stepped back and barked something in his own guttural language
before engaging Valdor again.

Valdor had only the time for a quick glance to his right as two
of the men on horseback were skewered by spears. There would be
no chance of defending themselves from up there. The captain must
have realised this as he roared the command to dismount.

Valdor turned his attention back to the Ve-Karn.

His natural choice would have been to advance and send a flurry
of sword strokes at his enemy. He knew that a few of them would
have found their way through his opponent's defences. But he was
not willing to leave the side of the princess while two others were
hacking their way into the men at his side.

Instead, he waited for the Ve-Karn to attack him, but his opponent
seemed to pick up on the reason why Valdor didn't advance. Instead
of attacking, he took a few steps back from him. Close enough to
move in and kill the princess if Valdor moved to help the others,
but far enough to avoid any chance of Valdor attacking him without
leaving the princess vulnerable to attack.

Valdor looked across again at the men fighting the other two.
Only four remained standing, but they had formed up closer and
were now able to fight two against one, the captain amongst them.

Valdor was surprised, but gladdened, that they had not all been
killed yet. These Ve-Karn were determined.

Yet he knew that could all change in an instant. If those men
fell, he would have three of them on him, all attacking the princess.

He was just thinking that the other two were almost close enough
for him to move to help the captain and his men, when another of
them fell to the spear of one of the Ve-Karn.

He knew if he was going to do something it would have to be
now, but for the first time in his life, he was undecided.

He couldn't leave the princess. If he did then she would die and
the Ve-Karn standing before him knew it. He need only stand there

poised with his sword and wait for his companions to finish off the remaining three soldiers.

Valdor looked quickly to the east and knew the carriage and his reinforcements would not get here in time. They would find only the corpses of those who now fought.

'Why are you just standing there, Valdor?' a familiar voice bellowed at him from the opposite direction. 'I thought I taught you better than that!'

Valdor turned his attention back to the three men fighting the Ve-Karn. Another had fallen, leaving only the captain and one other, until Thaiden and Catlin appeared from behind the Ve-Karn and drove their swords through the gaps in their armour, killing them both instantly.

Valdor immediately turned his attention back to the one that stood out of his reach. He didn't hesitate this time.

The Ve-Karn began backing further away, his defensive moves no match for Valdor's sword as it snaked in several times between his defences. Each strike slowed the Ve-Karn until Valdor found his mark under his sword arm, driving it deep into his body and stopping his heart.

He kicked him off his sword and looked across at where Thaiden and Catlin were checking on those men that had been struck down. Not all of those that had fallen were dead.

Valdor stepped back over to where he had left the princess and quickly checked on her welfare before picking her up into his arms and moving off at a jog once more.

It was only a few minutes more when the carriage for the princess met him on the track.

First out of the carriage was Derekia. Valdor had hoped their strongest wizard would be there to attend to the princess. He began to stride towards him when one of the lead guards pulled his horse up next to Valdor and jumped to the ground.

'Give the wizard space,' Valdor said to him and held out his arm to politely push him away.

The guard removed his helmet. 'I will see my daughter if I may Valdor.'

Valdor dropped to his knee without hesitation and gently laid the princess on the ground before his king.

He only looked up when the wizard got to her side, looked her over, and spoke to King Dayhen in a hushed voice.

'It is remarkable that she is still alive, Dayhen. We need to get her back to the capital. Fast.' Valdor heard the urgency in his voice and saw the fear in his eyes.

'If you need to give her strength, Wizard, as Heridah did, then you can use mine.' He looked intently at the wizard kneeling in front of the princess.

Valdor saw him look more closely at her then and place his hands to her face and chest.

'Ahh, he is right, Dayhen.' The wizard looked almost relieved. 'Heridah has augmented her constitution with that of another. It is why she yet lives. I saw only the wounds before.'

Dayhen waited for him to continue. When he didn't, he yelled at him.

'So what does that mean?!' He didn't look like he was in a patient mood.

'Will she make it to Lakerth?' The last spoken in a lighter voice, full of concern.

'She will, Your Majesty,' Derekia answered. 'Yet her strength fails her again. If I may, I would like to do what your Shield suggested.'

Dayhen looked at Valdor. 'What are you suggesting?' he asked him and then added, 'and where is Heridah?' His voice betrayed his fear for the other wizard. He knew he would not willingly have left the princess.

It was Thaiden who stepped forward to address his king.

'My king,' he said as he bowed. 'Heridah sent myself and Catlin forward to assist Valdor, augmenting our strengths with his own this time.' He paused to catch his breath. 'He was in need of rest when we left him, but he had those Shield that remained to watch over him.' Thaiden bowed again and withdrew to speak with the captain and others of the king's soldiers that had arrived with the carriage.

Valdor then answered his king's first question.

'My king, I wish to give what is left of my strength to the princess Areana. The wizard is able to transfer it to her.' He gave a short bow again and moved in close to where the wizard knelt next to the princess.

'Do it,' was all the king said and Derekia immediately grabbed hold of Valdor's arm. Valdor's head snapped back, but other than that, he showed no emotion. He looked at Thaiden, who in return looked at him wide-eyed.

After a couple of minutes, Derekia let go of him.

Valdor's head fell forward for a moment before he lifted it back up again and looked down at the princess. She had even more colour to her skin now than when Thaiden had given her his strength.

As he looked at her, she opened her eyes.

'Areana,' the king said and her eyes were immediately drawn to him. Tears welled up in them and she tried to speak, but it only came out as a croak through the dryness in her mouth.

'Father. . .' she managed before her eyes closed again. Her chest rose strongly now and to Valdor she looked remarkable compared to how she had been only minutes earlier.

He felt more fatigued than he ever had before, but still strong enough to stand and walk over to where Thaiden was still staring at him.

'What are you doing, Valdor, you should be resting!' He looked at him in a way that made Valdor a little uncomfortable.

'I am fine, my Lord, but I have a question to ask of you.'

Thaiden just looked at him for a time and then shook his head before replying.

'What is it?' he asked, still recovering himself from his own mad dash to get to them.

'My Lord, this may seem a strange request, but I need to leave.' He didn't know what else he could say.

Thaiden thought he was joking at first until he realised who it was he was speaking to.

'Where do you need to go, Valdor?' Thaiden had no idea where this was going. 'The princess is safe for now, but we still need to escort her and the king safely back to the capital.

'Yes, my Lord, I know. However, they have the wizard with them, yourself, Catlin, and thirty soldiers. I don't see that she is in any further danger for now.' Valdor was abashed at the words coming out of his mouth, but he couldn't shake the need within him now to find the idol. He had become convinced as to who it was that had given him the message.

Looking at Valdor, Thaiden knew he had to tread lightly with him at this moment, but he knew also there was no way he was going to let his finest monk just up and leave.

'Where do you need to go, Valdor?' He asked again.

'East of the dwarven realm, my Lord. Into the plains.' Valdor knew that he would have to tell Thaiden why, but he didn't know how to just yet.

Thaiden made no disguise of his surprise this time. His patience with his man flew out the window.

'The Eastern Plains! Have you gone mad!' He exploded. He paused then and looked around at the eyes of the men that were on him. His king and the wizard were already escorting the princess to her carriage, in the arms of four of his men and had paid him no heed. They were used to him yelling at his men.

'Do I need to find you all something to do!' he roared at them. Scurrying away, each of them suddenly found a crucial task that needed attending. If he was yelling at one of his Shield, they all dreaded to think what he would do to them if they caught his attention.

Even those caring for the injured and dead tried to look busier.

Valdor felt his cheeks redden as his face heated, but he wasn't afraid of his commander. He was chastened, but his beliefs were too strong for him to be daunted. Still he hesitated before answering.

'Lord Thaiden. A man came to me and gave me instructions that I need to journey to the plains and seek an item. He told me not why I had to, just that it needed to be achieved before I could look beyond it.' He expected a further outburst.

'A man came to you,' Thaiden repeated it to himself. 'Was this man your king?' He asked in a gruff, but serious tone.

'No, my Lord,' Valdor replied.

'Was this man your commander?' Thaiden asked again in the same voice, with no trace of mockery.

'No, my Lord.' Valdor again replied with no expression and a steady tone.

'Was it your God?' Thaiden asked, in a slightly louder voice this time.

It was then Valdor paused. He looked down, something he never did when conversing with Thaiden before raising his head again, looking his commander directly in the eye when he spoke.

'I believe that it may have been, my Lord.' He continued to stare then, unblinking and unsure of his commander's response.

Thaiden was taken aback. He hadn't expected that. He took a moment to let it sink in.

'Tell me about your meeting with this man.' He finally said in a voice that meant he wanted to know everything and would hear it all.

'He came upon me as the princess lay on the ground resting.' Valdor would leave nothing out.

He told his commander everything the man had said, his appearance, his demeanour, and his vanishing into thin air.

'I have felt a compulsion ever since, my Lord, and it grows steadily stronger. I see no other explanation and I find I cannot resist it.' He finished speaking and waited for his Lord's response. He was no longer torn by what he must do, but without Thaiden's permission, he would be considered a deserter.

A number of the king's soldiers had deserted their posts in the past, some had refused orders. Each occasion had resulted in their death.

No King's Shield had ever deserted or disobeyed an order. It never happened and none believed it ever would. Until now.

Thaiden appeared to hear the meaning behind the last words Valdor had spoken and wasn't sure if he was afraid or appalled at the implication behind them.

This was not a time for him to speak in haste.

'Wait here. I will speak to the king.' Thaiden walked away then, as sure as he ever was that his order would be obeyed.

As he neared the carriage, he chanced a look over his shoulder to make sure Valdor was still there.

'The world had definitely changed,' he thought, as he informed Dayhen's personal guard that he wished to speak to the king.

It seemed an age to Thaiden before King Dayhen finally emerged from the carriage, his wizard in tow.

'Make it fast, Thaiden, I want us to depart straight away.' Thaiden not only obeyed his king's every wish, but he also liked him. He didn't waste words.

'How is she, my king?' Thaiden asked.

'She is still sleeping, but she seems strong.' Thaiden could see the relief in his king's eyes.

'That is not what you wanted to speak to me about, is it Commander? Out with it.' He must have been able to sense whatever emotion it was radiating from him.

'In private, if I may be so bold?' Thaiden didn't want anyone else hearing what he was about to say.

Dayhen looked at him seriously for a moment and then beckoned him with a gesture to a spot a short distance away from the carriage. Derekia followed. Thaiden was about to say something about that but bit his tongue.

When they were out of earshot, he turned to his king.

'My king, one of your Shield wishes to go into the Eastern Plains. He feels there is something important there that he needs to retrieve.' There, he had said it. It was in his king's hands now.

Dayhen tilted his head a little in thought.

'He wants to go into the East?' I'm not following you, Thaiden. Speak clearly.' Thaiden knew his king didn't suffer fools.

'He told me that someone or something came to him on his journey here with your daughter and told him he needed to go into the Eastern Plains and find an idol.' Thaiden hadn't realised just how foolish it sounded until the words had come out of his own mouth. If it hadn't been Valdor who had spoken them to him, he would have thrashed the man for speaking like a fool.

'You speak of Valdor?' Dayhen was genuinely surprised. His surprise quickly turned into anger.

'You wish to send off our greatest King's Shield?! Now?! At a time when the elves have just been destroyed and my daughter was almost killed under the protection of twenty King's Shield and a wizard?' His voice was still low, but the heat behind the words intensified with each sentence he spoke. 'At a time when I have called in every able-bodied man to bolster my army. An army which will likely be called into battle any day now!'

Thaiden hadn't known about the elves. That one had him reeling, but he quickly brought himself under control. It could wait. This could not.

'My king. I understand what you are saying and I agree with you in everything you say.' He didn't know how to say the next bit, or how his king would react.

'Out with it, Thaiden. I don't have the time.' Dayhen was losing patience. Thaiden couldn't have handled this any worse than he already had.

'He believes the one that came to him was his deity, Your Majesty. He is convinced of it.' Thaiden waited for the explosion, but he should have known better of his king.

After a short pause, while he collected himself, Dayhen looked at his wizard and then back to Thaiden. The frustration and anger had left his features.

'So then, rather than have him killed as a deserter you want me to sanction this expedition of his as something crucial to the safety of my realm?' Thaiden realised it wasn't a question he was asking of him.

Derekia leaned in close and spoke something to Dayhen which Thaiden wasn't supposed to hear.

'Yes, yes, Derekia. You don't have to whisper it to me.' He turned back from his wizard to Thaiden.

'The man saved my daughter . . . again and is a legend among the people and my soldiers, Thaiden. I realise what having him killed would do to morale and their opinion of me. That is something I have no intention of doing.'

Thaiden let go of a huge sigh. That had been an order he would have had difficulty doing, both in terms of obeying the order and of being physically capable of performing the feat. It wasn't just that he couldn't think of any among them that would agree to do it, but he honestly believed there were none here capable of carrying it out.

Then he looked at the wizard and re-evaluated that thought. Derekia could and would do it at his king's behest.

As if the thought had summoned him to speak, Derekia touched his king's shoulder as he put forth a suggestion.

'Dayhen, I believe that we should not send him off alone and not before we are back safely within the capital.' He spoke slowly but in a manner that demanded his advice be heeded.

'I don't see that we can spare anyone to send with him,' Dayhen replied, 'but I agree he will come with us to the capital. I will need to send some men to meet with Heridah and the others, to take horses to speed their journey. I shall need everyone else, especially Valdor, to come with us.' He looked to Thaiden then. 'Will that be a problem, Commander?' he asked, but again it wasn't meant as a question.

'No, my king,' he answered. I hope not he thought, as he bowed to his king and walked back over to where Valdor waited.

The journey back to Lakerth was without incident, but it was nearing dark as they arrived.

Valdor had accepted his commander's request to travel with them to the capital, before he left for his journey into the plains. He knew it wasn't a request as such, but he wasn't going to defy his king when the direction they travelled wasn't far removed from the path he intended on going anyway.

Yet now they had arrived, he was keen to keep moving.

He felt his full strength had returned to him on their way back here. He had been given a strong horse to ride and hoped that he could keep him. It would make his progress much quicker.

As they entered the courtyard to the castle, he looked for and located Thaiden riding up front near the carriage. He rode up to him.

'Just give me a minute,' his commander said to him as he approached.

The carriage came to a halt and the king exited and helped with his daughter. She had obviously woken while they made their way here, but still looked fragile as she stepped down on to the cobbled stones below.

'The king wants to speak to you before you go, but he needs to see to the princess Areana before he does that.'

Valdor nodded his head and waited atop his horse.

A boy approached him and took hold of the reins to his mount.

'I'll take him for you, my Lord,' the boy said as he waited for Valdor to dismount.

'There is no need for that,' he replied. 'Just fetch a bag of feed and bring it to him here.'

The boy didn't move.

'It's late, my Lord, and the master will be angry with me if I don't have the horses fed and in their stalls before dark.' He lowered his head, but he didn't let go of the reins.

'This horse isn't going to the stables tonight, so please fetch the feed. Bring it back here and I'll feed him myself.' Valdor was polite, but his patience was wearing thin. He needed to be away from here shortly.

The boy left at a run towards the large stable complex in the distance.

By the time he returned, the sun had fallen below the horizon. He had a full bag of chaff for Kabir's mount.

'Just tie it around his head and you can go finish your chores. Tell the Stable Master if he should be angry with you that Valdor required your urgent assistance and he is to come and see myself or Lord Thaiden if there is a problem.'

The boys' eyes lit up when he realised who it was he was helping. He knew this man was one of the King's Shield, but not *the* Valdor.

He smiled, nodded several times, and flew off at a run back in the direction he had come from.

It was almost an hour later when one of the King's Guards came outside and told him the king was ready to receive him.

He should have known the king wouldn't come out here, but he had been hopeful.

With a sigh, he got down from his horse and walked inside the main doors towards the throne room.

When he got to the main doors, he saw there was only the king, his wizard Derekia, Lord Thaiden, and his chamberlain still present.

He was ushered inside by the guards and the door was closed behind him.

The king looked in slightly better spirits. Valdor assumed it was because his daughter was now home and her health had improved remarkably.

Valdor stopped at the steps leading up to the throne. Thaiden was to his side and the chamberlain behind him now. Derekia stood next to the king where he always did.

'Valdor,' the king began. 'I have given in to the wishes of your commander and to the advice of Derekia and allowed your wish to seek out this idol you speak of.'

Valdor bowed his head in thanks.

'I appreciate the urgency you feel to be on your way, but I would request you wait until the morning. It is not wise to travel at night

during the best of times and these are far from the best of times.'
Dayhen looked to wait for the response he expected would come.

'I would prefer to be on my way now, Your Majesty,' was all
Valdor said.

Dayhen sighed and looked at his wizard, before turning his
attention back to Valdor.

'I intend to send someone with you, Valdor, much to my
displeasure. As they have not yet returned, I would beseech you
wait until the morning before you depart.' Valdor knew again that he
meant it to be more than a request. He was the king and his requests
were the same as orders.

Valdor was torn, but also curious who his king intended to send
with him. He guessed it was probably Catlin, as she was among the
group that hadn't yet returned.

'Derekia has convinced me this may be something very important
to our realm. That what you seek may be of such importance that we
must find it and bring it back.' He hesitated. 'I agree, but not with
the one he would have me send with you.'

Valdor was confused now and even more curious.

'None here question your skills, or your legendary constitution,
but it has been pointed out to me that the creatures or other enemies
you face may have at their disposal such magic even your abilities
may be no match for.'

They want to send a wizard with me? Valdor was not pleased.
He knew straight away that a wizard would slow his progress and he
already had so much time he needed to make up. He didn't interrupt
his king and waited for him to continue.

'Derekia has also made it clear to me,' the king continued in a
voice that showed his displeasure at the advice he had been given,
'that now my daughter is safe behind the walls of the palace, that
Heridah should be the one to accompany you.'

Valdor waited to make sure his king had finished speaking before
he replied.

'I am humbled, Your Majesty, that you have given me your
blessing for this task I must undertake.' He bowed before he spoke
and then looked directly at his king. 'Yet I fear such a delay may
prove to be a costly one.'

His king didn't speak for a time.

'You would be best to remember who it is you speak to, Valdor,' the king finally managed to say to his Shield. 'You will await the arrival of Heridah in the morning and then once he is sufficiently rested you will leave.'

He stood then, which all of those present knew to mean this meeting was over.

'If I may say one more thing, Your Majesty?' Valdor was as surprised as everyone there that he had spoken his thoughts out loud.

Dayhen had already begun to step from the dais when he stopped and looked at Valdor.

'We are done here, Valdor,' Thaiden spoke into the silence.

King Dayhen raised a hand to Thaiden but didn't take his eyes from the monk standing in front of him.

'My king. I know the evil that threatens is real and I think as we all do, that it is coming fast. I hope to return as quickly as I can, but to do that I need to leave now and travel as fast as I am able to.' He didn't bow his head this time.

'There is a pulse inside me that feels as if it is pulling me away. I mean no insult.'

'I agree with haste Valdor, but you are no good to me or anyone else if you are dead! Now I am leaving.' He began striding out of the room again.

'King Dayhen..' Derekia began, but was interrupted.

'If anyone else utters another word before I am gone,' Dayhen said loudly without turning around, 'I will have them stripped and flogged.'

Derekia looked to Thaiden, who just shrugged. He didn't think he would do it, but then he wouldn't be surprised if he did.

Not another word was spoken until the king had left and the doors were closed behind him.

CHAPTER 33

The Time Has Come

THE CHAPEL BILSONT walked into was austere. There was nothing extravagant inside or out. The people of the village in which he lived did not covet wealth, nor did they covet power.

Situated in the south west corner of the King's Realm, they were subjects of the king, but no one from the capital ever journeyed there.

They grew their own food and raised and cared for their own animals. They were completely self-sufficient and secluded from the rest of civilisation.

There was one well-worn track that led out of their village and into the hills beyond, but there were no trails that branched off from that track until it met with the main road that headed to the capital.

Every few months, those that made the journey from this village would turn west towards Loftenberg once they reached the main track. Once there, they would stay but a short time before leaving and heading straight back to their village.

They traded nothing and got nothing in return from these journeys.

The old man walked slowly up to another man seated on a chair at the front of the chapel. They worshipped no particular deity in the King's Realm, but rather paid their respects to whatever divine being each man or woman believed in their own heart was there to protect and nurture the people of the land. It was decreed many,

many years ago that because none had actually seen their 'god', it would be disrespectful and far too self-indulgent to try and represent any kind of figure or idol of the one responsible for their existence.

Instead they had crafted 'chapels', a place where one could go for the peace and serenity they required to ask for or offer whatever was in their heart.

The man seated at the front of the chapel had been in this village for longer than any other. None knew exactly how long. No one had ever asked and he had never said. He was considered wise and a spiritual leader to those that sought him out.

The man who approached took a seat next to him.

'You asked to speak with me, Claden?'

Claden turned his head and smiled at the man as he sat.

'Thank you for coming, Bilsont. I do need to have words with you, as I did many years ago with the one who held your position before you.'

Bilsont nodded his head in understanding.

'The time is nearing, my friend,' Claden continued. 'A rider must be sent now to seek out the next to take your place here.'

'You know who that is?' Bilsont asked.

The old man nodded and continued to look at the man seated next to him. His hair was all grey now, the last streaks of black had left him years before. Yet his physical stature had not diminished. He was still incredibly strong and agile, his martial prowess no less now in his later years than it had been when he was a younger man. Claden could see that without the need for any demonstration. Bilsont was the strongest and best of them, but now his time here was at an end. It had always been that way and it always would be.

'One was chosen many years ago, Bilsont.' Claden paused then. He could tell that the man next to him wanted to ask another question, but he knew that he refrained out of respect.

'You wish to ask me what is to happen to you now,' Claden said, saving him from the embarrassment of asking.

Bilsont raised his eyebrows in feigned surprise and Claden smiled.

'You will return to your king, Bilsont. He is in need of all those able to fight in his service. I believe you will be most welcome there.'

Bilsont's smile feigned nothing this time. Claden had never before seen a look of pure delight on the face of one of the King's Shield.

CHAPTER 34

Into the Plains

BRINDEL HAD ARRIVED at the last of the foothills before finally stepping out on to the plains. His journey through the mountains had taken him less time than he thought it would. He hadn't met anything that slowed his progress or threatened his wellbeing.

There had been times after he spoke to the old man that his heart had gone into his mouth. Sudden snowstorms were usually the first and only indication that a *Krickshen* was present. He had wards that he hoped would give him a fighting chance, but he never wanted to have to test their worth. The snow beasts were still a mystery to the dwarves and although none had been taken in recent years, this was the mountain range where most of the attacks had occurred in the past and he didn't see any reason why they wouldn't still haunt these parts.

Food was scarce, but he had been able to trap a couple of smaller animals that had sustained him sufficiently.

He had to admit to himself that he didn't like what he was looking at. There was way too much open space for one born and raised in the mountains. For someone who had spent most of their life inside the confines of the mountain, the wide open grasses were daunting.

He didn't know what to expect once he got down there. He could see there was not a lot of cover, just a sea of long grass and small, spindly trees.

He had no idea what kind of animals or otherworldly monsters made their home within the plains, but he figured they would be well adapted to live and hunt there. He would need to be on his guard.

He took a deep breath and made his way down into the plains.

The first thing he noticed when he reached the beginning of the plains was the heat. The second was the grass.

He was short in stature, but from up high the grass hadn't looked this tall. It was over the top of his head, which would make progress very slow and even more dangerous. He wouldn't be able to see if anything was out there stalking him. He wouldn't even be able to see anything if it weren't! He may actually simply run in to some ferocious predator before he even knew it was there.

On the positive side, the fact that the grass towered over him would reduce the sun's oppressive heat a little bit. Even this close to the mountains, it was hot.

He dreaded to think how much hotter it would get as he moved further in. His charm that he made to ward off heat was keeping him cool now, but it needed to be recharged. To do that, he needed cold weather.

Whenever he was working his forge, he would simply lay down tools when it had depleted itself and find the nearest exit out into the cold air.

Here in the plains, he knew he wouldn't find any cool air until the sun had disappeared over the horizon. He figured he would have only a few hours of relief in the morning before he started to cook.

To top things off, he had no idea which direction the idol was. Not that it would have helped all that much even if he did. He would probably walk straight past it anyway.

His best hope was that the grass would thin out and he might run into someone or something that would help point him in the right direction.

Something that didn't want to kill and eat him would be a bonus.

He had been walking for hours after his charm had ran out and he wondered not for the first time what he was doing here. Dwarves didn't belong walking through tall grass under a hot, blistering sun.

He began to hope there were no predators nearby in these plains. Even with his dwarven constitution, he knew if he was forced to wander around here for days on end, he would eventually run out of energy and would be easy prey for even the weakest of them.

They would also have the element of surprise if they were to come upon him now. He began to doubt there would be many creatures that could or would want to live in this awful land and so his level of alertness had steadily diminished.

As had his hydration. Even drinking sparingly, his water wouldn't last long at this rate. He had finished his first canteen already and only had two others.

He should probably begin rationing his supplies, especially the water. He didn't know how long he would be here, wandering aimlessly through these plains. He didn't hold out too much hope of finding a hidden oasis among the grass.

His plan when he had looked out at the plains from his last high vantage point before he left the mountain had been to walk as far as he could in a north-easterly direction. He couldn't see where the grasses ended and he figured it would take days at least to get beyond where his eyesight had left off.

During the first day of walking, nothing had changed. The grass continued to sway in the warm breeze and he continued to push his way through it.

As night approached, he came across a larger, but still spindly tree. It would offer little protection from the sun during the day and little protection from the cold during the night. Already as the sun made its way below the horizon, the temperature began to drop dramatically.

Brindel let out a sigh of relief. The cold he could handle. At least he would get a decent night's sleep and his charm would be able to recharge itself.

He lay his bedroll out beneath the branches, for no other reason than it made him feel a little less exposed than he would just lying in the middle of the plains. There may be predators out at night that didn't show themselves during the day. At least he would have something to his back if such a beast were to find him during the hours of darkness.

With his axe in his hand, he lay on his back and fell into an exhausted sleep.

He awoke to the uncomfortable sensation of sweat coming out of every pore of his body. Already the sun was above the horizon and the heat had well and truly taken away the chill of the night.

He took a swig from one of his drink bottles, walked a short distance away to relieve himself, and then quickly scouted the immediate area for any signs that anything had been close to him last night.

He saw no footprints or other indications that there had been, so he went back to his tree and supplies and stripped his armour off.

The relief from the heat was immediate and intense. The sun was still hot, but his body could breathe again. He decided he would sit here for a bit and let his body recover before continuing on. He put the charm back around his neck and ate some of the stale bread and a little of the salted meat.

He packed up all of the belongings he hadn't taken out the night before and with a sigh put his armour back on. Picking up his sack of belongings with another exaggerated sigh, Brindel headed off into the plains for one more day of aimless walking.

He hadn't walked more than a league when he heard a sound behind him. Before he had time to turn around, he was grabbed by the shoulders and hoisted into the air.

One of the talons had snuck underneath his shoulder plate somehow and dug into his flesh. He let out a roar of pain as he looked up at the scaled belly of the flying reptile that had grabbed him.

He knew straight away what it was and knew he had better work out a way to sink his own claws into it before it climbed too much higher into the air.

It was a *palcyl* and it was moving at break neck speed as it soared higher and higher into the sky, banking around as it swept back towards the mountains. They were long like a snake, but with two legs ending in sharp talons. The face was that of a snake, except it had sharp teeth instead of fangs. The *palcyl* didn't bite and poison its prey like it's smaller, land bound cousins. They had a unique, but extremely effective method to kill their prey.

Living in the upper reaches of the same mountains where Brindel did, he had seen them many times on the other side of the ranges. They would often hunt in the lowlands where prey was plentiful. He had heard of dwarves being taken from time to time, but it was a rare event. They weren't huge and smaller prey was easier for them to carry.

If he had known they came out this side of the mountains to hunt, he would have kept an eye out for them. That thought didn't comfort him at present.

As they rapidly neared the mountains, he tried desperately to get his axe out of his belt. The flying reptile was lifting him up by the shoulders, which made it difficult for him to push his hands down far enough to clasp it, let alone remove it from his belt. He hoped that once he did get it out that he would be able to hook the rear of it somewhere on the creatures body, without killing it or injuring it badly enough that it couldn't fly. He would have to avoid the wings, the head, and any vital organs. He realised he would need to be incredibly lucky to get out of this one.

He had to try though and he needed it done before they reached the hard, rocky ground of the mountains. If he didn't succeed, then the *palcyl* would let him fall from their lofty place in the sky. They had their own 'drop' points, guarded by others in its group. None of the *palcyl* lived alone. Brindel had been fortunate on one of his past expeditions to see them at work and he had thought it fascinating. The skill to drop their prey into a small target zone from such a height had greatly impressed him at the time.

Not so much at the moment.

They were high above the lower mountains and there was little cloud cover at present, even at this height. Brindel knew he probably wouldn't be able to see the point where he would be dropped until he was on his way down to it, free falling to his death. He knew they would be close now and he was no nearer to getting his axe out. He had nothing else he could think of that might help him hook on to it.

Then without warning, the *palcyl* let go. Reflexively, he swung his left arm upwards and through some kind of miracle, grabbed hold of its right leg. The *palcyl* started to shake its leg frantically, as it dawned on Brindel that the talon that had pierced his shoulder had been caught between his armoured shoulder plate and the side of his helm. As he had lifted his shoulder up when it grabbed him, his helm had pushed down on the plate and caught its foot.

Brindel bellowed a laugh. He couldn't help it. It was the funniest thing he had ever seen.

'Ha,' he yelled out to the reptile, when his laughter subsided.

It continued to try and shake him off, but with Brindel's hand gripping him as well, there was no letting go of him while they were in the air.

Eventually, the *palcyl* realised it as well and stopped trying to shake the dwarf free. Instead, it turned its head and snapped at him with its razor-sharp teeth.

Fortunately for Brindel, it couldn't put too much force into this endeavour. It still needed to concentrate on flying and its efforts here also proved fruitless. It quickly snapped at the dwarf a few times, but his armour and charms were strong enough to repel its attempt to kill or maim him before they landed.

After flying around above the mountains for a time, the *palcyl* finally decided it would need to touch ground again before it would be able to shake the dwarf loose. The best place to do that was at the point it was going to drop him.

Brindel saw it quickly come into view, and as it slowed its speed in preparation for its landing, he was able to count at least four others waiting for them to arrive.

The 'drop zone' was a plateau, still high on the slopes, but it was long, if not very wide. The four that he could see were perched above it a short distance from the base of the plateau, spaced out along it.

The *palcyl* that carried him had banked around and now moved in directly along the ridge line so that it could land without crashing into the slope.

When it had almost touched the ground, Brindel felt it loosen its grip on his shoulders again and this time he let go of its leg and lowered his arm, letting the claw retract from under his armour. It had slowed its speed considerably by the time he let go, but Brindel still hit the ground hard, rolling without grace as he crashed into the hard rock of the mountain.

He stood and shook himself, quickly checking he had no serious hurts, before turning his attention to his surroundings.

His first thought as he had let go was that he needed to find himself a position where the mountain side was at his back. If they were able to surround him, he would not be so lucky a second time.

He saw he wasn't too far from the side of the mountain, but already two of the creatures had made their way down to the plateau that he stood on and were slithering their way to him. When on the ground, they tucked their legs into their bodies and moved as a snake would and they moved fast. He backed over to the side as one slipped down only a few paces in front of him.

Drawing his axe, he waited for the nearest one to attack.

Much to his disappointment, it stayed out of reach, hissing at him instead while it waited for the others to come to them.

He would have preferred to take them on one at a time, but they obviously weren't stupid and saw their advantage in numbers.

He also noticed, as the one that had grabbed him came back around and slithered to a halt further back from the rest, that they were smaller than the one that had grabbed him. They must be its offspring and were waiting for the parent to arrive before attacking. The larger one made a hissing sound as it approached and the others all slithered back a few paces.

The larger one continued past them and without hesitation lifted itself up and sprang at him, quick and straight as an arrow.

Brindel was taken by surprise at the speed in which it attacked. He had been anticipating some kind of stand-off first and then a group attack from all sides.

The beast somehow managed to grab hold of the handle to his axe and almost tugged it from his grasp. Brindel was pulled off balance and only luck saved him as one of the smaller ones struck at his torso.

He had just pulled his hammer from his belt and the small *palcyl* struck the head of it instead as he lifted it to strike the parent.

The larger one quickly let go of the axe handle when it realised that Brindel still had hold of it and had another weapon in his other free hand. As it let go, Brindel stepped forward and swung his axe in a sidewards arc towards it. The large *palcyl* pulled back as his blade swung past, striking only air and then quickly snapped forward at his face.

Yet as Brindel swung his axe, he followed it with a downward stroke of his hammer. He had anticipated that it may strike again quickly and the hammer struck it clean on the top of its head. He heard its skull clang into the hard rock of the ground and Brindel followed it with another downward strike of his hammer. This time, he heard the skull crack and knew the creature wouldn't be attempting to strike him again.

All of the others slithered backwards straight away. They each began making horrible hissing sounds but made no move towards him.

Brindel raised both his weapons and roared his own battle cry at them as he took a small step forward. He stopped and looked at them for a little longer as they continued to hiss and then struck the head of their dead parent again without taking his eyes off them.

'That was for dropping me in this place and making me have to start my walk across those bloody plains again.'

One of the *palcyl* made a different sound, before turning and leaping into the sky in the opposite direction to the plains.

The others stayed where they were and continued to hiss at him.

Brindel walked backwards until he reached the edge of the plateau. None of them had made any move towards him, so he turned all the way around and looked down.

He was a long way up and there was no easy path down that he could see.

He didn't have any equipment that would allow him to rope his way down. It suddenly dawned on him that he had no equipment at all except for what he was wearing and those few items that hung from his belt. His sack must have fallen during his flight here.

He cursed to himself and thought about going back to hit the dead serpent a few more times, but he wanted to be off this part of the mountain before the one that had left came back with more of them. He assumed it was off to get some help. Probably its other parent.

Looking back once more, he saw they still hadn't made any move towards him. They continued to spray their hateful hisses at him, as Brindel began the arduous task of climbing back down the mountain.

The *palcyl* had obviously chosen the plateau so they could leave their young there without fear of any potential predators making their way up to them.

Brindel was adept at mountain climbing, as were most dwarves, but usually they carried ropes with them and spikes to hammer into the side of the mountain. Brindel was left to try and find hand and toe holds and his progress initially was very slow. He wasn't fearful of being picked off by any of the *palcyl* as he climbed. Their wings would make it too risky for them to attempt to snatch him from the side of a cliff face. Their hunting was done down in the plains or in the valleys, where they could swoop down and take off in the same direction.

For now, he just needed to concentrate on getting through this part and hopefully finding a gentler slope or even a track of some description to walk along.

His armour didn't help his progress. It made it extremely difficult in parts to move his body at angles to the cliff face and there were a few times he had to go back up and try for another way, but the strength in his arms, shoulders, and legs were enough to keep him from falling to his death.

A short time before the sun found its way below the horizon, Brindel came across a place where he could rest for the night. If it had gotten dark before he found the gentle slope he was now on, he was certain he would have died on the cliff face above him.

His luck was finally starting to turn, although he was too tired to feel grateful.

Lying down, he was able to close his eyes and sleep despite the shivering cold.

He knew when he had lain down that it wasn't cold enough to freeze him during the night, but he was stiff and very uncomfortable when he awoke in the morning. The mountain above him shaded him from the sun and would do the same throughout the morning, but it was light enough for him to continue his journey.

He was mercilessly hungry and in need of some proper rest, but he knew until he got a lot further down he would get neither.

If all went relatively well, he estimated he should make it on to gentler ground before the day was half gone. It would probably take the rest of the day and half of the next before he was back out on the plains again.

He swore a few more curses at the creature that had plucked him from the plains before he started out again.

Although he was unfamiliar with this part of the Mountain Range, he was still familiar with all the pitfalls and such associated with travelling in the mountains, so he was able to make fairly good progress for the rest of the day.

By the time nightfall was approaching, he had made even better progress than he had hoped and could see the plains now in the distance. He didn't have all that far to go before he reached the lower hills and his first chance to find something to eat.

His only concern this far had been the lack of anything moving within the mountains. He hadn't seen any of those beasts that made their homes here and he was a little disconcerted by what it all meant. He had also never been this hungry before.

He reached the first of the fir trees and was looking around for somewhere to hole up for the night when he finally saw something moving ahead of him.

It had been a fleeting glimpse and he wasn't exactly sure what it was, but it was quite large. Perhaps a deer of some kind.

He decided it was worth the risk for him to track it for a distance, even if he found nowhere suitable to sleep as a result. Food in his stomach was more important than a comfortable place to sleep. His stomach would probably keep him awake anyway.

He moved to where he had glimpsed it and looked for the tracks it left on the ground.

They were cloven hooves, so he guessed his assumption had been correct. It was a large one, too. That would make it harder to catch and harder to take down if he was lucky enough to get close enough to throw his axe.

The trees were relatively sparse, but there were enough to prevent him seeing where it had gone. He was at least pleased to see it was going down the slope and not up.

After a short time, he heard the sounds of a struggle up ahead, just over a small rise. He wasn't sure what it meant but he walked cautiously to a spot where he could look down on what was happening. Standing next to a tree, he peered around it. About forty paces ahead of him, he saw the deer. It was on the ground and its struggling had stopped.

Around it were three other deer, tearing into the carcass as if they were a pack of wolves. They were smaller than the one on the ground, but other than their size, they looked exactly the same.

Brindel looked away and put his back to the bark of the tree. 'What did I just see?' he exclaimed to himself in a quiet voice.

Shaking his head, he peered around the tree again. It was exactly as he had seen it the first time, only this time he saw the face of one as it looked up from its feasting. It saw him at the same time.

It still had its jaws open, showing Brindel a set of sharp teeth with two longer fangs in the centre. The eyes were a bright blue, contrasting vividly with the blood smeared across its face and the white backdrop of snow.

It snarled at him and the other two lifted their heads and turned their eyes towards the dwarf.

Brindel stepped away from the tree. He saw the folly in trying to outrun them. Speed wasn't his greatest asset, so he pulled his hammer free of his belt and stood ready for them to attack.

'Come on you freaks. Let's see how you go against something that fights back.' He always liked to speak with his foes before a fight. He told himself it was to help mentally prepare, that it focused his mind.

Deep down, he knew it was because he simply liked to taunt them, to try and unsettle them.

It usually helped if they knew what he was saying and he doubted these monsters did.

'You three have got to be the ugliest, misbegotten creations I have seen in a very long time.' They didn't react to his words, but taunting was a habit for him now. 'Who wants to die first?'

All three attacked at once.

They died one at a time though.

Brindel hardly broke a sweat as he hammered their brains into the ground, breaking a few bones in the process. Their teeth were sharp and deadly against a fleeing deer. The dwarf's armour was a different proposition and their fangs didn't find an opening. They weren't quick like the *palcyl* and never stood a chance.

Brindel was left with the decision whether to eat those he had just killed and risk getting sick if they were suffering some kind of disease, or he could try and find some meat on the slain deer that the freaks hadn't already torn their way into. Their deformity may be natural, but he doubted it.

He walked over to the fallen deer and inspected the carcass. There was plenty of untainted flesh left on it, so he pulled out his dagger and went to work.

He cleared some ground after he had cut away some choice steaks and quickly had a small fire lit.

By the time he had eaten his fill, it was well and truly dark. The fire was a risk, but he decided to leave it burning a little longer while he warmed his bones.

When he was done warming himself, he moved back over to the tree and sat against the trunk. With a full stomach, he slept well.

CHAPTER 35

The Undead

VALDOR WAS UP early the next morning. He had slept well for the time that he did, but he was desperate to begin his journey to the Eastern Plains.

He went straight to the stables to get his horse. The same young stable hand that had greeted him the evening before was there again raking out one of the stables.

He threw down his rake when he noticed the King's Shield enter the complex and raced up to him.

'Your horse, sir?' he asked.

Valdor nodded and the boy raced to the stall half way down, where he had put his horse last night. Valdor walked over to where all the gear was kept and grabbed his own saddle and the rest of his gear.

By the time he turned around, his horse was waiting there for him, the stableboy holding the lead rope.

'What time did Heridah and the other King's Shield ride in?' Valdor asked him.

'They came in during the late hours of the night,' he said. 'I'm on the night duties at the moment, sir. Any that come in late I have to escort in. There is a bunk set up for me near the courtyard. When the princess' tutor and three of the King's Shield came in, I had to look to all of their horses myself. There were none others to help me. Just me, sir, but they were all washed down, watered, and fed before I went back to the bunk, sir. I take my duties very seriously, sir.'

Valdor eventually held his hand up. He thought the boy would have run out of breath sooner and he had thought better not to be rude and interrupt him, but then realised he would never stop if he didn't get him to.

'Can you take out Heridah's mount, please boy, and have him ready to ride.' Valdor didn't intend to waste any more time.

The boy looked unsure of himself.

'His horse was near exhaustion when he brought him in, sir. He isn't really rested enough to ride again yet. Forgive me my forwardness.' The boy lowered his head, embarrassed by his words.

Valdor looked at him for a short time but wasn't angry. He respected the concern he showed at the health of those it was his duty to look after. Valdor understood what duty meant more than most.

'What is your name?' Valdor asked.

'Markel,' the stable hand replied. He lifted his head a little so he could see Valdor from the top corner of his eyes.

'I appreciate what you say, but get him out anyway if you would. I will speak to Heridah about it when he arrives.' He indicated for Markel to go and get the other mount as he took the rope from his hands and started to get his own horse ready to ride.

After he had wiped him down and put the saddle and reins on, he looked up and saw exactly what the boy had meant.

The horse he led was a fine animal, a prince among horses, in fact. Yet Valdor could see he was in no condition to be ridden. He hadn't thought the young man had been lying to him, but he hoped he may have exaggerated the fatigue the horse was feeling. He wasn't lame, but Valdor could see that he had been ridden to the ends of his endurance.

The stallion held his head high, but the King's Shield knew that Heridah wouldn't be riding him today. That would be too cruel and he wouldn't be able to keep up with him anyway.

'Is there another he can ride?' Valdor asked. 'I'm sure you have plenty of noble steeds here in the king's stable.'

'We have many,' the stable hand said brightly, 'yet very few as powerful and with the endurance of this one. His name is Arrow.' He spoke lovingly as he said his name, stroking his mane and feeding him a few small treats from his other hand that he pulled from a pouch at his belt.

'Also,' he began and then paused. 'His Lord Heridah has never ridden any other horse but Arrow and no other person has ever ridden him.'

Valdor had suspected as much and his hopes of an early start were beginning to look less and less likely.

He decided to see if he couldn't speed things up a little bit.

Hauling himself up on to his own horse, he looked down at Markel.

'Put Arrow back in his stall,' he said and then trotted out of the stables and up to the main courtyard in front of the main doors.

He stayed on his horse as he called over one of those standing guard at the door.

The soldier walked down the steps to where he waited and looked up at Valdor.

'Please send word to Heridah that I am waiting for him here and that I am ready to depart.'

The soldier began to turn and then hesitated before turning back to look at the King's Shield.

'I have heard it told that you are leaving to seek something that will help us in the coming battles?' He looked nervous. Valdor wasn't sure if it was the evil that threatened or the fact he hadn't yet left to deliver Valdor's message.

Valdor knew the importance of morale, especially at a time like this, so he didn't chastise him.

'I do seek something,' he replied. 'And I hope to be back before anything of note happens here.' He gave the man a look which he understood to be the end of the conversation and walked back to the doors and inside them.

He returned shortly after and stood back in his place to one side of the entry.

While Valdor waited, he took the time to think about the journey he was about to embark upon.

He had never been to the Eastern Plains before. There had never been any reason to. Most of his time had been spent within the King's Realm or directly to the east of it fighting goblins. He had also spent some time roaming along the border of the Western Realm, fighting whatever warped monster or misbegotten men came close to the king's lands.

He hoped Heridah would have a greater understanding of the lands they were travelling to. Those of his order were supposed to be knowledgeable about many things within the realms. He conceded it was one of the advantages in sending the wizard with him.

Yet as the minutes went by, he was more inclined to concentrate on the disadvantages, time being the main one.

He was about to call the guard over again when one of the doors opened and Catlin walked out.

She looked healthy, although he could see she still favoured one side of her body slightly. One of her more serious wounds still hadn't healed properly. He knew to most people she would look in perfect health, but Valdor was trained to look for weaknesses and he had the added advantage in this case of knowing the woman walking down to him quite intimately. They had trained and fought with each other most of their lives.

She raised a hand in greeting as she approached and he returned the gesture.

'Do you have news on the wizard's whereabouts?' he asked her in a quiet voice. It was meant for her ears only. It wasn't a well-known fact that Heridah was a wizard. He was held in high regard by the people for his position as mentor to the king's firstborn, but he preferred to keep his other skills a secret. It helped keep the first born safer from those who may wish him or her harm, as they would be less careful in their planning if they thought him only a simple tutor. In the past, there had been a couple of occasions when a would-be assassin had received quite a shock when they realised her mentor was in fact one of the most powerful wizards in the human realm. The shock had been short-lived of course and none had lived to pass on his secret.

Only the most senior and trustworthy were aware of his true standing. Any of the King's Shield that rode with him were also made aware of it. It enabled them to do their roles more efficiently and there were none more trustworthy in the land.

'I went and roused him a short time ago, Valdor,' she replied. 'He was not pleased by it. He was less pleased when the king informed him last night of your plans and that he was to accompany you.'

Valdor had guessed as much. Heridah had spent the last sixteen years of his life responsible for the safekeeping of Princess Areana.

He would not be pleased to be leaving her side, now more than ever. The dangers in the land were real, the king's armies were preparing for war, and she had been almost killed on her way to the capital while he was elsewhere. 'Not pleased' was understating it by a long way.

Still Valdor was satisfied he would finally be coming outside soon. The predicament of what he would do for a mount was less pleasing.

'I have my mount to attend to,' Catlin said to him as she walked past him on her way to the stables.

Valdor watched her go and then turned his attention back to the doors in front of him.

Valdor was about to step off his horse again, this time intending to walk straight inside himself, when Heridah finally made his way outside.

He stopped two steps outside and looked directly at Valdor standing up in his saddle. Valdor read the look in his eyes straight away and decided it best not to say anything in relation to his horse just yet. He would walk with him to the stables and see what Heridah intended first.

Heridah made no move to get his horse, instead he turned his attention to the sound of horses approaching from that direction.

Valdor followed his gaze and saw Catlin trotting towards them. She sat on her own horse Firth, with two horses trotting behind her. One of those she led was Arrow and the other a dark stallion similar in appearance to the wizard's.

Valdor noticed straight away that Catlin's horse had saddlebags at its side. She hadn't walked out carrying anything so she must have prepared everything before she retired for the night. He surmised she may not have even slept yet. He had always admired and respected her strength.

He had mixed feelings on her accompanying them, which she obviously intended on doing. He was intrigued how she had convinced Lord Thaiden to allow it. He was happy for the extra sword, but it would be leaving the capital further weakened. She was a fearless warrior and a more than capable leader of men. Her presence here would have been worth dozens of the king's soldiers.

As she pulled her horse up next to his, Heridah made his way down the steps and walked over to Arrow. He ran his hands over the stallion and stood in front of him with his hands either side of the horses face. He spoke softly to him for a time and then moved easily into the saddle of the other horse that Catlin had brought from the stables.

Valdor gave an inward sigh of relief.

'Well then, let us not dally about all day,' Heridah said to Valdor and Catlin, as he turned the horse he was on towards the exit to the courtyard. He had tied Arrow to the saddle of his horse.

'How is the princess Areana?' Valdor asked the wizard as he drew level with him.

Heridah shot him a harsh look, which quickly faded to one of sadness. Valdor remembered as he looked at him, that he would not have been pleased to be leaving her. He winced slightly.

'My apologies, Heridah,' Valdor said.

Heridah waved his hand quickly in front of himself as if he were swatting away an insect. He shouldn't be angry at this man. He should be angry at his king for sending him away from his daughter. A great evil walks the land and he chooses now to send him away. He didn't even know what they were looking for?'

He couldn't stop thinking about the moment both his king and Derekia had informed him he would be accompanying Valdor into the Eastern Plains. He was a little embarrassed at how he had reacted, but he was not long returned and hadn't slept for many days. He was worn out from exertion, stressed at not knowing the fate of the princess and was then told he needed to leave first thing in the morning.

He realised that both Dayhen and Derekia must have seen the exhaustion in his appearance, as neither had reprimanded him for his outburst.

He only got a few hours rest after his audience with the king and his temper was still stretched, but he did his best to reign it in now while talking to the King's Shield in front of him.

'There is no need for you to apologise, Valdor.' Heridah said seriously. 'The princess awoke before I left. That is the reason I had to keep you waiting. Her strength returns. In fact, she is looking remarkable considering the wounds she received and how close to death she was.' He stopped his horse and looked intently at Valdor. 'Derekia told me what you did for her. All of it,' he added. Derekia had told him briefly of Valdor giving his strength to the princess. It wasn't only how stoic he was during the process that had impressed his fellow wizard, where even the strongest of men would scream out in pain and be left exhausted afterwards. The strength that had been returned to the princess was remarkable. She was as strong of body as if she had been without hurt and had a night of uninterrupted rest. That she had only recently been mortally wounded was inconceivable.

'I performed my duty. That is all.' There was no arrogance or false bravado in his words. The man continued to amaze him. His would be a huge loss if they didn't return in time. There was so much more to this man than even his deeds spoke of.

He fervently hoped that whatever threatened the land didn't show itself at the capital before he returned. Before all three of them returned.

They rode in silence for the first part of their journey. Heridah and Catlin were still fatigued and Valdor was left to his own thoughts.

The pace they set wasn't a fast one. Heridah wasn't going to over exert Arrow, even without a rider or supplies on his back. Valdor didn't press the issue. He understood the wizard's concern for his horse. He was satisfied the wizard had taken it upon himself to ride a different mount and not wait until his was better rested.

He was more at ease now they were headed in the right direction. It had been difficult for him since the old man had come to him and he had been forced to attend to other matters first.

They would now ride for a couple of days until a decision would have to be made on which direction they would take from there.

When they reached the town of Havern, they would have to decide whether they would brave the trails at the edge of the Dwarven Southern Mountain Range or go directly east into the lands of the goblins and head north from there.

The first option would take them through trails where the weather was unpredictable and the paths they took went high into the mountains. These would make every decision a dangerous one. Avalanches, snowstorms, and trails hardly wide enough to walk along would make this choice a risky one. If all went well, it would save them time and they would be in to the Eastern Realm sooner.

If they continued further east then their journey would take them around the dwarven realm. They would have only to navigate through the hills at the end of the Mountain Range. The weather there wouldn't be a problem. They might get thoroughly soaked through from the rains, but they wouldn't be risking death on every winding path they walked along.

It would take longer to go all the way around and Valdor was loathe to take more time than was required.

There was also the goblin problem to consider. Although their main settlements were further south and closer to the centre of their lands, with the way things stood in the lands these days, it would be no surprise if they were to bump into a goblin war party. Goblins were a lot stronger and more dangerous foes than the tree-swinging creatures that had caused them so much trouble only days before. He didn't fancy being hunted by a large group of them. They had some resistance to the magic Heridah would cast at them and they were competent-enough fighters with their wicked swords and spears.

On top of that, there were other creatures that would abound within that god-forsaken realm.

The choice wouldn't be an easy one, but for the next couple of days, they could sit back and relax as best they could on horseback. They would all need to be strong and well rested, whichever route they took.

'Can you tell me about the one who spoke to you, Valdor?' Catlin asked him, snapping him out of his own thoughts.

He looked across at his fellow King's Shield.

'He was not remarkable to look upon, Catlin,' Valdor replied. 'He was a simple-looking man, but there was something otherworldly about him. I don't know if he was who you think I believe he was, yet I am having some difficulty thinking of him any other way.' He crinkled his brow as he thought again about what the old man had said to him.

'So we journey east because of what he said to you?' She looked genuinely interested in Valdor telling her about him and what he had said. He could tell by the way she looked at him. He imagined it was probably how he looked when he spoke about him.

'Yes it is, but there is more to it.' He paused to think about what he would say. 'I wouldn't jump at the words of anyone, but there is a compulsion within me now. It is difficult to describe, but it didn't begin to ease until we left this morning and started heading towards whatever it is he wants me to find.'

'An idol of mud?' Catlin turned back to face the road ahead. The question was not directed at Valdor but rather a thought she said out loud. Valdor answered her anyway.

'He told me it needs to be found before anything can be revealed.' He paused again before continuing. 'The idol may not be what we actually need. That is my greatest concern. This is one of the reasons why I need to find it as soon as we are able.'

'I agree we need to make haste. I fear that our king will be needing us sooner rather than later,' Catlin thought she echoed his thoughts, but Valdor's next words confused her.

'He also told me that I need to make haste, but I don't think he was referring to my need to get back to the king.' He was confused about much of what he had been told, but the need to get there quickly was one of the few things he was sure of.

Catlin looked as confused as he felt.

'Why the hurry then?' she asked.

'I don't know,' he replied. 'The elves have been destroyed and there are things travelling the land that have never been seen in those parts before. Some monsters that have never been seen at all. Perhaps what we seek is something that will help us fight against the true force behind these evils.' He looked at his companion. Her features were showing the strain of little sleep and constant exertions. Her willpower alone couldn't remove the darkness under her eyes.

'I fear that returning without the item will avail us little, even if we return in time.' Valdor's voice had the sound of an omen about it.

'I fear that talking about it will avail us nothing,' Heridah said, as he pulled up beside the two of them on Valdor's side. The track was wide here and there was plenty of room for them to ride three abreast.

'Whoever or whatever it was,' the wizard continued, 'he was deliberately vague. I don't think he wanted us to know any more about it at this point in time.'

Valdor heard the wisdom in his words, but he knew it would continue to niggle at him no matter how hard he tried to put it from his mind.

'Now,' Heridah continued. 'Although we are some distance still from Havern, I think it prudent to discuss which way we will be heading to get into the plains.'

Valdor nodded in agreement. He had already decided which way he wanted to go, but he would take the wizard's thoughts into consideration. He would be foolish to dismiss him outright.

'I would like to go through the mountains,' Valdor said.

Heridah gave a slight nod. 'Why?' was he all he said.

'A route through the mountain will get us there faster and there will be less risk of running into anything particularly powerful. Or of anything roaming in large numbers, as we would meet in the goblin lands.'

'Really?' Heridah said in response, rising his eyebrows in surprise.

'Yes,' Valdor said, a little taken aback by his reaction. 'Although the conditions we encounter may delay us somewhat, it will still have us in the plains much sooner than were we to go around them.'

'Oh, I agree with you there, Valdor. My surprise was in relation to your comment that you expect not to run into anything nasty in the mountains.'

Valdor waited for him to continue. Catlin was also listening intently to their conversation.

'There is more than one reason why the dwarves don't venture much into the Eastern Plains, Valdor. The obvious one is that there is little trade with the plainsmen and barbarians, therefore no wealth to be made and shared. The second is that even if there was, they would probably take a more Northern route than the one you intend to take us through.'

'Surely nothing you would fear so much that you would choose to bypass it completely?' Valdor saw threats and dangers everywhere. He had always been able to combat them. In the company of one of the most powerful human wizards and another of his order, he wondered what kind of beast there was that would make Heridah quail at the thought of it.

'There is magic scattered throughout the land, Valdor, and there are plenty that have worked out how to use it. Many lack the skills and powers to be much of a threat to us, but there are some that have been around for a very long time and they have developed it to a level where I would consider them masters of their craft.'

Neither Valdor nor Catlin interrupted him as he spoke. Both of them had always been intrigued by those that use magic.

'Within their own environment, none are more powerful with magic than the elves. I still find it difficult to fathom that something has wiped them out so ruthlessly.' He paused as if in thought. 'Yet if they were to have left their forest and entered into an environment alien to them, their powers would also have been diminished.'

'They would still be incredibly dangerous to any who came upon them, but my point here is that even if an elf lord were to venture through the part of the mountains you intend and he were to cross paths with that which concerns me, then he would be sorely pressed to escape with his life.'

'What is it?' Catlin asked. Like Valdor, she wouldn't be afraid of the monster that he spoke of, but even those of the King's Shield knew their limits. If even Heridah was loathe to come across it, then maybe it would be foolish to attempt it.

'I don't know,' was all he said.

Valdor knew Catlin would have the same perplexed look on her face that he now had.

'I don't know what they look like and I don't know what they are called in the common tongue. The dwarves speak of them in hushed tones to scare their young, but they also speak of them when there are no children about. They call them *Krickshen*, which loosely translated into the common language means, *The Bringer of Death.* I have no doubt they exist and the dwarves have lost many of their people to them throughout the ages.'

Heridah looked seriously at Valdor now.

'I would not choose to go through the mountains,' he said at last.

Valdor turned his eyes back to the track they were travelling along. He needed to think about what the wizard had just said.

He was basically saying that if they were to meet any of these *Krickshen*, then it would be death for them all.

There was of course no guarantee they would meet anything if they were to go that way. The dwarven mountains were vast and the trail he intended on taking would see them journey through only one small part of them. There would be no peaks to traverse and the Southern dwarven stronghold was further to the west.

He still wasn't convinced they should go through the Goblin lands.

As the sun began to sink beneath the horizon and they found a suitable spot to camp for the night, Valdor was still no closer to deciding which way they would go.

The next day, they were all up early and set off again after a small breakfast. Arrow was looking remarkably well rested and in much better spirits, but the wizard chose to ride the other stallion still.

They were able to travel at a slightly quicker pace and Valdor was content.

They had passed a few refugees, making their way to the capital the day before, but they had little news of worth. The same tales of creatures attacking in all parts and that the land wasn't safe anymore.

Heridah had asked them why they risked travelling to Lakerth when Havern had been closer. Their fear was greater for their families being caught there than in the capital. They thought it would be safer in the Realm's largest city than within the walls of Havern. One comment in particular, from a man who had abandoned his bakery to travel the dangerous tracks to Lakerth, had concerned them all.

'When the goblins attack, there will be no help from the capital, sir. They won't be able to help, and Havern won't survive against a goblin army.' Valdor had seen the terror in the eyes of the children sitting in the back of their cart as they passed.

During the second morning out of the capital, they passed no more people looking for refuge at Lakerth.

By midday, they had been travelling for hours through farming land and had seen no farmers anywhere. The land was deserted, abandoned by those who were needed to provide for the sustenance of the realm.

After each farmhouse he passed, Valdor knew with a greater certainty that they would have no choice but to venture through the mountains. Time was critical or they would have nothing to come back to. Some of the farmhouses had been burnt to the ground and there were signs of violence and death all around them.

He was surprised they had come across none of those responsible so far. Perhaps they had finished their work here and moved on to try and wreak their havoc elsewhere.

They all remained vigilant.

In the early afternoon, they stopped. Screams rang out from the other side of a small hill they traversed. Without hesitation, they put heels into their mounts and galloped forward as fast as they were able.

Within minutes, they came to the top of the rise and looked down upon a farmhouse. The screaming had stopped a short time before they could see what was happening and they knew they were probably too late to help the poor souls below.

'Goblins!' Catlin said out loud in disbelief. 'How could they be so far inside the realm?'

They could see only six of them. The farmer and his family were all grouped together. They looked to be tied to each other in a circle, on a patch of dirt in front of their house. The six goblins stood in a circle surrounding them, making some kind of chanting noise. None of them had noticed the wizard and two King's Shields as they looked down upon them.

'Not goblins,' Heridah said in a quiet voice.

Even Valdor was confused. They looked like goblins to him and he had fought many.

'These creatures come from the southern parts of that realm and are much more dangerous than your average goblin,' Heridah continued.

'They are tough to kill, even for me,' he finished.

'What are they?' Catlin asked, the confusion and frustration at Heridah's vague comments obvious in her voice.

'Goblin wights,' he answered.

Valdor had heard of these evil monsters before, but he had never come across one. The stories he heard told weren't pleasant ones.

They were long forgotten goblin spell casters who had delved too deeply into the magic found in the southern mountains of their land. It was said they had killed themselves in their pursuit of dark magic but instead of dying, the magic brought them back and then sustained them in some kind of half dead state.

'How do we kill them?' Valdor asked and Heridah looked at him.

'I think it best if we go around,' he suggested. 'It is a risk we don't have to take. They haven't yet seen us.'

Valdor was surprised and a little shocked.

'They may still be alive down there,' he said. He made no attempt to hide the shock he felt at Heridah's words. He looked over at Catlin and saw the same look of disbelief on her face that he knew was on his.

'Don't you two look at me like that,' he returned, with some fire of his own in his voice. 'They are beyond our help now. The creatures are chanting their thanks to the powers that sustain them for the lives they have just taken. The magic keeps them from death, but they still need to feed. Those people are already dead.'

'Then I will make sure their bodies are treated with respect and their souls sent on in peace,' Valdor replied. 'I'm not going to watch as those vile creatures tear the bodies of these innocents to pieces.'

'You will not go down there,' Heridah said in a quiet voice, but with his jaws locked together and his eyes shooting daggers at the King Shield.

'I ask you again, wizard, how do we kill them?' Valdor said.

Heridah continued to stare at him. Valdor assumed by the look on his face that he wasn't used to having his advice ignored.

'I don't know,' he said finally. 'I have never fought them before.'

Valdor didn't know if that was a good thing or not.

'It is not worth the risk, Valdor,' he persisted. 'We have a more important task, don't forget.'

Valdor knew he was right. The people down there were already beyond their help. Yet he couldn't help the feeling he needed to do something. He had sworn an oath to protect the King's Realm from threat. Those things down there were definitely a threat.

'What about the next helpless souls those things come across?' Catlin spoke up.

Valdor and Heridah both looked at her.

Valdor nodded his head slightly at her words and then turned back to the goblin wights who were still chanting their eerie words.

He took out his sword and held it up to the sunlight shining from above. He moved the sword enough so that the glare from the blade shone directly on the creatures down below. As one they stopped their chanting and turned to look at the three sitting astride their horses above them.

Without a sound, they began to move towards Valdor and his companions.

Heridah shook his head as he fired a stream of liquid fire at the one who had made his way to the front of the others.

Even though they were still one hundred paces from them, the liquid fire tore through the chest of his target and the goblin wight fell to the ground. Wisps of smoke came from its prone body, as the others loped past him in ungainly fashion. Another two fell in the same fashion before they had covered half the distance. It wasn't until those two fell that Valdor and Catlin began their charge.

The creatures looked awkward, but they moved fast and their long arms ended in huge hands with claws that looked razor sharp. The two King's Shield were upon them quickly, swinging their swords at the two remaining wights. Heridah had already punctured the chest of another before Valdor and Catlin hacked the arms from the two that had swung their claws at them. Valdor could hear a muted, buzz of energy about them as he struck.

They wheeled their steeds around for another pass and saw the Wights bend down to where their arms were on the ground below them, severed just below the elbows.

The two of them looked on in disbelief as they pushed the stumps of their severed arms onto the ends of the limbs. Valdor and Catlin stopped their horses and watched as the limbs looked to attach themselves again. A darkness enveloped the area where the swords had cut them and the wights stood again.

They continued to watch as the blackness slowly dissipated and the arm looked whole again.

'Let us take their heads,' he said to Catlin, as he dug his heels into his mount.

He didn't fail to notice as his horse took off at a starting gallop that Catlin hadn't followed him. He heard the wizard yell 'look out' from where he still stood on his horse at the top of the rise.

Valdor continued his run at the two that had just reattached their arms and with lightning fast strokes of his sword took the heads from both of them. He thundered past them and again turned his mount, sending the ground beneath flying from the impact of its hooves. He looked back at where Catlin lay on the ground. Her horse was lying next to her on the ground, one of the wights slashing at its neck and body, tearing the flesh from it in chunks.

Valdor saw another stream of the liquid fire crash into the body of the wight after it halted its slashing and moved towards Catlin. She picked herself up from the ground, her sword still in hand.

Valdor saw the other wights making their way towards her. The holes in their chests were gone.

He galloped over to Catlin, lifted her on to the back of his horse as the Wights got near, and turned back up towards where the wizard still sat, firing out his liquid fire.

As he raced past them, Valdor looked at the two he had decapitated moments before. Their bodies were stooped over, the necks pushed up against their severed heads, the darkness again covering the wounds.

When the two King's Shields reached the wizards' side, they looked back down from the rise and saw all six wights whole again and making their way towards them.

'I feared as much,' was all Heridah said, as he jumped from his stallion and onto Arrow. Fortunately, he had kept his saddle on him. Catlin dropped from the back of Valdor's mount and gracefully slid into the saddle of the stallion Heridah had been riding.

Heridah moved in front of the two King's Shield and cast a wall of air at the approaching wights. It didn't knock them back as he had hoped, but it did stop them from advancing. He continued to push the air at them as they dug their heels into the dirt to stop themselves being pushed backwards. He was thankful they were unable to use any magic themselves, but the magic they had within them was effectively countering his spell of air. He wouldn't be able to keep it up indefinitely, but it at least gave him time to think.

'You two stay where you are,' Heridah barked. 'You will only get in my way now.' He was thankful they heeded his words this time.

He dropped the wind for a moment and sent a fierce wall of fire at them. It was intended to set them on fire, so that the next wall of air he sent would burn them with a heat too intense for their bodies to sustain.

Yet as soon as the fire hit them, it was extinguished. It rolled off their bodies and dissipated into nothing. The wall of air that followed did no more than hold them back as it had before.

They were resistant to plain fire as well as death. That was one less way to finish them off and Heridah was quickly running out of ideas.

He cursed as he struggled to hold the barrier of air in place. The magic within them continued to repel his efforts, forcing him to increase its strength to stop them advancing.

'We need to ride from here,' he said between clenched teeth, as he looked behind at Valdor and Catlin.

Valdor nodded his head as both he and Catlin dug their heels into their mounts and set off at a gallop south.

Heridah did the same as he dropped his wall of air.

Looking back over his shoulder, Heridah saw the wights continuing to follow them. They weren't as fast as the horses, but still moved at a pace quicker than Heridah had hoped.

He didn't know how long they would chase them for and he wasn't keen on pushing his horse too hard.

He quickly caught up to the others and drew level with Valdor.

'I agree with you, Valdor,' Heridah said. 'These creatures need to be destroyed.'

Valdor turned his head to look back.

'Indeed,' the King's Shield replied. 'They don't appear to be giving up the chase.'

Heridah looked back over his shoulder. Although they were dropping behind, they weren't showing any sign of fatigue.

'I have an idea,' Heridah said. 'We need to change direction and head back towards Havern.' He was confident Valdor wouldn't object to that.

'There is a forest between us and the town and I will need the trees.'

'I think we are far enough in front of them now' was all Valdor said, as he dug his right heel into his mount and gently pulled the reins to the left. The others followed him.

The wights immediately changed direction, looking to head them off.

Heridah could see Valdor had calculated correctly. As they got to the bottom of the valley, they spurred their horses on until they were back on the trail again.

The wights were closer again, but soon enough, they put enough distance between them and they fell quickly out of sight.

It wasn't long before the first thick pocket of trees came into view.

Their pace as they entered slowed and Heridah began to look intensely about.

'Are you looking for anything in particular, wizard?' Valdor asked.

'Yes,' was all he said.

He needed a certain type of tree. He knew they grew in these parts and it wasn't long before he saw one growing along the side of the trail they were on.

'I want you two further up the trail in case this doesn't work,' he said as he dismounted. 'And take Arrow with you.'

Valdor looked at him a moment, appeared about to say something, before giving a small nod and taking the reins to the wizard's horse. He and Catlin walked their horses further along the path before stopping and turning back.

Heridah noticed Valdor hand Arrow's reins to Catlin, before turning his attention to the tree.

He took a few paces back from the tree he had selected and began steadily unwrapping the thick vines that were entwined around the trunk of the tree.

He used a combination of wind to gently pry them off and other magical arts he had learnt to communicate with the tree.

It wasn't the same as the bond those of the elven forest had with the trees of Glorfiden. He instead coaxed it in a fashion, to allow him to use the vines to assist with his purpose.

It didn't take him long before he had all of the vines free of the tree, only their thick stalks holding them fast to the trunk.

They hung limp, trailing along the ground around the base of the tree, as the wights bounded into view.

Heridah was surprised how quickly they had caught up. He doubted they would have ever given up the chase. They seemed hell bent on catching them.

Their speed remained constant as they ambled forward.

They seemed to have no fear and showed no surprise as the thick vines of the tree lashed out at them. Numerous vines grabbed hold of the Wights, stopping them in their tracks.

As they struck, the vines wrapped their ends around whatever part of the wights they held. Several of them grabbed each of the wights and held them where they stood.

Heridah waited several moments until he was satisfied they wouldn't be able to tear themselves loose, before turning to Valdor and signalling him forward. He saw their bodies strain as they strove to break free, but they weren't physically powerful enough and couldn't free their hands to shred the vines.

Catlin let the reins of Arrow fall and rode forward with Valdor. She knew the wizard's horse wouldn't run away or bolt in panic.

'What do you need?' Valdor asked, as they approached Heridah.

'I need you to chop the arms from that one's body to start with,' he answered. He fervently hoped this would work. As Valdor drew his sword and stepped forward, Heridah grabbed his arm.

'Be careful not to cut any of the vines. I cannot emphasise that enough.' The wizard knew if it felt any pain the vines would withdraw straight away, leaving them vulnerable to attack from all six goblin wights and no horses to outrun them.

Valdor stepped forward and carefully inspected where he should cut that was clear of vines, but high enough so it wouldn't be able to use the remainder of its arm. The smaller the stump the better.

Cutting one arm just above the elbow and the other almost to the shoulder, he turned to the wizard.

'Do the same for the legs,' Heridah said.

Valdor turned back and saw the vines still had hold of each appendage as they were cut away. There would be no reattaching of limbs while the vines still had hold of them.

He delivered two more precise cuts and the Wight's legs were lifted away.

Valdor stood and awaited his next instruction.

The torso now rested on the ground. The vines had let it fall as the legs were removed, but two still held it in place.

'Now wait,' Heridah said.

Valdor looked at the body and head of the one he had hacked the limbs from. A dark cloud began to form at the severed part of each limb, as it had earlier each time one of them had been critically injured. He saw movement in the middle of the path and looked across at where both arms and legs tugged at the vines that held them. They were trying to pull themselves towards the body that lay on the ground. Whatever dark magic was at play, it wasn't strong enough to break free of the vines.

Satisfied, Heridah turned his attention back to the torso and the head.

'Now give me a moment and you can remove the head,' Heridah said.

Valdor looked on as the vine around its neck unwound and dropped to the ground.

Without waiting for Heridah's instruction, Valdor took the head from its shoulders and kicked it towards where the limbs were being held. The same vine that had just released it snapped around it once more and held it at bay.

The last vine released the torso and Heridah walked over to stand next to Valdor.

'Now I need you to open it up for me. I need to see inside. Let us hope our answer is in there,' the wizard said in a pleasant tone.

Valdor stepped up to the torso and began slicing it open. His sword was sharp and he didn't need to hack at it to open it up. His sword slid through the breast plate without difficulty and he pried the front of the chest open using his hands.

There was no mess. With no blood being pumped around its body, the only thing that appeared to keep it functioning was the black mist-like substance inside. It didn't leak out as Valdor opened it up.

'Now you can step back,' Heridah said, as he moved to stand above it.

He reached towards it with one hand and a fire began inside the Wight's body. It continued to burn this time, much to Heridah's relief.

He intensified the fire, turning up the heat within its outer protections.

As the wizard had hoped, the wights supernaturally enhanced fire protection didn't extend to its insides.

They burned and crackled now until the outer shell was just that. He had the vines let go of the arms and legs and he nodded to himself as they lay limp and unmoving on the ground.

He looked again at Valdor and stood back.

'Five more to go,' was all he said. That and 'be very careful not to cut the vines,' again.

Valdor looked at him without expression, before turning to cut up the rest of the wights. Heridah sent the vines back to the empty torso. They snaked their way around the shell and squeezed tight. Hardened from the wizards' fire, the husks crumbled into small fragments.

Catlin watched for a short time before casually walking back to collect Arrow.

They mounted again after the last of the wights had been dispatched.

The track was wide and all three rode side by side.

'That was well done, wizard,' Valdor said to him after a time of riding in silence.

'I remember telling you before that there are those who use magic that are much stronger within their own element.' He looked at the King's Shield with a fierce look on his face. 'This is my homeland, Valdor, and those abominations should never have come here.'

CHAPTER 36

A Happy Reunion?

JARKENE CAME BACK to himself in time to extinguish the feeble lightning bolt Mort had cast at him. He didn't think it would have caused much hurt even had it struck.

Neither Mendina nor his son made any further move, as he stood there staring at the child he believed had been killed many years ago.

He also made no move towards them.

All three stood there staring at one another for what seemed an eternity until Mendina finally broke the silence.

'Why?' she asked in a voice full of the sadness and horror he suddenly guessed she would have felt eat away at her since the storm arrived over Glorfiden.

Jarkene didn't know how to respond. Anger or contempt he would have known how to handle, but the despair he heard in her voice left him mute.

Faced by the one responsible for the death of her family and home, Mendina was no longer sure of the feelings she felt towards him. He was a lord of the elves and one of the strongest of their kind. He had been one of those responsible for keeping them all safe within their woodland realm since Glorfiden first rose from the ground.

She had been told he died many years ago as punishment for his betrayal of the Lord Nurturer and Protector. Yet here he stood, having just saved them both from a horrible death.

For days, she had felt nothing but hatred for him and disbelief that an elf had been responsible for sending the storm.

Her emotions were at war as he briefly turned his attention to her. His look was without expression or emotion, yet she had seen the look on his face the moment he recognised Mort. It was a look of both shock and extreme sadness. She couldn't reconcile those emotions with what he had done only days before.

He turned back to look at Mort without answering, so she asked her question again.

'Lord Jarkene, why did you do it?' Her voice was still soft and without the hostility she had expected to feel.

He didn't look at her this time, but he finally found his voice. His answer was directed to his son and not to her.

'I thought you were dead,' was all he said.

Hearing him speak, Mort also finally found his voice.

'You abandoned us!' Mort said, with all of the hostility Mendina had been lacking.

'I would never!' Jarkene said in a soft voice, but with renewed passion at hearing his son's accusation. 'I would have given everything I had and more for you and for your mother. Everything.'

'Then why did you leave? Why did you never return? A mighty Lord of the Forest and you couldn't even let us know you were alive!' Mort was screaming at him now, his own pent-up emotions flowing freely.

'I could not, Mortinan, I was. . .' Jarkene paused mid-sentence and looked startled once again.

'Where is your mother?' he asked. He looked desperately at his son now.

Mort looked taken aback by his question but answered him in a voice that Mendina knew. It told her he was far from satisfied with anything his father had told him. 'She is at home still. I left her there after *your* storm killed the elves.'

Jarkene's shock and concern suddenly turned to anger and consternation.

'You left her there alone?! You fool.' He looked at Mendina again. 'The two of you, stay here until I return. Better still, get back to the others that have gone to the centre of the forest. You will be safer with them.'

'What?' Mort responded, still furious at his father. 'She is safe there.'

His father's words took a moment longer to sink in before it dawned on him, for the first time since the creatures had attacked them, that the forest was no longer safe now the elven population had been decimated.

He had been a fool.

Without another word, Jarkene bounded away from the stunned half-elf and his companion and disappeared into the trees of the forest.

After his father vanished amongst the trees, Mort looked to Mendina.

'What have I done?' he said.

'You weren't to know, Mort. Neither of us were.' Mendina was still shocked by what had just happened.

'How could I have left her there?' He lowered his eyes to the ground. 'I should have known it wouldn't be safe there any longer.'

Mendina put her hand on his arm.

Mort looked up at her with a frantic look on his face.

'We have to go back for her.' He walked over to their pack. Mendina followed and grabbed his arm more firmly this time.

'You know we can't, Mort,' she said. Mort looked at her and knew she was right and he hated himself for it. The words the old man had spoken still burned within him.

'Jarkene will get there long before we could. Even after everything he has done, I saw his eyes before he turned to leave. If it is within his powers, he will not let anything happen to her.'

Mort knew she was right again, but he still didn't like it. There was too much he didn't know about why his father had left them and why he had sent the storm to Glorfiden. His need to know was as strong as the compulsion the old man had bestowed upon him. Almost.

If anything happened to his mother, there was nothing else he wanted to hear from his father. He would be dead to him again.

Mort's stomach churned and his thoughts were in turmoil as they collected up their supplies and continued their journey.

He didn't notice the look of consternation on the face of Mendina as they approached the boundary of the forest and the look of terror as she stepped beyond the last of the trees and into a field of grass.

There was no track for them to follow. There were no tracks into or out of Glorfiden.

Neither of them knew where they were headed, nor who or what they would meet on their travels.

They knew only the need to follow the compulsion in their mind and the constant pull to a land far beyond their own.

'How is it?' Mort asked, when he finally looked at Mendina and saw the fear and pain in her eyes. 'I apologise for not checking with you earlier.'

'It is bearable, Mort, and not as bad as I thought it would be. It is a strange feeling and pains me only a little, but it still feels wrong. I don't belong here and I fear it is only going to get worse.' She looked to put a brave face on, trying to smile for Mort's benefit, but all it did was shift his concern from his mother to her.

'If I could help you with it, I would.' He felt helpless. The son of an elven lord indeed. He couldn't even protect her from wolves.

Mendina sighed and shook her head slowly from side to side.

'Mort, we both need to try and forget those worries we have no control over and concentrate on what we can do to get to the end of this journey. I fear it will not be an easy one.' He agreed with that assumption.

'I know,' he said. 'I am not ready to fight anything. We will be an easy target for anything evil walking the land and it will be slow going without horses.'

Mendina looked at him sharply. 'You can be ready, Mort, but you need time to practice . . . and you need a staff.'

He gave her a confused look and then recalled that his father had carried one with him.

'What do I need a staff for?' he asked.

'All of the elven lords carry one, Mort. Each lord shapes one for himself using wood from our oldest trees. From those trees found in the centre of Glorfiden.' They continued walking as they spoke, the terrain not difficult. Mainly grass and gentle slopes were all they had to traverse as they travelled.

'Those trees are no more,' Mort said in response, knowing it was a harsh thing to say. He was still in a foul mood and he was too tired to fully think through the words coming out of his mouth.

Mendina didn't react to it as he had feared she would, after he realised what he had said.

'I know, Mort, but the staves were crafted from fallen branches, not cut from the living tree itself. Unfortunately, there is only one person left who would be able to help you with its making.' Neither of them needed to say who that one person was.

'So what do I need a staff for?' Mort asked.

'The staves the lords have store large reserves of the magic that lives in Glorfiden,' Mendina explained. 'It is absorbed into the wood and allows the user to draw magic from it no matter where they travel. They can augment their own reserves of magic.'

Mort could see how that would assist them in their travels. Without question he knew that he needed one.

'There is nothing we can do about it now, Mendina. It could take us days to track down Jarkene. Even then I don't know if I would allow him to help me. You and I still have many questions we have yet to ask him.'

Mendina knew they couldn't turn around even if they chose to. The pull the idol had over them was too strong. It wasn't something either of them could fight against by returning to the forest and waiting for Jarkene to return.

Mendina would have to do her best helping his powers reach the next level and she knew he would need to learn fast.

Neither of them were familiar with the land they now moved through or the lands they would have to go through in order to reach their destination.

Mendina was away from Glorfiden for the first time in her life and she was terrified. Without magic, all they had to defend themselves was the knife she carried on her belt. A pitiful defence.

'Mortinan?' Mendina broke the silence and Mort stopped to look at her.

'We should stop for a while if we can. You need instruction on your magic.' She was trying hard to keep it together and a distraction now would help with that.

Mort nodded his head but didn't say anything. Mendina realised he, too, was fighting his own internal demons.

'As I said before, Mort, concentration and confidence are very important aspects of using magic.' She was gladdened by the serious look on his face, regardless of the reason for it. She hoped he could use the anger and sadness to focus on what he was doing.

He remained silent as she stood there looking at him.

'First of all, you need to know that you are very powerful.' She needed him to believe that now. It was time for him to grow up.

He raised his eyebrows to her. 'So people keep telling me,' he said.

'If your father hadn't arrived when he did, Mort, we would have been killed in the forest. Killed in the place where you are most powerful.' She had no time to be gentle with him. He had to stop feeling sorry for himself.

'I am well aware of that, Mendina,' he said in a quiet voice, a little of the anger she was after coming through in his words. There was still self-pity though, and she needed to get rid of that.

'So when it happens next, will you freeze again, Mort, or will you step up and fight?'

She tried to keep any emotion from her face as she spoke.

Mort looked confused at her words and a little hurt.

'Do you think I did it deliberately?' he asked. 'I have no experience fighting evil men and blood wolves. What did you expect me to do?' His voice got louder as he spoke.

'It doesn't matter what I expected, Mort. What happened is over. You can dwell on it and feel sorry for yourself, or you can learn from it and try to do better next time.' She didn't take her eyes from his. She could see in his eyes he was afraid.

'How did you cast a lightning bolt at your father?' She intended to keep at him. The compulsion within her was a small, dull ache only. They had time for this. They needed to make time for this.

'I can see the magic, remember,' he still spoke as if the world were on his shoulders. 'I didn't just see the lightning, Mendina, I saw how the magic formed to create it. It looked complex, but when I cast it at him it didn't seem so hard. It was pitifully weak, but the form was how it should be.'

'So we need to focus on putting more power into it.' She didn't know how she could teach him that. In truth, she didn't really know how she could do anything other than try and get him to concentrate at a time when he needed to the most.

'I guess so,' he said, still not sounding convinced. 'So why were you unable to do anything against the wolves or those things that cast magic?'

Mendina didn't think he meant for his words to sound so condescending and rude, so she tried not to look at him too harshly.

'In Glorfiden, there were those of us trained in battle. Trained to use magic and weapons to defend our home. Those of us, such as Palir and the group he was with, would also go hunting and range along the borders of the forest to protect it against those foolish enough to try and enter.' She could see he was listening intently to her now.

'There were also those among us that weren't trained this way. I was among those elves that grew up learning about the forest and the creatures within it. My skills range from communicating with the trees and fey creatures, to collecting the berries and plants that can be made into powerful tonics and potions, or simply to add as a spice to flavour the meals we eat.' This was the reason she felt so helpless trying to help Mort now. He needed someone such as Palir to teach him. This was one reason she was so saddened when she realised he would never accept Mort as one of them.

Mendina looked at him intently now. His features and eyes didn't portray any disappointment in them, which surprised her.

'This is why it will be difficult for me to help you, Mort,' she continued. 'You need to learn how to use your magic to fight. To slay our enemies and keep us safe until we reach where it is the idol is located. I fear I will be nothing more than a burden on our travels.' She looked away from him this time. She didn't know why his acceptance of her was so important. He was young and foolish and at times a complete idiot.

When she felt his hand cup her chin and lift her face to look at him, she no longer felt the anger and resentment she had before when he touched her.

'You will never be a burden to me, Mendina.' He spoke in a very serious voice, yet with the same mischievous look in his eyes as when she first looked upon him. 'I will do better.'

She kept looking at him for longer than was proper, until she gently moved his hand from her face and stepped back from him.

He grinned at her. A genuine smile that made her forget her pain and frustration for that moment.

'Teach me how to focus my powers and the next time something attempts to harm you . . . us,' he added after a short pause, 'it will regret doing so.'

'Now that it comes time to help you, I am at a loss as to how I can.' Mendina knew she must look pitiful to him right now, yet he persisted.

'I'm aware you can sense the trees and their emotions, but how else do you communicate with them? Can you control them or other creatures?' The intensity was back in his voice now, but Mendina was horrified as she thought about what he suggested.

'Never!' she said. 'I do not ever try to control them. They are free and beautiful and cherished by all elves, not slaves to our whims.'

Mort didn't look taken aback by her reply, instead he had a small smile on his face.

'Yet I assume you can make your feelings known to them?' he asked. 'How do you do that?'

'It is just something I do, Mort. I reach out to them and they know what I am thinking, in a fashion.' She didn't know why he looked so pleased with himself. 'How can any of that help you?'

'Have you tried to communicate with anything since we left Glorfiden?' he asked.

'No,' she replied. She had been too busy trying to control her feelings to even attempt it. Plus none of the trees or creatures looked the same as those within her home. She didn't think she could, so she hadn't tried.

'Even if I could,' she continued, 'I still don't see why I would need to try.'

'Come with me,' was all he said, as he gently took her arm and walked her over to the nearest tree. It was a pine tree, the floor underneath padded with its fallen needles. There were a number of them scattered throughout the lands here. Closer to the Dwarven Mountains, they grew in much thicker groves.

'Can you sense what it is feeling, Mendina?' he asked her, as he let her arm go and turned around to look at it.

She looked at the tree and reached her senses out to it. To her surprise, it responded as clearly as if she were still standing within Glorfiden.

'What is it thinking?' Mort asked without even turning to look at her.

'It is healthy and it is content. The soil it reaches its roots into is fertile and the ground solid. It wants for nothing.' She stopped as he turned to look at her with a smile on his face. 'But you already knew that,' she said.

'I did,' he confessed to her, 'but this next part I do not.' He looked back at the tree. 'There is a family of parfils living inside this tree. I can see one of them on one of the higher branches. Can you see it?'

Mendina looked up and saw him. A small animal, they had long, soft fur and lived off the seeds within the pine cones. They were harmless, but rather shy. They lived in trees on the outskirts of Glorfiden, but sometimes came further in to collect other foods when the cones weren't in season.

'I do, Mort, but why are we wasting our time doing this? You need to learn other magic, not amuse yourself with what I can do.'

'Can you get him to come down to us?' Mort continued to ignore her. 'Please?' he asked, obviously seeing the frustrated look on her face.

Mendina sighed and turned back to the parfil. She sent a small wave of magic towards it, filling it with feelings of security and trust towards her. As soon as it reached the parfil, it began scurrying along the branch it was on and down the trunk of the tree. It stopped at a level on the trunk equal to their faces and turned its head to look at Mendina.

'Now get it to come to you,' Mort said, his voice serious again.

Mendina put forth feelings of need and a small amount of urgency and the parfil scurried to the ground and stopped at her feet, its large eyes looking up at her.

'Can we get back to what we should be doing now?' Mendina asked, as she thanked the parfil with feelings of gratitude, letting it know all was well again.

'We are already doing it,' Mort said.

'Mort, you need to take this seriously. Our lives depend on it!' Mendina's patience had run dry.

'I saw how you controlled it,' he said.

'I did not control it,' she replied, offended he would even suggest it.

'Would it have come to you otherwise?' Mort asked.

'Of course not,' she said. 'But I didn't make it come to me. I simply conveyed how I was feeling and it reacted accordingly.'

'Did it?' Mort asked, holding up his hand to stop her responding. 'Let me explain how I see it,' he said.

'Go ahead,' Mendina said in a sharp voice.

'I understand it could sense your intentions were not to cause it any harm. It may even have sensed you have a good and peaceful heart. However, it doesn't know you, it couldn't know you. Now tell me if I am wrong,' he continued, 'but the parfil's natural instinct is to flee from anything bigger than it, anything that could be a danger. They certainly don't go out of their way to help people.'

Mendina was trying to understand where he was going, but her frustration just seemed to be growing.

'I'm not following you. Will you get to the point, Mort?'

He stopped and looked to be thinking for a moment.

'I watched you with the parfil, Mendina. I saw exactly what you did and it is magic that you used. I could see it.' He paused again before continuing. 'I saw that man that shot the fireballs in the forest doing exactly the same thing with the blood wolves that attacked us.'

'Do what?' she asked. She was not comfortable at where he was going with this.

'He did what you did, but instead of sending a magical wave of good intention, I am guessing he was sending waves of evil intent. I'm almost certain he would have put the suggestion in the wolves' heads that he was much stronger and would kill them if they didn't do what they were ordered to. Wolves follow the strongest within their pack. That man made sure through his magical suggestion that the wolves knew who their pack leader was.' Mort was looking intently at her now.

He was comparing me to that foul Dark-Mage?!

Yet before she said the first thing that came to mind, Mendina thought more on what he was saying. Was what she did truly magic that compelled creatures to do what she wanted?

Mort must have anticipated what she might be thinking and spoke again before she responded.

'I am not insulting you, Mendina. I don't for a moment think what you do is in any way wrong or evil. Befriending the creatures of the forest is a far cry from controlling wild beasts to do your bidding. However, it could be important to our chances of survival.'

'How?' she asked, still not happy with him comparing her to the Mage.

'What if I could use it on people?' He spoke as if it were something he would like to do, was almost excited at the prospect.

Mendina was speechless and the shock must have shown on her face.

'If I could do it, Mendina, I would only do it on our enemies.' He was defensive now.

'I don't think it can be done,' was all she could say.

'How do you know that?' he persisted. 'Have you ever tried it before? Has anyone ever tried it before that you know of?'

She couldn't think of a time when she had ever contemplated performing such an act. It seemed evil to her and she had never heard it spoken of by any elf before.

'Of course not, Mort. Those who fight to defend our borders use more direct methods, which is what I think you should concentrate on.' She knew he wouldn't be able to convince her to feel differently about it. 'You already know how to use electricity. You just need to learn how to focus your power more. To channel the magic that is within you and control it, so it becomes a natural part of you. Only then will you be able to do more with it.'

He appeared to think about what she was saying and eventually nodded his head.

'Okay,' he said finally. 'Let's get started then.'

Mort looked around at their surroundings and pointed to a large group of rocks at the base of a gentle slope only about thirty paces away.

'Let's see if I can hit them with a bolt of lightning shall we?'

Mendina nodded. She was still sceptical. He had agreed with her far too quickly and easily, but this is what she wanted. She let their previous conversation go. For now.

She looked on as he furrowed his brow and held his hands out before him.

The air in front of him crackled as his magic pulsed and a short burst of electrical power shot forth from his outstretched hands. It sizzled through the air and hit the rocks with a muffled crack before dissipating into nothing.

Mort took a deep breath and tried again before Mendina could say anything, but the result was the same. If there was something alive and resting on the nearest rock, then it may have received a mild tickle.

'I don't understand why it isn't working?' Mort said, obviously frustrated with his effort. 'It looks the same as that which Jarkene cast, but without any force behind it.'

He looked at Mendina.

'What is the most difficult thing you do when you use your magic?' he asked. 'What is it that takes the most out of you?'

Mendina thought for a moment.

'If a plant or tree is sick or dying I can use my magic to heal it?' she replied.

'How big does it need to be to make it really hard for you?' Mort asked.

'It doesn't matter what size it is, Mort. Even a sapling takes a lot to nurse it quickly back to health.' She was regularly using her magic for these tasks. She hated seeing one of the trees or plants within Glorfiden suffering.

'So if I were to break a branch off this tree, you would need to use a lot of magic to heal it?'

Mendina's eyes widened in shock and anger.

'Don't you dare speak of doing such a thing.' What was wrong with him? Hurting trees and taking over the minds of people. She was starting to worry where his mind was at.

Mort blushed and looked down at the ground.

'I'm sorry, Mendina. I spoke without thinking.' He looked up at her again and she saw he was truly abashed at what he had said.

'But I need to see you heal something.' He began looking around them again. 'Can you see anything you might be able to help?'

Mendina looked around and swept the area with her senses, trying to locate anything that appeared to be in distress.

'I see nothing,' she said eventually. 'Usually when there are many trees together there are those that struggle to get enough sunlight, or the ground they are in is too soggy or dry. There aren't enough trees around here and the ground is fertile.'

Mort continued to look at her. 'What else then? What else can you do?'

Again, she knew he didn't mean it to sound so insulting, but she was still annoyed at his earlier suggestions.

'What else is this worthless female elf capable of?' She snapped at him. 'Is that what you meant to ask?'

His eyes opened wide and then narrowed.

'You know that isn't what I meant, but if you want to act like a child then we aren't going to achieve anything today.'

'I think it is time we kept moving,' she said and he nodded in agreement, picking up his backpack and flinging it over his shoulder. They started off again towards the east.

Neither of them said anything more for the rest of the day. They left each other to their own thoughts.

The following morning, they awoke and walked out of the small cave they had spent the night in. Mendina had stumbled upon it as the sun was making its final farewell the previous day. Although bone tired, they had checked it carefully and were both relieved to find nothing appeared to have inhabited it for a few seasons at least.

They saw that the weather had changed as soon as they opened their eyes and looked out of the opening. The rain wasn't heavy, but it had settled in. Mort knew they were going to be drenched before they got far.

'This may give me the opportunity to show you that which I was unable to do yesterday,' Mendina said as she stood and stretched.

Mort looked at her as she held her arms out. Her figure was silhouetted in the opening behind her and he failed to comprehend what she had said. He lay there staring at her instead. He had slept well for the first time in many days and was feeling better than he had since the storm had first struck the forest and changed his life forever.

'Did you hear what I said?' Mendina said to him. Her face came into focus as she stooped down to talk to him.

'Oh,' Mort stammered. 'Ah, no I didn't sorry. Something about yesterday?'

He saw her eyes narrow before she stood up straight again and turned to pick up her things.

'The rain may be a blessing for us.' She spoke in a louder voice this time.

Mort stretched as he lay on his bedroll.

'There is no hurry, is there? I don't feel the pull at all yet.' He felt no urgency to step out into the rain.

She turned to him again.

'This is the time we need to practice, Mort,' she said impatiently. 'And now that it is raining, I can show you something with my magic. Something that takes quite a bit of effort on my part.'

That certainly got his attention. Mort hopped up and quickly packed his bedroll. He didn't even bother grabbing something to eat. They could do that while they were travelling.

'Show me,' he said. He hoped that whatever she showed him would help with his own magic. If it didn't, then he was terrified he would never get the opportunity to wield magic in a way they were both in sore need of. They would be next to helpless against anything with considerable strength or powers.

'There are seasons when there is little rain in some parts of the forest.' Mendina started talking as they both stood at the entrance. Mort waited for her to step out, but she stayed in the dry cave for now.

'When it does come, much of it is captured by those trees that reach taller into the canopy. Those at the bottom get less or none at all. It is my job to distribute that water so that none of the plants or smaller trees go without.'

Mort was intrigued and his excitement was building as he listened to her.

'There is obviously no need for me to do that here, but I can still show you how it is done. It can be taxing on me.' She looked at him as she finished speaking.

'You know I will help if you are too fatigued afterward,' he said. He hoped he had read her expression correctly. She nodded to him and turned back to the entrance, before stepping out into the rain.

She stopped after only a few paces and held out both of her hands, her palms facing outward as if she were trying to push something. Mort followed her into the rain and stood next to her, but far enough to her side so he could see clearly everything she did.

He saw the magic begin to flow from her hands and spread out into the air before her. The raindrops falling in front of her slowed and then stopped. Before long, there was a pool of water hovering in the air, which continued to grow as more and more drops were collected into it.

Mort watched as the pool of water was steadily moved to her right and lowered towards the ground. He saw how she was able to direct it into the soil. Not with a splash, but in a controlled flow. He saw how much of her magic she used while doing it and it didn't seem a great deal to him. He was about to voice his disappointment when he noticed a greater flow come from her hands as she moved each one separately. The water that had pooled above the ground was now branching off in different directions, as a river of water would do if it come up against a barrier of some sort. The barrier this water was coming up against was her magic. She was forming not only several shields, but she was using the magic to help it into the ground as well.

Mort was fascinated at the control she was displaying and also with the amount of magic she was now having to use.

This continued for several minutes, Mendina progressively putting up more shields and redirecting the flow, while all the while increasing the amount of water she was pooling from the rain drops as they fell.

She didn't stop until Mort finally put his hand on her shoulder. 'I have seen enough,' he said softly to her. She would have fallen hard into the turf if Mort hadn't been quick enough to grab her.

'I'm just a little dizzy,' she said, as she gently pushed out of his embrace. 'Just give me a moment.'

Mort let her stand by herself but remained hovering at her side in case she hadn't fully recovered herself.

When he was satisfied she was okay, he stepped back a couple of paces, but kept his eyes focused on her.

She eventually looked up at him with a faint smile. 'That was more taxing than I remember,' she finally said.

'You are away from Glorfiden now,' Mort said. 'There is no source here to supplement your strength.'

Mendina nodded at his words. 'Did it help?' she asked.

'You tell me,' he said, as he turned his attention to a large boulder sitting atop a nearby rise.

Although he couldn't see the magic that was inside Mendina, he had seen how it looked as it left her. The moment it was released he saw that the strands were connected. What was most pleasing to him, however, was that when Mendina drew more magic out, those strands pulled sharply and their speed increased. Up until now when he had tried to increase his strength, he had tried to draw the magic out in greater quantities all at once. To pool it and force it out. He had been trying to make those strands bulge with the magic and release them in a burst. He saw now they didn't work that way.

The strands couldn't expand, they just moved faster as they exited the body. Once released, the magic could then be treated accordingly. It could be sent in different directions or it could be intermingled with the environment and made to impact en masse at a target. But not until it was out. That was where Mort's frustration and failures had stemmed from.

He stretched only one of his arms out now and pointed it directly at the large rock. He saw the magic begin to leave him and as it did he drew the moisture and heat to him. Then with a powerful gust of wind, he sent a crackling bolt of lightning straight at the rock. He didn't attempt to force the magic out this time but simply pulled at it as he had seen Mendina do.

Small fragments of rock flew away from the boulder as his lightning bolt impacted it. He was surprised at how little damage it did, though. He thought for sure it had been a powerful one.

He looked across at Mendina and saw a smile on her face.

'You did it,' she said to him in a soft voice, full of emotion.

Mort wasn't as thrilled, but his attention was quickly drawn back to the boulder his bolt had struck. It made a loud roaring noise, a sound like a roar of pain and anger. The large rock looked to unfurl itself, as he saw a tail and then a huge head, as it turned around to look at them.

He knew his eyes would have been as wide as Mendina's as he looked back at her.

'What is that?!' he said in disbelief.

She shook her head. 'I have no idea. But I don't think it is happy.'

Mort looked back at the boulder as it turned two dark and baleful eyes in his direction. It was unlike anything he had ever seen before.

He had seen felines before. There were many small ones in Mayfield. Not all friendly, but none of them large enough or aggressive enough to ever be a threat. Some people even kept them as companions.

He had also seen larger ones in the wild around his home. This looked very similar to a feline, only it was bigger than a horse and was covered from head to toe in something that made it look like it was made of rock.

So far, it hadn't made any move towards them. After turning its head towards them, it had remained standing where it was. The eyes continued to stare though, unblinking eyes that put the fear of death into both of them.

Mort felt the compulsion for them to move hit him strongly at that moment and he groaned. Not from the pain, but from the knowledge that their new friend was in their line of travel. They would need to make a wide berth and it may take them well out of their way. That is if it didn't just charge at them.

'Now would be a good time to see if you can charm this delightful-looking creature,' Mort said as he began to walk slowly around it.

'It might be hard to convince after you just sent a lightning bolt into it,' she replied as she kept pace with him.

Mort kept his eyes focused on the rock feline, but still saw Mendina out of the corner of his eye as she reached out a hand towards it.

'I can't read its thoughts at all,' she said to him in a panicked voice. 'You need to try something, Mort.'

His mind was racing. The lightning bolt had little effect on it, other than angering it. He assumed it was angry, even though it had made no move towards them yet.

They had gone barely fifteen paces when a man crested the rise in front of them and stood next to the black-eyed beast.

'I would advise neither of you come any closer,' he said to them. He was an older man, with long strands of grey hair shooting out from his skull in all directions. He was dressed in a ripped and dirty robe but he spoke in a clear voice, full of confidence and sanity.

'We have already decided to heed that advice, I assure you,' Mort said to him as they both stopped. 'I meant no harm to your friend. I thought it just a rock.'

He saw the old man frown and then furrow his brow in confusion.

'I can assure you we are not a threat.' Mendina said loudly to him. 'We are happy to continue on our way.'

They both started walking again.

'You can stop for a moment to talk?' the old man asked. 'It is not often I get to see an elf from Glorfiden in these parts. Or should I say ever.' He paused before finishing. 'And whatever it is you are, no disrespect intended.'

Mort was a little insulted, but he understood his confusion. Many people in Mayfield had looked at him the same, even after they knew who he was.

'We are in kind of a hurry,' Mort said to him as they continued walking. 'Also, I'm not sure how delighted your friend is with the lightning bolt I just hit him with.'

'Her,' the old man said.

'What?' Mort replied.

'My friend is a "she" and "she" is no longer angered at what you did. She assures me you have no evil intent within your heart. No evil towards her or me anyway,' he added.

Mendina grabbed Mort by the arm to stop him walking. 'Maybe we should speak with him for a short time,' she said. 'I think if they meant us harm they would have tried already.'

Mort wasn't so convinced. He had grown up as a friendly and welcoming person, but recent events had taught him caution and mistrust. Plus he had Mendina to worry about now. He intended to keep her out of harm's way as best he could.

'We are in a hurry, Mendina. We need to get back to the forest.' Mort still didn't trust the way the female rock-cat was looking at him.

'He may be able to help you with your magic,' she said.

Mort looked more intently at Mendina now. 'I have already learnt a lot, Mendina. The greatest obstacle I had I have already overcome. Plus how do you know he even uses magic?' He was beginning to wonder why she was so keen to speak with him.

'Do you think that thing with him was born that way?' she asked. 'Plus I think he is controlling it. Can you see whether he is?'

Mort looked back at the old man. Neither he nor his companion had moved. He seemed content for Mort and Mendina to chat first. He couldn't see any magic coming from either the man or the beast.

'Nothing,' he said to her.

'Well you were the one who was so curious about compelling people. This may be your opportunity to find out if you can?' Mendina persisted. 'I definitely think we should speak with him.'

Mort thought for a moment before nodding his head. She smiled at him, which he thought odd, but followed her as she started walking towards them.

Mort had to pull her up a short distance from them.

'I think this is close enough,' he said to her softly.

'Even up close I am unable to say what race of men you are from,' he said. Mort was feeling a little uncomfortable at the way the man was staring at him. He had a strange look on his face. This close he was more than a little unnerved at the size of the rock feline. Its entire body was covered in rock plating, but unlike any rock he had seen before. It was all fairly smooth, but followed the contours of its different body parts. The only thing not covered were its eyes, ears, and mouth.

He could see now that the darkness of its eyes came from something glowing at the edge of where the rocks covered them. The eyes themselves were a dark yellow and not black. The darkness had him confused, but he couldn't say if it were magic or not. It was nothing he had seen before.

'I am of no race,' was all Mort said in reply.

The old man smiled, nodded slowly and turned his focus to Mendina.

'It is truly a pleasure to finally meet one of the elves of Glorfiden.' He bowed in welcome. 'My name is Travis and I once lived in the greatest city of men, but chose the isolation of this area instead, many years ago.'

'Hello, Travis,' Mendina said pleasantly to him. 'I am Mendina.'

'Well met, Mendina,' he said, still smiling. 'And who is your charming companion?'

'This is Mortinan,' she said. 'His mother is human and his father an elf, which is why you were confused as to his heritage. Unfortunately, most of my people have been wiped out during an evil storm only days before and we venture to the east to retrieve. . .'

Mort was shocked as the words kept pouring out of her mouth. He grabbed her arm and turned her a little too forcefully to face him. She didn't even look angry at him for doing it.

Mort looked at Travis.

'What do you want?' he asked harshly. He knew he had done something to Mendina.

The old man continued to look at him as if he were trying to work out what to say.

'A half-breed,' he said. It sounded like he was talking more to himself than to Mort. 'Absolutely fascinating.'

Mort waited for him to continue.

'I am simply curious as to why the two of you are here, walking towards my home and away from your own.' Travis said. He didn't sound threatening, but Mort was on edge. It wasn't just the large rock-cat either. Something felt very wrong about Travis.

'If we are intruding then I apologise. We obviously don't know this area. If you could show me the best way to go to avoid your home, we will walk that way.' Mort didn't think that he would.

'Nonsense. We aren't far from my home actually, so you may as well come and rest a while before you continue. It can be a dangerous place for those who don't know what to look out for.' His smile didn't leave his face.

'I think we should take him up on his offer, Mort,' Mendina chimed in. 'I trust him, so can you.'

'That did it,' Mort thought. No more games.

'What have you done to her?' he asked.

Travis actually looked surprised and a little hurt by his words.

'I don't know what you mean?' he replied. 'I mean neither of you harm. As I said, I am fascinated to meet an elf and a. . .' he left the sentence incomplete.

'My name is Mortinan,' Mort replied. 'And we need to be on our way.'

The smile finally left Travis' face.

'I must insist,' he said, as he turned to Mendina and held his hand out. 'Come with me my beautiful elf.'

Mort saw it this time. Whatever magic he had been using had been invisible to him before for some reason, but as he reached his hand out to Mendina, Mort saw the tiniest of black strands flow from his hand and surround her head. The strands gently seeped into her as she started walking towards him.

Mort knew he had to be careful. He knew Travis' companion, although still, was ready to move at a moment's notice. He also knew it would be able to kill him with very little effort.

'I can't let you take her,' Mort said to him with all the bravado he could muster.

'Oh you'll be coming, too,' he said nonchalantly. 'You fascinate me even more than she does. Yet you don't even know why.'

Mort's mind was churning, but he decided force wasn't his best choice . . . yet.

'Of course I know why,' Mort said, as Mendina reached Travis' side and turned back to face Mort, a smile on her face and a blank look in her eyes.

Mort almost lost it at that moment, but pulled himself together before he did something that might get them both killed.

Travis didn't reply, he just looked at him with a funny look on his face.

'Do you know why it doesn't work on me?' Mort asked, trying to sound as calm as he could. 'I assume we can end the charade now?' he added.

'I guess we can,' Travis replied. 'I assume it is because you are a half-breed and have some kind of immunity. I am looking forward to finding out how that works.'

'I can tell you and save you the trouble,' Mort said.

'I'm listening,' Travis replied.

'After I have told you, I will not ask you again. I will expect you to release Mendina and send your pet away. I won't give you any more chances after that.' Even though he knew it was a bluff, deep inside Mort could feel the anger burning within him. He knew he wasn't going to let this man take her with him.

'I believe if you were capable of that young man, you would have done it already. The bolt you cast at my "pet" didn't appear very effective to me.' His smile was back.

'I was simply showing Mendina something,' Mort said. He hoped he was a good bluffer. He hadn't ever had to try and bluff people much before.

'So what is it you have to tell me?' Travis asked.

'Mendina forgot to tell you something about my elven heritage.' Here goes he thought. 'My father's name is Jarkene. The last remaining lord of the elves and the new Protector and Nurturer. I assume that is why your paltry spell has no effect on me.'

Mort saw Travis' eyes open wide. He didn't even try to mask his surprise.

'Let her go and we will be on our way,' Mort said in a voice full of the anger he now felt surfacing.

'The son of an elven lord,' Travis said. He sounded even more excited. Not the reaction Mort had been hoping for. 'That is something truly amazing. Not yet into his full powers either I am assuming.'

Mort readied himself.

'You two will be the crowning glory to my collection. Hopefully I will be able to use your services one day, my elven prince.' He turned to his companion. 'Don't hurt him too badly. I want him in one piece.'

The great stone-covered feline leapt at Mort as soon as the words had left Travis' mouth. It was so close Mort knew it would be on him in a single bound.

'He is trying to get you killed. I am not your enemy.' Unlike Mendina's gentle coaxing with the parfil, Mort used very little finesse. It was almost like a blow, as he sent all the magic he could into the mind of the beast. He saw the smaller black strands that Travis used seep from its head as his magic forced it out.

The beast landed on the ground in front of him and stopped. It was so close Mort could feel its breath on his face.

'Run while you can!' He poured more of his magic into it, his words filled with as much urgency as he could muster. He had no idea what effect so much would have on the beast, but it suddenly turned and ran, bounding away with huge leaps towards the mountains in the distance.

Mort saw the threads of Travis' magic reaching after it, but he blew them away with a gust of wind, his hands outstretched now as he turned his attention back to the old man.

He noticed he was no longer smiling. It had been replaced with a panicked look.

'I warned you, old man,' Mort said to him. He heard his own voice but didn't recognise it. There was no emotion in it.

Travis held his hands up in front of himself, but not in a threatening manner.

'I have released her,' he said and then looked down in horror at the small dagger embedded in his stomach, just below his rib cage.

Mendina pulled the knife out and stepped back from him.

'Your death won't be quick,' she spat the words at him. 'You don't deserve a quick one.'

Mort watched on in satisfaction as Travis collapsed to his knees, his hands pushed into his stomach trying to stem the flow of blood.

'Let's go,' Mort said quietly to Mendina. He had seen that look on her face before. Luckily for him, her dagger had only pricked him on that occasion.

Mendina stooped over and wiped her blade on the grass before returning it to the sheath on her belt. She followed Mort as he walked to the crest of the rise and they both looked down into the hidden valley below them.

The first thing they noticed was the house situated at the bottom. It was a large one, with several chimneys and a sizeable stable next to it.

The second thing they noticed were the myriad of boulders scattered around the house and throughout the small valley. The valley wasn't a deep one, but it was almost circular, as if something had dropped a large, round rock on to the ground from a great height. Mort looked around and saw one large boulder at each point of the compass, at the top of each rise. It appeared that Travis had guards surrounding his entire home. Mort also noticed the distinct lack of any trees. The old man was certainly not trusting of strangers. From the house he would be able to see everything that moved within his little valley.

They looked at each other.

'Should we go around?' Mendina asked.

Mort thought it would be probably be a good idea, but he was curious to see what was down there. Some of the rock formations were scattered about the valley, but closer to the house they were formed up in rows. From this distance, he could see that many differed in sizes and shape, but he was unable to tell exactly what they were.

'I would like to have a closer look,' he said and Mendina eventually nodded in agreement.

'I admit I would like to see what that evil man has been up to. Maybe there are some other creatures down there you can free, Mort. It looks like he has more of those big cats around the top.'

Mort nodded and they began walking down, ignoring the weakened pleas for help coming from behind them.

Neither of them knew what manner of creature the first rock was they came to. It appeared curled up and showed only the plates of rock covering its long body. Except for the human-like head staring emptily into the sky. The eyes were open and had pupils that stretched across the entire eye, as a snake does. It also had no nose, only small slits. Its mouth was closed, but the lips stretched across its face, much larger than that of a man.

'Can you read the thoughts of this one?' Mort asked Mendina, but she shook her head.

'There is only darkness, almost like a fog. I cannot help it.'

Mendina continued walking and Mort followed her.

Mort had tried to look into its mind as well and saw the same thing. It was different to how the big cats' mind had looked. He assumed it was because Travis had been controlling it at the time. It had allowed Mort to access it and send his own magic inside.

They came across several other creatures on their way to the first of the rows close to the house. Some they vaguely recognised, others were even stranger than the snake with the human-like head. They all had the same blackness within their minds.

The rocks formed up were in rows and a well-worn path ran in between them. They were like statues, Mort thought.

Unlike most of those they had seen so far, neither had difficulty recognising what these all were. Some were standing, some sitting, and some looked posed. They were all human and each one was covered in the same rock plates, only their faces showing.

Most of them looked like soldiers dressed in full battle armour, some of them holding weapons in their hands. The weapons, like their faces, were the only parts not covered in stone.

Mort counted twelve on either side. Six were women of varying ages and four children, the youngest no older than five.

'What is going on here?' Mendina voiced what they were both thinking. 'Who are all these people?'

Mort didn't answer her straight away. He saw there were rows of people leading away from the house on both sides and he assumed they would be there on the other side of the house as well. He couldn't help notice that the row leading towards the mountain consisted entirely of children.

'I don't know,' Mort said, standing in front of the youngest child within the row.

'We have to help them,' Mendina said. 'We can't leave them like this. I know what it feels like to be violated by that man.' She looked at Mort and her eyes looked haunted. 'The horror of their existence is almost too much to describe.'

'Their minds are the same as the other creatures in the valley,' Mort said. 'I don't know how to get rid of the darkness that shrouds their heads.'

Then a thought occurred to him.

'Perhaps there is another way to release them,' he said. 'But it could be dangerous. We don't know what could happen if all those other things out there are released from their bonding.'

'You think if we kill him then the enchantment will end?' Mendina had obviously been thinking the same thing.

'I think it likely that it will,' Mort said. 'I think the stones are bound to them with a dark magic similar to that he was using to control the big cat. I could see it around the eyes when it came close to me.'

'Should we go back up there and finish him?' Mendina asked. 'That will keep us at a safe distance.'

Mort didn't know what they should do. The ones in this row might be able to defend themselves, but the children in the other row would not. Some of the beasts scattered around looked powerful and unlikely to be friendly after their captivity.

'Those down here may not be able to protect themselves from the horrors in this valley,' he said. 'Also, some of these men may turn on us,' Mort said. 'I think we should wait over where the row of children are, unless it takes him longer to die than I hope.'

Mendina nodded in agreement and they walked over to the other row.

'They're not children,' Mort said as he got close to the first one.

Mendina stopped where she was as soon as she saw the first one.

'We definitely don't want to be here if these are set free,' was all she said, walking back over to the other row. Mort followed her.

'I think those dwarves will be more than capable of looking after themselves,' he said unnecessarily.

'We should go back up to Travis,' she said to him. 'I got a glimpse of what was on the other side of the house, Mort. They are definitely not human.'

Mort led the way back up the rise.

They had just passed the human-headed snake when they heard a noise behind them.

Mort turned and saw the remaining stones that covered the creature fall to the ground around it.

Two green-coloured eyes looked at him and held a look of murder within them.

It hissed and the head lifted up high, its body coiling underneath it.

A bright yellow substance shot from its mouth as it spat at him. Mort jumped clear just in time, as Mendina leapt the other way.

As soon as he settled his stance again, Mort shot out a lightning bolt before it could move towards them or spit once again. The bolt struck it just under the head and it crumpled to the ground.

'Back away,' Mort said, as he watched carefully to see if it moved. It looked to be dead, as his attention was quickly drawn to what was happening beyond the snake-woman.

'I think Travis is dead,' Mendina said, as she walked backwards at his side. 'It looks like your theory was correct,' she added, the shock at what they were looking at obvious in her voice.

The entire valley had come to life.

The humans, dwarves, and other creatures had shed their hardened exteriors all at the same time and chaos now ensued.

Mort's attention was drawn to the people first. They had initially huddled together, the men amongst them standing to their outside.

The dwarves had also moved together, but with less panic. There didn't appear to be many children among their ranks, if any. It was difficult to tell.

Mort hadn't paid much notice to the row of statues that were opposite the dwarves, but they were moving towards the humans as a group and they were all definitely adult. He couldn't be sure what race of people or otherwise they were, but the way the humans were backing away meant they obviously weren't friendly.

As for the other creatures spread throughout the valley, they were moving in all directions. Some moved towards the groups at the bottom, others fled at speed towards the top of the valley.

It was difficult for Mort to take it all in at once and his eyes kept darting from one set of movements to the next. Until one creature in particular started getting bigger as it made its way towards where he and Mendina were headed. He looked across at Mendina and saw that beyond her another large cat was making its way towards them.

They were moving fast and would be on them in less than a minute.

'I hope your lightning bolt does more damage now they are without their armoured hide,' Mendina said. She had seen them as well.

Mort took a moment to look back down the valley. He was relieved to see that nothing was coming at them from there at least. Perhaps the creatures had seen what was making its way to them along the ridge.

'They will have more impact if I wait until they are closer,' Mort said to her. 'I hope.'

He was looking back at the one coming from his left and didn't see the one coming behind him. Not until it jumped between him and the one heading their way, only paces in front of him.

In his shock, he almost cast a bolt at it. It was only because it was facing away from him that he didn't.

It took a few steps away from him and roared at the one approaching it. The other cat slowed in its approach and then began walking.

Mort looked over his shoulder and saw that the other one had slowed to a walk as well.

'What is going on?' Mort said. He thought about trying to communicate with her, but he knew Mendina was much better at it than he was, so he left it to her.

'It seems she remembers us and is appreciative of you freeing both herself and her kin from their captivity. I am fairly certain she just informed the others what you did for her.' Mendina no longer sounded afraid. She had a joy in her voice that Mort hadn't heard in some time.

The one Mort had freed turned to face him, while she waited for the others to join her. Suddenly, there came a roar from the bottom of the valley. It stood out from the other noises and screams coming out of the chaos below.

The three huge cats took off as one down into the valley. Mort looked down and saw the fourth one amongst those creatures that were now slaughtering the humans.

He couldn't tell if it was trying to help the people or whether it had just been caught up in the fight as it tried to make its way through the valley to join its brethren.

Whatever the reason, it was surrounded now by at least six of them as they took turns attacking it and retreating.

The roar of the three other cats as they raced down into the valley got the attention of whatever they were and as one they took off in the opposite direction.

The one they had been attacking stayed where it was as its fellow cats reached it. One of them stayed with it; Mort assumed to check on its wounds, while the other two chased down those that fled.

Bereft of any structured defence, the creatures were mercilessly taken down one at a time before the fastest of them had even made it half way up the other side of the valley.

After he saw the last of them fall, Mort's attention was drawn to what was happening where the dwarves had been.

Those that had been at the back of the house had moved into his line of sight and were positioned a short distance from where the dwarves now huddled together.

The smaller statured folk had bunched together. Mort assumed they hadn't ran because they would have been chased down easily by their larger foes. There were also a number of other creatures loitering around further away from the main house in the centre.

'Mort,' Mendina said to him from his side. 'Should we go down there and help the humans?'

Now that the creatures who had attacked them had been dispatched, the humans presently had nothing threatening them. They were cautiously making their way out of the valley, to the right of where Mort and Mendina looked down.

'I don't think they need our help,' he said. 'As for the dwarves and those other things. I am happy to let them fight each other.'

'I hope they all kill one another,' Mendina said with feeling in her voice.

'What is that?' Mort said, pointing into the sky. Something was heading towards them at a fast speed. There had been a few birds and other things with wings in the valley, but they had all taken flight the moment they were freed. Whatever this was, it had seen something that brought it back and he sensed it may have chosen Mendina and himself as its long overdue meal.

'It is big,' she said. 'I think it may be a dragon!' she exclaimed as it moved over the house, flying no higher than where they stood at the top of the valley.

'What is a dragon?' he said quickly. 'What should I do?' It was closing fast and was a lot bigger than he thought. It must have been a long way off when he first caught sight of it.

'Most breathe fire, but some have acid that burns the flesh.' Mendina sounded panicked and Mort could understand why as it came even closer.

It was a dull red and larger than anything he had seen before in the sky.

He quickly drew in as much of the moisture around them as he could and saw Mendina do the same.

As the dragon closed, it spat forth a fierce ball of fire. Mort squeezed the water together and pushed it hard at the fire as it left the dragon's mouth.

His magic sizzled and steamed as the fire struck, but it failed to stop it completely. The flames that penetrated his defence were enough to knock them both off their feet, their clothes catching alight and Mort's exposed skin blistering painfully.

Mort rolled frantically on the ground and the flames were quickly put out. He sat up and looked over at Mendina. She was already standing. She must have used her magic to extinguish her own clothing. He cursed himself. He should have thought of that. He got to his feet and looked to the sky to see where the dragon had gone.

It had flown a fair distance already, but he could see it banking around for another pass at them.

'Follow me,' Mendina said. 'Hurry!'

Mort watched her run down into the valley a short distance.

'What are you doing?' he shouted as he followed after her.

She stopped at the pile of rocks discarded by the snake monster and raised one of them into the air above their heads.

'At the dragon, Mort!' she said loudly, with urgency in her voice.

Mort looked at the rock, then at the rapidly approaching dragon. With as much effort as he was able, he sent the rock hurtling at the dragon with a strong gust of wind. He had to push it for the first part and then just let the momentum take it.

The dragon had plenty of time to see it coming and easily banked out of the way, the rock falling harmlessly to the ground a short distance past it.

Mort looked back and saw there were now three rocks in the air, all close to each other.

He looked to the dragon and knew it was about to shoot them with fire again. He had no time for anything defensive this time.

He gave the three rocks, all about the size of a human head, everything he had. They were close enough together that he was able to send them flying at it with the same gust. As they sped through the air, they began to spread apart. Mort stared wide-eyed as they did, his heart sinking.

Banking again to dodge one of them, the dragon didn't have time to evade them all. As it opened its mouth, Mort saw the fire inside its throat bubbling. One of the rocks bounced off its hide, while another missed it completely. The third went straight through its left wing, leaving a gaping hole in the membrane and flesh.

Instead of fire, it let out a screeching sound, unceremoniously crashing into the ground behind where they were standing, further on down the valley.

Mort didn't wait to see what happened next. He started pulling together all of the moisture he could from the air around them.

Mendina looked at him and at the rocks she had lifted into the air again.

'Mort, now is not the time to defend. Finish it off. It won't be able to dodge any of them this time.' The panic in her voice and eyes had been replaced with a steely determination.

'No,' Mort said. 'The rock bounced off its hide. They won't kill it.'

'They are still dangerous on the ground,' she said. 'We need to kill it or it will kill us.' Mort was confused at the raw panic in her voice. Did she not see them?

'We need to be ready in case it tries to burn us again,' he replied in a steady voice. 'Will you help me with this?' he asked.

The dragon was on its feet now and had folded its wings in to its body, one more carefully than the other.

It began to walk in an awkward fashion towards where Mort and Mendina stood waiting for it.

Mendina added her own magic to the water Mort had begun to draw out of the air in front of them.

The dragon stopped walking when it was close enough to strike and lifted itself up on to its back legs.

Mort sent a concentrated stream of water as it prepared to breathe its fire, striking it in the face. It momentarily stopped its attack, but did it no hurt.

Mendina looked across at Mort, horrified at what he had done.

'Why did you do that?!' she shrieked at him. 'I thought it was to be a shield. You have killed us both.'

He smiled at her briefly before looking back at the dragon.

Mendina turned her attention back to it, expecting to see a ball of flame headed their way.

Instead, she saw the dragon writhing on the ground. One of the big cats had its jaws clasped around its neck, while another tore at its belly with its claws and teeth.

'I'm sorry,' Mort said, a bashful look replacing his smile. 'I thought you must have seen them. The water was to distract it while they attacked. So they wouldn't get scorched if it sensed them approaching.'

She looked at him. Going by the look on his face, his apology seemed sincere. She didn't know whether to be angry at him or relieved they both weren't smouldering corpses.

She decided to say nothing and instead turned back to the dragon.

It looked to be dead. The cats had made quick work of it. They really were huge, she thought to herself. Neither was as large as the dragon, but they weren't a lot smaller than it either.

She watched as they stepped back from its carcass and looked up at Mort and Mendina. She reached her senses out to the one that began slowly walking towards them. The other had already taken off to re-unite with the other two at the bottom of the valley.

'She is checking that we are okay.' Mendina said to Mort before smiling at the cat and relaying that everything was okay now. She gave out a sense of gratitude for the help they had given them.

A feeling of home, of running free came through to her and she assumed it was telling her they were all going home now. She smiled and nodded, her own feelings of the journey she and Mort must now make foremost in her thoughts. She hadn't meant for that part to be communicated to it.

'What is she saying?' Mort asked.

Mendina looked at him. 'I can't speak with them, Mort. I can see pictures in her mind and sense feelings. That is the best way to describe it. I assume she sees the same from me.'

'Okay then,' he said. 'So I assume you are thanking her.'

'Yes,' Mendina said smiling.

'We should go and check out the house down there.' Mort said, completely changing the subject. 'And the stables. I hope he had some horses.'

Mendina nodded and the three of them began walking down into the valley.

CHAPTER 37

Too Late

JARKENE HAD NEVER moved as quickly as he did now.

Corein was alive! After all this time, after all the anguish and suffering he had gone through, he would once again hold her in his arms. He had never dared to dream this chance would come to him again.

He knew she would not look upon him with the same hatred and contempt his son had. She knew the man he was and she knew exactly how he felt about her. She would at least understand the decisions and choices he had made. She would still choose to love him.

He came across no other creatures foreign to Glorfiden in his dash through the southern trees of the forest. Nothing took his mind from his destination and the woman that would be waiting there for him.

His heart beat fast and his breathing was laboured, but his legs showed no weariness as he neared the place he had once called home. A home where he had briefly raised a son with the human woman he had taken as his wife.

Not until he at last came upon the orchard behind the house did his pace slow to a walk.

He knew straight away something was wrong.

Although it was outside the elven forest, he knew it had always been cared for and the creatures of the forest welcome. He was aware things had changed since he sent the storm and the animals and other fey creatures had fled to their holes and burrows to wait out the fires and whatever else may come in its wake.

Yet on his flight here he had seen and heard plenty of birds and other small creatures of the forest, carefully returning to the life they had enjoyed before.

As he stepped among the first apple trees, he was acutely attuned to the fact there were no sounds. No birds sang and nothing moved in the trees. The apples were almost ripe. It was the perfect time for birds to gorge themselves.

He heard footsteps and mumbled voices coming from where the house was and he grew wary. The voices belonged to neither human nor elf.

By the time he was halfway through the orchard, he began to pick up words and his speed increased. He sprinted through the other citrus trees and grape vines without sound and came to Corein's backyard.

Everything was as he remembered it. The house and gardens were still as perfect as he knew they would be. As he *hoped* they would be.

He saw two of the creatures walking around the backyard, kicking over items and ripping out plants. 'Dark-Goblins'. He almost spat the words from his mouth.

Smaller cousins to those in the east, these ones were less prolific, but more skilful fighters and some could use magic. Their skin was a dark, slimy brown, and they smelt like the cesspools they lived in further north. He would have smelt them a lot earlier if the wind had been blowing towards Glorfiden.

He could hear that the rest of the pack were inside. Neither of those in the backyard knew Jarkene was there. They wouldn't have seen him even had they been staring intently in his direction, yet it wouldn't have altered their fate even had they seen him standing in the shadows.

Before either of the dark-goblins knew what was happening, they were being dragged along the ground, neither of them able to make a sound as Jarkene wrapped their bodies in shells of air. He had done the same with the Ve-Karn earlier and within moments they were at the elf lord's feet, their eyes wide open in shock. Jarkene could see them both straining to scream as they saw who their captor was and the dagger in his hand.

The elf lord leant down to the first and released the spell moments before he slid his knife along the throat of the terrified dark-goblin.

He took a step towards the second and dealt him the same fate as his companion, before moving off towards the house.

As he walked around to the front of the home and came upon the front door, he still hadn't heard any noise that indicated to him his beloved Corein was inside. He knew she could be unconscious or that she could be dead. As he walked through the door to the living room, he fervently hoped she had gone somewhere else before these filthy creatures had arrived.

He knew it would be too much for him to cope with if something had happened to her. He had only just found out she was alive.

He didn't know what he would do afterwards, but for now, he would kill everything that had dared enter their home.

He walked inside and before even registering those that were inside he took in the destruction. All of the furniture and trinkets had been thrown around, many of them broken and shattered.

His eyes were drawn to the porcelain vase lying in pieces on the floor in the centre of the room. He had given that to Corein for their third anniversary. He remembered the effort he put into the creation of that piece and the subsequent passion they shared that night together. It was as if the memory of his wife and their time together, all of the special moments they had shared, lay shattered on the floor in front of him.

Regardless of the fate of his wife, they were all going to die slowly and painfully.

There were two in the living room as he stepped in. After their initial shock at seeing an elf walk in, they quickly moved to attack.

Only a few paces away and already with their wickedly curved blades at the ready, the two swung viciously as they advanced.

Jarkene looked away from the broken vase as the sword of the first one swung at his head. He had decided when he entered he wouldn't use any spells this time.

Although not the master of weapons that his brother had been, Jarkene's skills were still far above most others within the realms of Dark Swell.

Using only his dagger, he moved easily out of the way of the swinging sword, bending down and slicing the back of its leg just above the ankle. It sprawled on the ground screaming as the second thrust his sword straight at Jarkene's chest. The elf again moved seamlessly out of the way, his body moving with a fluidity few others could match. This time he grabbed the wrist of the dark-goblin's sword hand and sliced his dagger through the flesh of his elbow. The blade moved on to open the shoulder, as his weapon continued its arc. The skin peeled back, revealing the severed muscles underneath. The sword fell from its hand as Jarkene let go of the wrist and then sliced along the elbow of its other arm as it reached across to cradle the injured one.

They were no longer presently a threat to him.

He turned to look at the last of them as it stepped out of the doorway leading into his bedroom. The same room he shared with the human woman he had given his heart to. He stood there for a moment staring at the dark-goblin as it looked to its companions, writhing in agony from their hurts.

This one would die last.

Corein wasn't there and he didn't think she had been for a couple of days now. He quickly determined that none of the foul creatures he found in their house knew where she had gone or when. He had no doubt they would have told him anything before he had finally let the life run from each of them. He felt no satisfaction from their suffering or from their deaths, but he still had a lot of anger and frustration within him and it needed an outlet.

If she had chosen to leave and not been taken by anything then she would have made for the nearest human settlement. She would have gone to Mayfield.

Even though he would be away from the forest and his power source, he had a staff brimming with magic and reserves within himself. He was confident there would be nothing in these parts that could threaten his powers.

There was nothing anywhere that was going to stop him from finding his wife.

Pointing his staff at the pile of dark goblins he had stacked away from the house, an intense fire spewed from it and set the bodies alight.

He looked at them briefly as the fire burnt hot.

He then turned and started to run again, this time into the realm of men.

As he ran, Jarkene could still see Glorfiden to his left for the first part of his journey. He hated looking at it again from the outside. It reminded him too strongly of all those years he had only been able to look at it from afar.

He belonged within it now. He was the new Nurturer of Glorfiden and its Protector. There were few elves left alive and he intended to make sure no more died.

He thought of how exciting it would be to take Corein with him back to the centre of the forest. Glorfiden would grow again and he needed her there with him when it did. She would be able to talk to Mortinan and eventually make things right between them. He believed in his heart she could make him see that what he had done didn't define the man that he was.

He refused to believe anything untoward had happened to her.

His pace didn't waver as the day began to turn into night. He had left the views of Glorfiden behind when he stopped moving east and began the part of his journey that took him south instead.

By the time the first of the farm houses came into view, the sun had almost disappeared below the horizon.

There were no fires burning. He was disappointed to see that everyone had abandoned their homes. He had hoped that Corcin had stopped at one of these places.

He wasn't sure how he would be welcomed approaching the larger settlement at night. Even during the day, he knew they would be suspicious of him. He doubted they would let him within speaking distance at night.

He wasn't concerned about his ability to enter the town, but he would rather not have to force his way in. He didn't want to risk Corein thinking worse of him than she would already, after he eventually told her he was responsible for the storm.

He walked on a trail now and his progress quickened. The farmers needed a well-worn track to transport their goods and this was that.

There was none left in any of the houses that he passed. There were no animals and no people.

He noticed before it grew dark that it had been an organised exodus. There had been no obvious signs of violence.

They had been forewarned that something was coming.

He had noticed little outside of his own existence in the last few years, consumed instead with his own losses and misery.

He wondered now what was going on in the world. What evils had forced all of these people from their homes? What had made Corein want to leave the place they had made their home? It may have been the storm he sent that had spooked them all into thinking there was some unspeakable horror unleashed upon the land.

He didn't really believe that. It looked to him that most had left weeks ago, not days.

A storm directed at the elves also wouldn't make these people leave their homes. Lands they had farmed for many years and needed to harvest in order to feed themselves and sustain the people in the larger towns where they now found themselves.

He suddenly realised that he needed to get back to Glorfiden. If there was something else out there threatening the lands and that something knew of the demise of his people, there would be none there to stop them entering the forest. The Ve-Karn and the Dark-Mage had thought themselves safe to enter. It dawned on him how unlucky they were he had been so close to where they entered. Even with the warning the trees gave, he couldn't protect each and every border of the forest with only himself and a handful of others.

Yet without him there, enough creatures entering at once would have the run of the place. Those he had left there would need to hide or they would die defending their home. Probably the latter. No elf he knew would let any creature foreign to the forest remain within its borders, whether they be friend or foe. It was what had kept them strong and feared for so many centuries. The forest had always been death to any who entered without their permission.

He needed to find Corein as quickly as he could. He needed to get to Mayfield so that he could then get back to Glorfiden.

Yet he knew that travelling in the dark would be risky, even for him.

He couldn't see in the dark and he knew there were creatures out there that could. He had devised ways of keeping himself safe while he had been in exile, but he hadn't been running headlong through the night in unfamiliar territory during those times. He could keep himself to the path and easily find his way to Mayfield, but he had to consider there may be things in the night lying in wait for those foolish enough to be out and about.

The sun had completely disappeared now and only a sliver of moon was out. It was dark and he could only just make out the trail he ran on.

He slowed to a walk. He would at least be able to hear if something came at him. Probably.

He retained his skills at moving without sound even out of the forest and he was able to pick up the sound of movement ahead well before it came into sight. There were trees either side of the trail here and the sound he heard was coming from around a bend in the trail. He could make out a dim, bobbing light as it moved in his direction. He thought of moving into the trees for cover, but it was only the unknown that concerned him. If he could see his enemy then he could kill it.

He stopped in the middle of the track and waited for whatever it was to come to him.

As the light rounded the bend he saw several dark shapes behind it before everything went dark again.

They had seen him.

Prior to the night taking over, Jarkene had collected a couple of large, thick branches, in case he had need of light.

He flung one out in front and sent a small burst of fire at it, lighting the path ahead. He forced more heat into it and the track he walked on became brighter still.

As the flames grew, he saw that whatever they were, they moved fast and would be upon him much quicker than he had first anticipated. The flames showed only shadows, as they crashed into the wall of air he set only metres in front of himself. The air was thick and it only just held against their impact.

These were not men, nor normal beasts. Both the speed of their movement and the fact they had nearly pushed through his barrier told him they were creatures of magic and probably in their element during the dark hours.

Jarkene wasn't panicked though. He had lived for hundreds of years and was confident in his magical ability. It was that same long accumulated knowledge that also made him wary. There were certain spells he found were more effective against certain types and some that did little or nothing at all. So far he had no idea what he was up against, other than they were quick and they liked the dark.

Thickened air was a safe bet against most, but it wasn't much of a weapon. It gave him time to see what he was up against.

The branch continued to burn strongly, but it didn't illuminate whatever it was that had moved back from his shield. They seemed to be reassessing their own plan of attack.

Jarkene reached out to the fire and took the light from within it. The energy within the flames that created the light was easy for him to feed and suddenly the whole path in front of him was lit up. Two of the creatures stood back from his barrier of air, not moving. The light forced them to tuck their faces into their chests and lower them towards the ground.

It also momentarily halted the other four, two on each side of him. They had moved silently around the barrier already. If he hadn't illuminated the whole place, they would have been on him in seconds and he wouldn't have known until they had begun shredding his body. He saw the razor-sharp blade at the end of their arms, as they shielded their eyes from the light.

Jarkene poured more of his power into illuminating the track and it grew even brighter. He nearly had to shield his own eyes.

The shadow beasts to either side of him were suddenly pushed back, as he formed another air barrier. This time he pushed it back against them and then swung it around to the left, flinging them back near to where the other two in front of his shield were now kneeling.

These air barriers he joined seamlessly with the one he already had up. He continued pushing the ends of his barrier forward, forcing it to swing around so that it moved to the side of them and then eventually encircled them.

Before long he had six human shadows trapped inside his prison of air, all of them kneeling on the dirt with their heads bowed.

He hadn't seen their like before, but he knew they were abominations and shouldn't be walking free in the lands of men, certainly not this close to his own forest.

They were shaped like men, but their bodies were encased in a shadow that made it appear as if a dark cloud enshrouded their forms. When they moved, he could see the long arms that ended in a claw, like a small, curved dagger. The orbs that held their dark eyes were sunken and they were without noses. The mouths moved constantly but no sound came from them and he could see no teeth and no lips. They were hideous to look upon. Their legs were solid, too thick and muscly and not in proportion to the rest of their body, but it was what gave them their incredible speed.

As he tried to figure out how he would safely finish them off, they all turned to each other. They were still on their knees and facing down, but they each now sat with their backs to his wall of air.

Jarkene didn't like it when they all started to make a gurgling noise. It sounded like a chant as they reached their arms forward and touched palms with the one on either side of them.

'Time to put an end to this,' the elf lord said quietly to himself.

He raised his own arms and slowly brought them together as the air barrier started to move closer to them. It would soon squeeze them all together into one big pool of bones and pulp.

As he squeezed he saw a darkness begin to seep from each of them. It quickly spread beyond their prison of air and before his barrier could push together, the darkness extinguished his light. Within a few heartbeats of first seeing the darkness come from them, he was thrown back into a world where he couldn't see.

The moment the light vanished, the noise they made also stopped.

So, too, did his shield. It still held where it was, but somehow they found the strength to stop it moving any closer to them. It was like it was bogged in mud. He tried to keep it moving, but it wouldn't budge. Rather than stopping his magic directly, they had put some sort of shield of their own up which was stopping his from moving.

Whatever these were, they were definitely far more powerful in the dark.

Jarkene was acutely aware if he didn't throw some permanent light on what was happening here, these creatures were a genuine threat to his life.

He reached towards where he had thrown the first branch, but there was no heat source remaining. The darkness had smothered it and it still remained there. He quickly searched it, looking to get some idea of how this darkness worked, but all he got from it was an emptiness. It was like the air itself had been sucked away. As if the air had been completely removed from that space.

He heard the chanting begin again. He didn't need sight to know what they would be doing next.

They were going to take his shield down.

What were they? What weakness did they have, other than light? Light stunned them and reduced their powers, but it didn't kill them. He needed to know what it would take to vanquish them and he needed the answer quickly.

He felt the barrier of air surrounding them crumble. As it did, he fired lightning bolts in quick succession at the area where they had been while the shield had still held.

The bolts lit up the night sky, even the place where the darkness still lingered after *consuming* his shield.

The bolts struck three of the shadow creatures and knocked them backwards, sizzling. The clouds that appeared to surround them crackled and seethed as would a true storm cloud. They were knocked off their feet and backwards several paces. None of them got straight back up.

In his peripheral vision, Jarkene saw the others had already moved away and to either side of him. He continued to fire lightning bolts at both sides until he had knocked all of them down. None of them got close to him.

As he fired off his last bolt, he threw out his other branch and lit it strongly as he had the first.

The creatures remained lying on their backs and the darkness surrounding them continued to roil with what looked like the left over charge from his lightning strikes.

Then one of them sat up. It was soon followed by the others and in quick succession they all found their feet again and stood in front of him.

None of them made to move at him yet. They shielded their faces from the light, but it no longer had the same debilitating effect as before.

The lightning bolts he had fired into them seemed to have augmented their powers. That had certainly not been his intention.

Jarkene clenched his jaw and quickly assessed what his next move was going to be.

While his thoughts raced and he stood looking at them, the ones that had moved to the outer side of the trail slowly returned to the centre of the track with the others.

By the time Jarkene was ready, they were all standing side by side again in front of him, crackling and roiling like thunderclouds.

The elven lord casually reached inside his jacket and pulled forth his storm rod. He noticed them tilt their heads back, as if sniffing the air.

He pointed it at them and although not fully restored, he was aware it still contained within it enormous power. He was hoping to have it fully recharged before using it again, but these beings had left him little choice.

They all leaned forward as he pointed it at them and as one suddenly charged.

Attuned to his thoughts, the rod answered his call and a strong gust of wind burst forth. It knocked them back along the trail, tumbling over one another as they catapulted backwards.

They were flung back at least thirty paces from him as he reined the powers back in.

They slowly got back to their feet. They still didn't flee, but this time they didn't move forward at him either.

It gave Jarkene time to ponder what he could do to end this. They were taking up time he didn't have.

Now that he had time to focus away from the creatures in front of him, he looked around again and noticed a thin film of fog rolling in along the ground from the trees.

There was a lot of moisture available to him now and it was a cold night.

He sucked the heat out of the fog as he drew it towards himself and this time with the wind blast he sent tiny ice particles.

With a gust as strong as the rod would allow, he sent it towards them and watched satisfied as their bodies were shredded by the impact.

The force with which they hit made it look as if their bodies simply shattered. Like glass, the fragments burst apart in a scintillating display lit up by the burning branch in front of him.

Jarkene looked again in awe at the rod, before safely tucking it away.

Without hesitation, he set off at a jog, this time not as worried at what may be waiting for him on the track. He doubted there would be anything to threaten him where these shadow creatures had just been.

He knew he wasn't far from Mayfield now.

He would be there in a few hours and she would be there waiting for him.

CHAPTER 38

Shadow Hill

THEY WERE READY to leave early the next afternoon. Both Brax and Linf had slept peacefully during the night. The two men they had tied up were of no concern to either of them. Neither had the strength to attempt any sort of escape.

They continued to drain them throughout the morning and then sucked the life out of them completely just before they departed the farm.

Linf felt newly born. The goblin she had been before was a memory only, as she stretched her arms while walking to the cart. Clenching her hands, she hopped up into the back. Brax hadn't even asked her to get in the back. She was in such a mood she didn't care. Linf preferred her own company anyhow and would much rather be in the back than up front with the smelly human.

'I need to bind your wrists,' Brax said to her as he walked to the back of the cart.

Linf just smiled at him as she answered.

'I know you're stronger than me, old man, but I don't think you'll be putting those on me today.'

Brax just looked at her. Linf knew he was unsure, so she thought she would see how long she could leave him wondering. Just for a laugh, nothing more.

'I have told you already why you need these on,' Brax said. 'Nothing has changed since then. We will be coming across more men as we journey further into their lands.'

Linf just continued to smile and shook her head.

'Why then?' Brax finally asked.

'Why don't you just get up front and get us moving again instead of worrying about why I no longer want to be shackled to the side of this cart.' Linf could see he was getting more than a little annoyed with her.

'Don't try me, goblin,' Brax warned. 'I can still do what I need to without you. Your presence will make it easier, but don't make me rethink it is worth the effort on my part.'

Linf smiled at him again and chuckled. It was good to give him a bit of his own back after all those times he had made her angry for no reason.

Linf placed her wrist into the cuff and let the old man secure it.

'Can you leave this one out?' Linf asked, indicating her free hand. 'Sometimes I can't reach where I need to scratch and it annoys me.'

The old man took a deep breath and stared at Linf like he wanted to skin her alive.

Again, Linf just smiled at him and put her other wrist into the cuff.

Brax didn't even look at her as he secured the second wrist and then walked back to the front of the cart.

They made good time for the rest of that afternoon and found a deserted farmhouse to spend the night in. They stopped in time for Brax to see to the horses and cook himself up a hot meal before it got dark. Even the old man didn't want to be out at night. Linf had a sense all was not well in the land.

They were up early the next morning and continued on after a quick breakfast of dried meats and bread.

They both needed food to sustain their bodies, but neither of them needed it for energy. They both brimmed with it and Brax was keen to get to the first town on his planned journey.

They saw no one else on the road as they made their way towards Shadow Hill. No houses were occupied even this close to town.

Brax wasn't upset about it. It made their progress easier and it gave his story extra impetus knowing the people within the walls of the town would be happy to believe anything that may help their king combat the evils abroad.

It was mid-afternoon when the towers and then the walls of Shadow Hill came into view.

The excitement within Brax felt like it was bubbling just below the surface of his skin. He almost tingled in anticipation. Coupled with the strength he had gained so far on this trip, was the thought of all the people he had to choose from once he got within the walls of the town.

He knew they would be watched carefully with the goblin as his prisoner, but that wasn't a concern once he had Linf locked away in a room somewhere.

He had his cloak. None would see him.

'Goblin,' he said over his shoulder as the cart rumbled on towards the gates of the lower settlement. 'We are nearly there. Tonight, you will feed on your first human child.'

He didn't need to look to know the goblin would have a large grin on her face.

There were numerous small houses on the final road before the gates to the town. These were still occupied, many of which had stalls out the front selling all kinds of food and wares. This close to the safety of the walls the people felt safe enough. If danger were to approach, they would have time to find their way inside. The towers above the walls allowed those inside to see a great distance in all directions.

Brax had no interest in purchasing anything and went directly to the main gates. There were several guards both inside and out. They were both older and younger than the soldiers Brax remembered from when he was last in the King's Realm. He guessed most of the real soldiers had left this area and would be in the larger town of Havern, or even called back to the capital.

The older ones were probably ex-soldiers that had come in from their farms. The younger ones more than likely their sons, those that had been training for only a short time.

One of the older ones approached Brax and held his arm up, indicating for him to stop his cart.

Brax pulled his horses up and looked down at the man.

'You come from the East, sir?' he asked in a voice full of suspicion.

'I am in the king's employ, good man,' Brax said in a soft voice, but full of confidence and with an edge that relayed to the old man he was on an important and secret mission.

He could almost see the old man's brain ticking over. Brax had assumed they would be desperate for any news to show them the king was out there helping in some way. He also knew they would be suspicious of anyone they didn't know.

'I am no monster to threaten the good people of this town,' Brax continued. 'I have journeyed far to collect information for our king and I bring with me items to help fight the evils in the land and a special gift for his wizard.'

Brax could literally see the fear fall away from the man as his story took hold of his imagination and the desperate hope he felt.

Brax hopped down on to the ground and went to the back of his cart. The guard followed him, as did two other guards. There wasn't a lot happening there this morning.

He grabbed hold of the blanket he had thrown over Linf when they came into view of the walls.

He turned to the old guard and spoke to him before flinging back the blanket.

'It is very important that none of you are alarmed when I show you what I have.' He looked at each of the men in turn. 'This is a gift for a mighty wizard and he would not be pleased if any of you here did anything to harm it.'

He could see the anticipation on the faces of each man as they all took a couple of steps back and put their hands on the grips of their swords.

'It is secure and cannot hurt you,' Brax said as he removed the blanket with a flourish.

Linf had been less than impressed when Brax had explained to her the need for him to cover her with a blanket as they neared the town.

She understood nothing of what was being said as they stopped outside of the main gate. When the blanket was finally flung from her, she took a moment to adjust her vision to the sudden light and then quickly sat back as far as she could go with the restraints on. There were a number of armed men standing there looking at her and she could see the anger and fear flowing freely in waves from each of them.

The old one at the front drew his sword and took a step towards her before Brax stood in front of him and said something Linf couldn't understand.

The fear this one had shortly disappeared, as did the anger. Linf had no idea what the man was feeling right now, but she was suspicious of everyone.

The goblin suddenly wished she wasn't tied to the wagon. The old man had better not betray her, she thought. It occurred to her that she had no idea what he was up to, or why he had brought her with him in the first place. For the first time in days, she began to feel the stirrings of fear again. She didn't like it and she decided she needed to be away from here as soon as the first opportunity presented itself. Looking at the human and his fellow guards, she knew she didn't belong among men. The urge to go back the way they had come and into the plains was stronger than it had ever been.

Yet she would taste a child before she left. That she was sure of, no matter the fear she felt or the urge to run.

'A goblin!' the old guard hissed. 'Kill it!' he said to the others, as he drew his sword and stepped towards Linf. Brax moved to stand in front of the man and put his hand gently on his shoulder. The drain he caused was small only, enough to slightly weaken him and stop him in his advance.

'I said that this is a gift for a wizard,' Brax said in a voice slightly louder, but still not threatening. 'You must not harm it.'

The guard looked at him for a time and stepped back. He turned to one of the younger guards.

'Go and fetch the wizard,' he said to him and the boy took off at a run. The guard turned back to Brax. 'You see, old man, we have our own wizard here. I think whatever information this goblin has he will be sufficient to draw from it.'

Brax needed to rethink his brilliant strategy. There hadn't been a wizard this far out from the capital when he was last here. He hadn't considered this turn of events, although looking at the old guard now he knew that he should have.

'The king has forsaken us traveller,' he continued talking to Brax. 'He has called back nearly all of the strong fighters to Havern and the capital, leaving us to defend ourselves best we can. We shall need everything we can to turn the upcoming fight in our favour.'

Brax just stared at him and smiled thinly. He really needed to think fast.

They were escorted away from the gates, off to the side so that others were able to enter unhindered. Brax freed his horses from the cart and a few of the soldiers pushed the cart towards the wall, the rear of it facing away from the road. The old guard didn't want anyone else seeing what was in the back.

Brax found some posts nearby to tie up Dark Star and Storm Cloud, keeping a close eye on the cart to ensure none tried to do anything untoward to his companion in the back.

He needn't have feared. None of those present wanted to get too close to the goblin.

After reassuring both horses, he walked back to the cart to wait for their wizard to arrive.

The time waiting gave him time to think and reassess his plans.

The more he thought about it, the more he was convinced he should be safe, as should Linf. It was very unlikely the wizard would be able to understand the goblin language, yet even if he was he knew his goblin well enough to know she wouldn't be forthcoming. His greatest concern was that Linf would say or do something stupid enough to enrage the wizard or another with influence within the town.

They didn't have to wait long for the wizard to arrive. His appearance gave Brax some relief. He wouldn't have been much older than the farmer he had come across on their journey here. He saw this as a positive, as the skills and knowledge base of the wizard wouldn't be as broad as those in his order with more years of experience and study behind them.

The suspicion of older men, gained through years of life experiences, would hopefully be less in this man.

Brax's gaze was drawn to the men walking behind the wizard and his heart sunk. He had also not expected to see them this far from the capital and his mind began frantically trying to reassess his plans and options once more.

Their kind were the reason he had fled the lands of men all those years ago. Wizards he could handle. Although often without fear due to their arrogance, they were susceptible to anger. In fact, the arrogance that took away their fear usually increased the anger they felt against those who stood against them. He had faced wizards back when he lived amongst men and he had defeated them.

The men escorting the wizard also had no fear, but unlike wizards, they didn't possess the same arrogance. Their demeanour suggested otherwise, but Brax knew they rarely radiated anger. This lack of fear and anger made them extremely dangerous adversaries to him. His strength alone would usually be enough without the emotions to feed on, but these men had elite martial prowess and they were naturally very strong. Much stronger than other men. He had faced a couple of the King's Shield before and both times had been forced to flee.

As the wizard and his King's Shield walked up to him, he knew if he were unable to talk his way out of this he wouldn't be fighting his way out. He was trapped and he knew it.

Linf's life was now in the hands of the young wizard and Brax wasn't pleased about it.

He stood next to the old guard as they approached and the grizzled soldier stepped forward and nodded his head in respect to the wizard.

'Ethan, this is the stranger who has come from the East. I thought it best to get you before letting him into town.' He reminded Brax of a dog waiting for his master to pet him.

'Very good, Helbot,' he said to the guard. 'You can go and keep an eye on his pet now.' He paid no further mind to the old man as he turned his attention to Brax. The old man nodded his head again and walked off with a self-satisfied step to his gait.

The wizard didn't speak as he looked Brax up and down. Brax wasn't disturbed by the attention. He was concentrating on clearing his mind and slowing his heart rate. Panic and worry were wasted emotions, and this was going to be a very important conversation.

'Your name, stranger?' the wizard Ethan asked.

Brax inclined his head in a show of respect, much as the old guard had done. He knew the pompous wizards appreciated a show of deference.

'My name is Brax, sir. I am in the employ of the king and I am seeking a bed for the night to rest before continuing on to the capital.' He kept his voice steady and polite.

'You come from the East. Where have you been?' Ethan asked.

Brax was a little surprised the wizard didn't straight up ask about Linf. He surmised this one may have some wits about him. He would need to tread very carefully.

'I have journeyed quite a distance in my travels and been through many lands since I left the capital.' He decided he wouldn't offer much unless pressed.

'Answer my question, Brax.' the wizard said to him. He spoke in a sharp voice. Brax knew he needed to assuage any suspicions he might have and do it quickly.

'I have been through the Southern lands of the dwarves, spending some time in their Southern Halls and mountain range, before travelling through the plains of the horsemen. From there I went south, carefully negotiating my way through parts of the goblin lands, before finally making my way back here.' He thought to stop there, but the look on the wizards' face and the sudden wave of anger he gave off told Brax he was less than happy with his succinct tale. 'I was sent on a trek to collect whatever items I deemed could be valuable for the defence of the realm and bring them back to the king with as much haste as possible.'

Brax sighed in mock disappointment.

'I fear it has taken me a great deal longer than I had hoped and going by what I have seen in my travels, especially since entering the King's Realm again, the evil has well and truly shown itself.'

He left it at that. The anger had dissipated a little, but this wizard still wasn't happy. Brax didn't know why, but he figured he would find out soon enough. He didn't want to say too much for fear he would be tripped up. The less he said the easier he could cover his story.

'You are not a wizard, that is obvious to me.' Ethan continued to stare at him as he spoke, not taking his eyes from his face. 'You also don't look to be a soldier or even an assassin. So I am very curious. What skills do you have that would enable you to travel unscathed through such dark lands?' He paused, but Brax didn't think he was finished talking, so he waited for the wizard to continue.

Until he saw a huge wave of anger flow from him.

Brax jumped in before the wizard did something hasty.

'I was given several valuable items when I left and have collected several more during my travels. These have assisted me in avoiding any unwelcome advances. Luck has also played a large part, of that I have no doubt.' Brax was worried now. He had left himself vulnerable and he was finding it difficult to understand exactly where the anger Ethan was feeling stemmed from. He hadn't wanted to mention he possessed items of considerable value. He had assumed the wizard would be too afraid to defy his king.

'I will have those items you speak of. Now.' Ethan's tone and his emotions did not give Brax any more wriggle room, yet he decided to risk the 'insult to his king card'.

'I offer no disrespect, Wizard Ethan, but these are items for the king. I fear he may have need of them and the hour is late.' He lowered his head as he finished speaking.

'Helbot,' was all the wizard said in response.

The old guard ran to stand in front of him.

'Yes, sir?'

'Get a sack and put it over the goblin's head, then cover it again with a blanket in the back of that wagon. Gather more of your men and take that wagon to the rear of the main hall. I want everything on there removed and placed into the hall. No one is to touch anything other than to move it and no one is to go in there after it is all placed inside.'

'At once,' Helbot said and raced off to gather more men.

Ethan turned his attention back to Brax.

He continued to stare at him as he spoke. 'You have a silver tongue Brax and this may have served you well through your travels. You may be in the king's employ, but I have my doubts there. I still have many more questions for you and you had better answer me straight. Trust me when I say your life depends on it.'

Brax steadied the beating in his skull and the strong desire to smash the wizard's face through to the back of his head. All was still not lost. It had taken a turn for the worse, no doubt about that, but he was still confident he could get himself out of this one.

'I hope we can have this situation sorted quickly, but I do understand your suspicions. Shall I see to my horses and find a place to rest while you sift through my belongings?' Brax was fuming, but he wasn't stupid enough to show it.

'No need,' Ethan replied, still with that same steely stare. 'I will have your horses seen to. We already have a place for you to rest.' He turned to one of the King's Shield and flicked his head. An indication for a predetermined arrangement. Brax realised as soon as the two King's Shield moved towards him that this had been the wizard's intent before he had even arrived to speak with him.

It was certainly rather more disconcerting.

Looking intently at the wizard, Brax suddenly realised the reason for the wizard's hostility and the intensity of his anger.

Ethan was desperate.

A desperate man in a dangerous land and Brax knew how unpredictable desperate people could be.

Things had just gotten much worse for not only the goblin, but for himself as well.

The King's Shield walked him through the main gates and into the town of Shadow Hill.

It wasn't a large settlement when compared to Havern or the capital, but it was large enough to house thousands of people.

He noticed it still wasn't an ostentatious place. Back when he had been here last it had been smaller and far less populated, but rather than the garish houses and buildings in the Capitol, Shadow Hill retained its austerity.

It looked more like a large soldiers camp that a settlement of men celebrating the grandness of architecture. The walls were higher and had been made more solid. The buildings themselves were solid and plain, built to withstand whatever an attacking host may fire over the walls.

It wasn't until he got to the centre of town that the stalls and parlours brought a little colour to the place. They would be well out of range of anything flung over the walls and they had the small mountain at their backs to protect them from that side.

Once through this part of town, Brax was brought to another set of smaller gates leading into a courtyard. He could see the great hall beyond as he walked through the gates.

It also hadn't changed much since he had been here last. A few more defences was all that had been altered.

He looked behind as he walked through, to make sure the cart containing Linf and his belongings was still behind him.

He was surprised at the lack of protest and anger the goblin had shown when she was hooded and then covered again with the blanket. He saw quite a bit of fear emanating from her, but very little anger. He didn't think it was self-control and smarts that prevented her from lashing out, but he was glad nonetheless.

He still needed her. Both to get out of this predicament and for when they made it to Havern.

He was taken into the main hall. It had been cleared of people, other than one elderly male who was seated at the very back. He sat at a large table which went all along the back and down both sides, almost to the front. There was an empty floor space in the middle of it and breaks at both of the rear corners for people to move between.

One of the King's Shield walked behind the table at the back and removed a chair, which he put inside the space near the back. Brax was ordered to sit before he had his wrists tied to the arms of the chair.

He made no protest. He knew he would be wasting his breath with these men.

He sat in silence as the guardsmen brought all of his belongings in from the cart and stacked them up in front of him.

The last thing they brought in was Linf. She was still complacent, held by two guardsman with the sack over her head. Brax was happy they had brought her in here with him and not taken her away to a lock up within the hall. He was fairly certain things were not going to go well here and he would have need of her before this had played itself out.

When the last of his chests and other belongings had been brought in, the guards all left through the front door and closed it after them.

Ethan, the two King's Shield, and the old man seated at the table were all that remained in the hall. The old man still hadn't moved nor spoken. He just sat there with a look of disinterest on his face.

The wizard moved to stand in front of Brax and looked at what had been brought in.

'Tell me which of these are so valuable to our king and why?'

'Not a word of apology for treating him as a prisoner,' Brax thought. He really didn't like him.

Before waiting for an answer, he walked over to the pile and selected the Green Bear pelt.

'This looks fresh,' he said, turning now to look at Brax, holding the pelt up in front of him.

'Yes. A recent acquisition,' Brax smiled as he spoke. Good manners and an acquiescent attitude had proven to be of no value, so he decided he wouldn't bother with it any further. 'Something for myself. For all my hard work.'

Ethan smiled at him now, a look of satisfaction on his face.

'So we finally start to hear from the real man behind the façade. Good. I have a particular dislike towards those that wear two faces.' The smile remained. 'Do tell me how you managed to kill a Green Bear.'

'Not a particularly interesting story, I'm afraid. We were travelling through a forested part of the goblin lands and I heard him coming from a long way away. I assumed he had only just awoken and was very hungry. You know how they can get.' Brax' smile also remained. Two old friends having a chat about old times. 'It gave me time to hide myself, so that when he saw the goblin in the back of the cart and my two horses, his mind was focused on an easy feed and not where I was hiding in wait.'

Ethan put down the pelt and walked up to Brax. He leant down so his face was at a level with his own and spoke, still in a pleasant voice.

'You keep telling me parts of a story, but never the whole thing. This is not helpful.' His smile disappeared and he grabbed Brax by the chin and squeezed. 'How did you kill it?' He spoke the question in a soft voice, almost a whisper.

'I put the spiked end of a club into the back of its skull.' Brax said through clenched teeth. He had no intentions of telling him anything about his true gifts. That would be the end of any goodwill right there. He also didn't want to let him know about any of his other, more valuable items that may have made his tale far more believable.

He was through playing the wizards game. He was waiting now. He had one shot at this and nothing he said between now and then would influence that outcome.

The wizard flung his head back as he released his grip and turned back to the stacked pile.

'Keep your secrets then, old man. I will find out exactly how you did it after I have been through all of this.' He extended his arms out in a gesture to encompass all of Brax's worldly possessions.

'How about you take the Green Bear pelt as a gesture of my good will and we go on our way with the "King's" property.' Brax didn't believe for a moment that any more of his words would matter to the wizard. This time, however, he spoke directly to the nearest of the King's Shield.

He saw the man twitch. It was only momentary, but he had seen it. The lack of any emotions coming from the man were inconsequential so far as his powers went, but he saw the smallest trace of anger seep out. He could never have used it to weaken the man, but it gave him hope he may be able to use it against the wizard.

Ethan turned quickly. Time enough for him to see Brax turn his eyes from the King's Shield.

Brax saw the wizard's eyes narrow in suspicion and awareness. A new wave of anger also flew from him.

'This town is a very important strategic point for the defence of the realm, Brax. You know that, as does everyone else here.' He was no longer smiling. 'Anything of the king's which you possess here and is of value will be used in the defence of this town, thus defending the king himself.'

'I appreciate what you are saying, Wizard Ethan.' Brax also took on a serious tone. The conversation had suddenly turned to one of indirectly trying to influence the two warriors that were present in the room. 'However, do you believe yourself more competent than the king himself and his trusted advisors, to determine the true worth of what I possess? I'm sure your skills are at least equal to those of the finest wizards in the land and you will be able to best use those items I have.'

'Tell me what items you are referring to specifically,' Ethan said. The anger had stopped flowing from him. Brax realised the wizard had turned the conversation full circle and now had him where he had wanted him to begin with. 'Clever boy,' Brax thought to himself.

He stared back at the wizard, who this time just looked back at him without speaking. He seemed content to wait for Brax to speak next.

'Okay,' he said. 'There is a box in that small blue case there.' Brax indicated as best he could with a movement of his head towards a case near the bottom of the pile in front of them.

One of the King's Shield picked it up and placed it at the feet of the wizard.

'This one?' Ethan asked.

Brax nodded.

'What is in it?' he asked.

'In that case are various trinkets, but inside the small box are a selection of rings.' Brax looked at the wizard and sighed. 'They each have unique qualities imbued into them I'm sure, but I have only worked out the qualities possessed by three of them. No doubt you will be able to figure out exactly what the others do.'

The wizard narrowed his eyes and looked down at the case.

'If there is any charm or similar protection on this case, then these two men will put a sword through your heart.'

Brax remained silent as the wizard stooped down and opened the case. He grabbed the box and stood up again, holding it in both hands.

The box had only a latch on it. There was no lock.

He reached out with it and turned the latch towards Brax, holding it out in front of his face.

He flicked the latch and pulled the box open. Nothing happened, so he turned it around and looked inside.

There were five rings inside, all different in shape and design. There was a plain gold ring, a silver ring with a red stone sunken into it, and a bronze ring with runes on it. Another was a chain-linked ring, both gold and silver and the last made of emerald or jade. It was green and shaped in a square. None of them looked particularly valuable at first glance.

Brax watched as the wizard turned his gaze back to him, then down to look at his hands that were tied to the chair.

'Why do you not wear them if you know what they are?'

'They are not mine to use now that I am back in the King's Realm,' he replied. 'The ones whose uses I am aware of are the square emerald one, the silver ring with the ruby in it and the one made of bronze.'

'Go on,' the wizard said after Brax paused again.

'The emerald one enables you to blend into your surroundings,' he said.

Ethan's eyebrows rose. 'An invisibility ring,' he said to himself, smiling as he looked at it.

'No,' Brax said. 'That would be ridiculous.' He watched with some satisfaction as a wave of anger emanated from the wizard. 'It simply lets the wearer blend in with whatever background they have behind them. You must be touching something solid and you cannot move while you do so. As soon as you break contact with it or you move, then the effect is broken.' Brax smirked as he finished. 'It is good for hiding.'

Brax watched as the wizard reigned in his temper and calmed himself.

'And the silver ruby ring?' Ethan asked.

'That one let me start my fires. Especially helpful when I was traversing the Southern Dwarven realm. Perhaps it may be useful to augment the powers of one that can already use magical fire.' He saw the wizard's anger and fear completely disappear. He knew he would be pleased with that one.

Ethan picked up the ruby ring and slid it on a finger. He reached out his hand and fire flared up in front of him. The fire didn't scorch anything as the wizard let it burn only in the air in front of himself. He had it under his control and steadily increased the intensity. Brax watched as the fire quickly changed colour from a light orange to a searing white.

The flames disappeared as quickly as they had appeared and the wizard turned back to Brax. An intense but satisfied look on his face now.

'A powerful trinket indeed, Brax. One that will certainly help in the defence of this town.'

Brax smiled back at him and hoped he wouldn't be able to work out what the other two rings did. Brax certainly didn't want him to have too much augmented power for when he needed to force his escape from this hall.

He had a feeling Ethan wouldn't be satisfied with just a few powerful items to assist with the defence of Shadow Hill. He strongly suspected that this wizard intended to take for himself everything of use that he could find within Brax's things.

Eventually, he would attempt to open the chest he had booby-trapped and held within it his cloak. His most prized possession. He would risk death before allowing this carrion to have it.

Ethan took the ruby ring off, placed it back into the box, and closed it. He handed it to the King's Shield at his side, who in turn went and placed it on the end table.

'I will inspect the other rings later,' he said, before walking back over to the pile. 'Now what else are you willing to share with me?'

'I beseech you one last time, wizard Ethan,' Brax said. 'All of those items of value are for the king and his more powerful wizards. Could you not satisfy yourself with the rings you have. They will help with your defence of this town.' He knew what the response would be.

'I will decide what is needed here and what can be taken forth to the capital. As I said, this town is crucial to the defence of the entire realm.' Ethan's temper was under control now. Brax assumed he was feeling better now with the rings in his possession and the promise of more.

'The threat won't come from just this direction, Ethan,' Brax persisted. 'It will come from the south, the north, and the west. The other two items I have that are of considerable power will be needed by the king.'

'Tell me where they are,' Ethan said.

'You are not listening,' Brax said. 'I'm sure the king won't begrudge your taking of the rings, but these other two will be a whole different matter.'

'I won't ask you again,' Ethan said. Brax could see that his temper and anger were returning. His chance was almost upon him.

He sat there silently, deciding not to answer him at all this time. He hoped the wizard was seeing stubbornness in his behaviour and nothing more sinister.

'Atriol,' Ethan said, looking at the King's Shield standing behind his right shoulder.

'Yes, wizard?' Atriol replied.

'Kill the goblin,' Ethan ordered, no emotion in his voice.

Brax watched as Atriol drew his sword and began walking towards Linf.

'Curse you, wizard,' Brax said. 'The large chest with the lock on the outside of it.' He spoke loudly and in a voice traced with anger. 'I have made it clear that what is inside should be taken to the Capitol. Your guards have heard me.'

Atriol stopped as Brax began to speak and now walked to the pile again. He picked up the large chest with little effort and sat it down on the ground in front of Ethan.

'Now,' the wizard began. Brax could see he was still trying his hardest to contain his anger and frustration, but there was enough there for Brax to take hold of when he was ready. 'What treasure is inside this one?'

'Inside that is a cloak and it is something that could turn any battle for the one who wears it.' He saw all of the anger disappear again and knew the wizard was excited about this one.

'Atriol,' he said, indicating for the King's Shield to open it.

His guard pulled open the lid, reached inside, and pulled out the cloak that sat on top of a number of other nondescript clothing items.

The wizard turned to him with a suspicious look on his face.

'It looks rather plain to me. I sense no magical qualities within it at all.'

'I can't attest to your skills at determining what is and isn't magical great wizard, but I can assure you,' he continued quickly as the wizard took a step towards him, 'that it will give the wearer something quite unique.'

Ethan said nothing as the King's Shield handed him the cloak.

'Put it on and it will strike fear in your enemies. A fear so great it can be quite debilitating to any who would seek you harm.'

Ethan's eyebrows rose.

'Perhaps,' Brax continued, 'that one skilled in the use of magic could enhance it more than I was able to, which was still quite substantial. It is the true reason I was able to pass unscathed through the perilous lands in which I travelled. Why I was able to defeat a green bear and capture this loathsome creature.'

He looked at Linf and saw her curl her lip at him.

He looked at the wizard and was glad he hadn't noticed the look she gave him. If the wizard suspected Linf could understand him, then his whole plan was at risk of failing before it began.

'So am I to just take your word for this?' Ethan said to him.

'What would I gain for making such a thing up?' Brax countered. 'I am well aware that you intend to go through everything I own. Lying to you about this serves me no purpose,' he finished with a thin smile.

'As to how I can prove it to you.' Brax looked again in the direction of Linf.

'Put it on and see what it does to the goblin over there. I am quite sure she would love to get her hands on you if given the chance.'

There it was. His plan now rested on whether the goblin would be smart enough to catch on to what he had said and the way he now looked at her.

Ethan waited a while, looking at the goblin while he seemed to be deciding what he would do next.

'Be warned though,' Brax said to him. 'Whenever I used the cloak it tended to have a weakening effect on me, as if it were drawing some of my own energies to power itself.'

As the wizard began to put it on, Brax spoke again.

'No offence, but you don't look terribly strong. It may be best to have only a quick go of it.' He smiled as the wizard looked at him with a contemptuous sneer.

'You'll pay for that comment, old man,' he said, as he turned to Linf with the cloak now on, a wave of anger from his last comment clearly visible.

Brax looked over and was glad to see the goblin with a sudden terrified look on her face. She even leaned back in the seat she was on, as if she were trying to move away from the wizard.

Then to his horror, he saw her grab hold of the wizard's anger and begin to draw it into herself. She must have thought he meant for her to drain the wizard as well. He certainly hadn't meant that. He had intended to do that part himself. His control was much greater than that of the goblin and he feared she would go too far.

Both of the King's Guard tensed as the wizard suddenly went white in the face and began to sway a little on his feet.

As he began to rapidly weaken, the wizard began to panic a little as well, which the goblin also started to draw in to herself.

The one positive was that both of the wizards' guards believed it to be the cloak responsible and not the goblin or himself.

'You need to get the cloak off him,' Brax barked at them. 'It is draining him far too quickly!'

Both of the King's Shield moved quickly to the wizard and took a sleeve each. As they began to remove it from him Brax nodded to Linf, who was fortunately now looking at him.

As one they both snapped the bonds that held them.

Brax also latched on to the fear emanating from the wizard now and shot a pulse of that energy into both of the King's Shield. It struck the one nearest to him and knocked him off his feet and onto the ground.

Linf did the same to the one closest to her; however, her effort only stunned him. It knocked him back a short distance but he managed to keep his feet and also his wits.

Brax' second pulse only just knocked him over in time, as his sword was poised to run through the goblin.

Before either of them were back on their feet, Brax stepped quickly over to the wizard and lifted him to his feet. He curled his right arm around his throat from behind and turned in the direction of the King's Shield, as both of them jumped back to their feet.

'If you move,' Brax said quickly, 'I will snap his neck like a twig.'

He could see both men tense. He knew they were measuring their chances of preventing him from carrying out his threat.

'I am stronger than I look,' he continued in a serious voice, 'and he will be dead before you get half way.'

They didn't try to move against him, but Brax knew it would be just a matter of time before they would chance it.

'I didn't come here to fight you or this wizard,' he went on. 'I only want to return to the capital and finish the task that has been set for me.'

He knew these men understood duty and he had already planted the seeds in their heads earlier that his was a just and ordered mission for their king.

'I have seen enough.' The voice came from the left of Brax and it took him by surprise, but he kept his eyes on the two men spaced out in front of him.

'Put your weapons away and stand down,' the voice said with authority.

To Brax's surprise, the two King's Shields put their swords back into their sheaths and took a couple of steps back, their bodies no longer poised to attack.

Brax turned his head to look at the old man now standing behind the seats at the end of the hall. He had forgotten he was even there.

'You may keep hold of the wizard until you feel comfortable enough to let him go, but my men will not attack. You have my word on that.'

Brax had no intention of letting the wizard go, yet he suddenly realised who had been in charge here all along.

'I just have a few questions before you are sent on your way stranger.'

Brax had assumed he was some dithering old man, just a figurehead that answered to the wizard. Looking at him now, standing upright and proud with a spark in his gaze, he knew this man had definitely been in control all along.

'The Wizard Ethan serves a purpose and is crucial to the survival of my town; however, he can be a little arrogant and over the top at times.'

He looked at and indicated with an outstretched hand the two King's Shield.

'These two bear witness. You will suffer no more harm or indignity while you remain here. I swear this to you.' He turned his gaze back to where Brax stood holding the stricken wizard. 'You can release him now.' It was as much an order now as it was a request.

Brax looked across at Linf. He saw the confusion on her face. She wouldn't have understood anything the old man had said and was still drawing strength from the wizard, ready to continue their attack.

'I believe your words, good sir, and I thank you, belatedly, for the welcome you give both myself and the goblin into your town.'

He looked at the old man. 'I assume correctly that your protection extends to her?'

Brax saw him pause for a moment and then nodded his acceptance.

'I'm still not sure what your purpose with this creature is, but you seem to have some control over it. It will not be harmed.'

'Very good,' Brax said and let the wizard fall from his grasp. Linf had drained so much that he wasn't able to steady himself on his feet, but he remained conscious. Atriol moved forward and helped him to his feet, taking him to the nearest chair and putting him in it.

Brax couldn't help giving Ethan a small grin as the wizard glared hatred at him.

'Now, the first of my questions, Master Brax, if I may?' the old man walked around the table he was behind and into the centre area where the rest of them stood. He stopped next to the pile of Brax's belongings.

'Does that cloak actually do anything other than help keep the chill out?' he smiled as he finished. Brax knew this man definitely ruled these parts. If he didn't, then he wouldn't be smiling at the trick Brax had played on his wizard. A wizard who was seething with so much anger right now and looked ready to explode.

'It is actually made of a wonderful fibre, woven by the dwarves in the Southern Kingdom. It does a remarkable job of keeping out more than just the chill. You could walk through snow in that and be kept relatively warm.' He spoke seriously, but he knew the wizard had probably gone purple in the face now.

The old man smiled again, but Brax saw the humour didn't reach his eyes this time. He was still very suspicious of him, but Brax wasn't worried anymore. He had been given the old man's word that he would be safe and he knew none would dare break their word in front of the two stone-faced men present in the hall.

'You have given me a gift of the rings, for which I am grateful. The wizard in his haste forgot to ask what the other ring accomplished. I assume also that you know exactly what properties the final two possess.' Brax was impressed with this man already, but also a little wary. He was a smart one and there was something about him he couldn't put his finger on.

'He knows nothing, Lord Marcus, he is a charlatan and a thief!' The wizard practically spat the words out.

'Yet he bested you, Ethan,' Marcus replied in a level voice, seemingly unperturbed at the interruption.

'All the more reason to hold them and find out exactly how he did it!' The wizard was so angry it was blinding him to the ire that Brax saw building within Marcus' stance.

'I have given my word they will not be molested further!' Lord Marcus bellowed this time. The wizard went silent.

'However, he being able to beat you, Ethan, is not my concern today. We have battles to prepare for, most probably a siege of such proportions it will be difficult to imagine.' He turned back to Brax. 'I appreciate there are items amongst your little hoard here that will be of benefit to the king, but what Ethan said earlier was true. If we are able to repel those that will advance here, it will strengthen the chances those at Havern have and ultimately the Capitol itself.'

Brax looked at him. He knew there was something he had that would certainly help this man and those he protected within the walls of his town, but it was also something worth a small fortune. He also knew he couldn't ask for payment now. His story that he was a king's man would hold no water if he started bartering.

He decided the good will it would provide was worth it at this point in time.

'At the bottom of the chest that cloak was in is a helm.'

Atriol stepped over to the chest again and rummaged inside. He pulled out a very plain helm. It was dented and looked to be very old, which it was.

In the centre of it was a plain gem, translucent and dull.

'I assume it can be worn by anyone, as I myself was able to use it,' Brax said. 'It is now yours.'

Atriol handed it to his Lord and stepped back.

Lord Marcus looked at it and then put it on his head. Brax suddenly had a sinking feeling he would use it against him, but he still believed he would keep his word and the moment of dread passed quickly.

It was too large for his head and sat loosely. There was no chin strap.

'So how do I use it and what does it do?' Marcus asked.

'I once used it on a raiding party of goblins. If was effective against them all, maybe a dozen of them. I'm not sure how many more it would work on.' He paused before continuing, still a small sliver of doubt within him.

He sighed but continued.

'I was able to control them, Lord Marcus. They turned from menacing foe into loyal allies.'

He saw the eyebrows rise on Marcus' face and a broad smile appear.

'I spoke in my own language, but they understood when I told them they weren't to fight against me. It stopped them in their tracks. When I told them to turn and leave, they did so without hesitation.' Brax remembered it well. He wanted to try it on greater numbers but the risk was too great if it didn't work. 'I don't know how long the control lasted or on how many more it would work against, or whether it would even work on those creatures more powerful than a goblin, but there you have it. You can have your enemies fighting themselves before they even reach your walls.'

'I won't lie and say I am not intrigued as to how you came to be in possession of so many rare and powerful artefacts, but I will restrain myself in thanks for those that you have given me. However reluctantly those gifts were bestowed,' he added.

He took the helm off and Brax was sure it was a look of mischief he now gave him.

'Ethan,' Marcus turned again to his wizard, who looked to have regained at least some of his strength, if not his good humour.

'I would like you to shake hands with Master Brax here and give him a hug for the troubles you have caused him.' He said it with a smile.

A look of shock and amazement appeared on the wizard's face, replaced quickly by one of indignation and rage.

'That is one order I will not take from you my Lord. I am here to assist with the defence of this town, not pander to miscreants and liars such as this. . .'

Brax saw him put the helm back on as the wizard spoke.

'Shake hands with Brax and give him a hug. Then you can go and sit down again,' Lord Marcus interrupted.

The wizard stopped talking immediately, stood up and walked over to Brax. He held out his hand and Brax shook it. He then embraced him before walking back to his chair and sitting down again.

His eyes showed that the power of compulsion ended the moment he was seated back in his chair.

'My Lord, you go too far!' The anger coming off the wizard was remarkable Brax thought. He looked at the goblin and gave her such a look that Linf immediately ceased the drain she had started.

Brax chuckled on the inside though.

Marcus ignored the protestations of his wizard. He again took the helm off and handed it to one of the King's Shield.

'Trevain, fetch the guardsmen back in here and have them load all of Master Brax's belongings back on to his cart.' The King's Shield left with a small nod of his head in acknowledgement.

'You are welcome to spend the night,' he said. 'I will have the goblin held somewhere secure if you would prefer it?' He tilted his head as he waited for Brax to reply.

Brax wasn't too keen on staying the night now. He felt it would be prudent for them to move on after what had transpired here today. The wizard had certainly made no promise they would be left alone. His look held murder in it.

'A night to rest would be appreciated, Lord Marcus, but I am comfortable having the goblin stay with me. She is no threat.' He left it at that. Let him think what he would about their situation.

'Very well,' Marcus said. 'Atriol will take you to where you can rest before departing in the morning.' He turned to go and then stopped.

'It might be best if you didn't wander about tonight.' He didn't wait for a reply but left through a door near the back of the hall.

'If you would follow me,' Atriol said. 'Trevain will ensure your things are kept secure.'

He began walking towards the main entrance at the end of the hall.

Brax indicated for Linf to follow and they walked after the King's Shield.

It was almost dark outside as they left the hall. Brax only then realised how tired he was.

'What happened in there, old man?' Linf asked him as soon as they were left alone in their humble lodging for the night. 'Why didn't we kill them all?!'

Brax could understand somewhat why the goblin was upset but he was in no mood to put up with her right now. There was no way he was going to get at his invisibility robe. There would be no stealing away any children tonight or feeding on anyone else for that matter.

'It wasn't worth the risk, goblin. We may have been able to overpower the two King's Shields, but I wasn't sure of the old man. There is something about him that I can't quite work out. It is enough that we will get away from here relatively unscathed.' He spoke the last part with a bitterness in his voice. He was less than pleased with what he had been forced to part with. The helm and rings were incredibly valuable, in both coin and the magic they had within them. He had to reassure himself once again that compared to the prize he sought in Havern they were objects well spent.

'You promised me a child while we were here!' The goblin still wasn't done.

'Enough!' Brax said. 'You will need to wait a little longer yet, that is all.' He lay down on one of the beds.

'I'm sleeping now. We will talk more when we leave in the morning.' Brax was surprised when Linf made no further comment.

Brax awoke before it was light outside and walked over to where Linf was sleeping in her cot. He nudged the mattress and she sat up, a startled look on her face.

'What do you want?' she snarled. 'Is something wrong?'

'It is time to go,' he said and turned to grab the few things he had brought with him to their room.

'It's still night time,' the goblin said and rolled back over again.

'I'm leaving now,' he said. 'You can wait for the sun to come out. Good luck walking out of town on your own.'

He didn't have time nor was he in the mood to argue with her this morning.

He turned before opening the door and saw that Linf had thrown her blanket on to the floor and was standing now, glaring at him.

'It's dark. Why are we going so early?' the goblin didn't sound happy. 'Is this because I drained the wizard yesterday?'

Brax was going to respond, but he knew it would just lead to more complaining and more questions.

Instead, he turned back to the door and opened it. Linf was still talking as he walked outside.

'You're angry because I did a better job than you.'

He preferred her with the sack over her head.

They made their way to the back of the place they had been put up at. Brax was pleased to see the two guards posted there still looked relatively alert. They didn't seem surprised to see him and one turned to open the door to the shed.

His horses had been housed in the shed along with his cart. He didn't speak to either of them as he hitched Storm Cloud and Dark Star to the cart. Linf jumped in the back. He didn't see the need to cuff her this time and the look she had given him as she hopped in indicated she felt the same way.

Within a short time, they were ready to leave. Brax planned to stop when they were clear of the town and then feed the horses. He wanted to be away from this place.

Their next stop was going to be Havern and he wanted to be ready when they arrived. There was still a lot of planning to be done and the goblin wasn't quite ready, although her progress was beyond what he had hoped for when they had first left his home.

There were very few people about as they rolled out of the large shed and into the main street. The sun hadn't risen above the horizon yet, but the deep dark of the night was gone. The morning wasn't far away.

No one paid them any attention as they made their way to the western guard house. Brax was certain they would have been watched throughout the night. He figured their progress through the town had also been noted, but as they approached the large gates, they weren't stopped. Challenging those leaving was far less important than those who were looking to enter.

All of the farms they passed on this side of the town looked to be occupied still. There were farmers already out in their fields, guards standing watch at the paths leading into each farmhouse. Brax wasn't even tempted to stop at them. They were still far too close to Shadow Hill.

Once they had travelled past the final farmhouse with guards out front, Brax finally pulled the cart to a halt. It was mid-morning already and his horses needed taking care of.

Linf jumped down as he stopped and stretched her arms.

'How long will it take us to get to this town you are desperate to see?' she asked. He noticed she looked a little anxious.

'We should be there before it is dark tomorrow,' he said, studying her more closely. 'What is wrong with you?'

'Nothing old man,' she replied sharply. 'This better be worth it. I still think we should be heading the other way.'

'What is it with you and going east?' he asked, not for the first time. 'You don't know anyone there and I have told you already there is nothing but the Eastern Plains in that part of the world. Not a fun place.'

'I don't care what isn't there,' she persisted. 'I just have this annoying feeling we need to go there. You said yourself there are men in the plains. That means there are children as well and you promised me one of those!'

'I also told you that the men that live in the plains won't even bother asking what we are doing there. If they see you, then you'll be dead before you can decide whether to run or hide.' He wasn't sure if she was saying it just to annoy him or whether there was another reason she wanted to go there. Either way, once they had accomplished their task in Havern, she could go wherever she pleased. He would be glad to be rid of her.

'I have things to do now anyway, so go and annoy someone else.' He pulled some feed out of the back and walked over to Storm Cloud.

The 'annoying feeling' she had was growing stronger the further west they went and Linf couldn't shake it. It was really starting to get to her.

Another day and a half stuck in the back of the cart with nothing to do but think about how much she wanted to travel in the opposite direction. If he didn't get her a human child to feed on before they got there, things were going to get ugly. She knew her powers continued to grow and her control was getting better every time she used them.

The only thing stopping her taking her frustrations out on Brax was the uncertainty. She knew he was powerful, but just how much greater his power was to hers shrunk every day. It would be stupid to do something until she was sure she could beat him and that probably wasn't going to be before they got to Havern.

She decided it might be best if she waited to see what happened in Havern and take it from there. She knew he wouldn't need her after that, whatever that was. She also didn't know if he would risk trying to kill her after it was over. Maybe it would be best if they just said good-bye after that.

There was only one thing wrong with that happening. She really didn't want to be a lone goblin stuck in the middle of the human realm, no matter how strong she had become.

She needed Brax, if for no other reason than to keep her alive until she could get out of here and back into her own lands. Or into the plains, if that was where she needed to go.

She snarled at his back, silently cursing him for not getting her a human child and for bringing her here. Walking over to some trees to relieve herself, she decided she would wait for Brax to finish looking after his stupid horses before getting him to tell her what it was they were going to be doing when they got to the next town.

As she got back into the back of the cart and was about to ask her question, Brax threw her some food. She decided to wait a little longer as she made short work of it.

When they were on their way again, she carefully made her way to the other end of the cart, balancing precariously on a couple of his cases.

'What are you looking for?' Linf asked loudly. She knew he heard her, yet he said nothing.

'Why are we going to this town!' she yelled at him. 'I know you're not deaf,' she added. 'Stupid, but not deaf.'

He didn't even turn his head to look at her. She could see waves of anger coming from him and for a moment she was tempted to try and drain him a little, just to get his attention. Only for a moment though.

'Why are you ignoring me?' she asked in a quieter voice.

This time he did turn his head.

'Because I am thinking,' he said to her in a harsh voice. 'Because I am trying to work out a few things in my mind before we get there, so that we both aren't killed the moment we arrive.'

He turned back around.

Normally, Linf would have sat back down and brooded, but she'd had enough of him being in control and leaving her in the dark. She knew she had proven herself already. When they put that stinking hood over her head, she had accepted it. When he had wanted her to drain the wizard and fight the human without any anger or fear, she had done it without hesitating. She was smart and strong and she was tired of him not telling her anything!

'Like I nearly was back where we just came from,' she retorted, not moving from her perch. 'I want to know what we are going there for or I am getting off now!' She wasn't sure if she meant it, but she had reached her breaking point. The further they went, the worse her temper seemed to get.

The cart came to a sudden stop and she watched as Brax stepped down from the front and walked around to the back. She scurried over his things to the back of the cart.

She refrained from saying anything. She just glared at him, knowing he would be able to see how angry she was.

The anger coming from him was greater than she had ever seen it before, but before he said anything, the anger quickly dissipated. His look changed from an angry one to something she wasn't too sure of.

'Why are you so afraid?' he asked her.

Linf wasn't expecting that. Afraid? She wasn't scared. She just wanted to know what was going on!

'Are you trying to make me angry? You don't have to, because I already am. Just stop acting like you know it all, you ugly swine, and tell me why we're going to Havern!' She noticed his look hadn't changed.

'We go there to get something that belongs to me,' he said in a normal voice. There was no mocking and no anger. 'And before you ask, I am not going to tell you what it is. I am going to retrieve it and you are going to help me get it. It is for this reason alone I let you live after I saved your life.'

'I didn't ask to be saved,' Linf retorted, but without the same venom as before.

'Nevertheless,' he continued, 'you owe me, whether you agree with that or not.'

'Not,' was all Linf said.

'Like I said, I don't care whether you agree with me or not. I also know you aren't going to walk off, whether I answer you or not. You and I both know you wouldn't get far, Linf, not in the middle of the King's Realm.' Brax still didn't smile nor say it in his usual mocking tone.

Linf decided to try a different tactic.

'Why do you need my help? What do you want me to do?' Linf looked at him suspiciously now. 'It better not be as your prisoner again! I'm not going through that again.'

'You'll do whatever I tell you to do, goblin, and you'll do it well. Or else you'll die,' he said nonchalantly, 'and not necessarily by my hand.'

She tried not to let her anger get the better of her. She had tried hard to keep it in check on several occasions now and it had helped her situation then. She took a bit longer to respond this time though.

'What do you want me to do?' she asked again.

'When we are nearly at Havern I want you to try and kill as many people as you can.' He did smile this time.

Linf was struck dumb for a short time.

'What are you talking about?' she said finally. 'You're not funny. I'm not getting myself killed to help you, you scum. If you want me to get myself killed you bear's ass, you can just do it now. Or at least try,' she added, trying to calm herself before he could draw the anger from her.

He just continued smiling.

'You can try and stop the anger goblin, but the fear in you is intense at the moment. I could drain you before you even began to fight me.'

'You lie, old man,' she spat back at him. 'I am not afraid of going to the human dung heap.'

He looked at her with that strange look again.

'You don't even realise you are exuding such fear do you?' he said. Linf wasn't sure if he said it to her or to himself.

Either way, she'd had enough.

'I don't even know what that word is,' she said. 'I've had enough for real this time you old fool. Let's get this over with.'

He had no fear emanating from him and the anger wasn't enough for her to draw strength from him or debilitate him in any way.

As soon as she saw this, she decided to simply charge at him. She was a goblin and was physically stronger than him. If she caught him off guard she could tear his throat out before he even knew what was happening.

Unfortunately, for the goblin, he was more than ready for her.

As she leapt from the back of the cart, a pulse of energy struck her in the chest, knocking her back into the old man's belongings. It stunned her for just a moment, but before she could look to stand up again, Brax began to drain her. She tried futilely to resist what he was doing, but even to her stubborn brain, she knew it was no use. She lay back against one of his large chests as her life force was steadily drained from her.

Before she lost consciousness, the drain stopped. She looked at him as he stood at the back of the cart, still with very little expression on his face.

'I'm not going to kill you, Linf. Not just yet. Not until you have heard me out, you foolish goblin child.'

She knew listening to him was about all she had the strength to do right now, so she didn't even try to move as he continued speaking.

'I need you to kill as many people as you can so that I can get an audience with the Lord of Havern. I will be the one to stop your killing frenzy and will convince his guards to take us to see him. I won't hurt you any worse than I just did. A bit of play acting will reduce any real hurt you may otherwise receive.'

Linf was still too angry to reply. A little too weak as well.

'I know it sounds a bit like how we got into the other town, but I believe it will be a little harder to get the opportunity to see the lord this time. I think we will actually need to convince him of your worth. Slaughtering a lot of people should be enough to do that.'

'Just kill me now,' she managed to say to him. He may as well, she thought. If she was taken to their lord after killing so many of his people, there was no chance they would let her leave afterwards 'I'm not helping just so you can have another kill me and save you the trouble.'

'I agree, it's a great risk you will be taking,' Brax said. He looked much calmer now. 'But at least it gives you a chance.'

He stepped up on to the cart. Linf didn't see what he had in his hand. Even as she saw his arm swinging, she didn't have the strength to raise her hands to try and block it. Something crashed into the side of her skull and the world went dark.

Brax hopped back onto the front of the cart and got his horses moving again. He was furious with how things had panned out. He hadn't intended on telling the goblin his plans. She would need to be kept subdued until they reached the outskirts now and that would take more effort than he was hoping to expend. He would need all the power he could muster if he hoped to survive the upcoming conflict in Havern.

He also wanted Linf to be at her own peak strength when she went on her killing spree. He understood she could regain that strength quickly enough, but he was still concerned. She would be weakened when they arrived and she would look to fight against him rather than with him.

He needed to think how he could overcome this new dilemma. At present, he couldn't think of anything, but he had more than a day to think on it and to work on getting Linf to trust him again.

He took a deep breath and looked ahead, brought suddenly out of his inner thoughts as he caught sight of three mounted horses on the horizon ahead.

They were the first people he had seen since they left Shadow Hill and he was surprised to see anyone this far out of the town. No one was travelling during these times. He was curious what might be so important they had left the relative safety of Havern to travel to Shadow Hill.

He pulled up his horses and walked quickly to the back of the cart. Linf was still unconscious and cuffed to the side. He grabbed a blanket and put it over the top of her.

Getting back up on the front of the cart, he hoped she didn't wake before they passed these travellers. He couldn't be bothered trying to explain again why he had a goblin in the back of his cart.

CHAPTER 39

Havern

THEY RODE IN relative silence for the next few hours until they reached the first of the farms on the fringe of Havern. Rather, the first that showed signs of still being occupied. Valdor knew it would be dangerous for those who remained and very stressful, but the large town still needed to feed itself. They were approached on the well-worn trail they now rode on by several of the king's soldiers.

The soldiers soon recognised that two of those on horseback were King's Shields and one of them broke from the rest to ride up and meet them, a large smile on his face.

'Greetings,' he beamed, as he stopped several strides in front of them.

To be polite, Valdor and his companions stopped their horses to speak with him.

'It gladdens me to see you here,' he said. 'We haven't heard word from the capital in several days now and swords such as yours will be invaluable in the coming conflict. My name is Brenshan and I am in charge of the protection of these farms.'

'Greetings to you,' Valdor said. It had been agreed he would do the talking, as it would be better if no one were to start asking questions about why the Princess' steward was riding in the company of two King's Shield.

'It is fortunate I have no bad news to relay, but our journey requires some haste.'

The man looked as if he was waiting for something more, but when Valdor offered nothing, he turned his horse around.

'I will escort you to the next guard post then.' He prodded his horse into a trot.

It didn't take them long to arrive at the next set of soldiers. Valdor saw the advantage in having them so close together and in smaller numbers. It was better than having them grouped together in one force at the first stop.

The Lord of Havern knew he had to keep as many farms operating as he could and these along the main trail would be the easiest to defend. The creatures plaguing the realm could attack from anywhere, so if any of the posts were attacked, then the others were close enough to come quickly to their aid. The men all looked alert, which Valdor appreciated.

He knew some of the King's Shield were housed at Havern. He had no doubt their counsel was being listened to. They were trained in more than just combat.

As they trotted along past the third guard post Valdor noticed a cart at the front of one of the farms with several people getting in. He had seen similar carts at the farms they had already passed.

'Why are they getting into the wagon?' he asked the soldier escorting them to the next guard post.

'No one sleeps at the farmhouses, sir. Those that work them are all transported back to Havern every evening.' He didn't need to explain why.

Valdor nodded his head and they continued on.

After another two guard posts they finally came in sight of the large walls of Havern.

Over the previous few hundred years, Havern had grown much larger and as it did, so too did the walls that surrounded it. Ten times the height of a man and surrounding the entire town, they were a formidable defence, which they needed to be.

Unlike other large towns within the realm, Havern had no other natural defences to augment its own. There was no cliff at its back, not even a hill or similar rise to build it on. The land around these parts was quite flat, with a couple of good size rivers running past the town on either side. They were the reason Havern had grown where it did. The ground was extremely fertile.

The two rivers started out as one where they flowed off the mountain, then forked and stayed divided as they moved through the King's Realm.

Havern itself had grown between the two rivers. It marked the point where the two came closest to rejoining one another. Nowhere else did they meet again before they flowed into the black waters of the Dark Swell.

Before recent events, much of Havern's resources had been sent to the capital. They had grown wealthy as a result and their farmlands had grown and diversified. This in turn had attracted Dwarves from the Southern Mountain Kingdom and enabled them to produce enough to trade with them also. This had increased the wealth of the region remarkably, both in the coin the Dwarves sold and also the magic they dealt in.

Valdor wondered how the recent halt in trade had affected the people in Havern. They were at no risk of going without, but he had seen first-hand how the loss of wealth could drive a man to do foolish things.

He hoped the threat of creatures that haunted the realm would galvanise those that remained instead of causing unrest.

As they approached the gates, two men on horseback rode out to meet them.

Valdor recognised them both before he could see their faces. The way they rode and the build of each was enough to tell him which of the King's Shield these men were.

He knew if anyone had recognised Heridah on their way in then others would have accompanied them, but for a couple of King's Shield and an old man, these two were all that propriety dictated.

As they came into sight, Valdor saw a flicker of surprise pass across the face of Talor, a stocky man that Valdor knew well. They had fought together a number of times on the goblin borders. He was in his fifties now but still as fit any man thirty years his junior.

'Well met, Valdor,' he said. He inclined his head to Catlin. 'Well met to you as well, Catlin.'

'Talor,' they both said in unison.

The other man, a few years senior to Talor, looked straight at the wizard as he came to a halt.

'Heridah?' he said it as a question.

'All is well, Handor,' Heridah replied to the lean and much taller King's Shield. He looked almost skinny, such was the lightness of his frame, which was at odds to the strength and skill the man possessed. He was one of the finest of their order and had volunteered for the Havern assignment six months ago. Before that, he had been one of the King's personal guard. Valdor remembered at the time he told Dayhen he wished to give a younger man the honour he had been blessed with for so long. Havern was lucky to have him here.

'The princess is safe in the capital with her father,' Heridah finished.

Handor gave a small, satisfied nod and then a thin smile.

'Then let us not delay,' Handor said. 'Your rooms are being readied. I'm sure you'd like time to rest before meeting those you have come to speak with.'

'We won't be staying long, Handor,' Valdor said. 'We are passing through.'

'Even more reason for haste. I sense you are in a hurry to be on your way, if that is your assignment.'

Valdor knew neither man would ask what that assignment was. The fact Heridah accompanied both he and Catlin was enough for him to surmise that whatever their purpose, it was important to the welfare of the realm. The fact Heridah had left the princess back at the capital would have confirmed as much.

'I would like time to speak with Braylin before we continue our journey,' Heridah said to the King's Shield. 'If you could let him know. We will stay only as long as it takes to sufficiently rest our horses.'

Handor gave a small nod and Talor spurred his horse forward into the township of Havern.

Valdor knew the wizard would be waiting for them when they arrived at Lord Jaron's residence, which was in the centre of town next to the stables.

The rest of them rode in to Havern at a more relaxed pace, people making way on the streets when they saw the three King's Shield approaching.

As expected, Braylin was waiting for them at the steps to the residence, Lord Jaron standing beside him.

Jaron came down the steps as they reined in their horses.

'My apologies, Heridah,' he blustered, as the wizard dismounted. 'I wasn't told of your coming, otherwise, I would have organised a more fitting welcome for one of your standing.' He looked around. 'My guards are obviously fools if they failed to recognise you.' He continued to look around. 'Excuse my own foolishness, but where is the princess Areana?'

All knew while in public the two were inseparable.

'Pray tell me nothing untoward has happened to our beautiful princess?' He actually sounded genuinely concerned.

Heridah looked down at him and wondered, like he did every time he visited here, how this man was in charge of such an incredibly wealthy and prosperous town.

'No, Lord Jaron,' Heridah said to him as he walked past him, not caring about the proper greetings and protocols. 'She is safe in Lakerth and in very good health.' He paused and looked back at the startled Lord of Havern. A portly man, his face had gone red at the insult.

'I will be sure to pass on to your king the heartfelt and genuine concern you had for his daughter. He will be pleased to hear it from such a loyal man.'

He gave a small bow and walked inside with his fellow wizard.

He still possessed some diplomacy, Valdor thought to himself, as Lord Jaron's face returned to its normal pinkish colour and he smiled to Heridah's departing back.

'Lord Jaron,' Valdor spoke up, as the Lord moved to follow Heridah and Braylin inside. He knew the wizard wouldn't want Jaron looking over their shoulders as they spoke and he would be curious as to why Heridah was meeting with his wizard.

Jaron stopped and turned to face Valdor.

'Sir,' he said and then 'Ma'am' to Catlin. 'My good man Handor here will take you to freshen up from your journey.' He quickly turned again and started racing up the steps, obviously not wanting the other two men to get too far ahead of him.

'Lord Jaron,' Valdor said again, this time louder and with a very subtle note of annoyance in his voice.

Jaron was pompous, but he was a diplomat to the core and he recognised the severity of insulting one of the King's Shield. He stopped in his tracks and turned back once again. He made no move to go back down the steps, however.

Valdor was not insulted of course. Members of the King's Shield didn't tend to get annoyed easily, but he needed the man's attention.

'My apologies, Lord Jaron, but I didn't get a chance to introduce myself and my companion and to thank you for the hospitality you have forwarded us.' He didn't like to talk so much, but the sooner Heridah had the chance to complete his talks with his fellow wizard, the sooner they could continue with their journey.

'The King's Shield has no need to thank me for entering my town good sir, but I must try to catch up with my wizard.' He finished with a gracious smile.

'My name is Valdor and this is Catlin.' He wasn't surprised Jaron didn't recognise him. During those times he had been to Havern, he never had need to attend at Lord Jaron's residence.

Jaron stopped again in turning to leave and stared.

'*The* Valdor.' This time he not only turned back to Valdor and Catlin but made his way back down to the bottom of the steps again. 'My apologies, I should have recognised you.' He gave Handor a look. 'I would have hoped my own King's Shield would have informed me of the names of those they were bringing to my home.'

He walked over to Valdor and reached out his hand in greeting.

Valdor shook it and indicated Catlin with his other hand. He knew she would be aware of his intentions, as she also warmly shook hands.

'My Lord,' was all she offered, as Jaron turned his attentions back to Valdor.

'I haven't been here for many years, Lord Jaron, but I have heard some men in the capital speak of how your own stables are now as fine as those in Lakerth, if not more resplendent.' Valdor was keen to be out of this town and back on their way as soon as they could.

'I can show you them myself if you would be gracious enough to accompany me,' he beamed at Valdor.

'I would be honoured,' Valdor replied, as they walked away from the steps and towards the stables around the next corner.

'I must admit I am curious as to why the greatest King's Shield in the realm has travelled here with the princess' tutor and confidante.'

Valdor had expected nothing less from the man. It was this reason he had distracted him from following Heridah and saved the wizard from being bombarded with the same questions.

'Lord Jaron, it is nothing that specifically need concern you regarding the welfare of Havern, of that I can assure you.' Valdor had been around those whose days were consumed with political machinations and the sort. His military lifestyle and solitary nature helped whenever he needed to be obscure. Everyone knew the King's Shield were not inclined to speak of that which was not within their scope of concern. 'Our destination on this assignment will take us outside the King's Realm.'

Before Jaron Could ask any of the questions Valdor saw he was desperate to get out, he continued without pause. 'Such is the importance of the task set to us he has entrusted it with one of those closest to him, with one whom he trusts enough to care for the upbringing of his daughter. With the evil threatening the lands, he would be foolish to send one of his renowned wizards. Unfortunately, Heridah has not been able to disclose to either Catlin or myself exactly what the purpose is behind that which we seek.'

Jaron knew, as did everyone else, that a King's Shield never lied. Valdor was satisfied he also believed one of the King's Shield wouldn't hide the truth in clever words that spoke the truth but left out a lot more.

Yet he felt no guilt. Their quest for the idol had nothing to do with him and was not his business.

They turned the corner and before he could probe Valdor further Catlin sudden exclaimed, 'Lord Jaron, I see that those Valdor has spoken to did not lie. This complex is remarkable.'

Jaron's attention was turned from Valdor and his pomposity came to the fore once more.

'Thank you Lady Catlin,' he said, 'they are a wonder are they not?'

'May we see some of the horses Havern is also spoken of in high regard?' Valdor was glad she was also skilful at distraction. Her timing was as impressive as her sword stroke.

The next twenty minutes consisted of Lord Jaron regaling them with stories of horse bloodlines as well as other pursuits he liked to partake in on horseback, of which Havern was the equal to, if not slightly more advanced than those in Lakerth. Hunting and racing took up much of his story telling.

Valdor and Catlin were no longer required to think about their responses. Once Jaron got started, he seemed to go on and on. Valdor had obviously convinced him he knew nothing of any consequence in relation to the task their king had set them on, so he didn't bother trying to garnish anything further from them.

Eventually, they made their way out of the stables and back around the corner towards the front steps of Jaron's residence.

Valdor was pleased to see Heridah waiting for them on the steps. Braylin was no longer with him.

'Lord Jaron,' Heridah exclaimed in greeting. 'I was surprised you didn't join us, but I expect Valdor and Catlin were adequate company.'

'Of course, Heridah. I did mean to join you, but my attention was taken from me and the next thing I knew we were in the stables talking about horse racing and hunting.' He smiled, but also looked a little confused. Valdor suspected he had an inkling he might have been played, but was trying to work out whether those from the King's Shield would be capable of such a thing.

Eventually, he seemed to shrug it off as unlikely.

'Not to worry,' Jaron said with a large grin. 'You can join me for dinner in my private dining hall and we can converse then. I will have better rooms prepared for you.'

'You needn't bother, Lord Jaron,' Heridah cut in, before Jaron could start giving out orders to those waiting further up the steps. 'Unfortunately, our task is an urgent one and we are required to continue without further respite. I do hope you understand,' Heridah finished in a tone that suggested he would rather not have to leave so soon.

'I won't hear of it,' Jaron said, seemingly ignoring what Heridah had said and instead hearing only the regret in his voice. 'A short respite will not impact on your journey. If I know one thing and your companions are now only too well aware of it also, I know horses. The longer their rest, the faster you will be able to travel.' He winked at Heridah this time as he smiled. 'You certainly can't argue with that logic can you?'

'Believe me when I say if it were up to me I would spend many days here in this wonderful part of our King's Realm,' he emphasised the king part, 'however, it was King Dayhen himself who ordered us not to delay.' Heridah leaned in closer and spoke quietly, as if the words were for Jaron's ears only. Valdor heard him quite clearly. 'Would you like to be the one to tell Valdor we can make a small exception to his King's order?'

Jaron looked across at Valdor and seemed to think on it for longer than was truly necessary.

'A king's order to one of his Shield. I know that dilemma only too well,' he said in a voice far less cheery than the one he had used so far.

'So be it,' he said. 'Then I shall see you on your return through here and I will honour you as your station demands.' He was quickly back to his positive self.

'Until then,' Heridah said with a small bow. 'I look forward to it.'

They left shortly after with a larger escort than the one they had come in with. The two King's Shields were joined by ten of Jaron's own personal guard as they made their way back to the centre of town, before turning right this time towards the Northern Gates.

None of them spoke about their mission into the plains. Valdor and Catlin spoke in detail about Havern's defences and the threats they were facing, while Heridah kept his thoughts to himself.

As they approached the Northern Gates, Heridah's attention was drawn to a couple of small statured men walking slowly along the path. They had their hoods pulled down over their heads, covering their faces. They pulled a small cart behind them which looked to be full of their belongings and was covered by a blanket.

Heridah pulled up his horse and Valdor stopped.

'Go ahead,' Heridah said. 'I will meet you all at the gate. I won't be a moment. I think my horse has a stone in his shoe.'

Heridah knew Valdor wouldn't be deceived, nor would the other King's Shield with him, but the men with them were oblivious and they were the only ones that would report anything untoward back to Jaron. Not that Heridah was too concerned if they were to tell him he spoke to some dwarves, but he had always been wary of the Lord of Havern. He was a pompous man, unlike any other within the realm, but he knew that for the most part he was no fool.

Valdor nodded and indicated they should all continue. None of Jaron's men offered to stop with the wizard.

When they had moved on, Heridah got the attention of one of the dwarves that had already walked past him.

'A moment of your time, good dwarf,' he said in broken Dwarfish. Not many in Dayhen's realm knew any of their own language, so it was enough to get them to stop and turn around.

Looking closer at them as they turned around, Heridah was certain now they were from the Southern Kingdom, which is what he had expected and hoped. That crazy, foolhardy look wasn't present in the eyes of these two as it was in those from the North.

'My horse is lame and I was hoping you could help me look at it?' he said, this time in the common tongue. Their conversation would go much quicker if he didn't have to think so hard on what he was saying. His Dwarfish was passable but by no means fluent.

One of them stayed with their cart while the other walked over to him.

Heridah lifted the back leg of his horse as he did and showed him its foot.

The dwarf looked at it and then back to Heridah.

'The foot is fine,' he said in a gruff voice. 'What do you really want old man?'

Heridah smiled at him, but still kept hold of the leg.

'Just some information please. I can pay you of course.' Heridah knew these men gave away nothing for free.

'Show me the coin then. I have somewhere else I need to be.' He didn't waste words.

'What can you tell me about the southern pass through the mountains into the Eastern Plains?' Heridah reached inside his coat and pulled out a couple of silver coins.

The dwarf held his hand out and Heridah dropped them onto his palm.

'They are cold, windy, treacherous, and steep and did I mention very cold.' The dwarf gave a small smile and turned to walk away.

'I paid you for more than that.' Heridah said as the dwarf started to leave. 'Are you a thief to take someone's money for nothing in return?'

The dwarf rounded angrily on Heridah. 'Careful what you call me old man. I am here as a guest of Lord Jaron and he would be more upset with you than he would I if you were to be taught some manners right about now.'

'I paid you for information,' Heridah continued unabashed. 'I expect more than a poorly delivered weather report.'

The dwarf sniggered and turned around again.

Heridah put up a thin wall of air in front of the dwarf and watched with satisfaction as he tried without success to walk back to his companion. The dwarf turned back with an irritated look, but one decidedly less hostile.

'I am really going to need a little more,' Heridah said politely. 'Perhaps it was my fault for not being specific enough.' Inside, he was fuming at himself for having shown the dwarf he was a wizard, but he needed information about the mountain pass and this one was his best chance at getting it.

The dwarf glared at him but stayed where he was this time.

'Are they any worse of late than they have been in the past? Other than the details you have already provided to me free of charge.'

The dwarf continued to glare at him before answering.

'The weather is no worse and no better than it has always been. The tracks, trails, and paths to get into the plains are, as far as I have been told, also just as passable as they have always been.' The dwarf stopped again as if to say was that enough.

'Now for the part I paid you for,' Heridah said with a steely look. 'I will know if you are not totally truthful friend.'

Heridah realised the last part was not necessary. For all their bluster and thirst for riches, the dwarves were an honest race and Heridah was sure that whatever this dwarf told him would be a fact, as much as he was aware anyhow. He knew the thief accusation was going to get a rise out of him, as much as his last comment.

The dwarf looked furious now, but he was hesitant. To insult a wizard in the centre of Havern would have consequences. He had a typical Dwarven temper no doubt, yet he wasn't totally tactless either, unlike his northern cousins.

'I would not risk it if I had the choice to go another way,' he said. 'The evil you men speak about that is entering your realm seems to be festering within our own also.'

'Do tell,' Heridah said as he looked over his shoulder. Valdor and the others were almost at the gate now.

'A few new nasties and lots of the older ones,' he said. 'There will be new stories to frighten our children with soon, yet the oldest and scariest is also showing itself more than it ever has before.'

Heridah's heart sank. It was as he had feared. With a small wave of his hand he sent the dwarf on his way as he pulled himself back into his saddle.

He would need to convince Valdor the mountains were not their best route to take.

After they had said their farewells at the gate, the wizard and his companions started their ride north.

When they were no longer within sight Heridah pulled his horse up and the others followed suit.

'What did the dwarf say Heridah?' Valdor asked.

'Their realm is also under siege,' he replied. 'I would suggest, in the strongest sense I can, we turn east now and go around the mountains.'

Valdor wasn't pleased. They would have to turn south once they were well past the outskirts of Havern and find the main road to Shadow Hill. It would be faster than riding through the countryside below the shadow of the Southern Dwarven Mountains, but it would be a lot further than if they were to go through the mountains themselves.

Yet he had ignored the wizard one time already and he realised what he said now again made sense. If he were afraid of the *Krickshen*, then it would be folly to ignore him a second time.

'If we must go around, then we had best make haste,' Valdor replied as he looked at the wizard. Heridah nodded as they moved off again at a trot. They could gallop again once they were on level ground and try their best to make up for lost time.

CHAPTER 40

A Deal Is Done

'MASTER KEGAN,' LORD Jaron said pleasantly to the dwarf in front of him. 'It has been too long since you graced my hall.'

'Times have changed,' he said gruffly. 'The lands aren't as accommodating as they used to be. Even had a few of your people try to rob us before we were even half way here.'

'That is the sad truth of it, I'm afraid,' Jaron replied. 'Which is why it is so good to see you. I will no doubt have need of whatever it is you have brought to sell me.'

'I have some exceptional pieces for you,' Kegan said, his demeanour suddenly a little brighter. 'But they weren't easy to acquire.' The dwarf paused for a moment. 'And they weren't cheap.'

Jaron knew his words and the current state of the land would mean the dwarf's prices will have increased markedly, but he wasn't about to let this dwarf take advantage of him. He hadn't accumulated his wealth by giving it away.

'I have always paid a fair price,' Jaron said. 'I intend to offer you a fair price for these too. If they are what I am after.'

Kegan signalled his companion forward with the cart they had dragged with them. He pulled back the blanket to show Jaron what was inside.

Jaron walked over to it and looked inside.

There were all kinds of trinkets.

'How many of them have the special qualities you know I like so much?' he asked, not taking his eyes off what was inside.

'Several of them have been worked on by my brother,' Kegan replied. 'He tells me they are of the finest quality. You won't be disappointed.'

Jaron had always found it amusing how the dwarf's manner of speaking always changed when he was talking trade.

'Which ones?' Jaron asked. His usual patience was a little short today. The monsters that threatened his town were taking its toll on him. He didn't like feeling threatened.

Kegan picked up a bridle, which to the naked eye looked nothing more than a well-crafted piece.

'This will give extra strength and stamina to one of those beasts you enjoy riding around on so much. As requested.' Kegan added.

Jaron picked it up and had a closer look. He saw it had two small needles on the inside, where it would rest on top of its head.

'What are these?' he asked, indicating the needles.

'They need to be pressed into the skin,' Kegan replied patiently. 'So that the beast is joined to it. Won't work otherwise.'

'A little barbaric dwarf,' Jaron replied in a disgusted tone. 'I don't want to hurt him.'

'He won't feel a thing,' Kegan said. 'That is part of the charm. My brother Angus knows how much you care for them, so he added a little something to remove the pain it would've felt. Makes it even more valuable I'd say,' he finished with a grin.

Jaron just looked at him and put the piece aside as the dwarf reached in and grabbed out a long, slender dagger. It was made of a dark metal that Jaron hadn't seen before.

'This is the pick of the bunch,' Kegan said. 'One of the reasons why it took me so long getting here this time.'

Jaron's eyes opened wide as he looked at the blade the dwarf held up.

'For as long as I've been trading with your people, I have been told you do not forge armour or weapons for men. What is this?' he asked trying very hard to keep the excitement from his voice.

'Like I said,' the dwarf replied. 'Times are changing. We are all of us in danger these days. An exception has been made due to your long-standing patronage.'

Jaron studied the dwarf carefully now. He knew times were darker, but he didn't believe the dwarves would suddenly change their stance on arming men with their potent weapons. Even if it were just a dagger.

It suddenly dawned on him that Kegan was looking to make a large payday. He figured the dwarf may not know when it would be safe to return here again and he knew a weapon would guarantee him those sought-after riches. He wouldn't be surprised if he didn't even have his king's permission to sell it. Kegan might think no other dwarf would be coming here for quite some time so none could take back to his king what he had done.

'What does it do?' Jaron asked.

'If it comes into contact with blood, it burns as hot as the fiercest furnace. Stab someone with it and the flesh around the wound will practically melt.' Kegan smiled at him as he spoke.

'What is your price, Master Kegan?' Jaron asked him.

'For the dagger?' he asked.

'For everything in your cart.' Jaron said. He knew this was going to cost him a small fortune, so he may as well get an idea as to what the dwarf wanted.

Kegan looked surprised, as Jaron knew he would. He figured he might undersell if he got him off guard.

'You haven't even looked through it yet?' the dwarf said. Jaron knew that all dwarves preferred to sell each item individually. It improved the seller's chances of making an overall larger sum if he could haggle for each one. Plus he knew that dwarves loved to haggle as much as they loved amassing wealth.

'You have offered me something quite unique, my friend. I would like to return the gesture by purchasing everything you have brought with you.'

The dwarf turned to his companion and they spoke softly to each other for a short time.

'Your finest diamond, ten flawless dark rubies, and two of your smaller, but better horses.'

Jaron didn't even try to hide his surprise. Not only at the request of his finest diamond, but at the dwarf wanting horses. Everyone knew dwarves didn't ride.

'You ask a lot,' was all he said.

'I offer a lot,' was all the reply he got. Kegan would know that he was aware the weapon was offered without permission from his king. Jaron didn't know the punishment he would receive if he found out, but he knew it wouldn't be a pleasant one.

'My two finest ponies and the ten flawless rubies I can do,' Jaron replied, 'but you are obviously aware of the diamond you speak of and it's true worth.'

'That is my price,' the dwarf replied. 'It is a fair exchange.'

Jaron didn't reply straight away. He wanted the dagger and he would pay a small fortune for it. The magic it possessed was impressive, but the prestige he would hold being the first man to have in his possession a freely given, magical Dwarven weapon, was what drove him even more. Still he hesitated. The diamond was one of his greatest treasures and he would not give it up if there were something else he could offer in its stead.

'Instead of the diamond, I will offer you as many gold coins as you can comfortably pull in your cart.' It was a lot and far more than the items offered were worth.

'I have plenty of gold, Lord Jaron,' Kegan replied. He was stone-faced now the haggling had begun.

Jaron had done his homework over the years and he knew diamonds were in short supply within the Dwarven Mountains. The piece he had acquired had been brought to him from deep within the goblin lands and was like no other he had ever seen.

He also knew what other items were scarce in the Dwarven Kingdom.

'Very well,' Jaron said. 'I offer you five platinum wrought short swords. They are crafted by my personal smith and are very well constructed.' Platinum was rare and a metal that was stronger and able to be made sharper than any other material within the King's Realm. Again it was a higher price than he had wanted to make.

'You are welcome to add the swords to the deal, Lord Jaron, but my price is the diamond,' Kegan said. Jaron noticed that neither dwarf had spoken again since the first offer was made and the dwarf wasn't even considering his other offers.

It suddenly dawned on him that the dwarf had come solely for his diamond and that it was the only reason he had brought the dagger. Perhaps this expedition had been sanctioned by his king after all.

Neither of them spoke again for a long time. Both stared at the other, no expression crossing their faces as the battle of wills continued.

Finally, Jaron broke the silence.

'The diamond, the rubies, and two of my finer ponies.' Jaron said. 'And one more thing that will cost you nothing,' he added.

'You said the finest ponies,' Kegan replied.

'That was my first offer in response to yours, without the diamond,' Jaron said. The dwarf was trying his patience now.

'Very well,' Kegan said. 'It is a deal.' He reached out his hand to seal it.

'I said one smaller thing first,' Jaron said. His arms remained at his side.

The dwarf looked at him suspiciously, but said nothing.

'You met with a man as you entered my town,' Jaron said. 'What did he want of you?'

The dwarf hesitated for a moment but then obviously thought he was breaking no one's trust by telling Jaron what had been said. It was nothing of consequence anyway.

'Do you mean the wizard?' the dwarf said.

'No.' Jarod was beginning to become exasperated at the dwarf. 'I know nought of any wizard, Kegan. I refer to the man who asked you to look at his horse's foot.'

'I know who you are talking about, Jaron,' Kegan replied. 'The wizard asked me to look at his horse and then wanted to know about the weather in the Southern Mountain Pass.'

'If you would be so kind as to make the effort of telling me all that was said friend dwarf, then our bargain can be struck. If it were too much for you, then perhaps we can continue our discussions for a more equitable deal?' He had lost all patience now and was seriously considering withdrawing his offer.

'He wanted to know if it were safe to travel through the mountains to enter the Eastern Plains. That was all the information he wanted from me.' Kegan said quickly.

'And what did you tell him?' Jaron asked. Why would they be going into the Eastern Plains?

'I told him the mountains are more dangerous now than they have ever been before. That those who we don't like to talk about are roaming in greater numbers and that if they wanted to risk it they would probably die.'

'Do you think he knew about those?' Jaron asked. He had heard the stories about the *Krickshen*.

'He swore loudly when I told him, dropped the air shield that was stopping me from walking away, and then left without another word. I would say so.' Kegan finished.

Jaron didn't respond straight away. His thoughts were racing.

Heridah was a wizard! His own wizards had never informed him of that piece of information. It seemed the loyalty they had for their own kind was stronger than their loyalty to him. He would deal with that at a later time.

So it would be unlikely Heridah and his companions would go through the mountains then. Even the King's Shield wouldn't be foolish enough to risk crossing paths with a *Krickshen*. He needed to know what it was they sought now more than ever. If the king has sent a wizard with his strongest King's Shield then whatever they sought was something he wanted quite badly.

The dwarf's next words brought him out of his inner thoughts.

'It would seem this information has proven rather valuable to you Lord Jaron. We might have reached a worthy deal after all.' He held his hand out again.

This time, Jaron clasped hold of the dwarf's hand and shook it.

'I am curious about one more thing,' Jaron said as his thoughts focused again on the dwarf and his companion.

'Yes?' Kegan asked, smiling as their hands dropped.

'No offence to you or your companion,' he said and nodded at the other dwarf. 'But how did you manage to fight off those that tried to rob you? I know you have means to protect yourself, but hand to hand combat isn't what the Southern Dwarves are renowned for.'

'Ah,' Kegan said still smiling. 'I neglected to introduce you to my companion.' He turned and looked at the other dwarf. 'This is my distant cousin Granwen.'

'Greetings,' Jaron said, a little confused.

'He wasn't too happy about losing all of his armour before we left our Mountain homes, but even without it he still made short work of the four desperate robbers that thought us easy prey.'

Jaron looked again at Kagen's companion. As soon as Granwen smiled at him the penny dropped. The crazy was definitely in the eyes of that one now.

CHAPTER 41

The Plainsmen Ride

KABIR COULDN'T BELIEVE the stamina and speed of the mounts they rode on. Not one horse among them looked like it would ever tire.

They had been forced to slow a long time ago, but the speed was still enough for Kabir to voice his concerns out loud.

'How soon before we need to rest the horses?' he asked as he trotted beside Denizen. His riding had improved, but he was still sore from their pursuit.

Denizen looked across at him. The scowl had not left his face since they set off after the insect creatures. His determination to catch them was matched on the faces of all those he rode with; however, Kabir knew his desperation could lead to bad decision making.

'When we catch up to them Kabir,' he answered. 'Not before that.'

'I want you to keep your anger focused at the insects Denizen when I say this.' Kabir paused to give his words a chance to sink in.

Denizen made no response.

'Our urgency may be putting the health of the horses at risk. We won't be able to help if we don't make it there at all.'

'You do realise why we are pushing them don't you, highlander?' Denizen asked.

'Of course I do,' Kabir said, 'and I am aware that none know your horses better than your own people, but even I can see we are pushing them too hard.' He kept his voice level, without emotion.

He saw Denizen take a deep breath.

'We are almost at the point where they will turn off Kabir. We will reassess then and not before.' Denizen spurred his horse forward to ride next to another.

Reassess indeed, Kabir thought to himself.

He knew if the insect creatures had turned towards the plainsmen's training grounds, then it could easily lead to the death of most of those they rode.

Denizen was right when he said they were almost at the point he thought the insect creatures would change direction. They soon came upon the place he spoke of.

Kabir was neither relieved nor upset at what they found. He had thought they would do as much, as had Denizen.

'Hallor, take ten men with you and head for the camp. If you catch up to them do not get caught up in a battle. You will all need to fan out. Kill as many as you can, but keep riding. You need to warn them of what is coming.'

Hallor nodded and moved off to select those that would come with him.

'We will rest here only long enough to feed and water our mounts. They have been brave so far. They will not let us down.'

None of his men said anything. They all dismounted and began to take care of their horses. Each man carried with him a larger leather skin which contained more of the life-saving water that their horses needed. It wasn't much, but it would sustain them a little while longer.

Kabir noticed the men took only a small drink from their own water skins. He knew they would save it for their horses, even though they were all showing the effects of the hard ride and the long day so far.

It was now late in the afternoon and would be dark soon.

Kabir walked over to Denizen as his horse rested and fed.

'How far to the training grounds from here?' he asked. 'Will we be there before dark?'

Denizen had a harrowed look on his face now, made all the worse by his fatigue and worry.

'No,' was all he said and then his face drained of all colour as he looked off into the distance.

Kabir followed his gaze and saw a spiral of dust in the air some distance away.

'Cover your horses!' Denizen bellowed. 'Move fast!'

Kabir was confused and looked to see what the men were all doing.

'To your horse, Kabir,' he send in a voice filled with urgency. 'Do what the others do. Quickly!' he yelled, as he ran to his own horse.

They all took their sleeping blankets from the side of their saddles and were desperately trying to tie them around the heads of their horses.

Kabir raced over to his horse and quickly tried to do the same. Fortunately, his mount didn't fight him. Whether he was too tired from their journey or he was used to the plainsmen doing this, Kabir's horse didn't bat an eyelid as he tied the blanket as best he could.

The Barbarian looked over at the dust spiral and saw it was almost upon.

He looked around at the others and saw they were covering their own heads with the smaller horse blanket that sat under their saddles.

Kabir tugged his free from under his blanket, but before he could put it over his head, the cause of the spiral was upon them and he was too late to defend himself against it.

Digging flies were tiny and were adept at finding any opening that gave them access into the body of the one they were attacking. They attacked both man and animal, they weren't selective with their target. Moving in a swarm containing thousands, anything that breathed was their potential prey.

Denizen hadn't seen a swarm of them in at least twenty cycles.

On that occasion, they had lost many horses and almost as many men.

Some that had fallen victim had survived, but most either went mad or died shortly after the attack.

Denizen held the blanket as tightly as he could with one hand, while trying to secure his horses blanket with his other.

There was nothing else he could do now but wait.

After about five minutes, Denizen heard the swarm finally moving off further into the plains.

He swatted off those still clinging to his headgear and other parts of his body, before waiting a short time longer to make sure there weren't any remaining. If even one or two got inside the pain would still be considerable.

He knew from experience and the memory of it was still vivid in his mind.

He removed the blanket from his head and quickly checked his body, running his hands through his hair and over his face as did. When he was confident there were none on him, he removed the blanket from his horse and did the same to it. He checked its extremities, swatting a couple away from around its tail. He couldn't be sure that none had entered through there, but if only a few did at least his mount would still survive.

He then looked around, but knew already from the sounds of pain, that not all had been as quick to react as he had.

A few of his men were rolling around on the ground. Some were drinking their water and trying to force themselves to vomit it up again, hopefully expelling those that had made it into their stomachs. The ones inside their heads they could do little about. He knew that was the fate of those writhing on the ground.

He noticed several of the horses had bolted. He could see a couple of them in the distance, galloping hard. Others were already out of sight or had collapsed on the ground among the grasses, out of his vision.

Then he saw the Barbarian. He was sitting on the ground only a short distance away, his hands covering his face. His horse stood next to him. Somehow it had been spared and remained relatively calm.

Denizen walked over to him.

'How bad is it?' he asked as he stood over the top of him.

Kabir took his hands away and looked up at Denizen.

Denizen knew straight away he was going to die. The whites of his eyes were a dark red, an indication the flies were inside his head and feeding already. They didn't attack the brain to begin with, they started with the flesh before moving there. He had known men to survive hours before succumbing to their feeding and burrowing.

The rest of his face was bunched up into a grimace. They would be inside the rest of his body also he suspected. The barbarian looked like he was in excruciating pain.

'What can be done?' Kabir managed to say before wincing again and doubling over.

Denizen looked at him without answering.

Kabir managed to sit up again and look at the leader of their band of men.

'That bad?' he groaned.

Denizen nodded his head.

'Once they are inside you, there is no getting them out. They burrow inside and consume your flesh and organs.' He decided it was best to be blunt. The Barbarian already knew it wasn't good.

'Poison,' Kabir gasped at him.

'No,' Denizen replied. 'They have small pincers that tear at the flesh that allows them to consume it. Their size grows as their feeding increases.'

Kabir shook his head and groaned inwardly again.

'Do you have poison?' he managed to get out.

Denizen was confused. Why would he want poison?

He remembered then that some of those afflicted the worst had chosen to take their own lives rather than be slowly eaten to death from the inside.

'We don't have poison my friend, but we do have a toxin that paralyses the host for a time.' He thought about its effect for a moment. 'But I don't think that will help you.'

'Do it,' Kabir said to him. 'Cut me with it.'

'Cut you?' Denizen asked. He didn't know what he meant. The pain could be making him delirious.

'Cut me,' he repeated. 'Everywhere.' Then he screamed as his body began to spasm.

Denizen went quickly to his horse and pulled from his side bag a small vial of their potent toxin. He quickly dipped his dagger inside as he moved back to where Kabir was now lying on the ground.

He made several small cuts along his arms, legs, and chest. The toxin worked fast and his spasms soon stopped. He lay still then, his arms falling stiffly to his side.

Denizen looked closely and could see tiny movements under the skin, the digging flies still hard at work. Then as he looked on, their movement also stopped.

The flesh they consumed would now contain the toxin as his bloodstream pumped it throughout his body.

His breathing had slowed, but Denizen knew that was likely as a result of the toxin rather than the flies.

He turned to a couple of his men standing nearby. A couple of them had stopped to see what Denizen was doing.

'Did you see what I just did?' he asked one of them.

The man nodded.

'Then go and do the same for those who need it!' he yelled. He still wasn't sure if it would do much to the flies, but it would at least give his men the same respite from the pain that it had given the Barbarian.

He looked at Kabir again before moving off to check on the rest of his men and their horses.

He needed to see how many he would need to leave behind and how many he could take with him. He was still in a hurry to leave.

CHAPTER 42

Friends in Need

MENDINA COULD SEE that the humans had already began walking up the far side of the valley.

The dwarves and goblins had moved further to their left. Neither were yet brave enough to attack the other. It was a stand-off, but the dwarves were slowly making their way to the ridge at the top of the valley.

'What about them?' she said, still looking over at the goblins and dwarves.

'I don't think either of those groups will come anywhere near our new friends, do you?'

He was right, so she put them out of her mind.

They got to the bottom of the valley and walked over to where the other three cats were. One of them was lying on its side, blood seeping from several wounds. It looked to have been hurt quite badly.

'Can you help it?' Mort asked.

Mendina didn't think she could. She didn't have any of the vials of liquid and ointments she had made in Glorfiden. They took time to make and needed certain ingredients, which she doubted would be found around here. Her magic she used to augment the ingredients, she couldn't heal using her magic alone. Even if she could, she had used a lot of her magical reserves.

She looked at Mort and shook her head slowly.

'I don't think the wounds she has are fatal,' Mendina said. 'I can see nowhere that the blood is flowing freely.'

'That's good,' Mort said and turned his attention to the house. 'We should go.'

Mendina was taken aback by his callousness. These cats had just saved their lives, risking their own to do so and all he cared about was leaving.

'You just want to leave? They saved our lives,' she said.

'You said there is nothing we can do for it and that it won't die.' He looked a little taken aback by what she had said.

She knew he was right. It was her own guilt at not being able to help that was the reason for her sharp response.

'It is a "she"?' Mendina said to him. 'They are all females.'

Mort raised his eyebrows at that.

'I wonder how big the male ones are?' he said out loud.

Mendina didn't even bother commenting on that. Male didn't always mean bigger in the animal kingdom. Mort really was an idiot at times.

'We should check the stables first,' he said and began walking over to them without waiting to see if she was following.

Mendina turned back to the female cat they had freed first and conveyed their thanks for the help she and her companions had given them.

She couldn't be sure, but she thought it was conveying to her that it intended to travel with them until they got to the dry plains.

Mendina tried to tell her through her own thoughts that she should stay with her fellow cats, but the cat's own projection wasn't wavering. She doubted the male cats would be more stubborn than this one.

She turned and jogged to catch up with Mort. She wasn't surprised when she looked over her shoulder and saw the cat following along behind her, its head turning both ways as if it were surveying the area for any new threats that might show.

Mendina caught up with Mort as he pulled open the stable doors. She could hear there were horses inside before the door was even opened. They would have been spooked from all that was happening outside.

She saw straight away that it was a well-looked-after place. The outside had been neat and well maintained and the inside was no different.

She counted six stalls, three either side, but only three of them had horses inside.

She could hear one still prancing and snorting. She looked into its stall and saw it had injured itself, probably as it tried to kick its way out. There was a deep cut to its foreleg which was bleeding freely.

'Watch out,' she said to Mort as she prepared to slide open the gate to its stall.

'I don't think we should take that one,' Mort replied. 'I've checked the other two and they seem much more relaxed.'

'I know, Mort,' she replied in a patient voice. *Does he think me stupid?* 'I am letting it go. We can't leave it locked up. It will starve to death.'

Mort looked at her and nodded his head as he looked back the other way. 'Of course,' was all he said.

Mendina shook her head slowly at his attitude, as she unlatched the gate and stood back to let it out.

The horse took off at a gallop, ignoring the hurt to its leg as it stormed out of the stable and into the valley outside.

When she turned back to Mort, he was already leading one of the horses out towards the front of the stables where the horse gear was laid out.

'Do you know much about riding?' Mort asked as he passed her. 'My mother used to let me ride often whenever we visited Mayfield.'

Mendina shook her head. There hadn't been a need for horses in Glorfiden. Elves moved quickly enough through the forest using their own two feet.

'How hard can it be if you are able to do it?' she quipped, smiling innocently as she did.

Mort frowned at her before smiling himself.

'Excellent,' he said. 'I'll leave you to saddle yours, then.' Still smiling, he began to wipe down his mount with a brush.

Mendina quickly moved to where the other horse was and let it out of her stall.

'You might want to put a rope around her neck first,' Mort said. 'So that she doesn't run away from you.'

Mendina picked up some rope hanging next to the gate of the stall and slid it over its head. She didn't need to look at Mort to know he wore a smug look on his face.

She walked her horse next to where Mort was and tied it to the same railing he had. She then looked to see what he did before doing the same to hers.

Before long, both horses were saddled and Mendina followed Mort outside where the big cat was sitting, patiently waiting for them.

Mendina looked around and saw that the valley was now empty of anyone or anything except for themselves and their new companion.

She was given a vision from the big cat of her two fit companions chasing the stragglers away, until none remained. The third had been able to walk gingerly in their wake.

Mendina smiled at her and followed Mort to the front of the house.

'Shouldn't we be leaving?' she said to him, as he tied his horse to another wooden post at the front of the house. The nagging compulsion was strong again and was starting to give her a headache. 'I hope you're not thinking of staying here for the night?'

'We need supplies,' he said to her. 'It will be easier taking it from his stores than foraging for it ourselves.'

She knew he was right, so she tied her own horse up and followed him to the front door. She was worried about finding something nasty inside.

'He could have set traps,' she said, as Mort reached out to open the door.

He stopped and turned to look at her.

'I think his magic was more about control than anything else. I can't see anything around his house, nor was there any sign of magic inside the stables.

She had almost forgotten he could see the magic.

She nodded her head and indicated for him to lead the way.

A drawn-out 'wow' was all Mort said as he opened the front door and stepped inside.

Mendina followed him in and stopped in the doorway behind him. She looked around and was stunned.

There didn't look to be any rooms in this house, other than a small section near the back where there was a door that didn't look to go outside.

Mort eventually stepped forward and Mendina moved to the side of him, neither of them saying anything. They just stared.

'I'm very surprised the dwarves didn't come straight for this,' Mort finally said.

'We can thank our new friends for that,' Mendina replied, still looking around at the myriad of items and treasures that Travis had accumulated.

There were all kinds of weapons and armour, displayed tastefully on the walls. Carpets and rugs were strewn throughout, as were a myriad of objects and artefacts, all stacked neatly on top of tables. There were many exotic ones that she couldn't even guess what part of the world they came from.

'Do you see anything from Glorfiden?' Mort asked her.

Mendina was surprised by his question and looked around again.

'Nothing,' she said. 'It would appear my people may be the only ones he has never enslaved or stolen from.'

'Pity,' Mort said and Mendina shot him a baleful look.

'I just meant it would have been nice if he had somehow got himself an elven staff or similar.' He spoke defensively. 'It was a stupid thing to say I know.'

Mort began to make his way to the back of the house, where there were kitchen utensils and various herbs hanging by the window.

He walked over to the door and opened it.

'A pantry,' he said to Mendina as he walked inside. Mendina soon joined him. Her expertise as to what they should take with them would be greater than his in this.

Walking inside, she was surprised at the size of the room and the abundance of supplies there. She recognised many of the things he had in there. Although some weren't exactly the same as in Glorfiden, they were similar enough that she could confidently guess what they were.

'We'll need something to carry it in,' she said to Mort. 'Why don't you go and fetch us those. Make sure they can be hooked up to the horses easily enough.'

Mort left to do as he was bid and Mendina set to selecting those things she thought would be easiest to carry, would last more than a couple of days and would provide good nutrition. Hopefully none of it would poison either of them.

By the time Mort returned with a couple of woven sacks, Mendina had selected most of what she thought they would need.

In a short space of time, their new supplies were packed and tied to the saddle of their horses.

Mort paused as he stood next to his horse, ready to mount. 'Is there nothing else in there you think we might need?'

Mendina hoisted herself into the saddle of her horse and looked down at him.

'Do you mean should we be like the dwarves and take with us as many treasures as we can carry away with us?' Mendina's headache was getting worse.

'No,' Mort said, a little abashed. 'I mean the weapons, or the armour. Or anything else that might help us along the way.'

He mounted his horse after he finished answering her.

'Mort, we have our magic. More accurately, we have your magic.' She still knew she would be of little assistance if they met something truly powerful. 'Neither of us know how to use weapons Mort and any armour would just weigh us down and slow our progress. We don't know how far we need to go yet.'

'I guess so,' Mort said as he turned his horse away from where it had been tied up. 'There really were some nice pieces in there though. Maybe we will be able to grab some on our way back to Glorfiden,' he said cheerily.

'Sure,' she said, as she finally managed to get her own horse to move in the direction Mort's was going.

She had a feeling the small band of dwarves wouldn't have fled too far from the big cats and this house. She would be surprised if they didn't take the house itself when they deemed it safe to return.

They rode without incident for the rest of the day and were even able to travel slowly at night with the help of their new friend. The cat's night vision was as good as theirs was during the day and the thoughts projected back to Mendina were enough for them to navigate their way through the open terrain they traversed.

It was much the same the next day.

During the afternoon, they came upon a human dwelling set off the road. Mort knew it as a tavern. A place that welcomed travellers, sold them refreshments, and offered lodgings for the night.

Mendina took one look inside at the corpses strewn on the floor and turned around.

They continued on their way, skirting the mountains as they made their way towards the Eastern Plains.

Mort knew that without the mighty cat to show them the way, it would have taken them days longer to get to the plains. If they had made it there at all.

It not only led them, but took them through parts that weren't too onerous on their horses. Only a few times were they required to dismount and lead them through certain parts and across streams and rivers that were too risky to cross while riding.

Mort heard the cries in the night and sounds of combat when the cat would scout ahead. He was acutely aware she also gave them protection from those creatures that preferred to hunt during the darkest hours.

'How does she know the way so effortlessly?' Mort asked Mendina, not long after they had left the tavern with the slaughtered men inside.

'I think her kind are from there. Or at least an area near to where we are heading.' Mendina replied.

That made sense, Mort thought. They obviously hunted far and wide, or else Travis would never have caught them. Mort wondered whether Travis had actually travelled afar to obtain the creatures and wealth he had accumulated. If he had these cats to protect himself, then he saw no reason why he hadn't. He could have taken two with him and left two to guard his home.

'Why do you think he never tried to catch himself an elf?' Mort asked.

Mendina looked across at him for a time before answering. Mort raised his eyebrows, knowing he had spoken again before thinking.

'The magic,' he said, answering his own question before she could. 'But he wouldn't have known his powers would have no hold over the lords of Glorfiden?' he persisted. His question wasn't that silly, now he thought about it. His compulsion had worked on Mendina after all.

'Maybe he just didn't want to risk it!' Mendina answered sharply.

Mort belatedly realised she probably didn't want to be reminded that she had fallen victim to it herself.

'Sorry,' he said meekly and looked again at the big cat leading the way in front of them. He wondered not for the first time, whether she even liked him or only suffered him for his magic potential.

They travelled in relative silence for the rest of the day. Mort was surprised, but pleased, they had met nothing else to challenge them as they rode.

The temperature had been steadily dropping as they rode so close to the mountains and away from their home. Glancing regularly at Mendina, he noticed she was beginning to feel it. She held the reins with one hand, but held her other arm tight across her chest in an attempt to keep some of the cold out. He was very surprised at how quickly she had grasped the skill of riding.

Neither of them had known it would get this cold. Both had assumed it would be hotter as they rode towards the plains, but their ignorance in what was outside their own homes was clear to both of them.

Their companion didn't seem to feel the cold at all. She kept her steady lope going, seemingly moving without effort or fatigue. She stopped when they did to rest the horses, curling up and closing her eyes, but apart from that she was constantly on the move.

'We should have grabbed some coats from Travis' house,' Mort said as it neared dusk.

Mendina shot him a look which had him staring straight ahead once again.

He would never work her out, he thought to himself.

It was late on the next day when they finally caught sight of the plains ahead of them. The cat had led them a little closer to the mountains, but still within the hills below them. As they topped the rise of the valley they had just gone through, the wide spaces of the plains were suddenly spread out before them.

Mort had expected to feel the heat radiating from them, but it was even colder now where they stood. Colder than it had been anywhere else so far on their travels.

They stopped their horses and Mort sat there shivering next to Mendina. He could hear her teeth chattering.

'She is leaving us now,' Mendina said through clenched teeth, as she strived to keep her jaw still.

Mort knew his disappointment was clear. He was hoping that somehow she would be able to lead them directly to the idol itself.

'Her kind live further south from here and she is going back to join them.' Mendina had a funny looking smile on her face as she finished. Mort saw it as a combination of sadness and the cold.

Mort hopped down off his horse to give the cat a fond farewell, but it was already running away towards the plains.

Mendina chuckled. 'I think she really liked you,' she said to him.

Mort just scowled, shook his head, and got back up on to his mount.

'She must have forgotten who it was that saved her,' he said.

He looked at Mendina and saw a large grin on her face. 'Shouldn't we get going,' he said, as he prodded his horse to get it moving. He could hear her still chuckling to herself as she followed him down into the plains.

CHAPTER 43

Let's Try This Again

WHEN HE AWOKE in the morning, Brindel was feeling much better about his journey into the plains. It was amazing how a decent feed lifted the spirits.

He got up intending to cook up some more meat to take with him and saw that all four carcasses were gone. Something had dragged them away during the night. He cursed again, but then realised whatever it was that had removed them had also left him unmolested. He thought begrudgingly that he should be thankful for that.

The sun wasn't even halfway across the sky when he finally came out onto the lower hills at the foot of the mountain range.

There was a thick forest of trees between him and the plains, but he didn't foresee any troubles travelling through them. It was only a short walk and there wouldn't be any elves on this side of the mountain. A couple of hours at most and he would be back into the hot, arid plains beyond.

He looked over his shoulder at the mountains behind him and to either side. He wasn't close to where he had entered the plains the first time, much to his displeasure. He would have liked the opportunity to look for his backpack. There were treasures in there he wouldn't be able to replace in a hurry, if at all.

With a sigh, he tried to put it out of his mind. He'd already given away most of his things before he left his home. Someone else may as well have the rest of it.

He still had his best pieces of armour, his weapons and the few trinkets that he always wore. Things could be worse, he thought, and then regretted it straight away. Why tempt fate further by thinking such a thing?

It would be just his luck if things did get worse.

'Things could definitely get better,' he said out loud to the mountains behind him. He didn't feel any better saying that either.

'Let's get this over with then, shall we?' he said to himself and moved off towards the trees below.

The sun was directly above him when he left the trees and walked into the long grass that he had missed so much.

It wasn't as thick in this part and the going was easier than before, although it was already frightfully hot. His charm was keeping most of the heat at bay for now, but he could still feel the heat as it slowly began to cook him inside his armour again.

He regularly turned and looked to the skies as he walked, but so far, there had been no sighting of any *palcyl* scanning the plains.

He still had the nagging compulsion to guide him and he was pleased this time it was taking him directly east. At least the *palcyl* hadn't taken him further away from his destination, wherever that was. Perhaps his luck was beginning to change after all.

He needed to find what he was looking for fairly soon. The one water bladder he still had on him when the *palcyl* snatched him, he had filled just before he reached the trees. One water bladder wouldn't last very long in this place and it wouldn't take long for death to take anyone without water. Even with his Dwarven constitution he still needed water to survive.

The sun was three quarters of the way across the sky when he was brought out of his boredom and suffering by movement up ahead. The grass had thinned even more the further in he went and he could see quite a distance in some directions.

The thing that caught his attention was a long way in front of him and it had stopped moving at the same time he did.

'Obviously saw me too, didn't you,' he said quietly to himself.

He couldn't make out what it was yet, but it definitely wasn't shaped like a man. Whatever it was, he hoped it didn't have too many friends with it.

He was tired and uncomfortably hot and he didn't want to use what energy he had left fighting in these horrible grasslands.

If it was men then he might at least get some water and food out of it, but he doubted this creature would be carrying those things around with it.

It still hadn't moved again as he began walking slowly towards it.

He could have gone around, but he really couldn't be bothered. Best scenario was that it got spooked by his fierce demeanour and bad humour and took off.

He had halved the distance to fifty paces and the creature still hadn't moved, but he could see it more clearly now.

It was ugly and he had no idea what it was.

'What is with all these freakish mutants?' he said.

It looked like a giant insect, but with the body of a large cat.

He took ten more paces before stopping again.

It still hadn't moved since he first saw it and he was wondering why. He looked all around him and saw nothing else, but there were numerous small spindly trees and bushes among the tall grasses. Plenty of spots for its friends to hide if it wasn't alone.

Brindel took another ten paces closer. It was crouched and looked ready to attack, but still it wasn't moving. He was convinced now that it wasn't here by itself. He suspected it was drawing him towards it so that another, or several others, could attack him while his attention was on this one.

He took a few steps to his left but made sure he could still see it. After his third step, the creature took a few steps in the same direction, mirroring his own movements, before it also stopped. The dwarf looked around but saw no other movement among the grasses and bushes.

'I prefer to dance up close and personal,' Brindel said to it.

He moved back to his right again but took six paces this time. This time the insect cat moved back to where it was when he first saw it and stopped.

It didn't move across any further, but this time Brindel saw movement to his right. It was as far back as the other one, but still further to his right.

So there were at least two of them, but unlikely to be any that were closer than these two. That was enough for Brindel.

'I know you don't understand anything that I'm saying to you,' he said. 'But in fairness, I will give you this last opportunity to tuck your tails in and run.' He couldn't yet see if it had a tail, but he liked the phrase.

He ran straight at the one he had seen first. He had a good look at it now and saw that the body was powerful, but unlike a big cat, it had what looked like giant pincers rather than feet.

He anticipated it would be quick when it moved and so he was ready for it when it finally did. Brindel had taken his axe from his belt as he began his run at it and swung it directly over his head as if he were chopping up firewood. The insect creature had leapt at him after his first few steps towards it and the dwarf's blade bit deeply into its skull as he swung it downwards. It died instantly; however, the momentum carried it into the dwarf and knocked him back off his feet. Because of the way he struck it, Brindel was unable to dodge out of the way and so took the full impact front on.

The other one arrived as he was trying to push its dead companion off him.

Brindel managed to squeeze out from under it and only just had time to put out his gauntleted hand to stop it clasping on to his neck.

One of its front claws started slashing and stabbing his torso, but his armour was holding up under the onslaught.

It was taking all of his strength in one arm to keep its jaws from his throat, but he needed his other hand to pull his hammer free. His axe was still imbedded in the head of the other insect hybrid.

He managed to pull it free and grabbed it at the top of the handle, just under the steel head.

It was more of a tap than a swing, but it stunned the insect creature enough for it to step back. Enough time for Brindel to quickly get to his feet.

The insect cat took another step back from the dwarf. Brindel was surprised it had given him the opportunity to settle himself and not attack straight away.

The cunning way they had tried to entrap him earlier sent alarm bells ringing in his mind. Brindel held his breath a few seconds and froze. It was those valuable few seconds that enabled him to hear the movement behind him.

It also allowed him to step to his side, swinging his hammer as he did so. The creature failed to impact him as it had anticipated and at the last second its claws bit into the ground to try and turn in the direction Brindel had moved.

As it did, the head of Brindel's hammer smashed down on its back, shattering its spine and dropping it to the ground.

The one standing back didn't hesitate this time. The moment his hammer struck the back of the other it jumped at him.

The dwarf was balanced this time though. His killing blow on the second one was followed by a sideways swing the moment he saw the other one jump.

It impacted the side of its head, caving it in. He was able to comfortably side step this one as it crashed into the ground.

Brindel steadied his breathing and listened to the sounds around him, before turning and checking with his eyes.

There didn't appear to be any more of them around.

He walked over and pulled his axe free from the skull of the first one he had killed. He looked closely at it, both fascinated and disgusted with how it blended both feline and insect. It almost looked natural in the way it was designed, but he was pretty sure a large cat wouldn't be interested in mating with a giant insect. He doubted they even could, if they were warped enough to try in the first place.

He walked to the nearest bush and sat in the small amount of shade that it offered. He knew he needed to ration his water but he took a large mouthful. He needed it after the exercise he just had.

Hopefully his destination wasn't too far away, he thought for the hundredth time.

He didn't stay sitting under the bush for too long. He was still thirsty and it would only get worse the longer he stayed in the plains.

His armour felt like he was walking inside his furnace back home and he wasn't enjoying it. At least if he got too hot in the furnace, he could drink as much as he wanted or walk outside to cool off. There was no relief here in the plains.

If he knew where he was heading, it may have made things more bearable.

After an hour or so more he had stopped looking behind him. He decided if one of the *palcyl* found him and grabbed him again, then it was welcome to him.

The grass had become thicker after a couple more hours of walking and he had little to no vision of the land in front of or around him. He was easy prey once again to anything that might hear him coming.

It was much to his surprise when he pushed aside a particularly thick clump of grass and suddenly there were no more.

The ground before him was completely flat, just dirt and small stones. Completely desolate, except for the large ant nest sticking out of the ground about a league in front of him.

Even from this distance he guessed what it was, although if he hadn't just fought and killed three of them, he may have been confused as to what such a monument was sticking up out of the ground in the middle of plains.

A giant bloody ant's nest full of giant, freaky-looking insects. His luck was back where he had become accustomed to it being.

'A statue made of mud,' he said and laughed. A hearty laugh. Where else but inside a giant nest made of mud.

'I wonder how big their leader is?' he said out loud to himself. He was more curious than afraid. It would probably be huge. He looked forward to that challenge.

Brindel knew he would need to kill a lot more of them before he got to their leader, but at least it would be easier to kill bigger insects than it would to have thousands of tiny ones crawling all over him and inside his armour. The thought of that gave him shivers.

He was still too far away to see if there was much activity outside of the nest, but there were none of them near where he had come out of the grass. He was confident if there were some around that none of them had seen him yet.

Still, he didn't make any move forward just yet. He wasn't sure if he should attempt to go in now or wait until it got dark.

He didn't know whether they were like normal insects, which he knew all went back into their nests during the night. Or whether they were more like the big cats, which could see in the dark and liked to hunt at night.

He figured because they had the head of an insect and lived inside an insect dung pile, that the former was more likely and they would probably all be inside during the night. Plus, he had just been attacked by some of them and it was still day.

That would mean that *all* of them would be inside come dark. He may need to make his way through the entire population to get to his prize.

His decision was a fairly easy one in the end. He had to get out of this horrendous heat. At least inside the nest it would be much cooler.

He took another mouthful of his water and headed off, hoping that because they had the body of a cat, they also had a water supply somewhere in that monstrous labyrinth they called home.

He had crossed almost half the distance when the first few of them came into view. They were scurrying around outside a large opening at the front. He had no idea what they were doing, but he didn't really care so long as they weren't sprinting towards him. He had been regularly checking behind himself and so far none had emerged from the long grass surrounding the nest. He took another quick look at where he had come from and all was still quiet in that direction.

He looked back at the nest and saw that at least five others had joined those he had seen only moments before. They were no longer scurrying around. They were all standing still and appeared to be looking in his direction.

It was at that exact moment he wondered what had possessed him to think he would be able to just walk straight in through the front door, or hole as the case was here.

He hadn't had much trouble tackling three of them and he guessed that his confidence may have come from that. Perhaps he also surmised only a few of them would be able to attack him at once when he was inside the nest and walking along one of their tunnels.

'Bloody heat!' he said, looking up at the scorching sun above him. It was obviously to blame for him failing to realise there might be a few dozen of them waiting to stop him from even making it to the entrance.

They still hadn't moved, which was a little disconcerting, until another dozen or so suddenly appeared from out of the entrance. That was much better, he thought.

As soon as the others had joined up, they all moved off.

Maybe six moved off to the right of him, six to the left and the rest straight at him. He guessed it was prudent of them to think there may be more than one of him. After all, who in their right mind would attack their nest all on his own?

On the open ground, they moved fast. Much faster than his legs could carry him, so retreat was not going to be an option.

They had covered half the distance in less than thirty seconds when most of those heading for him suddenly broke away to his right. The others stopped where they were.

He looked to his right to see why and saw that two people on horses had entered the plain from the grasses.

They were a fair distance away and he couldn't make out who the riders were.

He turned his attention back to those in front of him. There were still six, maybe seven of them for him to contend with, plus the six that had gone left. Unless someone else came out of the grasses on their side, they would be back to add their numbers sooner rather than later.

And if the two on horses to his right fell quickly, then those ones would also come back for him.

He recognised this was his best chance and he didn't hesitate.

Pulling both axe and hammer from his belt, he wrapped the leather straps on the ends of each to his wrists. He then charged at them, in so far as his dwarfish legs pumping as fast as they would go could be considering charging.

He began twirling both as he ran, the axe head starting to burn hot as he did, the hammer sparking. Faster and faster they turned until the first two got to him.

Both couldn't jump at him directly, there simply wasn't enough of him to do so, so they instead leapt past his side, swiping their claws at him as they did.

The axe on his right side sliced through a limb as it would through butter, the hammer smashing the other leg away and sending electricity pulsing through the rest of its body. Both crashed to the ground behind him as Brindel's charge continued.

Once past those two he changed direction, as the next one leapt straight at him. His axe head again sliced through it, from its head right through to its tail. It didn't slow him, his weapons a blur now as they spun through the air.

He did have time for a mental note as he approached the next one. They did in fact have a tail.

The next one and the others behind it, stopped in their charge at him. They dug their claws into the ground and quickly took several steps away from the flaming and sparking blurs surrounding the dwarf.

Brindel ran at the one closest to him, but it moved easily away from him, turning and running a short distance before stopping to face him again.

Brindel was surrounded now, but he kept his weapons spinning and turned himself in a slow circle as he did so.

It was a stand-off. None of the insect creatures were brave enough to attack and he wasn't fast enough to chase them down.

He knew he wouldn't be able to do this all day, so he started making his way towards the nest.

'Perhaps this will give you the incentive to come closer,' he said to them as he continued to spin his weapons.

As he turned, the two horsemen came into his line of vision again. He had forgotten about them in the excitement of his own little battle.

They had gone past where he was now in their efforts to reach the nest and there were no insects around them. It was as if they had simply ridden straight over the top of them. He still couldn't make out who or what they were that rode them, but they would be at the nest much sooner than he.

It suddenly occurred to him that perhaps he wasn't the only one searching for this idol of mud. If he wasn't and they were also after it, then he needed to move faster.

'Hey!' he yelled at the two on horseback. 'That treasure is mine!' There was no way anyone else was going to steal the idol, not after everything he had been through to get here. Not a chance.

'You are such an embarrassment to your race,' he said in a quieter voice, after hearing himself refer to the idol of mud as treasure.

Nevertheless, he was not about to let these interlopers thieve what was rightly his to take first.

He began to lope towards the entrance of the nest, his weapons still spinning at his side. The insect creatures kept pace with him, but still none were willing to brave moving any closer to his weapons.

Brindel wasn't far from the entrance to the nest as the two on horseback dismounted and began walking inside. His eyes nearly popped out of his head when he saw that one of them was an elf. The other one looked human, but was shorter than most men he had seen.

His eyes quickly returned to the elf. He stared at her in a fury, until they walked into the nest and were lost to sight.

As he got near the entrance, the insects that were shadowing him finally decided to make their move. As one they attacked from different angles.

As one they died. Brindel crouched and swung his blurring weapons in circles over his head, turning as he did so.

He looked around as the last one stopped moving and saw the other six were on their way back, but were still some distance from where he was. He surmised they had been sent to check the fringe where he had entered from the grasses.

No more exited the nest after the elf and her friend had entered. Brindel assumed they were taking care of any they came across as they walked through the tunnels inside.

Brindel realised he may not be able to catch them, and even if he did, these two might actually be able to look after themselves. In his weakened state, he would rather get in there quick, snatch the idol, and leave. He certainly wasn't worried about confronting them, but he'd had enough conflict lately and he needed a rest.

A thought suddenly occurred to him that there might be a quicker way to achieve that outcome. If the leader's den was in the centre, where he hoped it would be, then the best route to make his way there was the direct one. The tunnels inside could be a maze to anyone that didn't know their way through. Which would be anyone that wasn't one of the insect creatures.

Instead of walking along the tunnel as he entered, Brindel went straight up to the wall and smashed it with his hammer. The clay was hardened, but it was mainly mud and it crumbled under the power of his blow.

It took him only a few blows to make a hole large enough to fit his body through. He risked putting his head through to look around and didn't see any of the insects in the next tunnel, so he stepped through. He looked back and saw the six insect creatures scramble in through the entrance. They paused at the hole he had made and then scurried away along the corridor.

He chuckled as he struck the next wall with his hammer. I hope the elf and her elf-loving friend don't hear those ones as they sneak up on them from behind.

It took him only a few strikes to break through the next wall and again he stuck his head through and found the next tunnel all clear.

It got darker the further in he went, but the insect creatures used some substance within their building material that gave off a faint glow.

It wasn't enough to let Brindel see facial features but it was enough for him to make out the outline of anything moving along the tunnel.

He stuck his head through the fifth wall he crashed through and nearly had it taken off. He only just managed to pull his head back through, as the insect creatures' claw crashed into the wall next to the hole he had made.

He decided to take a little longer at each wall so that he could step through without crouching and having to pull himself through.

He was better able to defend himself during the next few confrontations.

By the time he had crashed through about fifteen walls, he gave up counting after the first five, he had met barely ten of the insect creatures and never more than two at a time. He was surprised he had run into so few.

He was either going in the wrong direction, or they were all waiting for him closer to where their leader was. Either way, he was not feeling good about where he was going. The efforts he had expended and the lack of water were starting to take their toll on him. He hoped he would get there soon, regardless of the outcome when he did. He felt more comfortable with stone around him, not mud. Even so far into the nest it was still stifling.

After a few more walls, he began to think he was definitely going in the wrong direction and was seriously considering going back to the start and trying his luck along the tunnels.

'One more,' he thought, as he swung his hammer. It chipped away a huge chunk, but it didn't go through as all of his others had. This wall was thicker. He grinned inwardly and smashed at it again. It took him four more good strikes before he was finally through. The hole was only small, but he could already see that whatever was on the other side, it was far better lit than any of the tunnels he had been through.

He smashed away the wall around the hole he had made so that he could get his head in closer to peek through it.

Putting his eye up to the hole, he could see movement, but it was close to the hole and he couldn't make out any shapes. He stepped back and started chipping away at the wall. He wanted to thin it out to a size where he would be able to get through quickly when he finally breached it.

It didn't take him long. He had discovered a renewed fervour now that he was so close to his final destination. He was sure this was the main chamber. He refused to believe the idol would be anywhere but in the room beyond this wall.

When he was satisfied with his work, he stepped back and readied himself. He took a deep breath and flexed his arms, holding his hammer in a firm grip.

'Time to smash the king bug,' he said quietly to himself before raising his hammer and punching a huge hole in the wall. He swung it in a loop and took out the rest of the thin bit of mud left, as the insect creatures on the other side attacked.

His hammer continued up and smashed down on top of the first one as it came at him through the hole he had made. He then punched it forward at the second one as it jumped over the first one. The blow knocked it back and Brindel followed it inside, stepping carefully over the fallen one.

He knew he had only stunned it and was swinging again as it swiped at him with its front leg. He knocked it away from him and took another step forward, crushing its skull with his next blow.

Looking around quickly, he saw he was in a large chamber with a rounded roof. The ceiling reached quite a distance above him.

He was shocked this time to see there were no other insect creatures present, guarding the large one that stood at the far end of the chamber.

There were two entries into the chamber, both halfway along to the left and right of where he stood. Three entries now, he corrected. He stood there for a moment to make sure no more came inside, before slowly walking towards the insect leader. It was quite a bit larger than the ones he had met so far, but it wasn't as big as his mind had pictured it. He was a little disappointed.

As he moved closer, he was thrilled to see a staff stuck into the ground behind it. At the top of the staff was an idol. It looked to be made of mud.

He decided he wouldn't waste his breath giving it the same chance to leave, as he had the others when he was still outside.

He just needed to kill it, grab his idol, and leave.

It moved when he was within ten paces, leaping through the air at him, as was their wont. Brindel was ready with his hammer, but before he could swing, its front claw smashed into his chest plate and sent him sprawling across the floor. It was on him again before he had the chance to get up, grabbing his right leg by the ankle with its large pincers and flinging him sideways across the floor of the chamber.

This one was a lot quicker than the others, despite its size and it flung him like he was nothing more than a plaything.

It tossed him far enough that he was able to get to his feet before it struck him again. He adjusted his swing this time as it struck him once more. He was able to pummel its leg with it, but not before it struck him in the stomach, doubling him over as well as pushing him backwards.

The blow he struck had hurt it though. It stepped back from him this time, limping gingerly as it did.

Brindel sucked in some quick breaths as he tried to get his breathing back to normal.

This one was a lot tougher than any of the others.

It kept moving, walking backwards towards the staff where it had been standing when he came in. Brindel didn't know why. Maybe its leg was hurt worse than he thought. It was limping a little, but it had been beating him quite soundly. He was surprised it hadn't tried to finish him off.

It gave him the time to put his hammer back into his belt and take out his axe. It was his weapon of choice. A clean strike should finish it, no matter its size and strength. Aside from his armour, it was his finest work.

The insect leader stopped when it was back standing in the same spot it had been before it first attacked.

Brindel scoured the chamber looking for any booby traps or other nasty surprise. He could see nothing, but he still approached cautiously, looking at the ground where it stood.

His eye was adept at finding the smallest fissure in stones and rocks, but the properties this chamber was made of were something altogether different.

He couldn't tell if the ground around it was solid or not, or whether there was a trap door in the ground before where it stood.

'Get a hold of yourself,' he said to himself. 'It's a bloody insect.' He was giving it far too much respect. He had made it this far without much difficulty. Another few steps and he could be on his way.

It reared up as he was almost within striking distance. It caused Brindel to hesitate momentarily. He hadn't expected it to do that.

When it did nothing else, Brindel took two more quick steps and swung his axe at its lower torso. As he did so it turned its body to the side and its tail struck at him with lightning speed.

He barely registered that it had struck him as his axe bit deeply into its side. It slumped backwards on to the floor, knocking over the staff behind it.

Brindel looked at what had struck him and was shocked to see that unlike the smaller ones, this one didn't have the tail of a big cat. It had what looked like a wasp's stinger, or half a one at least. The first section was that of a cat, but halfway along, the stinger came out. He looked down at where it had struck him.

He could see exactly where it had struck, from the yellow substance left on his armour just above the waist. An inch lower and it might have snuck through where his chest armour linked with his thigh guard. There was a tiny gap there when he moved. He dreaded to think what the poison in that thing would have done to him.

His luck was well and truly back where he wanted it to be.

CHAPTER 44

The Idol Is Found

THE CREATURE CONTINUED to spasm at his feet for a short time until it finally stopped moving. Brindel gave it a final kick and walked over to where the idol had fallen to the ground. He had expected it to shatter on hitting the ground, but on closer inspection, he realised it wasn't made of mud at all. The outer covering had cracked and most had broken off. The remainder of the dirt fell away as he lifted it up, leaving behind the inner golden work that was really the idol.

He lifted the rod and touched it with his hands, searching the surface for some clue as to how it was supposed to help him. A clue he was told.

'A clue to what!?' he said out loud.

'I guess the lowly mind of a dwarf wouldn't be able to comprehend its true meaning.'

Brindel turned and saw the elf-lover and his bitch-elf enter the cavern from the hole he had made in the wall.

He knew they would be coming, but he had hoped he could get the idol and be gone from here before they arrived. Still, he wasn't concerned. He had battled elves before and only one of them standing in front of him gave him no fear. He recalculated. One and a half. Looking closely at her companion who had spoken, he could see that it was part elf.

He quickly tucked the idol into his belt and replaced it with his axe.

No witty retort came to mind, so he just stood there and waited for them to come closer or cast their first spell.

'I, on the other hand, will take that rod, cave dweller', the half-elf said to him in a pleasant tone.

Cave dweller? Funny, Brindel thought. This half-elf is as funny as those dwarves he had grown up with.

He hadn't liked them either.

In response, Brindel began to put on an exaggerated show of limbering up.

'Would you like to arm wrestle for it my mighty elf want-to-be', Brindel replied in the common tongue. He smiled at his own wit. Elf want-to-be. That was a good one.

The half-elf stiffened at that comment and the she-elf put her hand on his arm, saying something to him that Brindel couldn't hear.

'Yeah, listen to her boy, she's a real elf.' He smiled again, this time for the benefit of them both. 'At least I think she is. I don't know though, as I'm not sure there are any elves left.' He said this in a serious voice, tilting his head in query.

The elf took her hand from his arm and they looked at each other. She nodded and the half-elf turned to Brindel and a blast of air swept through the cavern at him as Mort swept his arms forward in an arc.

Brindel held his axe out in front and the wind split in two around him, crashing into the wall behind him with an impact that shook the cavern.

'How do you think this is going to end when your spells don't work on me, halfy?' Brindel mocked him. 'Not too late to take your elf-girl and leave this place. You could probably outrun me,' he chuckled.

Mort stopped and stared at the dwarf in front of him.

That was a powerful blast of air he had sent at him. It should have catapulted his body into the wall behind where he stood and shattered every bone in his body. Instead, it had slid past him as if he weren't there.

Mort knew he had to think fast. This dwarf was full of confidence and bad manners, but he knew he wouldn't hesitate for too long.

He didn't fancy him getting close enough to use that axe he held.

The edge looked unnaturally sharp and he had heard from Mendina what Dwarven weapons could do to flesh.

Mort tried to buy himself some time to think.

'Is there anything written on it, dwarf?' he asked pleasantly. 'I assume you can read a few words.'

The dwarf went back to limbering up, this time his neck and then his legs.

'How about I come over there and you can have a closer look at it,' he replied, swinging his torso from side to side.

Mort wasn't frantic, but he figured this dwarf wasn't stupid and he was far too confident. He was reaching down now to his feet, loosening up his back. Mort knew he had to try something a little unconventional with this one. No longer was his first priority the idol.

Before anything else, he needed to keep Mendina and himself alive and worry about the idol after that. The dwarf had the advantage here, underground. Mort was too far from the forest to draw on the powers it offered and his own reserves, although not low, weren't at their peak.

Also, this dwarf was strong. Or rather his weapons, armour, and other magically resistant items were. He could see that almost everything the dwarf wore had some kind of specific element to reflect or absorb the magic thrown at it.

Mort considered throwing parts of the wall at him, but it was made of dirt. Made strong with whatever substance the creatures had used to keep it together, but just dirt in its broken down form. It might make him sneeze, but not much else.

Then a thought occurred to him as he continued to look about at their surroundings in greater depth. They were in a catacomb of corridors and chambers. The dirt must have come from somewhere to have been built so high up. He wondered if there weren't tunnels also running underneath where they stood.

The dwarf finally stopped his posturing and gripped his axe firmly in both hands.

'Time's up, ladies,' he said in a casual voice and began his charge at them.

Brindel was enjoying the look of consternation on the face of the half-elf. He knew by the way he carried himself and spoke first that he was the strongest one in this duo. He immediately dismissed the female from his thoughts.

The wind gust had been strong, but not nearly enough to bother his wind charms.

He figured his other spells would be just as ineffective, so he had decided to enjoy himself a little before killing them both or watching them flee. It didn't bother him either way, but he would feel better about the fell deed if he at least first offered them the opportunity to leave.

'Time's up, ladies,' he said, as he began his casual lope towards them.

After about three paces, he saw the half-elf draw back his arms and he braced himself for whatever it was he was throwing at him.

There was a bright spark and the next thing he felt was that horrible feeling of falling, as the floor at his feet opened up. Down he went.

After what seemed an eternity, his body smashed into the floor of the corridor below. But instead of stopping there, his weight sent him crashing through that floor as well.

He let out a loud grunt at the first one. The protections he had in his armour protected him from the crushing impact. Unfortunately, he had nothing to repel gravity, so the speed at which his body stopped still sent his insides sprawling. His head rang and his lungs had the wind knocked out of them.

The second impact was no better, but luckily no worse and this time he stopped.

As soon as the dust cleared and he could see properly, he looked up. He could make out the forms of the half-elf and his girl looking down at him from the cavern above. He sucked in the deep breaths he needed to fill up his lungs again, as another bolt of lightning struck the ground next to where he lay sprawled.

He couldn't believe it, as he toppled over and into the large gap that had once again opened up underneath him.

Although stunned from a third impact and still sucking in great gasps of air, he managed to roll over several times before the dust settled again.

This time, he was well away from the floor as it opened up once more from a searing bolt where he had landed moments before.

After taking the time to get his breath back properly and dusting himself off, Brindel walked back to the hole in the floor and leaned his head over to look up.

He could make out the shape of the half-elf's head still looking down the first hole he made. Brindel was sure he could see a smile on his face.

'Very clever, boy,' he yelled up into the distance. 'You got me there, but we'll meet again I'm sure. Only the next time I'll make sure the floor is a solid one.' He tried to sound calm and carefree, but inside he was boiling with rage.

Oh he was going to enjoy splitting that one in two. There will be no toying with him next time.

On second thoughts, he decided next time he would use his hammer. He would beat all his limbs to a pulp before killing him.

He was still struggling to get air into his lungs as he stepped back from the hole.

'Good luck, dwarf, but the next time I'll be ready for you.' The half-elf sounded very pleased with himself. Oh he was going to suffer.

He felt inside his belt to make sure the idol was still there. It was and he felt a little better remembering it was the sole reason he had come here in the first place.

He couldn't resist another jibe before leaving, so he stuck his head around one more time, only just pulling it back in time to avoid the full weight of the insect leader as it brushed past his helmet and crashed into the hole below him.

Laughter came from above and Brindel seriously considered finding his way back up there to hammer the both of them into the floor right now.

He even started making his way along the corridor he was in before he managed to get himself under control again. He had the idol and he would be patient. He knew they would find him now, wherever he went.

With a low growl at the hole in the floor, he took his hammer from his belt and replaced it with his axe.

The dwarf walked to the side of the corridor that faced the direction in which he had entered this catacomb and started smashing his way out.

The half-elf could wait, but he pictured his smiling face every time his hammer smashed through the hardened mud, until finally he found himself back out under the hot sun of the plains. He had needed to find his way up to the same level as when he had entered, but it was no trouble for a dwarf.

He knew the elf and her half-elf protector would have made it out well before him and going by the horse tracks, would make it out of the plains well before he would.

He took off at a lope, deciding to wait until he was back in the safety of the mountains before studying the idol further.

Let's see how that cowardly half-an-elf copes with the hard rock of the mountain under his feet!

CHAPTER 45

The Answers Revealed

LL SIX GAMERS still sat at their respective *eyes*, engrossed by the events unfolding before them.

There was so much going on within the world of Dark Swell that at times some of them had difficulty watching it all.

They had expected it would take time for their champions to begin branching out, that some may even stay within their own realms for an indefinite period. What was occurring had them all not only watching the game without pause, but for the first time openly discussing it.

A great deal of that discussion was not only about their respective champions and those acquainted with them, but why things were unfolding the way they were.

They had all seen throughout the last 1,000 years a myriad of creatures spring to life in the desolate and unpopulated areas of their respective realms, both humanoid and monster.

They had known they were born there at the will of the creator but up until recently these creatures had impacted little throughout the land.

At times they moved around in greater numbers, combating those races chosen by the gamers, yet they had never posed much of a threat and had been of little consequence. The gamers had believed they were put there to offer practice and training for their races to increase the skills of their eventual champion.

Yet since the Naming Day, they had begun moving in greater numbers and new abominations had sprung forth that none had seen before.

However, the most disturbing and most talked about thing was they all seemed to be moving in the one direction now.

The same direction all of their champions had gone.

They knew the creator was responsible, but none of them were certain why they were now on the move. They all had theories but nothing conclusive.

Now the idol had been found and they all wondered what that meant. It was a clue, but like Brindel's champion, they had no idea what for.

Brindel, of course, was delighted that his champion had found it first. He sat back on the grass with a broad grin on his face and looked across at Mortinan and Mendina.

Neither of them looked at him. They were still engrossed in their *eyes*.

Not until he spoke out loud did they turn their attention to him.

'Your champions were both fortunate there,' he chuckled. 'I thought my man was about to do to you what he had done to that other elf back by the lake.' He was pleased with himself and had always enjoyed trying to get a rise out of the others, especially Mortinan.

'I could say the same for your dwarf, Brindel,' Mortinan replied, but without much conviction in his words. Mendina stayed silent. She had never risen to the bait.

'It may not matter though, Mortinan,' Brindel continued. 'My champion has the idol now. There may be nothing more for your champions to do but hail mine as the victor.' He hoped that the idol would give his champion a huge advantage in the game, but until the Creator intervened again to say as much he wouldn't get too excited.

Mortinan had very rarely spoken prior to Naming Day. He had always been the most serious and solitary of those competing, but since their involvement in the game had ended, he had suddenly opened up and was now happy to talk about any topic that came up.

This time he laughed at Brindel's words, with more confidence than he had shown moments before.

'I fear you may be getting ahead of yourself, Brindel,' he said. 'I believe there is a lot more yet to do before this game sees its conclusion.'

'Perhaps,' Brindel agreed still smirking, 'but I don't think your champion is going to measure up as much as you hoped he would.'

Mortinan didn't bite this time. Brindel had tried to throw that one in his face on more than one occasion since the game began on Naming Day.

He agreed his champion had a long way to go, but he was still confident he would get there and that when he did the dwarf wouldn't be a match for him. He hoped when they next met, it would be closer to an environment that would favour him. Glorfiden would be nice he thought.

'I agree it is unlikely the game will be decided because of this event or is even close to ending just yet.' Valdor was similar in many ways to Mortinan and took the game very seriously. He had little time for the taunts and jesting that the others seemed to enjoy, but he had always enjoyed talking about the contest.

'Although I confess, I am still not sure what purpose the creatures serve that are making their way out of the far reaches of our realms.'

'They are there to test our champions and nothing more.' Mortinan said.

'I think we all understand that,' Linf chimed in, 'but why do they move in such numbers and with such purpose?'

Mortinan looked to his fellow gamer. Linf had proven herself more thoughtful and knowledgeable than he had initially suspected. She liked to question the others and some of them probably thought her naive, as he once did. Mortinan had since realised she knew the answers to most of her own questions. He believed she simply enjoyed the conversations and debate they provoked.

'At the beginning, the Creator said that the strength of our realms was just as important as that of our champion,' Brindel was no longer smiling. He also believed the game had a long way to go. The Creator hadn't appeared to his champion yet, so he thought he would join in on this conversation as well. 'These creatures are spewing forth to test the strength of our realms, therefore weakening our champions if their realm is not up to the challenge.'

'Perhaps,' Mendina said, 'but why are they all following the path towards the idol?' All of them looked at her as she spoke. She didn't talk often.

'They are my thoughts,' Linf added. 'I'm quite sure they have been put on the same path as our champions.'

Several of the others nodded.

At that moment, the Creator appeared at the centre of the circle and all of their *eyes* became transparent. All present were shocked at his sudden appearance and the conversation ended. Each of them turned their attention to the one in front of them and waited for him to speak.

Brindel's heart raced. He may have been right after all.

'Greetings,' he said and looked around the circle.

'You are all wondering what is going on.' He paused, as he often liked to do. 'I am here to tell you,' he said quietly.

'It is not something I would usually do, speaking to you all again so soon after the Naming Day. Yet what I have done in this world is also not something I would usually do. In fact, this is something I have never done, so I consider it fair to explain.'

As intrigued as they had been with the game, none took their eyes from him as he spoke or thought of anything, but the words that came out of his mouth.

'I said to you all on Naming Day that it is an extraordinary field of champions. As such, I felt not only were you each deserving of a good show but you are all potential victors on this world.' There seemed to be a sparkle within the chasms which were his eyes. 'I still believe that,' he said looking straight at Brindel.

'They weren't done yet,' Brindel thought. He hoped he would at least tell him how the idol would help his champion.

'I decided then, that it was in the best interests of all present here, particularly myself,' he added with a grin, 'that this game be helped along to its fitting conclusion.' He continued to smile as he laid out what he had done.

'I have set tasks for each of your champions. Or more accurately, I have set them upon a path, a set of clues to which each is compelled to find, except for this next one I have planned.'

That had been the best guess of the gamers as they discussed why their champions had all headed for the same part of the world.

They all picked up on the 'set of clues' and 'except for the next one'.

How many clues were there to be? All of their thoughts were in tune on that question, but none asked it. No one ever interrupted the Creator.

'I gave each a clue to move them in the right direction. They were given nothing more and each one only at a certain time, depending on how long it would take them to journey there. If they didn't delay,' he added.

'I deemed this fair to all, although some had to pass through areas they weren't necessarily comfortable with and some had further to travel. This couldn't be helped.'

'Yet even those that didn't get near to the idol in time, as most have not, will still be given a clue to the next one.'

Brindel was not happy with that. Where was the reward his champion had earned for finding it first?

As if he heard his thoughts, the Creator turned his gaze to Brindel.

'Yet your champion found it first and is merited with an advantage to find the next.'

Brindel relaxed noticeably.

'The dwarf will receive the next clue shortly. No other will know it, until a time I deem fitting based upon their efforts and progress in their attempts to find the first one.'

'In answer to your next question,' he continued without pause, 'the moment the idol was found by the dwarf, all compulsions on each of your champions ceased. None can follow Brindel after he has received his next clue.'

Brindel nodded and smiled. A head start was a huge advantage.

'Now,' the Creator continued, looking around again at each of the gamers in turn. 'There is one more question I will answer for you all.'

'To add more spice to the game, some of those foes I have been adding to each realm were themselves given a compulsion at the time of the Naming Day.'

This had been the part that most of the gamers had failed to agree upon. Some thought they had simply been set loose upon the world, others that they too were sent to go wherever it was their champions had been sent.

'Not only were they made to test your races as they grew into power within each of their realms, but they have now been sent forth to test each of your champions. Luck will play some part in this game, but I don't want a champion winning that isn't worthy of the title.'

He paused again and looked around at them all.

'For many of those foes I have created and put upon this world, there is the compulsion to seek out the location of each of the clues I have given to your champions.' Some of those in the circle smiled, proud they had assumed right.

'Yet also within some of them I have planted a gift . . . of sorts.' The smiles quickly vanished.

'Whenever they are within a certain distance of any of your chosen champions, they will sense where they are. When they come within sight of that champion, they will look to the creature as if they are glowing, that there is a light which radiates from within.'

He smiled as he spoke next.

'When they see the light of that champion, it both hurts and taunts them and they will want very much to extinguish it.'

'You see,' he continued, as he looked upon six surprised faces, 'each of your champions are a shining beacon in more ways than one. They not only need to best each other, but many of the other dire creations I have planted into this world.'

'Good luck,' he said and disappeared.

END OF BOOK 1